PRAISE FOR
ALLIE R...

'As with her mind-blow... yet another tense, twisty, addic...'
JO SPAIN

'Fast paced, nail-bitingly tense and packed full of twists'
SARAH PEARSE

'A high-octane, addictive summer read, perfect
for your beach bag'
LUCY CLARKE

'Gave me the same sinister-yet-wish-you-were-
there vibes of The Beach'
AMY McCULLOCH

'A compulsive page-turner . . . had me until the very last page'
SALLY THORNE

'Unforgettable'
WOMAN & HOME

'A tour-de-force, a truly gripping chiller of a thriller,
genuinely impossible to put down'
PETER JAMES

'A clever, compelling story'
RACHEL ABOTT

'With classic Reynolds twists, this fast-paced novel will
have you second-guessing just who you can trust'
WOMEN'S WEEKLY

'Sun, sand, surf and suspense . . . drenched in
atmosphere, tension and intrigue'
EMMA HAUGHTON

'A tense and gripping thriller . . . kept me
guessing until the very end'
JO JAKEMAN

Also by Allie Reynolds

Shiver

Allie Reynolds

THE
BAY

HEADLINE

The right of Allie Reynolds to be identified as the Author of
the Work has been asserted by her in accordance with the
Copyright, Designs and Patents Act 1988.

First published in 2022 by
HEADLINE PUBLISHING GROUP

First published in paperback in 2023 by
HEADLINE PUBLISHING GROUP

1

Cataloguing in Publication Data is available from the British Library

ISBN 978 1 4722 7029 0

Typeset in 11.25/14 pt Sabon LT Std by Jouve (UK), Milton Keynes

Printed and bound in Great Britain by Clays Ltd, Elcograf S.p.A.

Headline's policy is to use papers that are natural, renewable and recyclable
products and made from wood grown in well-managed forests and other
controlled sources. The logging and manufacturing processes are expected
to conform to the environmental regulations of the country of origin.

HEADLINE PUBLISHING GROUP
An Hachette UK Company
Carmelite House
50 Victoria Embankment
London EC4Y 0DZ

www.headline.co.uk
www.hachette.co.uk

For my boys: Daniel and Lucas. Love you so much.

PROLOGUE

The tide's coming in. Every wave seems to lap a little higher. Erasing, bit by bit, the traces of what I did.

There's something soothing about putting one foot in front of the other, mashing my toes into the sand. Last night's storm has washed up all sorts of things onto the high-water line. Assorted leaves, seed pods, frangipani flowers. A whole orange that squishes when I step on it and turns out to be full of little but seawater.

The others are still sleeping – at least I hope they are. I scuffed the sand further up the beach, but if one of them came here now, they'd see it: the sign of something being dragged to the water. They might also wonder what I was doing on the beach so early without my board.

Not that it's surfable today. The ocean is a lumpy mess, water dark with sand churned up by the storm. The wind is still howling. The gulls face into it, eyes narrowed, feathers ruffling. One trots ahead of me, back end blown into a feather boa.

I pace the shoreline. Watching, waiting.

The sharks haven't found the body yet. But they will.

CHAPTER 1

KENNA

'Hey, you!' A blonde woman holds a flyer in my direction. 'Take one please!'

A slight accent: Dutch or Swedish or something.

I blink, dazzled by the sunlight after the shade of the train station. Why is it so bright? It feels like the middle of the night.

'Best Thai food!' shouts a young man.

'Looking for a room?' calls a girl with multiple facial piercings.

The touts stand there, holding their ground – or trying to – in the stream of people flooding from the station. Sydney may be on the other side of the world, but so far, arriving here is little different to arriving in London or Paris.

My heavy backpack makes me unsteady on my feet. The Thai restaurant guy tries to give me a flyer but I have my travel card in one hand and my daypack in the other so I shrug in apology and step around him.

3

'Happy hour!' shouts another voice. 'Six-dollar schooners.'

As I'm wondering what a schooner could be a hand grips my wrist. The Dutch woman. She's fiftyish with dark blonde hair and clear blue eyes. Pretty, or she would be if her face wasn't taut and unsmiling. I want to pull free and walk on – ignore her like everyone else – but the desperation in her eyes stops me. I glance at her flyers.

Missing! Elke Hartmann, German national.

The photo shows a smiling blonde girl clutching a surfboard.

'My daughter.' The woman's voice is raw.

Not Dutch then. I'm hopeless with accents. The tide of people divide and merge around us as I skim the flyer. Elke is twenty-nine – a year younger than me – and she's been missing for six months. I offer a tight smile of sympathy. I hope the bus stop isn't far because this backpack weighs a ton.

A briefcase bashes my calf. I spot the clock on the wall. Half past five: the evening rush hour. The realisation makes my brain hurt. I can never sleep on planes. I've been awake for two whole days.

'Have you ever lost someone you love?' the woman asks.

I turn back to her. Because I have. Lost someone.

'She was backpacking here.' The woman nods at my bags. 'Like you.'

I'm not backpacking, I want to tell her, but she doesn't give me a chance.

'They're in a foreign country and they don't know any-one. If they disappear, it's days before anyone notices. They're easy targets.'

With the final word, her voice cracks. She lowers her head, shoulders shaking. I drape my arms awkwardly around her. My palms are damp; I don't want to ruin her blouse. I need to get going, but I haven't got the heart to leave her like this. Should I take her somewhere – buy her a cup of tea? But I want to get to Mikki's place before it gets dark. I'll give her a minute and hope she cries herself out.

Office workers file past. The women seem better groomed than their British counterparts: all glossy hair and tanned legs in heels and short skirts. The men wear their shirts with the sleeves rolled up and top two buttons undone, suit jackets slung over their shoulders, ties nowhere in sight.

Sweat pools under my armpits. This sticky humidity, Mikki always moaned about it: *Nearly as bad as Japan.* It's March, the Australian autumn, and I hadn't expected it to be this hot.

I watch the touts handing out flyers. The Thai restaurant guy offers a flyer to anyone who'll take one but the others seem to be targeting backpackers. With their oversized backpacks and milk-white or sunburnt limbs, they stand out a mile. *Easy targets.*

Elke's mother sniffs. 'Sorry.' She hunts through her handbag and pulls out tissues.

'No problem,' I say. 'Are you okay?'

She dabs her eyes, sheepish now. 'I let you go. But you be careful, yes?'

'I will. And don't worry about me. I'm not a backpacker. I'm here to visit a friend. She's getting married.'

'Oh, my apologies. She'll be expecting you.'

'Yes,' I say.

She isn't, though.

CHAPTER 2

KENNA

'I'm going to kill you!' Mikki says.

I stand on her doorstep, hunched under the weight of my backpack. 'I knew you'd be mad.'

Freckles pepper Mikki's cheeks and forehead. Her long hair, previously glossy and black, is matted and burnt brown by the Australian sun. The flowering tree beside her front door scents the night air with an exotic smell, highlighting the fact that I'm on the other side of the world.

She's looking at me as though she can't decide if she's happy to see me or not. 'Why didn't you tell me you were coming?'

Because you told me not to come. But we won't get into that yet. 'I tried phoning, but you didn't answer.'

'I told you, there's no reception at the beach we go to.'

Her white Roxy top shows off her taut biceps and tan. As unobtrusively as I can, I look for bruises but don't see any. I let out my breath a little. Here she is, apparently safe and well. My best friend.

She breaks into a smile. 'Oh my God, Kenna! You're really here!'

I smile too. *Oh my God!* is her catchphrase and I can't count the number of times I've heard her say it – usually at the latest crazy thing I did.

She pulls me into a hug.

See? It's all right. Best friends do stuff like this. If your intentions are good, it's okay to overstep boundaries.

What is a friendship but a sum of the memories of the time you spent with someone? And the better the memories, the better the friendship. Memories of Mikki: me and her nude surfing one night when we were drunk; me push-starting her ancient Beetle down a narrow Cornish road above a cliff; a camping trip when she forgot to pack the tent so we chatted up the campers next-door and booted them out of one of their tents so we could borrow it.

All the hilarious things we got up to. And this will go down in our shared history as another of those things. The time I flew to Australia to pay her a surprise visit. At least that's what I'm trying to tell myself. She must have been surfing today – her hair is sticky with salt. I peel a strand from my mouth and pull back to look at her.

'I can't believe you came all this way,' she says. 'What if I wasn't here?'

The thought had crossed my mind. 'I'd have found a hotel.'

There's a stiffness between us. It could be because we haven't seen each other for over a year, yet it feels like more than that.

'Come on in,' she says.

I remove my shoes before I enter. Mikki hasn't lived in

Japan since she was six but she's acquired many of its customs from her parents. Dumping my bags, I glance around. Wooden floorboards, junk store furniture. Is her fiancé in? I hope not.

'Are you hungry?' she asks.

'Um. I don't know.'

She laughs.

'My body clock's all messed up. What time is it?'

She checks her watch. 'Nearly seven.'

'Seriously?' I strain to think. 'It's eight a.m. in England.'

'I'm making *nikujaga*. A monster batch.'

I follow her into the kitchen, where a rich and meaty smell hangs in the air, and realise I *am* hungry. My skin is slick with sweat. The windows are open, the back door too, but the draught coming through the flyscreen is as warm as the air in the room, and the ceiling fan only circulates the heat.

Mikki wafts her face as she stirs the pan on the stove. Now that she's got over her shock, she *seems* happy to see me, but you never can tell with Mikki. She comes from a culture of politeness before all else. I, on the other hand, have one of those faces that shows every emotion so I keep my gaze firmly on the surroundings.

Dishes are piled high in the sink; ants crawl over the worksurface. Strange. Mikki's a neat-freak – used to be anyway – and the place I shared with her in Cornwall was always spotless. She sees me looking and squashes ants with her finger.

My head throbs with a mixture of dehydration, tiredness and jetlag. 'Can I have some water?'

She fills a glass from the water dispenser on the fridge.

I slosh ice water over my fingers and T-shirt in my hurry to get it to my mouth but it feels so good I'm tempted to pour the whole lot over me.

Mikki mops her brow. She looks leaner and stronger than I ever saw her, even when she was competing. Below her denim cut-offs, her feet are bare, nails glossy with black polish.

'You look amazing,' I say.

'Thanks. So do you.'

'Don't lie. Especially after that flight. No wonder you don't want to come back to the UK. Who'd want to experience that flight again?' I'm trying my hardest to shift the tension, but it's still there.

'Your hair.' She reaches out to touch it. 'It's so—'

'Boring?' Since we met in the last year of primary school, my hair has been every colour of the rainbow except its natural mousy brown.

She laughs. 'I was going to say normal.'

I laugh too, even though 'normal' is probably not a compliment in her book – or mine.

Mikki spoons casserole onto plates. As she sets them on the breakfast bar, I spot the tattoo on the inside of her wrist. 'What is *that*?' I say.

She glances at it like it's no big deal.

We talked about tattoos before I got mine – a bird in flight that she designed for me, on my shoulder blade – and I told her she should get one.

'No way,' she'd told me. 'My parents would kill me. A lot of Japanese people think tattoos are dirty. You can't go in a gym or public swimming pool if you have them.'

'Still?'

'Yeah. Or you have to cover them. Many companies won't employ you if you have tattoos. It's not good for their image.'

So I couldn't be more shocked to see the ink on her wrist. 'Let me see,' I say now.

Mikki tilts her arm to show me. It's a butterfly in shades of black and brown with a stripy fat body and horned antennae. I should say something – tell her I like it. But I don't. It's *horrible*.

We pull up stools. There are so many things I want to ask her. Not yet, though. I don't want to kill the mood altogether.

It's weird to eat *nikujaga* in this poky overheated kitchen. We ate it so many times in our draughty, cold kitchen in Cornwall, shivering after a surf.

'How's the big smoke?' she asks.

I turned thirty recently and my birthday passed almost unnoticed. My new colleagues didn't know it was my birthday and I didn't tell them. Mum sent a card and a handful of friends texted or phoned, but that was it. 'I'm loving it. I've met a nice bunch of people there already.'

'And how's work?'

'Yeah, good. Busy. My clients smash themselves up on a regular basis.'

She looks disbelieving. 'In London?'

'Yeah. Rugby, yoga classes, stuff like that.' This at least is true. I tell her about some of the injuries I've treated recently but she seems like she's only half-listening. 'What about you? Are you still working at that nightclub?'

'No, I quit ages ago.'

Mikki must have inherited a small fortune when her

granddad died because she's mentioned she wants to buy a place here.

'So what are you doing?' I ask.

'Oh, this and that.' She swipes a flyer off the table (*McMorris surfboards: handcrafted boards for those who know the difference*) and fans herself with it. 'Fuck, it's hot.'

'Since when did you learn to swear?'

She smiles. 'Blame the Aussies.'

I smile too, teeth clamped together so hard it hurts my jaw.

All the things I want to say are rising up my throat, threatening to burst out.

CHAPTER 3

KENNA

Is he abusive, Mikki? Does he hurt you?

I hope I'm wrong, but there were so many red flags in our calls. How do I bring it up? Do I just come out and say it? She might get all defensive and deny it, so I wait for an opening as we chat about mutual friends, our parents, and the Brazilian Maya Gabeira surfing the biggest wave ever ridden by a woman.

There's a jingle of keys and a guy walks in, tall, blond and athletic-looking.

Mikki seems flustered. 'Um, this is Jack. Jack, this is Kenna.'

I'm on my guard immediately. So this is him. I glimpsed him during some of our FaceTime calls and heard his voice in the background but never properly saw his face.

He grips my hand with a confident smile. 'I've heard so much about you.'

The intense way he's looking at me makes me flush. I take in his strong frame, sizing him up. Nobody threatens

12

my best friend and gets away with it. *Calm down, Kenna. You don't know that.* But I sure as hell intend to find out.

He shoots an amused look at Mikki. 'Did you know she was coming?'

Mikki's smile seems forced. 'No.'

He turns back to me. 'First time in Australia?'

'Yeah.' I absolutely do not want to fancy this guy, but he's ridiculously good-looking. From his tan and the way his hair is bleached almost white in places, it's obvious he spends a lot of time outdoors. Cleanshaven with a strong jaw and a cleft in his chin, broad shoulders packing out a Quiksilver T-shirt, he could have stepped off the set of *Home and Away.*

'Never been to England,' he says. 'Too cold and all that. One of me mates went out there for a year and froze his nuts off. Imagine surfing in gloves and a balaclava. And that's in summer, hey?'

'How was work?' Mikki asks.

'It was all right.' Jack dishes himself a plate of casserole. He didn't kiss her, or even hug her – although who am I to judge how long-term couples should greet each other?

'You finished early.' There's an accusing note in Mikki's voice and I add this to my tally of black marks.

'Yep.' Jack peels off his T-shirt and slings it into a corner, then takes a beer from the fridge. 'Want one, Kenna?'

I battle to keep my eyes on his face, not his chest. 'Better not or I'll fall asleep.' And I need to keep my focus.

Jack sits beside me and takes a long drink. I'm torn between hating him and fancying him. I can't deny that they look great together. He: blond and athletic. She: dark

13

and a full head shorter. And they have a major interest – surfing – in common. But in our calls Mikki hardly mentioned him. If she was truly into him, she wouldn't be able to stop talking about him, surely?

From the way she moved in with him right after she met him and their rapid engagement, you'd think they were head-over-heels, but watching them now, I don't see it. She seems mildly irritated by him; he seems good-naturedly tolerant of her. Mikki's always been reserved when it comes to showing emotions, plus they've been together nearly a year, so the fire might have died down to a slow and steady flame. But her evasiveness about him suggests something is off.

The little I know about him I've had to drag out of her. He isn't working much – he has back problems – so she's 'helping him out' with the rent, and she's abandoned her plans to travel round Australia, because Jack's shown her 'the best beach'. He sounds way too controlling for my liking.

Her wedding announcement had slipped out when we spoke last week, as though she hadn't intended to tell me. It was the final straw.

'I'll fly out,' I said immediately.

'No, no. We don't want a fuss. It's not a big deal.' Her tone was one of weary resignation – sadness almost.

'Are you pregnant?'

I heard her splutter. 'No!'

So why, then? But she didn't explain. I was worried enough that I booked a flight as soon as the call ended. It meant taking a month off work, which wasn't ideal, but I work for myself so I can take holiday whenever I want, and besides, I've done nothing except work for the past eighteen months. I've been a rubbish friend, too caught up in my own misery for too long. Mikki was there for me two years ago when I needed her, so I owe it to her to help her now.

Before I left, I phoned her parents to say I was going to visit, and to sound them out. I didn't mention the wedding and neither did they, which suggested they didn't know about it: another red flag.

I'm worried Jack's pushing her into marriage because he's after her money. It wouldn't be the first time she's been taken advantage of. Mikki gets taken in by every sob story going. You know the sort: people who ask for money in the street because they lost their wallet and they need two-pound fifty for a bus home, then you see them the next day doing the exact same thing. Mikki gives them two-pound fifty, every damn time. She's the kindest-hearted person I know, but she never seems fully equipped for the adult world.

Does Jack know her family own a chain of successful surf stores? Even if she hasn't told him, he could have googled her.

He clasps a large hand over Mikki's lower arm. 'Paperwork all done?'

I stiffen immediately.

'Yep,' Mikki says.

There's no sign of fear in her body language but it doesn't mean it's not there.

'Two weeks today, hey?' Jack says.

Oh, shit. They must be talking about the wedding. I had no idea it was that soon. So I have fourteen days to convince her to change her mind. I check her finger for an engagement ring but her hand is bare. Which shouldn't surprise me, I guess, if Jack is skint. I don't imagine the lack of a ring bothers Mikki. She may be well-off but she's the most unmaterialistic person you could imagine.

I watch Jack eat. Her fiancé. I still can't get my head round it. In all the time I've known her, Mikki never had a serious boyfriend. She dated a guy briefly in high school and a few more since, but they never lasted long. For a while I wondered if she preferred women, but she didn't seem into them either. Perhaps surfing is enough for her, her one true passion.

Jack is nothing like the guys she's dated in the past – creative types mostly, bearded, with long hair and hippyish clothes. Jack's more . . . wholesome and athletic. Hotter. *Not a helpful thought, Kenna.*

His tattoos are the other weird thing. He's covered with them. Ornate sea creatures and mystical beasts, a snake curled round his wrist like a bracelet. Is that why she hasn't told her parents about the marriage – because they wouldn't approve?

Jack's staring at me again and it's creeping me out. I need to get Mikki alone and find out more about him. He collects the empty plates. At least he's house-trained. While he washes the dishes, I open my backpack and pull gifts out: bags of English chocolate – Minstrels and Revels – because Mikki mentioned missing them; books; a cute pair of Havaianas with a Japanese Manga girl on them.

Mikki slips her toes into them. 'Oh, I love them!'

'And . . .' Feeling shy, I pull out make-up – all the

16

brands she used to love when we lived together. 'I didn't know if you can get them out here. Or if you still wear it.'

She pops the top off the lippy and goes to the mirror in the living area to slick some on. 'You can, but thank you.'

Pink lips gleaming, Mikki gives me another hug and sits back down. There's still a weird tension between us but at least she looks more like herself.

'How's Tim?' she asks.

I'm impressed she even remembered his name. 'We only went out a few times. I broke up with him ages ago. Didn't I tell you?'

'Good. He sounded super boring.'

I laugh. She knows me so well. 'Why didn't you tell me that earlier?'

She laughs too. 'I wanted to.'

For a moment it's like old times. Me and her, best friends forever. I don't have a sister – only an older brother I'm not that close to – but Mikki's the next best thing.

'Was he too nice?' she asks.

'Not exactly.' I puzzle over her choice of question. Does it reveal something about her and Jack? 'Just . . . My heart wasn't in it.'

'So you're not seeing anyone?' Mikki asks.

Jack glances over his shoulder at me and I feel self-conscious. 'No.'

Drying his hands on a tea towel, he comes over. 'Lucky you arrived when you did, Kenna, because we're off up the coast tomorrow.'

I look at Mikki for confirmation. Her sheepish expression cuts me deep. I flew all the way out here to see her for a few *hours*?

'You got plans?' Jack asks.

'Um.' Hang out with my best friend. Find out about this dodgy Aussie guy she intends to marry. Talk sense into her and bring her home. 'Not really.'

'You should come along,' Jack says.

Mikki's eyes widen but he doesn't notice. She's giving off all kinds of weird vibes. Until she catches me looking at her and rearranges her expression. 'Yeah, you should totally come.'

'I wouldn't want to get in the way if it's just the two of you,' I say.

'Nah, there's six of us,' Jack says.

I tense. Mikki hasn't mentioned much about the group she surfs with, but I don't like what I've heard. I play for time. 'Where are you going?'

'Just a beach.' Jack grins, but it's a joke I'm not in on.

I turn to Mikki. 'Is it the surf beach you mentioned? The one with hardly anyone there?'

'Yeah.' Something passes between Mikki and Jack. She's flushing.

'How long are you planning to stay?' I ask.

'As long as possible,' Jack says. 'Right, Mikki?'

I wait for one of them to mention the wedding, but they don't. 'And you're camping?'

'Yep,' Jack says. 'You surf, right?'

'I used to but not any more.'

'How come?'

I don't want to get into this. 'I gave it up.'

Jack frowns. 'How can you give up surfing?'

Because I couldn't bear to see the ocean. Not after what happened. 'I moved away from the beach for work.'

'Well, you're not working now, are you?'

'I've not got a board.'

'What do you ride, shortboard or longboard?'

So many questions. 'Um, shortboard.'

'Wait there.' Jack leaves the room.

I turn to Mikki. 'If you don't want me to come, just say.'

'Of course I want you to come,' she says.

I lower my voice. 'Are you okay? Because if he . . . hurts you, I can help.' There. I've said it.

Mikki jolts. 'What? No.'

The rapidness of her response seems suspect. 'You don't seem that happy.'

'It's not that. Not at all. I was just surprised to see you.' She glances at the doorway. 'And there's been some weirdness in the Tribe.'

'The *what*?'

'It's just what we call ourselves. But you should totally come. It'll be so cool.'

She's overdoing it now. What has she got herself involved in? A panicky feeling grips me. 'I picked up the weirdness in our calls. That's why I flew out here. I want to bring you home.'

'No. I—'

Jack breezes back in gripping a shortboard by the rail. Damn. He stands it beside me. The deck is waxed but judging from its pristine condition, it's hardly been used. His palm clasps my shoulder. I jump at the unexpected contact. Anger flares inside me as he pushes me up against the board.

He looks from the top of my head to the tip of the board. 'What do you reckon? It's a five-eleven.'

I pull away, glaring at him.

He doesn't notice. He's looking at Mikki. 'Otherwise Mikki has a few.'

Mikki always had all the boards she wanted, thanks to her parents' surf chain. The week before I turned twenty-one, I snapped my only surfboard and couldn't afford a new one, and she gave me one for my birthday, beautifully wrapped. Must have used a whole roll of wrapping paper. She always gave me more than I could give her, another reason I'm determined to be here for her now.

Mikki nods her head vigorously. 'There's plenty to choose from.'

'Trust me,' Jack says. 'You see the waves where we're going and you'll surf them. We got a spare tent. We got spare everything. So. Ya coming?' His excitement is like that of a small child.

'Um.' I glance at Mikki again. It'll be super awkward to go along when she obviously doesn't want me to, but she's clearly in some sort of trouble. I need to do whatever it takes to get her home to safety.

CHAPTER 4

KENNA

Jack's car is so huge it's basically a small truck. Black and chrome, with a personalised numberplate – *Jack0* – it sits high off the ground on oversized wheels. How can he afford a car like this if he's skint? Or did Mikki pay for it?

The radio blares: *It's going to be a scorcher! If you're heading to the beaches today, there's one metre of southerly swell and light westerly winds.*

Jetlag woke me at 2 a.m. this morning. I lay wide awake, plotting how to get more out of Mikki, but by the time she got up, Jack was already up, packing the car, and I didn't manage to catch her alone. Still, she's all smiles this morning and now seems genuinely happy that I'm coming along.

Jack pulls around a corner. 'Bondi Beach,' he says, gesturing out the window.

The buildings part to reveal a glistening blue ocean lapping a horseshoe-shaped beach. It's only early, but people cluster on the pale sand. Lone runners pound barefoot; lifesavers in red and yellow hats stand guard. The sunlight is dazzling, the colours so vivid I have to shield my eyes. Place a photo of this beach beside one of an English beach and you'd think the English one needed flash.

A few hundred surfers bob in the ocean, chasing every wave that passes. I watch three people surfing the same wave: a longboarder, a shortboarder and, half-hidden in whitewash, a bodyboarder. The shortboarder pulls alongside the longboarder, gesturing angrily. Behind them, the bodyboarder darts about as though intending to cut up the middle. The wave shuts down, sending them flying in a tangle of limbs, boards and foam. I hold my breath until all three heads surface.

'Why are we driving this way?' Mikki asks, in the front passenger seat.

'Thought I'd give Kenna the tour,' Jack says. 'In case she doesn't come back here.'

'What do you mean?' I ask. 'I fly out from here, so I'll definitely be back.'

Jack glances over his shoulder at me, eyes hidden behind mirrored sunglasses. 'Who knows? You might like where we're going so much that you never want to leave.' There's a ghost of a smile on his lips.

A chill runs through me despite the stuffy heat of the car.

Jack pulls up at a supermarket. 'Remind me to get camping gas.'

He and Mikki head into the store and grab a trolley each. I follow behind them. Jack puts in bags of pasta and rice, tins of vegetables and fish and four huge water containers. Mikki checks items off a list.

'Broccoli or green beans?' Jack asks.

'Broccoli will keep longer,' she says.

He lifts a large yellow fruit I don't recognise.

'Eurgh, no,' she says, and he puts it back.

I watch the dynamic between them, looking for more red flags. So far, he's nothing like the dominating figure I'd feared but he could be putting on an act for my benefit. Behind closed doors he might be totally different.

I point to a bright pink spiky thing. 'What's *that*?'

Mikki grabs one. 'Dragon fruit. You'll love it.'

One of my favourite things to do when I get to a new country is check out their chocolate, but to my disappointment they wheel the trolleys straight past that aisle. Luckily, there's a selection beside the checkout, some familiar, others not. I pick out a couple as they load the conveyor. Jack winks at me and I feel like a small child smuggling sweeties into my parents' trolley.

He wheels his trolley out, leaving Mikki to pay. There was no debate between them, suggesting a long-ingrained habit: another black mark against him.

'Here, have this.' I peel off two hundred dollars from the five hundred I took out at the airport.

Mikki waves it away. 'No way! You might only stay a day or two.'

She wheels the trolley out before I can press her.

Jack has opened up the back of his truck to reveal a giant cool box, which we fill with milk, cheese and meat. The remains of Mikki's casserole are in there already.

I heave a bag of ice from the trolley. It's heavier than I expected and I totter sideways.

Jack's hands clamp over mine. 'I've got it.' He shoves his bare knee under the bag to take the weight.

My insides simmer at the bodily contact. I release my grip and he lifts it easily into the cool box.

He turns to Mikki. 'How's your sugar levels? Want a banana?'

'No, I'm fine,' she says.

I'm secretly impressed that he asked. Mikki's always had a thing with her sugar levels and has to eat regularly or she gets faint.

Jack takes a banana from a bag, peels it and bites into it. 'Want one, Kenna?'

'Not right now, thanks.'

The car is blisteringly hot. I yelp as I climb in. The leather is scorching.

'Sorry,' Jack says. 'The aircon's bust.'

The smell of cut grass mingles with petrol fumes as we drive through the suburbs. We pass cricket ovals and rugby fields. There are little snapshots of Australian life each time we stop at lights. A man in a straw hat stands on a riverbank, fishing rod dangling; a family of four lug an enormous cool box across the road. Every single vehicle seems to have some sort of watercraft inside it, on top of it or behind it on a trailer – jet-skis and surfboards, boats and canoes.

'You guys have known each other since primary school, right?' Jack says.

'Yeah,' I say. 'My family moved down from Scotland when my dad lost his job. Mum's brother ran a farm in

Cornwall and needed help, so I started a new school mid-term. I was the new girl with the funny Scottish accent. The teacher led me into class and I saw this girl with the same trainers as mine.'

'The same what?' Jack says.

'Running shoes.' Mikki throws a grin over her shoulder at me. 'Aussies are supposed to speak the same language as us but they don't really.'

They were Adidas. Black with white stripes.

Cool name, Mikki said as I sat down beside her.

It's short for McKenzie, I said. *I like your shoes.*

And that was it. Life's so simple at that age. If only it stayed that way.

I watch a bikini-clad woman strap a longboard onto her car. It sparks memories of Cornish summers in my late-teenage years, the roof-rack of Mikki's VW Beetle sagging under the weight of our boards.

The traffic is bumper to bumper as we approach the city centre.

'Come on! Move it!' Jack's knees jiggle beneath the wheel. 'I can't wait to be in the water.'

'Same,' Mikki says.

High rises slide past, casting the road in shadow. A woman in a burqa carries a tray of sushi rolls over a crossing; a Japanese girl carries a McDonald's bag. This could almost be a large English city until you look closely and see old men wearing shorts and surf brand baseball caps and old ladies with bare legs and sandals instead of thick brown stockings and sensible lace-ups.

A poster in a bus shelter catches my eye. *Missing: French national.* The photo shows a smiling dark-haired girl. The bus pulls away to reveal more of the wall and another *Missing* poster. And another.

'Wow! Missing backpackers. There's so many of them!' I think of Elke's mum and her sad eyes.

Mikki waves her fingers. 'Australia's a big country. Thirty thousand people go missing here every year.'

I stare back at the posters as Jack drives on: a trio of young women.

'Look!' Jack points.

Through the skyscrapers, I glimpse the brilliant white sails that top the Sydney Opera House, but right now I'm more interested in the missing backpackers. 'But where do they go?'

Mikki cranes round in her seat to look at me. The criss-cross supports of the Harbour Bridge stencil intricate patterns onto her face.

'Who knows? They get lost or just feel like disappearing. Most of them turn up eventually.'

CHAPTER 5

KENNA

When the traffic thins, Jack puts his foot down on the gas and a welcome breeze blows in the open windows. Copper-coloured cliffs tower on either side, the passage of the road hacked through the rock. They call Australia 'the lucky country' but I doubt the people who built this road felt that way.

'This beach.' I have to shout over the draught to make myself heard. 'How far is it?'

'Four or five hours,' Jack says. 'Depends on traffic.'

'Wow, that's quite a way.' Presumably I can get a bus or train back if I need to.

'Don't worry. It's worth it.'

Mikki nods. 'It's *so* worth it.'

Their excitement is catching. A beach. I haven't been to a beach since I left Cornwall eighteen months ago. 'Does it have a name?'

'Sorrow Bay,' Jack says. 'But we just call it the Bay.'

The road begins to climb. Deep gorges fork off here and there between swathes of forest.

'It's got a rocky point break at the south end,' Jack says. 'And a river mouth to the north. Little community on one side but on our side, there's nothing. It's an hour off the motorway and you need a four-wheel drive to even get near it. There's a dirt road but it's full of potholes. You have to know it's there or you wouldn't bother.'

I call up Google Earth on my phone. *Sorrow Bay.* Here we go. The tiny beige beach is backed by a wide expanse of green national park. Here's the river. 'Shark Creek? And are there? Sharks?'

Jack glances at Mikki as though he's not sure he should be telling me. 'There's been some attacks over the years but it works in our favour. It puts people off.'

'By attack, you mean . . .?'

'Well, they're great whites mostly. Hard to survive something like that. But it keeps the crowd down. It used to be a popular campground. Now it's only us that surf there.'

I swallow. 'Glad I don't intend to go in the water.'

'Wait till you see it.'

Sharks are something surfers try not to think about. We didn't have to worry about them in Cornwall but Mikki and I have both surfed in places where shark sightings are common and you just have to accept it as a risk of the sport, like skiers and snowboarders risk avalanches.

Mikki sits hunched over her phone in the front. So this is what she's been doing – surfing with sharks? It shouldn't really surprise me. Surfing has been her life the whole time I've known her. It was my life as well for many years, but Mikki took it further than I did and working as a surf instructor meant she was in the ocean all day, every day.

I swallow a yawn. Jetlag is setting in and once again it feels like the middle of the night despite the blinding sunlight. I email my parents and play about on social media. When I next check the window, I can almost imagine that we're in Cornwall. There are gently sloping fields speckled with dandelions, cows grazing beside snow-white geese. Only the odd palm tree gives the game away, plus the parched look of the vegetation, as though someone has turned the oven up to high and forgotten to turn it off.

Signs flash past. *Swans Creek, Herons Creek*. A creek, to me, is a muddy ditch, but most of the ones we drive over are big enough that I'd call them rivers. *Muddy Creek*. *Eight Mile Creek*.

Mikki's still on her phone.

I lean forward and tap her shoulder. 'You okay?'

'Yeah, why?'

'You're really quiet.' She's hardly spoken since we left Sydney.

'She hasn't had her coffee yet.' Jack nudges her. 'Eh, Mikki? We'll stop at the servo before the turn-off.'

I'm impressed once again by how well he knows her. Mikki can be a moody cow at times, especially when she needs a coffee. I turn my gaze back to the window. *Grassy Plains*. *Shallow Bay*. I like the straightforwardness of the place names around here. What you see is what you get. *Cow Creek* – had a cow once got stuck there? *Mosquito Creek*. I wouldn't want to fall in that one. *Rattle Creek*. Or that one.

29

At the service station Mikki and I go inside to use the bathroom while Jack fills up. When I emerge, Mikki's looking at something on the pinboard. It's covered with bits of paper, flapping in the air conditioning: weather bulletins and bush walks, yoga classes and Men's Group . . .

Missing, German national. Last seen on Bondi Beach on 2nd September.

A familiar set of eyes look out at me from the poster: *Elke*. A weird feeling runs through me. It's almost as though she's following me around.

Mikki jumps when she sees me and steers me to the coffee counter. 'What do you want?'

'Cappuccino,' I say. 'But I'll get them.'

'It's okay.' She seems distracted.

Jack comes up to the window.

Mikki waves him back to the car. 'I'll pay!' she shouts and steps forward to order. Her eyes flit back to the poster as we wait for our coffees.

I try to pay but once again Mikki doesn't let me. 'Thanks,' I say, taking a sip.

Outside, Jack is chatting to a couple of women beside a bright yellow Jeep with surfboards on the roof. *Rent-a-Jeep* it says on the side.

'You've got Bumble Bay to the north,' Jack tells them. 'That's a good one.'

'Wait,' one of the women says, flipping through a little pocket surf guide. 'Yeah, I got it.'

I force the missing backpackers from my mind for now. 'Hi. Are you American?'

'Canadian,' her friend says.

'Sorry,' I say. 'I'm terrible with accents.'

Clutching his coffee, Jack heads behind the taller of the two. 'Don't move.'

Her eyes go wide. A pretty redhead, she's wearing a denim playsuit.

Jack clamps his palm over her shoulder. 'Mozzie. Got it!'

She laughs. 'Thanks! The mozzies here are evil.'

'Wait!' Jack says. 'There's another one!'

He's all over her. I'm not convinced there really are any mosquitoes. I think it's just an excuse to touch her. I glance at Mikki, embarrassed on her behalf, but she doesn't react. Almost as if he does this a lot.

'My wife has good blood,' the dark-haired woman says.

'Did you tell them about Sorrow Bay?' I ask Jack.

'Hey, we need to go,' Jack says.

The woman consults her book. 'Sorrow Bay? It's not there.'

But Jack strides off. One minute he's flirting big time, yet the moment he heard the word 'wife' he suddenly had to go. As if it isn't bad enough to flirt in front of his fiancée, he's homophobic as well?

'It's probably too small to be listed,' I say.

'Let's go, Kenna,' Mikki says.

Her too? I want to show the women that I'm not like that. 'There's a campsite there. That's where we're off to.'

'Kenna!' Mikki tugs my arm sharply.

The woman takes her phone out. 'I'll google it.'

Jack toots the horn.

Mikki's nearly ripping my arm from its socket. 'God, Kenna. Come *on*!'

'Sorry,' I say. 'Better go. Have a great trip!'

'You too!' the woman calls.

Silence in the front of the car as Jack pulls back onto the motorway.

'Look at the trees,' Jack says. 'The southerly's blowing. Those bastards are getting all the waves.'

Dickhead. *Let it drop,* I tell myself.

Jack nudges Mikki. 'Want to check the forecast before the turn-off?'

Mikki pulls out her phone. I remember the missing backpackers and pull out *my* phone. There are various articles. I click on the first one. *Eight missing backpackers and counting . . .* I scan the photos. Most of the missing people are female. The two males couldn't look more different: one in a wetsuit, blond hair plastered to the sides of his face; the other in a suit and tie, so clean-cut he doesn't look like a backpacker at all. There's a mix of nationalities: American, Swedish, Irish . . . A couple of them hold surfboards. The coffee has had no effect on me whatsoever. I'm zoning out even though I try my hardest to keep awake.

'It's three to four foot today,' Mikki says. 'Dropping off tomorrow.'

'Damn!' Jack says.

I hold onto my seat as he turns.

A sign flashes past: *Welcome to Sorrow National Park.* We're on a single-track gravel road now. Between the trees, a glimpse of dark water. Shark Creek, I guess, though it looks like a full-blown river.

Another sign: *Road subject to flooding.*

'What's the wind doing?' Jack asks.

Mikki peers at her phone. 'South wind in the mornings, turning north in the afternoons.'

Yawning, I click on another article. Another missing backpacker was last seen in Bondi, just like Elke. Still, most backpackers probably visit Bondi.

'Better be quick,' Jack says when he sees what I'm doing. 'The phone signal runs out in a minute.'

'Seriously?' I say.

'There's nobody out here,' Jack says. 'Nobody except us, anyway.'

I'm starting to regret this whole idea. 'So there's no internet, no phone *at all*? Shit!'

The article refuses to load. Sure enough, there's no reception. I'm online all the time normally. Clients book me through my website. I posted to say I'm away all month but if any of my regulars hurt themselves, they're likely to message me anyway. And what if I want to leave? Without a phone line to call a taxi or an Uber, I'm reliant on a guy I hardly know.

But my eyelids are so heavy it hurts to keep them open. I can't fight the jetlag any longer. There's a black hooded top in the footwell. I pick it up, wad it against the window as a pillow and close my eyes. As I drift off, I hear Mikki's voice.

'She's sleeping,' she says accusingly. 'You didn't, did you?'

'*No!*' Jack says. 'Of course not. She's yer mate!'

Dimly I wonder what they're talking about. But I'm too tired to care.

CHAPTER 6

KENNA

My eyes fly open as I'm pitched forward. The car skids to a stop. A canopy of leaves obscures the sky, casting the road in shadow – if you can call it a road. It's just dirt and gravel.

A barrier blocks the track ahead: *Danger! Landslides. Road closed.*

Mikki opens her door, jumps out and drags the barrier sideways. Jack drives on, gravel crunching under the tyres. I panic, wide awake now, and crane my head to see where Mikki is. Jack jams the brakes on again and Mikki climbs back in. Behind her, the barrier is back in place. Jack continues down the dirt road.

I watch through the windscreen as we bump up and down. 'It said the road's closed.'

'Don't worry about it.' Jack drives on for long minutes, bouncing through potholes.

A grinding noise from under the car as we dip into a large crater. I grip my seat, terrified he'll pop a tyre – then

34

what? I check my phone. Still no reception, so it's not like we can call a tow truck.

The trees seem to go on forever in every direction, trunks bare and blackened in places, with brave new foliage sprouting forth. Around a corner, water streams across the track: a weir. Jack drives through it without slowing, sending water spraying past the windows. I'm freaking out a bit now. I didn't know it would be quite so remote.

'I don't have a sleeping bag,' I say.

'We have a spare,' Mikki says.

'I didn't bring any sunscreen.'

'You can borrow mine.' She glances over her shoulder at me. 'You never used to be such a worrier. I was like that too, the first time I came here. This place is going to be good for you.'

Jack slams on the brakes.

'What?' Mikki asks.

He points at a long dark object across the track. A stick. No – a snake.

Jack revs the engine but the snake doesn't move. 'Fuck.'

'Just drive over it,' Mikki says.

'I don't want to squash it.' Jack draws in slow breaths, knuckles white on the wheel.

'Want me to—' Mikki begins.

Jack opens the door and jumps out. 'No.'

'Careful!' Mikki shouts.

He slams the door. She and I watch through the windscreen.

'Is it poisonous?' I ask.

'Probably,' Mikki says. 'He's terrified of them.'

35

Jack scours the side of the track and picks up a dead leaf which he tosses at the snake. The snake doesn't move.

Jack aims another leaf. It bounces off the snake's back and the snake slithers off. Jack jumps back in, looking pale.

Mikki pats his shoulder. 'Good one.'

He grips the wheel for a long moment before setting off again.

I see vehicles parked ahead: a flashy red pick-up truck and a mud-splattered four-wheel drive. Jack crunches to a stop beside them. The earth is hard and dry under my feet as I step out. I smell bark and moss, and the still air rings with the buzzing of insects.

Jack throws the back of the truck open. 'Take what you can carry.'

Mikki sets off down a narrow trail, laden with bags. I haul my backpack on, slide out the board Jack showed me yesterday, grab my daypack and set off after Mikki. It's strange to carry a surfboard under my arm again. I don't plan to make a habit of it. Mikki turns a corner and disappears from view. Surfboard bashing against my hip, I speed up. The path splits into two, but Mikki's nowhere in sight.

A wooden sign: *Beach this way*. In the distance, the hiss of waves. Insects hum in my ears as I hurry along. The track is overgrown and branches scratch my face. A cobweb blocks the path ahead. I don't like spiders at the best of times but at least English ones aren't deadly. I look back, hoping to see Jack, but there's nothing. I can't hear the waves any more either, which is weird. Carefully I use the nose of the surfboard to scrape the cobweb aside.

Looking for spiders, I duck through. The trees are pressing in on either side, branches snagging in my hair as I push past. Did I choose the wrong path?

Around the next corner – a man.

I stop in my tracks. 'Hi.'

All he wears is a pair of board shorts. He has closely cropped dark hair and stunning grey-green eyes. And he's staring at me as though he's seen a ghost.

'I'm Kenna.'

He clears his throat. 'Clemente.'

Tanned and bare-chested, he has the narrow hips and strong upper body of a surfer, and tattoos down his arms and legs. He must be one of the group, surely – the Tribe.

'I'm looking for the beach,' I say. 'And my friend Mikki.'

Clemente seems to collect himself. 'Not this way.'

He has an accent – Spanish, I think.

'Oh,' I say. 'But the sign—'

'Come.' Before I can stop him, Clemente takes the surfboard from me. I follow him back through the bushes to the other fork. We reach a clearing where four tents are arranged around a wooden picnic bench and barbecue. A small concrete building stands to one side – a toilet block?

A girl strides towards me. 'Who the fuck are you?'

I try not to flinch. She has a strong Aussie accent, long blonde dreadlocks and skin that has seen too much sun.

'This is Kenna,' Jack says. 'Mikki's mate from England. Kenna, this is Sky.'

Sky turns on Mikki.

'*He* invited her, not me,' Mikki says quietly.

Hurt spikes my chest.

Jack wraps an arm around my waist and steers me to the pile of bags and boards. 'Just dump everything here for now.'

For once, I'm grateful that he's so bloody hands on. I brace myself as I pass Sky, almost expecting her to lash out. A skin-headed black guy with strong, proud cheekbones and serious muscles steps forward to join her and Clemente. The way they're looking me up and down makes me feel like an accused criminal standing before a jury.

Sky turns to Jack. 'You can't just bring people here unannounced.' Lean and muscular in a racerback top that shows off strong shoulders, she's a few inches shorter than me. Her feet are bare beneath ripped cargo shorts, her toenails sea blue.

The black guy shakes his head. 'Yeah, you can't keep doing this, brother.' He has an accent but I'm not sure what it is.

'She flew all the way out from England,' Jack says. 'Shame to come all that way to only spend a few hours with her friend.'

When Mikki had mentioned the group, I'd imagined a bunch of hippies who wore flowers in their hair, smoked weed and danced barefoot around a campfire. Not this. Clustered in close as they discuss what to do with me, they remind me of a sports team plotting how to wipe out the enemy.

Chapter 7

Kenna

Mikki shoots me a helpless look. *Say something, Mikki. Stand up for me.* But she says nothing. I sense she's embarrassed. My arrival has stirred up trouble for her.

Jack nudges Clemente. 'What do you reckon? She reminds me of—'

'*Don't!*' Clemente's gaze meets mine. Those incredible eyes . . . I can't look away. Or swallow. Or hardly even breathe. It's a relief when he whips around and strides off into the trees.

Sky sighs. 'What are we going to do?'

'Kenna's going to hang with us for a few days, then go off travelling,' Mikki says.

Finally. But it's too little too late.

'Yeah,' Jack says. 'And the next time we do a supply run, I'll drive her to the Greyhound stop.'

Trying not to show my discomfort, I sip water from my bottle and look around. A tarpaulin strung between the trees shelters exercise equipment: yoga mats, gym balls

39

and foam rollers similar to the ones I use in my studio. Surfboards lie about everywhere, face down, waxy surfaces shaded from the sunlight streaming through the leaves.

'But she knows about this place now,' the black guy says.

'Who's she going to tell, Victor?' Jack asks.

'That's the problem!' Victor raises his voice. 'We don't know, do we?'

A crow takes fright, flapping up, cawing an alarm over the treetops.

'Shush.' Sky clasps his shoulder and pads over to me. 'Victor's right. You can't tell anyone about this place, Kenna.'

Victor follows her over. 'What we have here is precious.' He slings his arm around her; apparently they're a couple.

'Who would I tell?' I say. 'I don't know anyone in Australia except Mikki and you guys.'

Jack turns to the others. 'See?'

'Surf's up!' a voice calls.

We all turn to look. Clemente jogs back down the track.

'It's too windy,' Sky says.

'It's changed direction.' Clemente starts waxing a surfboard.

Suddenly the others are picking up boards and passing the wax around. I wait for them to remember me, but Clemente jogs off down the track and the others run after him, one by one, leaving just me and Mikki.

Mikki seems flustered. 'Sorry. They're pretty protective of this place. They'll get over it.'

I force a smile. 'Sure.' It was always me and Mikki

against the world. I'm reeling at how her loyalties have shifted.

She rummages through her backpack, pulls a bikini top out, strips her T-shirt and bra off and wriggles into it. I blink in shock. She used to be such a prude.

She has surf shorts on already. She picks up her board and looks my way, apology in her face. 'Are you coming?'

For a moment I'm tempted. If only I could erase what happened and go back to the time before the ocean was poisoned for me. 'No. But have fun.'

'Thanks.' Mikki jogs off, leaving the clearing still and silent except for the sounds of nature: the rustle of leaves, the faint crash of waves.

A dark silhouette of a person careers towards me. What the—?

I let out my breath. It's just a wetsuit, swinging on a clothes hanger from an overhead branch. I stand there, trying to collect myself, but every movement of the trees and bushes makes my nerves jangle afresh.

My daypack has my wallet, passport and phone in it. I grab it and hurry down the track after the others. The trees start to thin; the crash of waves gets louder. A tang of salt in the air. I emerge from the undergrowth to a faded wooden sign: *Danger! Unpatrolled Beach. Strong currents.* Behind it, a sandy bay with jagged dark rocks at the south end. Waves wrap around the rocks, glassy and perfect. It's a bittersweet sight, like bumping into a lover you still have a thing for, even though you know they're bad for you. I moved to London to avoid having to see the ocean, yet here it is in front of me once again, its pull stronger than ever.

Mikki is scrambling over the rocks. The others are already in the water, paddling out. I kick my flip-flops off. The sand caresses my toes as I walk towards the rocks.

The water is the most incredible shade of turquoise. I used to think it was this colour that gave surfing its magic, then I surfed the grey water of dusk, black water by moonlight, silver water during a rainstorm and every shade of blue and green, all just as magical.

Clemente catches a wave and carves huge powerful turns almost to the shore. Sky is up and riding the wave behind. The ache builds. I could run back down the path, grab Jack's spare board and join them. Out of the shelter of the trees, the wind is stronger. It blasts me towards the water as though it can read my mind. I lean backwards, fighting it, and pick my way sideways across the rocks instead, looking for a flat one to sit on. Here we go.

The water is so clear I can see shells and pebbles on the seabed. I reach down to cup a handful. It's warmer than I expected – way warmer than Cornish seas, even in midsummer. I let it trickle through my fingers. Amazing to think these same water molecules might have washed past my local beach, crashed over Hawaiian reefs, or once been part of huge icebergs.

The glare off the water is dazzling. I should have put my sunglasses on. The brightness of this place; I'm not prepared for it. A larger wave splashes up against the rocks. My shorts get soaked but I don't care. I lick my lips and taste salt. God, I've missed that. I scoot forward until my feet are the water. And it's like I'm washing my soul.

Jack gets a wave, taking off with the white cap peeling over his head and disappearing into the barrel before shooting out the other end. Again, I contemplate going back to get that board, but I know what would happen if I did. I'd get smashed, for a start, because I'm massively out of practice, but far worse: I'd be sucked back into the sport I quit, obsessed all over again.

In my surfing years, I couldn't plan anything because my life revolved around the waves. A nine-to-five job? That's when the waves are least crowded. My cousin's wedding? The waves were amazing that day. A city-break with girlfriends? For two hundred quid I could fly to Biarritz! When I quit, in a way it was a relief because I could live my life again and focus on my career, although I can't say I'm happier for it.

A wave looms towards Mikki. She paddles sideways. *Don't take it, Mikki!* It's breaking right onto the rocks, the water in front of her sucking dry. If she falls, she's in trouble.

She paddles for it. The ocean pitches up behind her and for a moment it looks like it'll tip her in headfirst, but her knees compress in a sharp bottom turn and she somehow remains standing. A backwash rushes out from the shore, lending a few inches of water over the rocks as she zigzags over them.

A burst of pride washes over me. At thirty, she's just as hardcore as she was at twenty. The risks she's taking, though! The sooner I get her out of here the better. I fish in my bag for my phone. Still no reception. Without transportation of my own or even the ability to call an Uber, I'm at the mercy of the others. Behind me, cliffs rise up. If I get to higher ground, I might find some reception, but how do I get up there?

I set off back along the sand. The sun blazes down on my arms and head. I didn't think to put on a cap – or sunscreen. At the far end of the bay, a rock wall extends out into the water, the river presumably just beyond it. I note the calmness of the water beside the rocks and how the waves aren't breaking there. If I hadn't spent my teenage years surfing the treacherous Cornish coast, I wouldn't recognise it: a powerful rip that runs rapidly out to sea.

I retrieve my flip-flops and head into the trees. The shush-shush of leaves is soothing, the air several degrees cooler. The trail branches left, then right, with no sign of the trees ever ending. In places the undergrowth is so thick it obscures the path and I have to wade blindly forward until I glimpse it again. Clouds of mosquitoes rise up as I push through.

The sound of crickets grows deafening. It feels like I could walk for miles in any direction and never find my way out. Now and then, I glance back to make sure I can see the way I've come.

A movement catches my eye. A bright blue butterfly sits on a leaf, opening and closing its wings. Transfixed, I pause to watch it. Something buzzes past my ear and hits my cheek. I squeak and bat it away.

When I look up, I'm disoriented. I do a slow aboutturn. Green in all directions – so much green it's dizzying. Openings in the undergrowth on either side. Which track did I come in on? I glance left, then right, and they both look exactly the same. I can't hear the waves any more so I can't tell if the beach is behind me or in front of me.

I check my phone but there's still no signal. *Don't panic.* I walked for three or four minutes so I'll pick a path at random – the one on my right – and walk down it for five minutes. If it doesn't take me back to the clearing, I'll turn and walk back the other way. Easy.

I stride forward, and soon my T-shirt is sticking to my back and I'm desperately thirsty. I didn't think to bring my water bottle. A news headline springs to mind about a hiker lost in Australia's Blue Mountains for several days, who survived by drinking water that had collected in leaves. I peer into the nearest bushes but there's nothing – it's too hot.

Have five minutes passed yet? My head is spinning. I lean against the nearest tree trunk, trying to think. Should I wait here until it gets cooler or keep walking? I close my eyes.

Something buzzes in my ear and I jerk upright. I must have fallen asleep because I'm even thirstier now. My head hurts. The trees ahead look thicker so I press on into the shade. Through the bushes, I see something. It takes my brain a moment to make sense of it.

Lying on the ground, just discernible in the gaps between the leaves, is a body.

CHAPTER 8

KENNA

A scream breaks out of me.

The body scrambles up and a man with raggedy blond hair and a scruffy beard pushes his way towards me. I raise my hands instinctively as he nears me but he makes no move to attack me.

'Hi,' I say. It comes out as a squeak.

His eyes flit from my face to the trees around us. *California Dreaming* says the logo on his grubby white T-shirt. I can't decide if he's one of the Tribe or some kind of traveller or homeless person.

'I'm lost,' I say. 'Do you know the way back to the campsite?'

'Who are you?' There's anger in his tone.

'Kenna. Mikki's friend?'

He thinks about that. And skirts round me. 'This way.'

What was he doing, lying there like that? I hurry after him, trying to pull myself together. 'What's your name?'

'Ryan.'

'Are you Canadian?'

He glances over his shoulder. 'I'm American.'

'Oh. Where are you from?'

'Noo York.' He hams up the accent. 'No, I'm actually from California.'

Apparently he's one of those people who feel the need to make everything a joke. I hate it when people do that because you can never be sure if they're serious or not. It's a defence mechanism usually – if you keep everything jokey and light, you stay on the surface and avoid getting deep or personal – but it's bloody annoying.

Ryan stops dead and points. An orange thing in the tree ahead. Large and oval, some kind of fruit maybe. He shimmies up the tree, gripping the trunk between his thighs.

'What is it?' I ask.

'Papaya.' He twists it off, inspects it and hurls it sideways as though it burnt his fingers. He drops back down from the tree. 'Bats have been at it. They carry diseases.' He spits into his cupped hands and wipes them on the gnarled bark of the tree trunk.

A fierce chirruping erupts from a nearby bush. I back away. 'What's that?'

'Just crickets.'

We walk on.

'How do you know the way?' I ask. 'It all looks the same.'

'I've learnt my way around.' Ryan gestures to a huge ridged tree trunk a metre in diameter. 'You recognise the landmarks.'

'I'm surprised there aren't more signs.'

'There used to be.'

Flashes of green and red in the branches. I squint upwards at the birds above.

'Lorikeets.' Ryan tucks a straggly blond strand behind his ear. Every time our eyes meet he looks away.

He sets off again. The undergrowth gets thicker.

'Whistle,' he says.

'What?'

'To let the snakes know you're coming.'

Is he joking?

'Weather like this, they like to sunbathe. You don't want to step on one. If they hear you, they have time to get out of the way.'

I'm still not sure if he's winding me up but I whistle through my teeth, scanning the ground ahead as he leads me left and right. Damn jetlag. I'm all out of energy.

Suddenly we're in the clearing again. The others stand around in dripping swimwear. They fall silent when they see me. No prizes for guessing what they've been talking about. Mikki flashes me a sheepish smile.

Ryan strides towards them. 'Someone tell me what *she's* doing here?'

'It's all right,' Sky says. 'We've dealt with it. She's only here for a few days.'

'Nobody asked me about it,' he says.

I thought Sky and Victor were together but she slides her arm round Ryan's shoulder in a very intimate way and leads him into the trees to talk. The others disperse. Mikki gives me another smile and heads to a tent. I want to speak to her but she's probably getting changed.

Jetlag is hitting hard, now. I look at the tents, longing

to crawl into one and sleep. My water bottle is where I left it beside the mound of bags. I take long, beautiful gulps. It's the temperature of a hot bath and tastes of plastic but I don't care. Clemente and Jack are at the tap, improvising a shower by filling bottles and pouring them over their heads.

An intense pain suddenly radiates in my big toe. I look down and there's an enormous ant, brown and glossy, on my foot.

'Shit!' I brush it off and dance around, scared there are more.

'What happened?' Jack calls.

'An ant bit me.'

'Bull ants,' Jack says. 'Evil bastards.'

'God, it's burning.' My eyes are watering.

'Get some ice on it.' The cool box from Jack's car sits in the shade under a tree. He heads over to it and scoops out a handful. Before I can protest, he steers me to a tree stump, lifts my foot to his lap and presses the cubes to my toe. At some unseen signal, the lorikeets take off from their branch and fly a lap above the treetops, squawking madly.

The hairs on Jack's thigh rub my ankle. This guy has no sense of personal space. Clemente looks over at us, his expression dark. Then I notice Sky and Ryan watching me too.

I wrestle the ice from Jack. 'I'll do it.'

The lorikeets return to their branch and the squawks continue at a muted volume as though they're evaluating their lap. I press the ice to my toe.

'I saw you at the beach,' Jack says. 'What do you reckon? Nice, hey?'

'Yeah, really nice.'

Jack beams. 'Told ya!'

I'm struggling to work him out. Kind to snakes, even though he hates them, attentive to Mikki's needs, and so far nothing but friendly towards me. So what is it about him that prickles? Is it just that I think he's taking Mikki for a ride?

Mikki emerges from the tent with her wet gear and heads to a clothesline strung between the trees. Clemente is at the cool box. I watch him fill a sock with ice and wrap it round his fingers: a homemade icepack.

Ice cubes dripping from my fingers, I limp over to him. 'Have you hurt your hand?'

His damp hair sticks up in little dark spikes. He clicks his tongue. 'Is nothing.'

'Want me to look?'

'No,' Clemente says and walks off.

How rude is this guy? I head over to Mikki.

She nods in Clemente's direction. 'What did he want?'

'Nothing.'

Clemente is filling a bottle from one of the water containers we bought in the supermarket. I can't stop looking at him and every time I do, he's looking at me. Probably because he's noticed I'm staring. *Stop it, Kenna!*

I turn back to Mikki. 'What *is* this place? Who *are* these people?'

Something flickers over her face.

'What?'

'They were there for me when you weren't.'

'Are you mad with me?'

She draws in a shaky breath. 'You know how you felt

when you lost Kasim? That's how I felt when you moved to London. I mean I know it's not the same, but it's how I felt. You were just gone.'

I'm astonished by her outburst. She never says things like this. 'Yeah, it's not the same at all because you could phone me and FaceTime me . . .' Even as I say it, I remember how I shut myself away, not answering her calls. 'I'm sorry.'

Tears shine in her eyes. From the way her shoulders are shaking, I can tell just how much emotion she's holding back.

I hug her. 'I'm so sorry. Shit, you're going to make *me* cry.'

She hugs me back, then pulls away, still fighting for control. 'What you went through was much worse, I get that. But it hurt. I kept telling myself you'd come back one day, but it seemed like you'd moved to London for good.'

'I told you. Come and stay with me. You can stay as long as you like.'

'I'm a surf instructor. What could I do in London? I feel dead inside when I'm away from the ocean.'

Dead inside. I can definitely relate.

'Cornwall wasn't the same without you. I felt so alone.' A single tear rolls down Mikki's cheek. She wipes it angrily away. 'That's why I came here and now I'm actually happy again, even happier than I was in Cornwall, but you keep on at me about going home. And it's not going to happen.'

I try another tack. 'I saw you earlier, surfing in, like, one inch of water.' I expect her to look at least slightly guilty – or even simply acknowledge the danger.

51

'So?'

I feel like a mother interfering in her teen daughter's business. 'Do you know how risky that was? We're in the middle of nowhere. If something happens . . .'

'Seriously?' Mikki says. 'You of all people, telling me that?'

CHAPTER 9

KENNA

TWENTY YEARS AGO

Two pairs of Adidas trainers swinging back and forth in the pale winter sunshine. Me and Mikki side by side on the climbing frame on my first day at my new school. The air smelt of cowpats, so different to my old school, with its smell of diesel fumes from the busy bus lane beyond the gate.

'None of the other girls like me,' I whispered.

'Don't worry,' Mikki said. 'I'll be your friend.'

'Okay.' I fought tears. I missed my old school and my old house. My old life.

Mikki wrapped her arm round me. 'Let's stick together.'

'I hate this place. What even is there to do around here anyway?'

'Can you surf?'

'I've never tried.'

'I'll teach you.'

'Cool.' I could barely even swim but I wasn't about to tell her that. With her glossy black pigtails and mischievous

53

smile, Mikki seemed like a lot of fun. 'And I'll teach you to walk across the bars. Want to try?'

Mikki squealed as I stood up.

'Don't look directly down,' I said. 'That's the secret.'

Slowly, she got to her feet, her dark eyes all big and scared.

'Look at me. You can see the bars, right? Forget about the drop and just walk normally.'

Mikki took a cautious step forward.

'Hey!' a voice shouted. 'Stop that at once!'

Mikki wobbled and almost fell. Just in time I grabbed her hand. We sat down in a hurry and burst out laughing.

'Get down from there, girls!' Miss Rotterly stood below, waving her arms.

I spent the afternoon sitting outside the head teacher's office for my 'dangerous' behaviour. It was a relief when the bell rang. Outside school, my mum got chatting with Mikki's mum. While we waited for them, I climbed a tree.

'How did you get up there?' Mikki shouted.

'It's easy!' I slid down and showed her where to put her feet.

Mikki was shorter than me, so I had to give her a leg-up, then I climbed up to join her.

'Time to go,' Mikki's mum said.

But Mikki couldn't get down. I forgot how going up is always easier than going down. In the end, her mum had to call the fire brigade. Miss Rotterly came out to see what all the noise was about. When she learnt I was to blame, she went nuts.

'What is it with you?' she shouted. 'You keep this up and someone's going to get badly hurt.'

CHAPTER 10

KENNA

My ant bite throbs. I press the ice back down on it.

'Basically,' Mikki says, 'I'm doing the sort of stuff you used to do and you're giving me a hard time for it.'

'But he died,' I say. A fresh wave of guilt hits me.

'It wasn't your fault.'

That's debatable, but I don't say so. We've had this discussion so many times. A sting in my shoulder – a giant mosquito. I squish it and blood smears over my skin. 'God, the mosquitoes are shocking.'

'You get used to them,' Mikki says.

'And the ants. Don't you mind them?'

'Not especially. Only moths, and I'm not even that bad with them any more.'

'Really?' She's always been terrified of moths. Not butterflies. Just moths. I thought it was funny and kind of cute – they don't even bite! – until I witnessed her have a full-blown panic attack. 'Remember that time one got stuck in your hair?'

We had been on a narrow winding road, as most Cornish roads are, when a moth flew in the driver's side window, hitting Mikki in the face. She had screamed and lost control of the car, which shot forward, then – fortunately – stalled and lurched to a stop on the edge of the road.

I had tried to free the moth from the car but Mikki thrashed about while the moth flapped madly in the corner of the windscreen.

Mikki grins. 'Yeah, let's not talk about that.'

We're laughing about it now, but it was quite possibly the closest I've come to dying. Relieved to see Mikki looking more like her usual self, I slide my phone out. Still no signal. 'Do you get used to being offline?'

'I love it.'

'Seriously? It's killing me to think of all the notifications I've missed. I'd normally have checked my social media a dozen times by now. I'm trying to cut down, but I didn't plan to go cold turkey.'

I'm worrying about my clients too. Dom Williams had a frozen shoulder and I'm desperate to know if he's got any movement back; Jolanta Novak had knee surgery this week.

You never switch off, do you? Tim complained on our second date.

But if someone gets hurt, they might need me. I used to like being needed, but this past year, it became a bit overwhelming.

'Hang out with us for a few days,' Mikki says. 'Then you can go back to all that.'

'I guess.' How can I convince her to come home? I'm all out of ideas for now.

At least our conversation seems to have cleared the air a little. Mikki reaches for my hand and grips it as though she'll never let go.

Laughter rings out over by the trees. Sky has a really dirty laugh. The others have obviously heard it a million times because they don't react. She's with Victor, planking on a yoga mat in a string bikini that shows off her taut stomach muscles.

Mikki nudges me. 'You could even have a surf or two.'

'I told you. I don't do that kind of thing any more.'

'What, have fun?' Her tone is gentle. 'Whether you surf or not, it won't bring him back. You can't punish yourself forever.'

'But it could have been me or you.' I felt invincible surfing as a teenager. It took my boyfriend's death to bring home how dangerous it can be.

'We all die eventually.' Mikki is quoting one of my own catchphrases back at me and I don't know how to argue with her. 'All I know is right now, around these guys, doing the things we do, I feel more alive than I've ever felt. Anyway, nothing bad is going to happen again. Just surf small waves.'

'You know as well as I do that it doesn't work like that,' I say.

With sports like ours, you always want more. Bigger, faster, scarier. You have to keep upping the ante to feel the same buzz. Or maybe that's just me.

Mikki's tone softens. 'Don't you miss it?'

'So much.' A mosquito drones in my ear. I swish it away. 'But it's not my life any more. I've changed.'

'I know.'

I can tell from Mikki's face what she thinks about this.

'When was the last time you were truly happy?' she asks.

The answer is easy. The year I spent in Cornwall with her and Kasim. I've made a new life for myself in London but I can't say I'm happy there. My 'friends' in the building I work in, if I can call them that – the other therapists, the receptionist and the security guard who mans the door – seem to like me, but I have no idea why; they're probably just being polite. They don't know the real me, the person I was before tragedy struck.

On my days off, mostly all I do is lie in bed with my memories. *It's okay to do that,* I told myself at first. *You need time.* But that was two years ago. For the past year, I've become increasingly aware that it's not okay. I chew my lip, no longer so sure of myself.

'Perhaps you were meant to come here,' Mikki says. 'Open yourself to it and I think you'll love it as much as I do.'

I glance around, taking in the well-worn surf gear dripping from the line and the faded collection of tents. The tangled undergrowth dotted with blossom. Bushy white flowers that look like toilet brushes, pink ones with spiky petals that wave in the breeze like the tentacles of sea anemones. And the trees: hundreds and thousands of them.

There must be places where you can go to talk about bereavement, Dad said a while back. He was probably thinking of the local church hall or the community centre at the end of our street. I'm sure he never imagined somewhere like this.

Clemente and Victor stagger down the trail with stuff from Jack's car; Jack unloads the cool box into a small fridge.

'Why is there a fridge?' I ask. 'Is there electricity?'

'No,' Mikki says. 'They run it off camping gas. And the barbecue.'

Sure enough, Clemente deposits a gas cylinder beside the fridge and goes about changing it.

Ryan is at the barbecue, chopping vegetables with a scary-looking knife. Mikki's casserole sits nearby. I smell it on the breeze and suddenly I'm starving. Ryan glances up every so often as though he's waiting for something to happen. He's so twitchy. He catches my eye and quickly looks away. I picture him as I first spotted him, lying in the earth. What the hell was he doing?

Victor and Clemente head over. Victor clutches a mug of something with a metal straw poking out of it. It seems to be filled with green herbs. Marijuana?

'Yeah, Mikki!' Victor holds up his hand to give her a high five. 'You got a good wave today!'

Clemente pokes Mikki in the ribs. 'It was my wave! She snaked me.'

I haven't seen Clemente in playful mode. He's like a different person.

Mikki giggles and shoves him away. I can't help smiling with them. I love the easiness between Mikki and the two men. *She's found her tribe,* people say, and in Mikki's case, she really has. She's had to travel to the other side of the world to do it, but somehow she's hit upon a group of people with as much passion for surfing as her. But I can't overlook the risks she's taking.

'What bothers me is you're miles from the nearest hospital,' I say. 'Doesn't anyone ever get hurt?'

The smiles fade. An awkward silence. Mikki's eyes meet mine, reproachful.

I turn to Clemente. 'How's your hand?'

He tuts. 'Dislocated my finger but is fine. I clicked it back in. I done it many times.'

'I dislocated my finger once,' I say. 'And it bloody hurt.'

'I will strap it but first I ice it.' He's still clutching the ice pack.

'Can I see?'

Clemente raises an eyebrow.

'It could be broken.'

With a huff of exasperation, he lifts the ice pack off and I take his hand in mine. Dislocated fingers are common occurrences for the local rugby team, so I often see them at work, but examining someone has never felt so intimate. My throat tightens at the coolness of his palm and the pressure of his fingertips against my wrist. From the way his body stills, I think he feels it too.

Carefully I examine each finger. Over the birdsong, I hear him swallow. Even in the fading light, I can see which finger it is. His ring finger is purple and swollen. I'm extra-gentle when I manipulate it, but he doesn't flinch.

'It's not too bad,' I say. 'I'd ice it as much as you can and then strap it.'

'As I said,' he snaps.

'Have you got tape?'

'Yep.' Clemente yanks his hand free and stalks off.
Another awkward silence.

Victor breaks it. 'Do you surf, Kenna?'

'I used to.' I nod at his tea. 'What's that?'

'*Chimarrão*.'

'What?'

Victor laughs. 'Brazilian tea. Is a kind of herbs. Try.'
He holds it out.

'No thanks.'

'Is good. Try.'

Politely I take a sip. 'God!' The hot acrid liquid stings
my throat. 'It's strong.'

'Nice, huh? Have more.'

Since I seem to have no choice, I drink more. Maybe it
will help my jetlag.

'Where's your accent from?' Victor asks.

'Scotland,' I say, impressed that he can hear it. 'But I
left there when I was ten and I didn't think I still had it.'
The Cornish kids teased me so much I made a conscious
effort to get rid of it. 'Are you from Brazil?'

'Yeah, from Rio.'

'Your English is really good.'

Victor beams and hollers after Clemente. 'You hear
that? She says my English is really good.'

No response from Clemente.

'So what do you think?' Victor inclines his shaven head
in the direction of the beach.

He seems friendly enough but he's so loud. I want to
back away a bit but it would seem rude. 'Yeah. Beautiful
spot.'

He puffs out his chest. 'The most beautiful. And you

know the best thing about it?' He flings an arm wide, striking me in the shoulder. 'That it's all ours.' A bellowing laugh.

I force a smile but his words disturb me. As much as he'd like it to be, it isn't their wave. It's national park, so presumably it belongs to everyone. And yeah, it's a beautiful spot, so why isn't anyone else here? From the scraps of information wrestled from Mikki in our calls, I know she's been coming here nearly a year and the others have been coming longer still. The barrier across the road can't have been here that long, surely?

'How many surfers can say they have their own wave?' Victor isn't smiling any more. 'I tell you, I would kill for this wave, Kenna.'

From the look in his eyes, he's quite serious.

CHAPTER 11

KENNA

The only thing my phone is good for now is telling the time, and soon I won't even be able to do that unless I find a way to recharge it. I stuff it back in my bag. It's five o'clock and the heat of the day is finally beginning to fade. Lorikeets squawk in the treetops as though arguing about what they've done that day; mosquitoes dance in the shade.

Clemente is doing pull-ups from a bar lashed in place between two trees. You'd never know he'd just dislocated his finger.

I head over to him. 'You shouldn't be doing that.'

His eyes meet mine as he pulls up again. He replies through clamped jaws, without breaking his rhythm. 'Why not?'

Shaking my head, I go to my backpack. I'll swap my flip-flops for running shoes to keep the mosquitoes and ants off my toes. As I step on the ground, something prickles my heel. I lift my foot but I can't see anything.

Mikki comes to see. 'What's up?'

'There's something in my heel.'

'Is it a bindi?'

'A what? Ow. It hurts.'

'They have these prickly horrible seeds in the grass. Wait.' Mikki gets a torch from her tent and shines it at my heel. 'There, see? And another one here.'

She lifts her nail to show me a tiny spike as fine as one of the hairs on my arms. Amazing that it can irritate that much.

'They're all over the place,' Mikki says. 'So watch where you step. My feet have toughened up now so I don't feel them.'

She stoops down to pluck something from a plant. 'Want one?'

A cherry tomato. 'Thanks!' Sweetness explodes on my tongue as I bite into it. 'Are they wild?'

'No. We grow stuff.' She gestures to the bushes and I see various plants in neat rows.

Male laughter drifts our way. Clemente and Jack stand close, heads lowered. Clemente says something and Jack laughs again and slaps Clemente on the back.

'It's ready!' Ryan calls.

In a chipped assortment of bowls, Mikki's casserole nestles beside stir-fried vegetables.

Victor clasps his arms around his biceps. 'Is cold tonight. Let's light the fire.'

Brazilians have a different idea of cold, clearly.

Jack swats a mosquito. 'Yeah, it'll keep the mozzies off.'

Victor produces a lighter. He has a tattoo on the inside of his wrist – the same place that Mikki has hers – of a monstrous wave in striking shades of blue, with a thick white lip. He and Jack crouch over the fire pit, muttering and cursing.

Clemente pushes them aside. 'Let me.' The muscles in his back ripple with the movements of his arm. If you can't imagine a back being sexy, look at a surfer. They have the best backs.

Soon a small fire burns. We sit around it on an assortment of tree stumps and rocks. Sky sits beside Victor in a gauzy peach blouse and combat shorts. Jack eats one-handed, free hand rubbing up and down Mikki's inner thigh. Ryan sits a little apart from the rest of us, leaning forward over his plate, blond hair covering his face.

I turn to Clemente. 'Where are you from?'

'Spain,' he says without looking at me. 'Barcelona.'

Espain. Barth-elona. His accent is so hot. 'Do you go back there much?'

'Not for seven years.'

'Do you miss it?' I ask.

'No.'

Getting words out of Clemente is like drawing blood from a stone so I give up and watch him eat. Until I notice the others watching me watching him.

Sky breaks into a smile. 'Where are our manners? We should introduce ourselves to our guest. Okay, so I'm Sky and I used to be a competitive swimmer at high school, then I discovered surfing.'

That explains the shoulders. Useful too, for a surfer, to be a strong swimmer. I wish I was.

Victor gives her an adoring look.

'I'm a Gold Coast boy,' Jack says. 'The beach was down

the end of our street. I used to wag school and go surfing. The teachers reckoned I would come to nothing but I got sponsors before I turned twelve.'

'I'm Victor,' Victor says. 'I like big waves and I cannot lie.'

Everyone cracks up. Sky whacks Victor on the back of the head. She has tattoos around her biceps: a wild tangle of vines and flowers that remind me of the undergrowth here.

Clemente says nothing until Sky clasps his arm.

'I flew into Sydney five years ago for a working holiday and never went home,' Clemente says.

'You got residence?' I ask.

'Yep.' Clemente doesn't volunteer how.

Sky's fingers linger on his arm, skimming his olive skin. She seems a really touchy-feely person. When Victor notices, he wraps a possessive arm around her waist.

'How long are you in Australia, Kenna?' Sky asks.

Ryan hasn't introduced himself, but she doesn't prompt him. I glance at Mikki. 'About a month.' Or maybe less if I can convince her to leave.

'Mikki said you used to surf,' she says. 'Why did you stop?'

'My boyfriend drowned.'

A hush falls over them. Their gazes are sympathetic, yet curious.

'And now you're scared of the water?' Sky asks.

These Aussies are nothing if not direct. 'No. I just didn't feel like it.'

Sky looks at me thoughtfully. 'That's a shame, because the ocean is an incredible healer. That's why all of us are

66

here. We were broken in some way, or at points in our lives where we needed something, and we found it in the Bay and each other. We still have our issues, but we're working on them.'

I file this away, wondering what their issues might be. 'So what do you all do?'

'We surf, we train—'

'I meant what do you do for work?'

Sky frowns. 'Here at the Bay, we're not defined by our work, Kenna.'

I feel like I've been told off by the teacher but I try not to show it. 'How long have you been coming here?'

'A few years now.'

'And how often do you come?'

'I spend nearly half the year here. We all do.'

The others are nodding, even Mikki, which explains why I could never get hold of her on the phone. I wonder how they afford it, but it seems rude to ask.

'Who wants to surf in Sydney?' Jack says. 'It's crowded as hell.'

'Yeah,' Victor says. 'I couldn't surf at Bondi any more. Catch me on a bad day and I might just kill someone.'

I look at him uneasily. That's the second time he's mentioning killing. 'So who came here first?'

Their silence tells me I've hit on a sensitive topic.

Clemente clears his throat. 'Me, Jack and Victor.'

'And Sky,' Jack says.

Clemente gives him a sharp look. Another pointed silence.

'Not Ryan?' I say.

'No,' Jack says. 'Ryan turned up like a bad smell.'

Everyone laughs – a bit too much.

'We were down in Sydney for a couple of months, working,' Jack says. 'It was spring, when the wind turns the waves to mush. We left some things here, stashed out of sight. Food and some of the gym stuff, but when we came back, some had moved and some was missing.'

Victor raps a rhythm on his thighs with alternating hands. Knuckle, palm, knuckle, palm. I wish he'd stop. It's distracting me from what Jack's saying.

'We thought some campers had been here,' Jack says. 'Then more food went missing. Clemente went out for a piss a few nights later and heard someone crashing away through the trees. Chased after him and caught him. Ryan had arrived while we were away. When we showed up, he hid in the bushes.'

'Where was he sleeping?' I ask.

'He had a swag. Used to watch us surfing and wait until we'd gone in before surfing himself.'

I glance at the trees over Jack's head, realising that anyone could be out there watching us and we'd never know. Even in the daytime, the undergrowth offers so many hiding places.

'Eventually he joined.' Jack slings an arm around Ryan's neck and roughens up his hair. 'And you've only left here, what, once, since then?'

Ryan extricates himself, smiling stiffly. 'Yep.'

'We appointed him the Guardian,' Jack says.

'What?' I say.

'Didn't want it happening again. Someone robbing our stuff and all that. So when we're all back in Sydney working, he stays here, watching the place.'

I turn to Ryan. 'What would you do if someone else comes here while they're gone? It's not like you can phone them.'

Ryan hesitates. 'Stay out of sight and steal stuff from them, trash their tents, whatever. Luckily, it's never happened.'

Ryan gets up to collect the plates and I jump up to help.

'No, no,' he says. 'It's my turn.'

'It's all right.'

Ryan and I squat by the tap, washing up in a tub of water. The others remain by the fire.

'So whose idea was it to form the Tribe?' I ask.

Ryan lowers his head over the tub and I notice again how he really has a problem with looking me in the eyes. 'Clemente, I guess. Or his wife.'

I laugh obligingly. Another of his unfunny jokes.

Clemente's head turns my way. For all that he seems unfriendly, I catch him looking at me an awful lot.

'Or Victor,' Ryan says. 'You'd have to ask them.'

My laughter cuts as I realise he's serious. 'Clemente's wife?'

'Yup.'

'Where is she now?'

Ryan stares down at the plates. 'She died.'

'Oh, that's . . . When did she die?'

'Soon after I joined the Tribe.' Ryan tugs his beard. 'Nearly two years ago.'

Not that long. 'What was her name?'

But Ryan clams up. 'You'd better ask Clemente.'

He's gone red, as though he said something he wasn't supposed to say.

CHAPTER 12

KENNA

I look over at Clemente thoughtfully. Perhaps losing his wife is why he's so moody.

Jack is putting a tent up beside the tent Mikki went in earlier. I help him peg out the groundsheet, the smell of damp canvas taking me back to childhood camping trips in Scotland. Springy green grass and russet red bracken, delicate pink heather spread out beneath an eternally grey sky. Fleece jackets and muddy boots, cheeks glowing from windburn. Different in every way from the sub-tropical campsite here.

'I'll sleep in this one,' Jack says. 'You sleep in there with Mikki.'

I'm tempted – anything for a chance to get Mikki alone – but it's so close to the other tents that the others will hear everything we say, plus my jetlag will probably wake me super early again.

'It's okay,' I say. 'I'll sleep in this one.'

'Fair enough.' Jack slaps a mosquito off his shin.

He slots the frame rapidly together, the easy way he moves his body suggesting he'd be equally at ease with someone else's body. *Scratch that thought, Kenna.* He clearly has some kind of hold on Mikki, so the last thing I want is to let him get a hold of me too.

Sky approaches with a sleeping bag. 'Want this?'

'Thanks,' I say.

Jack lurches sideways and breaks into a grin. Sky is right behind him. Did she pinch his bum? He unzips the flyscreen door. I heave my backpack off the ground and crawl inside. Better find what I need for the night before it gets dark. I locate my sponge bag and a clean T-shirt to sleep in.

Mikki peers in. 'Here, put this down.' She passes in a yoga mat.

'Gather round!' Sky calls.

I crawl out to see what they're up to.

Sky reaches down to pick something. 'See this blade of grass? Now you find some.'

The others search around them, some more reluctantly than others. I watch from a distance. I think I know what they're about to do. I read about this technique in a former rugby player's memoir that one of my clients convinced me to read. Athletes need to clear their heads after they make a mistake during competition, so they look at the blade of grass and imagine it as the mistake, then throw it away to mentally let go of their failure. As unobtrusively as I can, I pull a piece of grass from under a nearby tree.

'Think about what you screwed up in the surf earlier.' Sky holds up her grass. 'Now focus on your grass and fill it with everything you did wrong.'

Long moments of silence as they mimic her. I look down at my blade of grass. I screwed up a lot of things today. I never foresaw what this place would be like – how remote it would be or the total lack of phone communication. Or that Mikki's friends would be this territorial. I need to stop feeling so intimidated by them.

'Now eat it,' Sky says.

I jerk my head up. Is she serious?

She stuffs the grass into her mouth and chews. There's rolling of eyes as the others do the same. I've never eaten grass before. I'm pretty sure we can't digest it. Is it even clean? I give it a sniff – and catch Sky and several of the others looking at me. Feeling like a total idiot – especially as I wasn't invited to join in, I put it in my mouth. It doesn't taste of anything much. I force it down.

Sky wipes her hands to show they're empty. 'That's how we deal with failure. Eat it and make it a part of you. Let it stew inside you and strengthen you.'

Well, that's different.

'Now draw yourselves up straight,' she says. 'We're doing a cliff race tonight.'

'Oh, come on,' Clemente says. 'It's almost dark.'

Sky smiles. 'Exactly.'

The others exchange looks. I have no idea what a cliff race is but I sense danger. I catch Mikki's expression as she heads to her tent. She doesn't look too thrilled.

I wait outside while she changes her shorts. 'Just say no, if you're not into it,' I tell her quietly.

Mikki huffs and reaches for something. Climbing shoes. Helplessly I watch her pull them on. Climbing was always *my* thing, not Mikki's. I grew up far from the sea in a damp, grey city. Mum's from Iceland and was – still is – a really good climber, so my brother and I lived at the local climbing wall from an early age. Warm and dry, climbing was way better than most of the other sports on offer. In summer we climbed outdoors on real rock.

'We taking head torches?' Ryan calls.

'Fuck no,' Sky says. 'The whole point is we're not seeing the rock, we're feeling it.'

Sounds like a load of crap to me. I wait for one of them to point that out but they don't. Clemente and Victor in particular seem like strong-minded, outspoken individuals. What does Sky have over them? They're grumbling, but in a resigned kind of way, like you do when your mum tells you to tidy your room.

They all wear climbing shoes by now. Shit – Clemente's finger. He's strapping it.

Giving up on Mikki for now, I head over to him. 'Want me to—'

'No,' he says without looking at me. 'Is fine.'

'If you make it worse, you won't be able to surf.'

Clemente ignores me and rips off a piece of blue tape with his teeth. *Rocktape*, it says on the roll. *Waterproof.*

I watch him wind it around his hands, binding his last three fingers together. The trees behind him are feathery black silhouettes, swaying in the breeze. 'Are you scared to say no?' Maybe goading him will work.

He raises his head, his expression dark. 'I feel nothing, okay?'

I can't tell if he means he can't feel his finger or that he feels nothing in general. I look around at the others in an attempt to gather myself. Silent and focussed, they fill water bottles and change clothing. Ryan removes a hair elastic from his wrist and scrapes his hair back into a ponytail. My breath catches in my throat. His face has been half-hidden by his hair up to this point. With his deep tan and the lower part of his face obscured by his beard and moustache, he bears little resemblance to the clean-cut guy I saw online earlier.

But there's no doubt about it. He's one of the missing backpackers.

CHAPTER 13

KENNA

One by one, they head down the trail to the beach, leaving me alone in the clearing once again. A movement flickers in the corner of my eye but it's just that damn wetsuit. Back and forth it swings, like a hanging man.

I'm all unnerved about Ryan. Foreigners need a visa to visit Australia. Presumably Ryan came here on holiday and liked it so much that he didn't want leave, so he stayed on beyond the date on his visa. Illegal – they'd throw him out if they caught him and probably ban him from returning – yet understandable, and hardly sinister. Still, from the poster I saw on my phone, someone back home misses him, enough to report him missing. What sort of person would disappear and not tell their family or friends?

And what about the other missing backpackers? I hug my arms around my chest, remembering Mikki's reaction to the posters. Was it because of Ryan?

The clearing is creepy with only the trees for company

so I hurry after the others, clutching my water bottle in one hand and swishing mosquitoes with the other. The light seems to fade with each step. By the time I reach the beach, the ocean gleams navy and the cliff face is dark brown, contours barely visible. Sky's wrong about not needing to see. Half the skill in rock climbing is in locating possible hand- and footholds and evaluating them before you move.

They're gazing upwards and left. The cliff must be forty or fifty metres high. Halfway up are two markers: one red, one blue. From my teen years in Cornwall, I know the dangers of sea cliffs well. Battered by the wind and waves, the rock quality will be variable, with loose bits liable to break off when you grab them. It's probably also greasy in places. I scan the group. No rope; no chalk. Are they serious? Freeclimbing up there in this light is borderline suicidal.

And surely they're not all climbing at once?

'Mikki,' I say quietly. 'This is madness.'

She gives me a pained look. 'I'm trying to focus.'

I search my brain for something – anything – I can say to stop her.

'Losers are on dinner duty for a week,' Sky calls.

Victor grimaces and clasps Jack's shoulder. 'You'd better not lose, brother.'

'Here we go,' Ryan says. 'Roo Bolognese again.'

Jack grins. 'Good Aussie tucker, mate.'

'Here are the teams,' Sky says. 'Red team is me, Mikki and Jack. Blue team: Clemente, Victor and Ryan.'

'Girls against boys.' Victor aims a playful punch at Jack's shoulder.

Once again, I wonder about Sky's position within the Tribe. If I was observing them from a distance, the feminist in me would be cheering her on. *Good on you, Sky! You've got all these big guys taking your orders.*

As it is, I'm wary of her, puzzled by the power she obviously wields.

The teams are conferring about who goes first, so apparently it's a relay with one person per team climbing in turn.

'Whoever's last, they're not going to see anything in this light,' Jack says.

'Great,' Sky says. 'Jack just volunteered to go last.'

The hard look in her eyes dares him to protest. Victor gives him another mock punch. I'm sensing that Sky's someone I need to stay on the right side of.

She punches the air. 'Fear is fuel!'

'Panic is lethal!' the others shout back.

Sky and Ryan take their positions at the foot of the cliff. I study Ryan again as he looks over his shoulder for Victor's signal. Do the others know he's 'missing'?

I catch Clemente staring at me. 'What?'

He jolts. 'Sorry. You remind me of someone.'

'Who?'

But he shakes his head and looks away.

We are interrupted by the beginning of the race. 'GO!' Victor shouts.

Ryan and Sky throw themselves at the cliff. I can tell immediately that they're proficient climbers – Ryan particularly. There's no sign of the nervous twitchiness I noticed earlier. He climbs with a smooth and confident rhythm, making it look effortless.

Victor pumps his arm. 'Go, go, go!'

My gaze drifts up the cliff face, searching out hand- and footholds as though I'm climbing it myself. A part of me I thought I'd left behind forever is sparking back to life.

Ryan and Sky are already high enough that a fall would do them serious injury. Ryan braces the side of his foot against the rock and climbs to the right. I spot the crack above. He's planned his route well. Soon he's almost level with his marker. *Be careful,* a voice in my head tells him. Fainter, another voice: *I want to do that.*

Clemente watches with arms folded. No sign of nerves, but he must be worried. *I'm* worried. How will he climb with three fingers strapped together? While Sky and Ryan have the ideal climber's build – lean yet muscular with strong, wiry forearms – Clemente is bulkier and heavier.

Sky reaches her marker soon after Ryan. Both of them are cutting rapidly left towards where the ocean laps the foot of the cliff. Sky glances down between her feet, water below her now. In the dark, it's impossible to tell how deep it is. She must be nearly twenty metres up, so I expect her to climb lower before she drops, yet she pushes off and leaps out over the ocean, twisting round in mid-air to face outwards.

Splash!

Mikki starts climbing. Victor dances from foot to foot, poised to launch himself at the cliff the moment Ryan hits the water. It's as though Victor has the energy of three people rolled into one. Perhaps it's his special tea. It's helped my jetlag anyway.

Ryan splashes down and Victor launches himself at the

wall. Mikki is partway up by now. I feel another burst of pride. She's clearly been practising because she's better than she used to be, but she's gasping for breath and toeing everything. Victor's making heavy work of it too.

Mikki raises her foot to waist height, without noticing a lower and easier foothold, and uses all her strength to haul herself upwards. By the time she reaches her marker, her arms are visibly shaking. Sky lets out a small cheer, but Mikki still has a long way to go before she's safely back at my side.

I glance at the rocks below her. *If she fell, what sound would it make?*

A sting of a mosquito on my ankle. I slap it without taking my eyes off Mikki. She's climbing left now. The waves are licking the bottom of the cliff below her but she's not far enough over yet. The water's too shallow. She continues left. Victor's close behind and she keeps looking at him. *Look where you're going, Mikki!*

She reaches sideways and her foot slips. For a terrible moment she's hanging by one hand, swinging back and forth, toes scrabbling for purchase and not finding it. She loses her grip, plummets downwards and lands messily in the water.

It's exactly – horribly – like something that happened over a decade ago.

CHAPTER 14

KENNA

THIRTEEN YEARS AGO

The fifteenth of September: a day I hate to remember. It was an Indian summer that year and the unusual heat was making us behave erratically. School had just gone back and the long Cornish winter was just around the corner, but a group of us had a free period and we wanted to soak up the last of the sunshine. The waves were flat, so we called in at the corner shop, where the young guy serving never asked for proof of age, then headed across the fields armed with cider and Pringles.

The scene plays out in technicolour whenever I think of it: the gold of the hayfields, the blood-red poppies in the hedgerow. Clouds drifting in slow motion across a brilliant blue sky. Hungerford Quarry had been a working one until recently and was all barricaded off but the workers and machines had gone. We were like a pack of street cats exploring new territory, climbing fences and ducking under barriers, passing the cider between us.

We didn't know if there'd be water in the quarry. We whooped when we saw it.

Danger! No swimming! said a sign.

Spoilsports, we thought. Compared to the Cornish seas with their treacherous currents and tides, what danger could there possibly be in that small water hole?

We hadn't brought swimwear.

'Let's skinny dip!' shouted Toby Wines and promptly stripped naked.

Most of the boys followed suit. Mikki and I knew Toby from surfing club and I'd had a crush on him for years. A strapping farm boy – and a naturally talented athlete – he'd talked to me in the corridor a few times and even walked me home from school recently. I was hoping he might ask me out.

Mikki and I stripped to our bras and knickers. Some of the girls went topless but I didn't because I knew Mikki wouldn't want to. We charged down the rocky shale and splashed straight in. The water was the same colour as the slate surrounding it and had a strange metallic smell, but the temperature was delicious: tepid on top, icy below.

'It takes your breath away!' Mikki gasped, treading water beside me.

We climbed out covered in goose bumps. The cider long gone by then, we sat in the sunshine eating Pringles while we warmed up, trying not to look too closely at the naked boys nearby.

The terraced sides were perfect for jumping off. We did some low-level jumps, then a few of us climbed higher. With the sun hot on my back, I carried on upwards, triggering a small rockslide. I climbed as high as I could go.

'Oh, my God, Kenna!' Mikki screeched. 'Be careful!'

Toby squinted up at me, shielding his eyes from the sun as I stood on the edge of the topmost ledge with my toes hanging off the edge. I wasn't scared of heights and wanted him to see that. Mikki was climbing slowly upwards, still shouting out her concern, but if Toby told me to be careful, it might mean he liked me.

He climbed up to join me. Mikki was just below him.

'Are you going to jump?' he asked.

'I don't know.' The water was a gleaming grey square from up there. Clouded with silt to begin with, it was even murkier now we'd stirred it all up.

'I will if you will,' he said.

Later, at the hospital, he would tell me he was joking. *I never thought you'd actually jump.*

'Okay,' I said. And jumped.

Terror filled me as I plummeted. I hit hard and surfaced spluttering.

Toby peered down at me.

'Come on then, jump!' My shout echoed around the quarry.

But Toby remained on the ledge.

'You chicken!' I shouted.

A couple of the others made chicken sounds.

I was mad now. He couldn't tell me to jump then pull out. 'Just do it,' I shouted. 'Jump!'

A chant started up. 'Jump! Jump!'

As I trod water, my toe made contact with something sharp. 'Wait!' I shouted. 'There's something—'

Too late. Toby had already jumped. His legs pedalled the air as he dropped, as though he'd heard me and tried to change his mind at the last minute. He entered the water neatly, both feet together. And surfaced with a strangled scream.

I swam to him as fast as I could and the others helped me drag him up the bank. His legs were mangled; that's the only way to put it. Someone phoned for help and we endured his screams until the paramedics arrived.

Unseen by us, there was an abandoned crane just below the surface, and he'd jumped directly on top of it. Toby had shattered both legs and several vertebrae. Weeks later, he left hospital in a wheelchair, his surfing career over before it began.

CHAPTER 15

KENNA

We bound over the rocks to get to Mikki. I have no idea if it's deep enough and the others clearly don't know either. I'm hyperventilating.

When Kasim died, my life as I knew it shattered into pieces. It was months until I found the strength to go round on hands and knees looking for them and trying to put them back together. Mikki was one of those pieces – the biggest one remaining. I've only just got her back in my life. I can't lose her. I just can't.

Mikki's head pops up.

'Are you okay?' I gasp.

'Whoo, that was fun!' Mikki sounds super shaky – as you would be if you'd narrowly escaped dashing your brains out. 'Go, Jack!'

I'm too relieved to be angry. Victor splashes down beside her, and Clemente and Jack set off up the cliff. My heart is still hammering. It's only when Mikki scrambles out and comes to join me, unhurt and flushed with excitement that I start breathing normally again.

The sky is royal blue by now, the ocean black, shimmering in the light of the half-moon. I can't see the mosquitoes any more but I can still feel them. I swish the air around me at regular intervals.

Ryan is next to me, wringing out his T-shirt. My thoughts return to the missing backpackers.

'I saw a photo of you online,' I say quietly. 'It said you were missing.'

Ryan turns his head sharply. 'Did it?'

I want to ask him who's looking for him, if he's let them know he's okay, but something in his tone warns me not to. So instead I ask, 'How long have you been in Australia?'

For a moment I don't think he's going to answer. 'Two years.'

So I guess he's an overstayer, just as I suspected. I want to find out more but I can't tear my eyes off the cliff. Clemente and Jack are good solid climbers but they lack the grace of Ryan and Sky.

It happens when Jack is a few metres up. As he reaches high for another handhold, a piece of rock breaks off in his other hand, leaving him gripping it uselessly as he falls backwards through the air. My mouth opens in shock. The crash of him landing on his back seems to reverberate through me.

We rush over.

Jack raises a hand. 'I'm okay.'

Clemente climbs back down the cliff. Wincing, Jack gets to his feet. From the stiffness of his movements, I can tell he's hurting. Clemente talks to him in a low voice. Jack rubs his back and nods.

'What now?' Victor says.

'He tries again,' Sky says.

Clemente turns to face her. 'Not a good idea. If he falls again—'

I note how he's positioned himself between Jack and Sky.

'We're not quitters,' Sky snaps.

'We're not idiots either,' Clemente says.

He's right. From the looks of it, Jack has at least badly bruised his back and may have also cracked ribs. If he falls again, he could do far worse. I wait, willing one of the others to speak out. Clemente seeks out Ryan's gaze, then Victor's, but they refuse to meet his eyes.

The way they interact reminds me of wolves. Sky's the alpha, but the betas are ready to attack if she shows a moment of weakness. Unlike wolves, though, their leadership is not about brute physical strength. If it was, Victor or Clemente would be in charge. Why then? Is it Sky's mental strength that maintains her role as leader – or something else?

Jack's handsome face is taut with pain. A wild idea forms, except I don't do that sort of thing any more. But maybe, just the once, I could.

'I'll climb for him,' I say.

In the silence that follows, Mikki's eyes search mine. Apparently satisfied with what she sees, she turns to Sky.

'Take your positions.' Sky's tone is one of boredom but I sense she won't forget about me defying her.

Victor whoops. 'We have a contender!'

Clemente frowns but says nothing.

I gaze up the cliff face, glad I opted for stretchy gym shorts for comfort during the car journey, rather than my denim cut-offs. My palms are sweating. I wipe them on my T-shirt. So far, all I feel is a mixture of bubbly excitement and guilt. I can kid myself that I'm doing this for Jack, but really I just needed an excuse to get back into the action.

You have no fear, Mum told me the first time she took me to a climbing wall.

I must have been about seven and I couldn't figure out what she meant. I had a rope and harness on. If I fell, the rope would hold me. I'd been climbing stuff for as long as I could remember – the trees and climbing frame in my garden, the bookcase at home to retrieve a toy my brother threw on top of it. It wasn't until a few years later that I realised fear of heights was even a thing.

My family would do bouldering sometimes – free-climbing large boulders without a rope, with a crash mat below on the harder climbs – but it wasn't a big deal. If I slipped, it was embarrassing and annoying rather than scary. I would scramble to my feet and try again, determined not to repeat the same mistake.

Climbing runs in her blood, Mum used to tell her friends. She was gutted when I swapped climbing for surfing.

I flex my fingers. They're strong from hours of regular use in my job as well as my daily strengthening exercises, but I haven't properly climbed for years and my other muscle groups will be badly out of practice.

'Go!' Victor shouts.

I reach upwards for the first handholds. In the dim

light I can see just enough. My running shoes don't have the same flex or grip as climbing shoes so I have to dig in hard with my toes, but soon my limbs are working of their own accord. Muscle memory is a beautiful thing. I've had newly injured clients phone me in tears – not from pain but from the perceived setback. *All that training time wasted.* It's not wasted, I tell them. Your body will remember.

I'm not looking down or thinking about how high I am, I'm simply focussing on where I need to go. Just a few metres higher, then sideways to the marker.

Clemente climbs alongside me. His marker is lower but further right than mine. I wince as he grips a handhold and propels himself upwards. That's got to hurt. His biceps flex but his face reveals nothing. He's blanking it out.

And I need to blank *him* out. I stretch upwards and touch the marker. A muted cheer from Mikki and Sky. My body runs on autopilot as I climb sideways. Winning should mean nothing to me – I don't mind being on dinner duty; they only have to ask and I'd do it – but I'm hyper-aware of the others' eyes on me. I hate myself for it, but I need to impress them.

The others jumped from this height, but I have no idea how deep the water is below so I climb rapidly downwards. A whoop from Victor: Clemente must have reached his marker. Not bad without the use of several fingers. He'll jump any moment so I twist and leap, bracing for the impact. The water folds itself around me like a cool sheet. I surface to Mikki and Jack's cheers. Sky nods as I scramble back over the rocks and I sense her looking at me with new eyes.

She saunters over to me. 'What do you think of our training session?'

'It was bloody dangerous,' I say.

She smiles. 'It looked to me like you enjoyed it. How long did you say you're in Australia?'

I hesitate. 'I work for myself so it's flexible really.'

Water rushes up over our toes, glossy and black.

'Perhaps you should think about staying here longer,' Sky says.

'Why?'

'There are two types of people in the world, Kenna. Put them on a clifftop with a big drop below and you'll see the difference. Most people will back away from the edge. A few will step closer.'

'Let me guess,' I say. 'You'll step closer.'

Sky gestures to the others who stand at the foot of the cliffs, dissecting the climb. 'All of us will step closer. I'm not saying it's a good way to be, that we're brave. You could say we're stupid. We suffer more injuries than other people and live shorter lives. We live hard and fast. If we fall and die, then so be it. We don't choose to be like that, any more than people in the other group choose to be careful. We're born this way.'

'Why are you telling me this?'

'Because I think you're one of us, Kenna.'

CHAPTER 16

JACK

It feels like someone's stuck a fucking knitting needle up my spine. I'm trying to remember how many codeine I've got left. My bitch of a doctor wouldn't prescribe any more until next month because I went through the last lot too quickly.

The danger is you'll get addicted.

Bit late for that, mate.

I hate the others seeing me like this. If they knew the state I was in, they wouldn't want me here. Mental note: *don't fall off any more cliffs*. But I have to keep up with them.

At least in the surf I can still hold my own. For now, anyway. Surfing is the only thing I've ever been good at. Everyone gives me shit for my attitude in the water, but the way my back is at the moment, every wave could be my last one.

It was my dad who got me into surfing, but not in the way you might think. He wasn't one of those dads you see pushing little kids onto waves on huge foam surf-boards and high-fiving them when they stand up. Or maybe he was, but I wasn't one of the kids he pushed.

I've never met my dad. Never even knew who he was, growing up – Mum wouldn't tell me. One day, my auntie Karen let slip that he was a surfer. I used to go down the beach every day after school after that and spend all arvo watching the blokes at the point. Surely I'd recognise him? See some sort of resemblance? My mates' dads all looked like them in some way – same hair or eyes or nose. I had white-blond hair at that age and Mum was brunette, so I figured my dad must be blond. Half the men round there were blond, though, so that didn't narrow it down much.

I watched the lines they carved into the waves: curvy and smooth, jagged and fast. Powerful yet graceful. Wanting to see the men from closer up, I asked Mum for a board, but she said: *No chance*. Fair enough; half the time we couldn't even afford lunch.

One day, a cyclone hit the coast and one of the likeliest dad candidates – he had the lightest blond hair and was a shit-hot surfer – got swallowed up by a giant blue cavern. When he surfaced, he paddled in to the beach, tossed his board onto the sand angrily, then removed the leg rope and set off up the dunes, leaving his board behind. I figured he'd leave it parked there while he went to buy a spare part, like my big bro often had to with his car.

'I'll watch your board for you,' I called.

'You can have it,' the guy said. 'I fucking creased it.'

Up close, I saw his dark roots and realised his hair colour came from a bottle, which probably ruled him out as my dad. The board was long and narrow, with a fine line – crease – at one end, but it still seemed usable. It was days before I could stand up on it. *Your dad can do it,* I'd tell myself as I wiped out yet again.

When I eventually made it out to the point, I sat amongst the prospective dads, listening to their banter. Gradually, I stopped looking at them and started looking at the waves. Later still, the men started looking at me. And one of them was a scout for Billabong.

'You silly duffer,' Mum said when I told her why I'd taken up surfing. 'Your dad was a Pommy backpacker. He wasn't even that good a surfer. He was long gone before I realised I was pregnant. I never knew his surname.'

But it didn't matter by then because he'd unknowingly given me the greatest gift on earth.

Sponsors fought over me as I followed the swell around the globe. The chicks came flocking and I had a different girl every week. I rented a beachfront penthouse, bought myself a brand-new car and all that. Jack Wilson was living the dream.

If the wave that broke my back had been a ten-point ride, that would have been some consolation. Go out with a bang, right? But the barrel shut down on me, folded me up like a fucking beach chair and mashed me into the coral. When I popped up, I could move my arms but not my legs. No sensation from the waist down. Scariest thing of all was not being able to feel my dick. I thought my life was over. Three long surgeries later, I got sensation back, but sometimes I wish I hadn't.

I don't know if I have a high or low pain threshold. All I know is I hurt.

Pain is hard to quantify; everyone has a different tolerance to it. As an athlete, you train yourself to blank it out. You might compete – and even win – with a broken bone. I've done it myself – won a heat with a broken toe. No big deal; I just focussed on the other side of my body and mentally cut off my toe. Adrenalin helps. When I got out of the water, I got my toe taped up, then went back out and won my next heat too.

Back pain is different, though. Your back's the centre of your body and it's a whole heap harder to ignore. Fear adds to the mix. If you know this is the worst it's going to be, you might be able to cope. It's the not knowing that's the killer. How much worse is it going to get?

After my accident, my sponsors ditched me so I had to give up my pad and crash on mates' sofas. Before long they started asking me for rent. I'd have been homeless if Clemente and his wife hadn't taken me in. I'd have lost my car as well, if Mikki hadn't taken over the monthly payments.

Mikki's nothing like the glamorous party girls I used to take to bed. The first time I slept with her was like losing my virginity all over again. I cried – mainly because it all still worked. Mikki has her issues but she's pretty cruisy, and who else would have me? I never had a problem getting the chicks, and they still look, but they've kept their distance since my injury. As though they can smell I've gone bad.

I'm a different person now. My world has shrunk so much. I do my best to be strong and brave, but the pain is wearing away at my soul. Even with the codeine it never completely goes away. All I want is a day – or an hour, or even a minute – of respite.

I *hate* the weakened piece of shit I've become, but pain has a way of bringing out your primal side. Trust me on this. When you experience pain at this level, you will beg, lie, steal, basically do whatever it takes to avoid it. Anything at all.

CHAPTER 17

KENNA

Jack's skin is smooth and warm under my hands, his lats so strong it's hard to tell what's damaged. It wasn't easy to convince him to let me look at him. I probe with my fingers.

He flinches. 'Fucking hell. Your hands are strong as fuck.'

'Sorry.' I ease the pressure. Now I see where Mikki learnt to swear. Still, it's not the first time I've been told that.

My brother used to tease me every time we climbed. *You'll never get up there with your tiddly little fingers!*

Mum showed me how to strengthen them. I did the exercises religiously – anything to prove my brother wrong – and I still do them subconsciously sometimes, when I'm watching TV or waiting for appointments. My hand strength came in useful when I switched to surfing – it takes a pretty strong wave to rip my board from my grasp – and proved useful again when I did a massage course.

You have iron fingers, the instructor told me. I quickly built up a client list – surfers, farmers, the local rugby team. Soon I had a waiting list, which meant I could pick and choose my hours around the waves. Enjoying the work and the freedom it gave me, I went on to train further.

Jack yelps. 'Not there. That's where I had it fused. Broke my back at Pipeline.'

I jerk my hands off him. The Hawaiian surf spot is the world's deadliest.

'I've got one working vertebra where everyone else has three.'

'I'm so sorry. I should have asked.'

'No worries.'

The tangy astringent smell of a nearby bush – tea tree or eucalyptus? – fills my nose as I work my way down his spine. I'm terrified of hurting him again.

Sky's voice makes me jump as she approaches from behind. 'You have training in that?' Her tone is sharp.

I glance around, amused by her protectiveness – or is it possessiveness? 'I'm a sports therapist, yeah.'

Her eyes narrow. She walks away.

'Do you know you favour your left leg?' I call.

Sky swings to face me. At first I think she's going to deny it. Then she caves. 'I tore my meniscus last year. I thought I'd fixed it.'

'I could give you some exercises.'

She nods warily.

I turn back to Jack. 'I don't think you've broken anything. It's just bruised.'

Jack flexes his back carefully. 'Thanks.'

'Get some ice on it and rest it for a bit.'

He grins. 'I'll rest when I'm dead.'

Something large and black flaps over my head. I duck.

'It's only a bat,' Jack says.

The toilet block is pitch dark. I need a wee but there's no way I'm going to grope my way about in there. Earlier I went in to find two cubicles that are basically holes in the ground with lids over them. Outside the building is a single tap. I turn it on and use the thin trickle of water to clean my teeth. I'll get my phone in a minute to light up the way, or maybe Mikki has a spare torch.

Footsteps behind me. 'That's not drinking water.' Clemente's voice.

'Damn.' I spit what I can onto the ground.

Clemente gestures to the roof. 'It's from the rainwater tank.' With that, he walks off.

I'm not naturally confrontational but adrenalin is pumping through me from the climb. I chase after him. 'Oi!'

Clemente turns with a scowl, grabs my arm and yanks me sideways. 'Careful!'

Just discernible in the near-darkness: a massive ants' nest right where I was about to tread. My wrist smarts where he grabbed it. Not as much as ant bites would hurt though.

'What's your problem with me?' I ask.

'I didn't invite you here.' His tone is cold.

I've had it with this guy. I refuse to let him faze me. 'You act tough, but that's all it is. An act.'

Unbelievably, he smiles. He's trying to wipe it but doesn't manage to. 'How do I act tough?'

I mimic his posture, folding my arms across my chest and planting my feet wider apart. Clemente drops his arms to his sides, slowly and casually, and gives me a steady look.

Warning bells are ringing but I ignore them.

This gritty patch of earth beneath my toes is my patch. I will not back away. 'I think you're scared of women.'

Clemente shifts in until he's as close as he can get without actually touching me. 'Do I look like I'm scared of you?' he whispers.

'No,' I whisper. 'But you are.'

He fights another smile, yet I sense pain there too. I have no idea what his story is, but his tough-guy act is his defence mechanism and I have no right to poke underneath it.

His smile vanishes. 'I don't want you here. So you should stay away from me.'

CHAPTER 18

KENNA

The smell of bacon wakes me. My limbs feel heavy, my eyes don't want to open, but I can hear the others eating breakfast so I crawl reluctantly out of the tent. I have days like this sometimes, when I can hardly summon the motivation to move and all I want to do is sink into nothingness and not be here.

The others are sitting around the unlit fire. I slip my feet into my flip-flops and something wraps itself round my face, soft and black, like the wings of a giant bat. It's that bloody wetsuit.

I wrestle it off. 'Whose *is* this thing?'

'Clemente's,' Jack says.

I lift it down. 'I'm going to move it. Every time I see it, I think someone's hanging there.' I hook it on a branch outside Clemente's tent.

The others have gone strangely quiet.

'What?' I say.

Clemente carries the remains of his breakfast to the bin, dumps it then enters the toilet block.

All eyes are on me as I sit down.

'You weren't to know,' Jack says quietly. 'But his wife hung herself. From that very tree.'

I sit there in horror, taking this in. The wetsuit morphs in my brain into a woman swinging back and forth.

Now I understand the darkness in Clemente's eyes and the reason he won't let me close, and I feel terrible for how I called him out on it. You'd never get over something like that, surely. How can he bear to stay here? I've never surfed on the beach where Kasim died. I just couldn't. I never surfed again anywhere.

'There's bacon and eggs in the pan,' Mikki says. 'Help yourself.'

I get up, glad to escape.

'We're going surfing,' Mikki calls. 'Want to come?'

'No thanks,' I say. Even though I want to.

The others head off, leaving the clearing empty except for Jack, who sits on a tree stump fixing a ding on his surfboard.

'How's your back?' I ask.

He flashes a smile. 'Great.'

'Really?' There are plenty of other boards lying around. If his back wasn't sore, I suspect he'd have taken one of them and gone with the others.

'I popped a painkiller,' he admits. 'I'm just waiting for it to kick in.'

The food is sealed away in bags and boxes to keep the wildlife out. I tip muesli into a bowl and reseal the bag carefully. I feel awkward helping myself to it. I must give them some money towards it. If Mikki won't take it, maybe Sky will. The milk is in the cool box – the esky as they seem to call it – bobbing in a sea of melted ice. I slice banana over the top and watch Jack while I eat.

Cradling his board across his lap, he squeezes resin from a little tube and spreads it on the fibreglass with a stick. As usual he's wearing just his board shorts. His biceps flex as he smears the resin. He tests his repair with a fingertip, then pulls out sandpaper and carefully sands it. When he's done sanding, he opens a fresh box of wax.

I watch, amused, as he lifts it to his nose and breathes in deep.

He sees me watching and grins. 'Best smell in the world.'

'So what do you do for work?' I feel nosy asking, but I'm looking after Mikki's interests.

'Mate of mine runs a business installing solar panels. Me and Clemente give him a call when we need something.'

'I hope you don't have to do any heavy lifting.' Mikki mentioned periods when he couldn't work and certainly any kind of physical labour would be hard with his injuries.

'I try not to.'

He gives you these blinding white smiles with his perfect teeth, but the look in his eyes never quite matches and I sense it's not just his back that's damaged. He was a professional surfer, but what is he now? He's still trying to figure it out. The last few years can't have been easy for him. I sense the sadness inside and long to help him.

He straightens and rubs his back. He looks a little spaced, actually. I wonder what painkillers he's on. Strong ones, clearly. 'Want me to check your back?'

'Yeah, would you?'

His eyes look particularly blue this morning. I get him lying on a mat. Sunlight filters through the leaves, dappling his skin. In the daylight I can see a deep vertical scar on his lower spine, along with bruising and a small graze. He's tightened up since yesterday.

'Have you got any oil?' I ask.

He hesitates. 'There's Deep Heat in my tent.'

'Can I get it?'

Another tiny delay, as though there's something in his tent that he doesn't want me to see. 'Sure. In the side pocket on the left.'

The tent smells of male deodorant. I glance around as I locate the Deep Heat. Mikki's clothes are in neat piles; Jack's are strewn everywhere.

Parrots flutter and squawk in the branches above as I smear Deep Heat either side of Jack's spine. 'Mikki said you competed in the WQS. How old were you when you had your accident?'

'Twenty-six.'

'Breathe into where I'm pressing. How old are you now?'

'Twenty-nine.'

On average, surfers peak in their late twenties. Surfing is *hard* and it seems to take that long to reach success. Jack's accident cut him down before he reached his peak.

In sports like surfing, you never know who's going to make it. You need natural talent, opportunity and the right mindset, but luck also plays a part. I guess the same applies to any sport, but with surfing in particular so much is outside your control. Every surf spot is different.

Every single wave is different. We paddle out into the unknown, a realm where nature is king.

Mikki was unlucky in that she never got the scores she needed – couldn't handle the pressure of competition maybe – and Jack had a different kind of bad luck. It's something else they have in common.

Straightening, I brush the dirt off my knees. 'There. Best I can do.'

'Thanks.' Jack eases himself up.

When you spend most of your working day around half-naked bodies, you get to see all the scars, flabby bits and other areas that would normally be hidden by clothing. Jack's body? Six feet of lean, muscled perfection. When I force my eyes from his chest to his face, I realise he's watching me with undisguised amusement.

I turn away. 'Sorry.'

'Hey, look all you want.'

My eyes flash back to his face. I breathe fast, shallow breaths as his eyes search mine. *What are you doing, Kenna?* A pair of lorikeets fly over our heads, side by side in bomber formation, as I back away from him.

Jack picks up his board 'Not coming?'

'No.'

'See ya later.' He jogs off down the trail.

I watch him disappear from view. A twig cracks behind me. I spin round and there's Ryan.

Did he see my moment with Jack just now? His expression reveals no clue either way.

'I thought you'd be surfing,' I say.

'I went earlier,' Ryan says.

He doesn't say where he's been but it wasn't the beach – it's the wrong direction. He drags his fingers through his sandy hair. There's something caught in it – a dead leaf.

'I want to go up on the cliffs,' I say. 'Is there a trail that leads up there?'

'Yeah,' Ryan says. 'I'll show you.'

'Oh. Okay.' I hadn't expected that, but I can't think of a good reason to refuse so I stuff my phone and water bottle in my bag, grab my cap and sunglasses.

Ryan leads me on a trail I haven't been on before. Pink and grey parrots toddle ahead of us on their funny short legs. We're faster than they are and when we get too close, they squawk and flutter upwards.

I'm dying to find out more about Ryan's situation. 'Do your family know you're here?'

Ryan's head jerks round. 'No.'

His parents must be frantic. I can't imagine why he would do that to them but it's very clear he doesn't want to talk about it. We're heading uphill now. I pant for breath.

Ryan stops ahead to pluck something from a tree – half a dozen or so purple things, small and oval – which he stuffs into his pockets. 'Passion fruit,' he says when he sees me watching.

Ahead, the trees thin and the ocean spreads out below like a sheet of blue corduroy. The others sit on their surf-boards near the point.

'Wow!' I breathe.

A rare smile from Ryan. 'I know, right?'

A rickety wooden railing marks the edge of the cliff. *Danger! Erosion! Do not cross barrier. $1000 fine.* The lopsided sign looks in danger of falling over the cliff itself. I suck in my breath as Ryan climbs onto the railing and sits on it, legs dangling over the drop. His bare feet are deeply tanned, his toenails overgrown. The breeze catches my hair, blowing it forward. My T-shirt flaps. I peer cautiously over the railing. We're roughly above the part we climbed up.

Surfers see the ocean in a totally different way to everyone else. I never thought about waves much before I started surfing. If I noticed them at all, they just seemed to rear up randomly. I certainly never noticed the patterns.

I remember sitting on the beach in Cornwall with water streaming from my nose after one of my humiliating early surfing attempts, waiting for Mikki and her mum to come in. An old man with white hair and a weather-beaten face stood nearby.

'How do they do that?' I asked, as one surfer after another carved smooth figure-of-eights. 'I couldn't even stand up.'

The old man smiled. 'You have to read the lines.'

'What do you mean?'

He pointed out the thick navy stripes of larger waves rolling in and explained how they arrive in sets of between three and ten. How there could be five minutes between sets or twenty-five. That waves break more slowly at high tide, making an easier take-off for beginners like me, while low tide waves are faster and more hollow.

It was a whole new language and one I vowed to learn.

'How do you know all that?' I asked.

'I've been surfing here since 1962.'

'Do you still surf?'

'I would if I could.' He gestured to his stick, which I hadn't noticed until then. 'Go on. Get back out there.'

I never saw him again. I saw his face, though, months later, smiling out from the back of Dad's newspaper. *Michael Cooper, 1965 surf champ, dies after battle with Parkinson's, aged 72*. I had to have a good long look in the cupboard after that for something I couldn't find so I didn't have to explain why I was crying about a man I'd barely known.

His words stayed with me like a legacy. *Read the lines . . .*

Ryan points. 'Look, here comes the set.'

Larger waves roll in below. It hurts to watch them peeling. I ache to be in the water again. Mikki paddles for a wave, but Jack snakes her and gets the wave himself. What a bastard! I can't believe he did that.

Mikki catches the wave behind. Shit, that's big. Judging from how she's surfing, she's been doing this kind of stuff for months, but it feels like if I take my eyes off her for a second she'll get smashed. When she dismounts neatly, I let out my breath.

Remembering why I came here, I pull my phone from my bag and hold it up. Damn. No reception. Ryan sees but doesn't comment. I stuff it back in my bag.

The stunted trees that line the clifftop twist in weird directions as though in eternal search for shelter from the wind.

'What did it say about me?' Ryan asks suddenly.

'What?' I ask, startled.

'The thing that said I'm missing.' He's all tensed up again.

'Oh.' I try to think. 'I only saw it for a second or two. All I remember is your photo.'

'Right.'

I can't tell if he's relieved or disappointed. 'How long do you think you'll stay in Australia?'

Ryan's eyes flit across my face. His eyebrows are bleached white in places and his face is covered in sun-spots. The Australian sun hasn't been kind to him – though maybe the Californian sun wasn't either. 'Who says I'm going back?'

His shoulders have tensed; his hands have curled into fists. I shouldn't ask any more but I can't resist. 'You don't plan to?'

'I can't.' His tone is sad yet resolute.

Dark possibilities creep into my mind as I contemplate what might make someone run to the other side of the world.

CHAPTER 19

KENNA

I spend the morning wandering the maze-like network of trails, trying to find a phone signal. Wary of getting lost again, I don't venture too far, but it's a waste of time. I don't find a signal, and now my phone has only seven per cent of battery left. I don't know why that bothers me so much – it's not as though I can use it – but it feels like my last link to civilisation.

Back in the clearing, something's happened. Mikki is kneeling on the ground, leaning over a tree stump, resting her palm on her forehead. Her lips move as she mutters something. Guilt flashes through me. Has Jack told her about earlier? Ryan is in the bushes, tending plants with his back to us. Has *he* told her?

I hurry over to her. 'Mikki?'

She doesn't seem to hear me so I clasp her shoulder.

Her head jerks up. 'God, you scared me!'

'What's wrong?'

'Nothing. Just doing my fear session.'

'Your what?'

Mikki looks sheepish. 'We have to work on our fears, part of the deal when we join. I look at my moth tattoo and visualise it being real.'

'Oh. I thought it was a butterfly.'

She tilts her wrist my way. And now I see it: the dreary brown wings and fat grub-like shape of the body.

'Does it help?' I ask.

'Yeah.'

I stare at the ugly creature splayed permanently across her wrist, marring her beautiful skin. Whether it works or not, it's a pretty extreme way to deal with a fear. 'How was the surf?'

'Amazing. I'd have stayed longer but I snapped a fin.'

'Shit! How?'

'I hit a rock. It's all right. I've fixed my board already. The others are all still out there.'

'It's not your board I'm worried about. If you fall on those rocks and smash your head . . .'

'You're *such* a worrier these days.'

I smile at the irony, because it used to be me calling her that. I'm finding it hard to look her in the eye after my experience with Jack. Mikki needs to know the sort of person she's about to marry. I take a deep breath. 'I was massaging Jack earlier. And he was kind of flirty.'

She rolls her eyes. 'Yeah, that's Jack.'

My face is burning up. 'I'm worried I might have encouraged him.'

'Don't worry. I'm used to it.' Her tone is resigned.

'Okay.' I don't feel any better about how I reacted, though, or how he treats her. There's a little piece of seaweed in her hair. I pick it carefully out. 'Twelve days until your wedding, right? Have you found a dress?'

'Yeah, the blue one I bought in Bali.'

I struggle to hide my surprise. 'Great.' That sounded weak even to me, so I try again. 'It's so you. Beachy vibe. I love it.'

'I thought I'd kill two birds with one stone. Something old and something blue.'

My heart breaks for her. A wedding shouldn't be about how many birds you can kill. It's not the well-worn four-year-old dress that upsets me, it's her total lack of enthusiasm, and it can't be a financial thing. I don't understand it. Why is she marrying him if she doesn't want to?

Mikki is a really private person, so even though we're close, I try not to pry – in fact, maybe that's *why* we're close, because I never press her – but right now I'm going to have to, because something's not right. 'Have you guys fallen out?'

Her forehead scrunches. 'No. Why do you think that?'

'You don't seem very excited.'

She twirls a strand of dark hair around her finger. 'I'm just not into weddings.'

I think about this and decide it's probably true. I'm not into weddings either – being laced into some heavy white gown and put on show is my personal idea of torture – yet there's clearly more to this story.

'I'd better finish my session.' Mikki returns to staring at her moth.

Here's Jack now, coming back from the beach with Clemente and Victor. I approach as he showers, keeping my eyes carefully averted from his chest.

'Mikki's tattoo,' I say. 'What did you think when she got it?'

'It's ugly as. But if it helps . . .' Jack flashes me *his* wrist, with the snake inked around it. 'See this? I got it eighteen months ago.'

'Oh yeah. Victor's got one too. The wave, right?'

'Yep. Hey, sorry if I made you uncomfortable earlier.'

I'm squirming now, and the sight of his smooth, bare chest, streaming with water doesn't help one bit. I force myself to say it. 'You're hot.'

He doesn't need me to tell him that. If you're as hot as he is, there's no way you wouldn't be aware of it, but I'm hoping that by voicing it out loud, I can clear the air and shut down the flirting. 'But I shouldn't have been looking at you like that.'

'As I said before, look all you want.'

I try again. 'When me and Mikki got our first place together, my boyfriend made a pass at her. Mikki came and told me, straight out.'

She'd looked at me with terrified eyes, like she thought I would blame her instead of him. *There's no easy way to say this. Connor made a pass at me last night after you'd gone to bed. He said I had beautiful hair.* I hugged her and kicked him out.

'I'm lucky I have such a faithful friend,' I say.

Across the clearing, Clemente and Victor are laughing about something; Victor throws his head back and slaps his thigh.

'It's all good,' Jack says. 'Anyway, I brought you here for Clemente. As well as Mikki, I mean.'

All the blood rushes to my face. 'Sorry?'

'I knew he'd like you,' Jack says.

I've gone hot all over. 'Well, he doesn't seem to.'

'Oh, don't worry. He does.'

I feel like my attraction must be marked on my forehead, for all the world to see. It's mortifying and exciting at the same time.

I leave Jack to finish his shower. Mikki is still staring at her moth. Her lips flutter like moth wings. That hideous design. How can she bear to have it on her skin? I can hardly look at it and I'm not even scared of moths.

CHAPTER 20

KENNA

Mikki and I sit in the shade watching Victor and Clemente kick a ball about. The leaves shift constantly above our heads, throwing kaleidoscopic patterns onto the ground.

Victor throws his hands up. 'Penalty!'

'No it wasn't,' Clemente shouts.

They thunder past.

'Where do they get all their energy?' I say. 'I'm knackered.'

'It's the heat,' Mikki says, combing her wet hair with her fingers. 'It took me a while to get used to it.'

'Do you know where Jack put my chocolate?'

We find it in the fridge.

'Don't let Sky see,' Mikki says, as we eat a piece. 'Sugar is a weakness.'

Victor and Clemente see, though, and come over.

'Wahoo! I love you, Kenna.' Victor wraps me in a bear hug, then sees my face. 'Sorry. Too much energy! I get like this when I haven't surfed enough.'

'Victor used to be a professional big wave surfer,' Mikki says once he and Clemente resume playing football.

'Oh yeah?' I say.

'He got PTSD after a wipeout.'

'But he still surfs?'

'Yeah. He gets shaky sometimes but Sky's working with him on it. You should talk to her. She's helped me with all sorts.'

'Like what?'

'We do a lot of underwater stuff, so I'm more comfortable in bigger swell.'

I can't believe you dropped that wave! Mikki used to say every time we surfed big waves. *Aren't you scared?*

But the waves we surfed were never *that* big.

'And I'm not good at sharing,' Mikki says. 'I'm too possessive. I was way out of my comfort zone to start with, living with these guys, sharing food and everything else.'

Mikki *is* kind of possessive at times. That's why it's so weird that she claims not to mind Jack's flirting.

'But Sky's helping me with that too.'

It's obvious she admires Sky a lot – worships her, almost – and that bothers me for a reason I can't quite explain.

Mikki nudges me. 'Go and talk to her. Tell her about Kasim.'

Sky is across the clearing doing a headstand, pale dreadlocks splayed across the mat.

Feeling shy, I go over to her, but I'm hardly going to start up a conversation about my dead boyfriend so instead I say: 'Want me to show you some exercises to rebalance your legs?'

Sky climbs up. 'Sure.'

She could be beautiful if she wanted to, but it's as though she goes out of her way not to be, with her asymmetric hair, shaven on one side, her edgy and unusual clothing and dominatrix-inspired accessories – leather armlets and chokers. When she wears something feminine like the blouse she had on last night, she pairs it with more masculine garments like the baggy combat shorts – possibly Victor's – held in with a studded belt. I admire her confidence.

Sky's wearing a crop top and gym shorts just now. I check her back and hips and get her doing bear crawls back and forth. It's a painful exercise to do – clients always hate it – but Sky does it without complaint.

'One more,' she says when I tell her to stop.

Her muscles flex as she moves. She's lean but, God, she's strong.

When I moved from Cornwall to London, my arm muscles attracted unwanted attention. People would stare. *You look strong. Are you a swimmer?* They feigned admiration, but I could tell I intimidated them, so I stopped dyeing my hair weird colours and started wearing more feminine clothes that hid my muscles, trying to pass myself off as one of them. Someone normal. Deep down, though, I felt like a fake. I love that Sky doesn't feel the need to conform.

When she straightens, her hands are covered in earth and bark.

'Did you see Jack snake Mikki today?' I ask, expecting her to share my outrage.

Sky wipes her hands on her shorts. 'I saw. But it was his wave.'

Strictly, this is true since Jack was closest to the breaking wave, but only because he snaked around her. 'Oh, come on. You don't do that.'

'Jack used to compete and he still has that mindset. The killer instinct.'

'What?' I say, startled.

'A ruthless determination to win. Everyone has it to some extent but if you train it, it becomes second nature. It's not a bad thing.'

I'm not sure about that, but I change the subject. 'Mikki told me about her tattoo.'

I think Sky senses my disapproval because she looks at me gravely. 'Fear is the greatest weakness we humans are born with. To overcome it we must experience it.'

'I don't know about that,' I say. 'If you go round triggering people's fears, they might panic. There was a girl in my class at school who was terrified of wasps. On a school trip when we were about twelve, we were eating ice creams and a wasp started chasing her. She ran into the road to escape it and got run over by a bus.'

'That's a sad story, but she ran from her fear and we can't escape our fears. We have to face them. That's what we try to do in our training sessions. Experts call it exposure therapy.'

Having her this close makes me a bit lost for words. 'I'm no psychologist but fear is different to a phobia, isn't it? I don't like wasps either – does anyone? – but I wouldn't call it a phobia like the girl at my school had or Mikki with moths.'

Sky frowns. 'Mikki's doing so well with her therapy. Have you seen how it's carried over to her surfing? By facing one fear, she's become braver in general.'

There's a hardness to Sky that you don't often see in women. I like it, but at the same time it scares the hell out of me.

Chapter 21

Kenna

After lunch, Mikki and Jack apply sunscreen to each other, as do Victor and Sky. Ryan's nowhere to be seen so Clemente applies sunscreen to himself. Why are men so hopeless at putting sunscreen on?

Unable to help myself, I go over to him. 'You've got big white streaks on your shoulders. Want me to fix it?'

Clemente just looks at me. Doesn't say yes but doesn't say no either. Approaching him right now would be like approaching a stray dog – he might snap – so I wait.

'Fine,' he says in an exasperated tone.

I step behind him to rub it in.

Clemente's olive skin is peeling in places and judging by the colour and heat, he's mildly burnt. 'You need more.'

Silently, he hands me the bottle. *Factor 50, 4 hours water resistant.* I squirt out a handful. It's gloopy and white, like school glue. Both hands working in tandem, I smear it over his shoulders. It's weird, touching him.

Some of my clients are hot, but there's not this . . . pull. There wasn't, even with Kasim. It's hugely distracting.

Soon the process takes over. My fingers do it automatically: seek out tightness. He inhales sharply as I find a knot. If I had my massage table, I'd go to work properly. He's unbelievably tight. I lift his arm and get him holding an overhead branch to give me better access. Ignoring the curious looks of the others, I work his muscles.

My fingers probe beneath his shoulder blade. 'Let me know if it's too hard.' Somehow I know he'd never admit it. And he doesn't make another sound, no matter how hard I go.

The others pick up their boards.

'I'll catch you up,' Clemente calls.

Mikki flashes me a wary smile. 'See you later.'

From Clemente's profile I can see he's working with me, focussing on the knots as I find them and willing them to submission. A line of sweat trickles down his temple. As I lift his other arm to the overhead branch, his gaze meets mine. It's intense, having his eyes on me while my fingers are pressed into him.

I still feel terrible about my unfortunate comment this morning. 'I'm sorry about your wife.'

In his eyes, there's not just sadness but guilt as well. He looks away, and now I wish I hadn't mentioned her. Clearly he blames himself. Perhaps he feels he should have seen it coming. That he should have been able to stop her, to make her happy. Or is it worse than that? Was *he* the one who'd made her unhappy? Once again I wonder how he could possibly stay here.

Clemente doesn't look at me again until I step back. 'Finished.'

'Thank you.'

A *cak-cak-cak* from a nearby tree makes me jump.

'Kookaburra,' Clemente says, looking for it. 'Over there. See?'

On a branch behind the tents is a brown and white bird with a funny, oversized head. It opens its mouth and lets out a peal of crazy laughter.

As Clemente waxes his surfboard, I glance around wondering what to do. Continue the search for mobile phone reception, maybe, except I'm scared of getting lost again.

Clemente picks up his board. 'You aren't coming?'

He's looking at me in that intense way of his. I hear Sky's voice in my head. *The ocean is an incredible healer.* One surf can't hurt, can it? Mikki will be thrilled to see me out there, and that way I can keep an eye on her from the water. That's how I justify it to myself. Deep down, I know I'm doing it for me, not her.

I duck into my tent to change into a bikini. My skin is still red from yesterday so I pull on a T-shirt and hastily rub on sunscreen.

As I follow Clemente down the track, fear sets in. I don't want to get sucked back into the sport that cost me so dearly. The other reason I'm scared? I can hear the waves from here. The rhythmic crash is loud enough to drown out the parrots.

'How big would you say the swell is?' I ask.

'A metre, metre and a half,' Clemente says.

When it comes to wave height, the custom is to be conservative, a tradition stemming from Hawaii, where waves are measured from the backs rather than the front. A metre and a half means waves that are well above head height. I'd hoped for tiny waves so I could ease back into it, but that's surfing for you: the ocean serves up what it wants when it wants.

'Shit,' I breathe when we reach the beach. Clouds have blown in and the waves are lining up in thick stripes under a steel-grey sky.

'What?' Clemente says.

'Nothing.'

He raises his eyebrow. His message is clear: if I don't feel confident in waves that size, I shouldn't go out there, but the others have seen me now. Mikki gives me a thumbs up.

The damp sea air folds itself around my face. 'Let's do it,' I say.

Clemente sets his surfboard on the sand and stretches his triceps. I've noticed how every surfer has a different pre-surf ritual regarding what they eat and drink, how they prepare their board, and their warm-up routine, often focussing on areas they've injured previously. Clemente's routine hints at shoulder issues.

I put my board beside his and rotate my arms in gentle circles. For me at least, the stretches prepare my mind as much as my body. I flex my neck from side to side, breathing in the salt spray. Usually by this point I'm mentally out in the ocean already, feeling the surge as a wave takes me, but there are too many distractions today. And Clemente is one of them.

He picks up his board. 'Okay, stay close to the rocks and the current will sweep you out.'

I grab a handful of sand and scrub my fingers to get the sunscreen off. There's nothing worse than trying to surf with slippery hands. Clemente scrambles over the rocks. Nerves jittering, I hurry after him. One minute he's ankle deep, the next he's in and paddling. He glances over his shoulder, beckoning me to follow. I step cautiously forward. The rocks are draped with stringy black seaweed. It's slimy under my toes.

The first wave hits me with more force than I expected, smashing me back over the rocks. Sharp edges slice my legs and feet. I scramble onto my board and paddle with as much force as I can muster. My shins sting but there's no time to check the damage. The next wave arrives and I dig my knee hard into the waxed fibreglass of my board to duck-dive under it, but my timing is off and the wave sucks me back with it. I surface and paddle hard, out of breath and out of practice.

The darkening sky is mirrored in the sea. Birds plummet into the water with a splash, only to burst out again a few seconds later, clutching fish. It's one of those days when every dark shape below me acquires multiple rows of teeth and a patent black eye and even a glimpse of my own reflection makes my stomach lurch.

Jack gets a wave. If his back is hurting, you'd never guess. He surfs as though he can see a few seconds into the future, making it look so damn easy. Clemente and Victor whoop as he lands an air reverse.

The next minutes are a game of one step forward, two steps back in a bizarre sort of dance with the Pacific. Another wave looms. I duck-dive, but it rips my board from my grasp, leaving me to flap for the surface. A dark shape speeds underwater towards me like a torpedo and I suck in my breath, but it's only a dolphin.

Yet another wave. Boardless, I swim down to avoid the worst of it, eyes clamped shut, hoping there are no hidden rocks in this dark void. They're all watching when I surface. *Pull yourself together, Kenna.*

I retrieve my board and paddle for my life. In the lull between waves, I somehow get out the back. My legs and feet sting. As unobtrusively as I can, I lift each leg in turn. I'm bleeding in a dozen places.

A dark shape shoots past, making me flinch. Bloody dolphins. It's as though they're doing it on purpose, just to freak me out. A grey shelf rears up. Half-heartedly I paddle for it. To my relief, Victor paddles for it too and I let him have it, but there's another wave behind, bigger than its sister. The others are watching, so I paddle again. Even as I push up, I know I'm not going to make it, but I'm already past the point of no return.

My board swings to vertical and beyond, tipping me off headfirst. I faceplant, then the wave pitches down, drilling me deep. When I pop up, I do a rapid audit of body parts. Miraculously, I seem to have escaped unscathed. Snorting water, I paddle back out.

'You okay?' Mikki asks.

'Never been better,' I say and everyone cracks up.

I sit there watching the others while I get my breath back. You can learn a lot about someone from the way they behave in the water; I noticed that in Cornwall. Jack drops in on everyone with no inhibitions; Clemente appears to have a death wish, taking off on every wave that comes his way; Victor sits at the back, waiting for the giants; Sky rips up and down, draining every last drop of energy from each wave. I haven't seen Ryan surfing before. Somehow I'd imagined he would sit on the outside, keeping his distance from the others like he does on land, but he's right in the thick of it, hassling for waves.

As for Mikki . . .

'You got so damn good,' I tell her as she paddles back out.

'I know.' Mikki beams in delight at saying something she considers so un-Japanese and I laugh with her.

Victor gets a wave. He's a goofy-footer, I notice, surfing with his right foot forward, unlike the rest of us. A wave comes Ryan's way and Jack drops in on him. I wince as their boards collide. The two men end up side by side in the water and Ryan grabs Jack by the hair. I saw Jack drop in on Victor yesterday, stealing his wave, and Victor laughed it off, but Ryan is really bloody mad.

'Hey!' Clemente calls. 'Calm down.'

'Incoming!' Victor shouts.

I turn to see a set rolling through. One wave, I tell myself. One decent wave and I'll be happy.

'Go, Kenna!' Mikki shouts.

I paddle hard, scrabble to my feet, then I'm riding it. Dancing over water. Unused to the board or the wave, I only manage a couple of turns before I overbalance, but it's enough.

Mikki throws her arm round my back as we walk up the sand later. 'It's so good to surf with you.'

I look down at myself. Blood streams from the cuts in my legs; my arms and back are seizing up, but for the first time in two years I feel happy.

CHAPTER 22

KENNA

Jack's on dinner duty tonight. My original fears about him being abusive seem unfounded but he's a total flirt and he snakes her in the surf. I don't get what Mikki sees in him. Surely it's about more than how he looks?

I head over, determined to get to the bottom of why she's marrying him.

He dumps a packet of meat on the barbecue.

'What's that?' I ask.

'Kangaroo mince,' Jack says.

With his blue eyes on my face, that unwelcome attraction flares up again. The meat sizzles, filling the humid air with a gamey smell. I screw up my nose.

'Aussies don't eat it much,' Jack says. 'They feed it to their pets, but Mum had five kids and she couldn't afford beef so I grew up on the stuff.'

Victor's groans drift across the clearing. Sky has him doing chin-ups.

Her voice rings out. 'Ten more!'

Victor's arms shake as he lifts back up.

'What else are you going to put in?' I ask.

'Chilli.' Jack points the wooden spoon. 'There's a bush over there. See if there's any ripe ones. I need three or four.'

Wary of spiders, I delve into the bush. 'Did you plant this?'

'Ryan did.'

As I hand Jack the chillies, I hear a noise from Victor that's almost a scream. Sky has him doing weighted squats now, clutching a rock to his chest.

'Again!' she shouts.

I watch, worried she's going too far. 'You met Sky in Sydney, right?'

'Yeah, she used to surf at Bondi.' Jack slices the chillies and scrapes them in. 'She hooked up with Victor. Me and Victor were living at Clemente's place in Bondi by then. When the lease on Sky's apartment ran out, she moved in with us.'

The acrid fumes make my eyes sting. 'So there were, what, five of you living there?'

'Yep. Six when Mikki arrived.'

No wonder their place was so messy. I'm beginning to understand why these guys are so close – they're together all the time. There were shared houses in Cornwall with people packed in together to save money on rent. Work less, surf more: every surfer's motto. But these guys are in their thirties, so you'd think they'd want their own space to focus on careers or start families. Mikki's more of an introvert than I am and I'm amazed she can cope with it.

Jack continues. 'One day, Sky said: *I could get you*

surfing a whole lot better but I don't know if you want to do the work. She laid it down like a challenge.'

'Right.'

'We'd gone stagnant, I guess. I'd done my back by then, Victor had torn his rotator cuff and Clemente had knee issues.' Jack scrapes the meat mixture into a casserole dish. 'We asked what it would involve. Training like hell, basically. I told her you only get better at surfing from surfing. *What if the waves are flat?* she said. *You sit on your arse and smoke weed?* Which was basically what I was doing. Clemente's wife had started smoking it too.'

I file this away. Do any of them still smoke? I haven't seen it.

Jack tips in tinned tomatoes. 'We told Sky we wanted it and she's pushed us like hell ever since.'

Victor flops to the ground and Sky heads off to begin a workout of her own. The girl never stops. No wonder she's so fit.

Over Jack's shoulder, I see Clemente and Mikki return from the beach, dripping wet. Must have been for a swim. They stand chatting as they towel themselves dry. I watch them with interest. Mikki's never had male friends before. Now they're pulling on boxing gloves. Mikki's a foot shorter than him. I bite my lip at first, but she gives him a pounding – and he lets her.

'Shit!' she cries when one of her punches catches him on the ear.

He doesn't even flinch. 'Don't stop.'

I love how gentle he is with her – his best friend's girl. *Fiancée,* I correct myself and my chest tightens.

Victor still hasn't moved. I head over to him. 'Are you okay?'

'Yeah.' He's gleaming with sweat.

I lower my voice. 'Why don't you just say no?'

Victor drags himself up to a sitting position. 'Have you ever had a trainer, Kenna?'

'No. I'm like a donkey. I hate being pushed.'

Victor mops his brow, his yellow and green Brazil wristband squeaking against his skin. His biceps are huge. 'I've had a lot.'

'Oh yeah?'

'My mum was Brazilian jujitsu champion and my dad loved surfing. I competed at both and I had trainers for each. When I was sixteen, I had to choose between them. I chose surfing.' Victor rubs his quads. 'Fuck, that hurts.'

'You've overdone it a bit, haven't you?' I say.

'If you have a trainer, you have to commit to their methods. It's your choice, but once you commit, they basically have the right to do whatever they want to you.'

'You need ice.' I collect a pair of socks from my tent, stuff them with ice and place them over Victor's thighs.

He winces as I press it down. 'There are good trainers and bad trainers, Kenna.'

I nod at Sky. 'And she's good?'

'One of the best.' Victor shoots another look in her direction. Clemente is on a mat, doing push-ups. With a cackle of laughter, Sky sits on his back. Clemente manages several more before he collapses.

Victor's face darkens. 'Some trainers can inspire you to pass your limits.'

'And she can?' I ask, noticing afresh how stunning she

is. Of course they want to impress her. Hell, *I* want to impress her.

'Yep. It's like she can get in your head.'

I lift the ice packs from Victor's thighs. 'Is it helping?'

'Yeah, give me more!'

A shadow falls over him as I press them down again and I turn to see Sky watching us.

'Have I killed him?' she asks.

'Yeah,' I say. 'You pretty much have.'

'Poor baby.' She strokes Victor's brow, smiling wickedly.

None of these guys are soft, but I sense somehow that she's the toughest of them all.

She leans over to say something in Victor's ear. I don't hear what it is, but his shoulders stiffen instantly.

'Now if you'll excuse us, Kenna,' Sky says.

She sets off towards one of the trails. Victor gets up to follow her with a look of pure fear.

CHAPTER 23

KENNA

As we eat, I look around at the happy faces of the others, in their tatty, well-worn clothes. These guys forgo the normal comforts: a soft bed to sleep in, pubs, clubs and screens. They don't need any of that because they have this. An incredible wave that's all theirs.

I don't know where Victor and Sky went earlier but they're side by side now, cuddled up close, apparently relaxed and content.

That evening, around the fire, we talk about the ugly side of surfing. Localism.

'I heard it's bad in California,' I say.

'Yeah, the locals were heavy at my local beach,' Ryan says.

'There is an area between Spain and France called the Basque country,' Clemente says.

God, that accent.

'If I surf there, they hate me because I am *Spanish*,' he says. 'And if I surf in France, they hate me because they think I am Basque. The last time I surfed Mundaka my car tyres got slashed.'

'Spewing!' Jack says.

'Brazil is the same,' Victor says. 'If you are from Rio and you surf the beaches of Sao Paulo . . .' He flips his fingers back and forth rapidly.

'Cornwall was pretty bad too,' Mikki says.

I glance at her, remembering the day someone wrote *Japs Out* in spray paint on the rocks above our local beach. We were only teenagers at the time and it wasn't aimed specifically at her – there were a number of local Japanese surfers – but it must have stung. The council were slow to clean it. When I couldn't bear to look at it any longer, I asked my dad how to remove spray paint and he came to the beach to help me scrub it off. But how do you clean a whole attitude?

'It's different if you're female,' Victor tells Mikki. 'They're not going to hit you.'

Sky rolls her eyes. 'Yeah, they just drop in on us, snake us, intimidate us and perv on us.'

Victor wraps an arm around her. 'One day I take you to Rio.'

Sky ignores him. 'That's why the Bay is so special. We don't have to deal with all that.'

'They should make female-only surf spots,' I say.

Sky and Mikki lean over to give me a high five. We laugh at the men's expressions.

'It's sad,' Clemente says. 'Surfers have always loved to travel, see other places and surf different waves.'

'Problem is there's too many of us and not enough waves,' Ryan says.

Clemente reaches out to Victor and Jack on either side of him. 'I wouldn't have met these guys if it wasn't for localism.'

'Oh yeah?' I say.

'I was surfing at Narrabeen,' Clemente says. 'And I could hear Victor getting hassle, basically because he's a bloody good surfer. *Not from here, are you?* one of them said. This skinny Aussie kid.'

Clemente looks at Jack and I realise he's talking about him.

'Victor unwisely got into a conversation with him,' Clemente says. 'And his English was even worse than mine and that's saying something.'

Victor's booming laugh makes me jump. 'What are you saying, brother? My English is better than yours any day.'

'He got a wave and Jack dropped in on him,' Clemente says.

'I drop in on everyone,' Jack says.

'You don't have to tell us that,' Ryan mutters.

'Victor was ready for the punch-up,' Clemente says. 'And I was worried about Jack's safety.'

Everyone's laughing now.

'So what happened?' I ask.

'I could see Victor was a nice guy,' Clemente says. 'I talked to him in Spanish so Jack wouldn't understand.'

'Can you speak Spanish?' I ask Victor.

'I can't speak it but I understand,' Victor says.

'I explained that Jack lives with me,' Clemente says. 'And I invited Victor round for dinner. I told him Jack would cook for him to apologise. You should have seen

Jack's face when the doorbell rang and Victor was standing there.'

The others laugh their heads off. Men are funny: quick to fight but equally quick to forgive. Jack and Victor seem like best buddies these days, so it's hard to believe how they met.

'God, I *hate* localism,' Mikki says.

And we all chime in in agreement. Still, if it hadn't been for localism, I wouldn't have met Kasim.

Then again, he might still be alive.

CHAPTER 24

KENNA

FOUR YEARS AGO

Mikki and I flew to France for the weekend, picking up a hire car from Biarritz Airport. She googled the surf spots as I drove north.

'*Wannasurf* says it's hollow and gnarly,' she read.

'Cool,' I said.

'*Localism is strong for this wave. Take a low profile.* Oh, shit.'

'What?'

'Some of the comments. *Someone smashed my mirror while I was in the water. If you have a hire car, I hope you have insurance.* Have we got insurance?'

'Yeah, but the excess is like five hundred euros.' Glimpses of the beach between the trees. I strained to see waves. 'Look for a park.'

Mikki grabbed my arm. 'Oh no, here's another. *When you sport a German licence plate like me, even the cops broke into my car.* I don't think we should park on the beachfront. You can't miss that this is a rental car.'

True – it had *Easy Rentals* in mile-high letters across the side.

'I'm sure it's not as bad as they make out,' I said.

'Please? I won't enjoy the surf if I'm worrying about the car.'

I sighed and turned down a side street. 'Happy now?'

We pulled on shortie wetsuits.

'Try to blend in,' Mikki said, as we jogged down the pavement.

But it wasn't easy to blend in when you had pink hair, and everyone stared at us as we paddled out. This beach was called La Gravière – The Gravel Pit – after the gravelly sand in the area. It was known as the world's heaviest beach break and had the crowd to prove it.

A commotion nearby as we waited for a wave. I freaked out, thinking it was a shark, then realised they were shouting at a guy with a camera. Now they were trying to get his camera off him. An arm shot out. Shit – someone threw a punch.

I paddled over. Mikki and I had different ways of dealing with aggression: she kept her head down, I kept my head up, so I was touched when she paddled after me, adding her voice to mine. The surfers backed off a bit and the camera guy paddled towards the beach. The surfers cast dirty looks at us and saw to it that for the rest of the session, neither Mikki nor I got any waves.

'Bastards,' Mikki muttered. 'I've had enough.'

'Me too.'

We paddled in.

The camera guy was on the beachfront, leaning against his car. He smiled as we approached. 'Thank you.' He gestured to his camera. 'I couldn't let them take this. Two thousand euros, just for the 'ousing.' He had wavy black hair and a thick French accent.

'Why were they shouting at you?' I asked.

'Because I am not from here. I am from Maroc.'

'Morocco?'

'Yeah.'

Then I noticed his right arm, hanging limply at his side. Dislocated in the battle to hang onto his camera. His dark eyes sparked with laughter as Mikki and I helped him take his wetsuit off, despite the pain he must have been in. The vulnerability of him got to me; this well-muscled and clearly very fit young guy unable to use his arm. We drove him to hospital and later to our campsite.

Kasim came from the desert, I come from a cold, damp, northern city. He was macho, I'm a feminist. He was emotional and hot-tempered, I'm logical and rational. We were complete opposites, from totally different cultures, but right from the start it was as though he was a part of me.

He didn't leave my side for the next two years.

Chapter 25

Kenna

Raised voices bring me back to the present. There's some kind of argument going on around the fire.

'Oh no,' Clemente says. 'You don't do this.'

'Let's put it to the vote,' Sky says.

'I think we all know this is no democracy,' Clemente says.

Sky throws him an amused look. 'What do you mean by that, honey?'

'Exactly what it sounds like.'

She slides her fingers through the hair at the back of his head. 'You're getting all riled up.'

Clemente slaps her hand away. 'Stop it.'

'I vote yes,' Victor says.

What are they voting for, and why do I have the feeling it involves me?

'What about you, Mikki?' Sky asks.

'Oh, come on!' Clemente says. 'She's Mikki's friend; of course Mikki's going to vote yes.'

Now I *know* it involves me.

Mikki's eyes flash my way. 'Yes.'

'You're voting no, I take it?' Sky asks Clemente.

'I am,' Clemente says.

'I side with Clemente,' Ryan says.

Sky turns to Jack. 'It's three-two on if we invite Kenna to join.'

I suck in my breath. I never saw that one coming.

Jack nods. 'Fine by me.'

Clemente explodes. 'Oh, come on, man. We agreed!'

'Four-two,' Sky says. 'Kenna, you're invited to join the Tribe.'

Adrenalin spikes in my stomach at the prospects this would offer. Surfing; climbing. And danger: lots of it. I catch myself. Much as I'm flattered to be asked to join this toughened group, I'm only here until I can persuade Mikki to leave. She's not safe with these guys. She's too trusting. Too kind-hearted. And why is she marrying Jack when she doesn't seem to want to?

'It's not a decision to take lightly,' Sky says. 'You're either all in or not in. There's no half-in. If you join us, each member has a duty to protect all the others and above all protect the Bay.'

I open my mouth to decline. But I need time to work on Mikki. They'll do another shopping trip eventually. Back in the real world, with internet and phone reception, more options will be available. If I go along with this for now, I'll have a chance of understanding the hold they seem to have on Mikki and how to break her free of it.

Sky's waiting. The whole Tribe is waiting.

Ryan – who voted 'no' – finds it even harder than usual

to meet my eyes. Victor watches me intently. *I'd kill for this wave.*

My gaze turns to Mikki. *There's some weirdness in the Tribe.*

She's clearly in over her head. Surrounded by these strong and forceful individuals – Sky, Victor, Clemente – she's overpowered and outnumbered. I have to help her.

Sky watches me as though aware of the battle going on in my mind.

'Yes,' I say. 'I accept.'

The calculating look in her eyes sends chills up my arms.

CHAPTER 26

KENNA

When I wake, it's still dark. The lumpy ground digging into my back and the musty smell of tent canvas reminds me where I am. I fumble for my phone, which now has only four per cent of battery left, and check the time. It's 4.30 a.m. Bloody jetlag. I close my eyes and will myself back to sleep.

A hissing sound, like a hand on canvas. My eyes fly open. Someone's out there. Notch by notch, they're slowly unzipping my tent. I sit up blinking into the darkness.

'Shh!' The quietest of whispers. 'It's me!'

'Who?' I whisper.

'Shh! Clemente. Come.'

Quietly as I can, I slither out of my sleeping bag. What on earth could he want? All I'm wearing is a T-shirt and knickers. I grope around for the shorts I wore yesterday, pull them on and crawl out of the tent, barefoot.

Clemente waits at the opening, his silhouette barely visible. 'Come,' he repeats.

Too sleepy to argue, I find myself following. I peer down

to try to see where I'm stepping, but the trees obscure most of the moonlight and I can't see a thing. Where is he?

As I grope forward, I remember how he voted against me. Fear flits across my stomach. It probably wasn't the best idea to follow him but I'm completely lost now and couldn't find my way back to my tent if I wanted to.

'Here!' he whispers.

I have no choice but to place one hand on his back and stumble after him. The heat of his skin radiates through his thin T-shirt. I think this is the trail to the beach. He must know it from memory.

Jetlag is working against me again. Instead of waking up wide awake like yesterday morning, my brain is slow and my body feels heavy. Something spikes my heel. I wish I'd put my flip-flops on. I used to go about barefoot in summer in Cornwall but these days my poor soles are tender from months of urban life.

The crash of waves gets louder. Light at the end of the trail. A half-moon hangs over the ocean, shockingly bright after the shadow of the trees. The sand is cool and gritty underfoot. The waves glow white as they crumble and I can tell straight away that we won't be surfing today – they're tiny and blown out.

When I turn, Clemente is looking at me.

'What are you scared of, Kenna?'

Once again, it's as though he's deliberately trying to faze me. 'Why do you want to know?'

'Because your fears are our fears.' Clemente makes quotation marks with his fingers. 'And whatever they are, Sky will find out.'

'If I tell you, how do I know you won't tell her?'

'You don't.'

I turn the question back on him. 'What are *you* scared of?'

Clemente gives me an exasperated look. 'Horses.'

I almost laugh.

He looks at me with intense irritation. 'It's something about their teeth.'

I try to wipe my smile. 'What else?'

He hesitates. 'Losing my vision.'

His gaze holds mine and I sense the truth in his words. The intimacy of the admission rocks me. Watch him surf or work out and you'd think he's invincible – he free-climbed a cliff with a dislocated finger! – yet here he is, admitting a deep fear.

'Amongst other things,' he says. 'What about you?'

'I'm not telling you.'

He lets out another exasperated sigh. 'Sky sniffs out your weak points, so be prepared.'

'You don't like her?'

He frowns. 'No, I like her. But some bad things have happened. Come.'

I follow Clemente to the water's edge. The moon lights up his profile as he studies the ocean.

He turns to face me. 'How long can you hold your breath?'

Over his shoulder the water gleams, black as ink. Suddenly I'm very aware of the loneliness of this spot. If I shouted, the sound would be drowned out by the wind and waves long before it reached the others. I fight back visions of him grabbing me and shoving me underwater. 'Why do you want to know?'

'There's an initiation test.'

A wave rolls in. Water laps around our ankles, a few degrees below blood temperature. I study Clemente's face for a clue as to his intentions, but all I can discern, from his regular glances at the trees, is that he really doesn't want us to be disturbed. He's seriously creeping me out right now but I try my hardest not to show it.

'Why?' I ask.

'Sky's idea. We're a tribe, so we don't want any weak links, they bring the whole tribe down. She will test you out today.'

We stand at arm's length, swatting at mosquitoes.

'Maybe two minutes,' I say finally.

Clemente looks at me sceptically.

'I've done some breath work.' I'm not sure whether I should be telling him this or not.

'In a swimming pool?'

'Yep.' When you work with sportspeople you have to keep up with the latest training techniques or risk looking stupid when you have no idea what they're talking about, in which case they lose confidence in you as a therapist. I do it out of personal interest too. Years before it became trendy, big wave surfers trained in breath control to prepare for the lengthy hold-downs that follow a wipeout. Now everyone's doing it: yoga studios, business people, even schoolkids. Kasim, Mikki and I did the course together – not that it saved him.

'It's totally different when you have waves throwing you about,' Clemente says.

'I get that. What does the test involve?'

'I don't know. It's different every time. But it will push you to your limit.'

'If you don't want me here, why are you telling me this?'

Clemente doesn't answer. He has a way of looking at me sometimes that scares me – really staring at me as though he isn't seeing me but someone else.

I fold my arms. 'I'm not doing it until you explain.'

He lets out a hiss of annoyance. 'The last girl who did the test panicked.'

My stomach spasms. The scene I'm picturing isn't pretty. Who was the last girl? They told me there was nobody else.

'I don't want it to happen again,' Clemente says. 'So you need to practise.'

'Okay!' I'm hurt that Mikki didn't warn me about the test. They really have her in their grasp.

Clemente takes me through some warm-up exercises similar to the ones I did on the breath control course: exhale twice as long as you inhale; three long breaths then hold. He whistles through his teeth as he exhales so I copy.

He checks the trees over my head again, then wades into the shallows. Warily, I follow him.

'Now under,' he says.

Is he getting off on this? There are some sick people out there. I study his face, but all I see is extreme reluctance, so I take a breath and duck down until I'm cross-legged on the seabed. My ears click and fill. Little bubbles fizzle from my nose, tickling my forehead. The waves rock me gently as they pass. I count the seconds in my head.

I'm barely under the surface but it's too dark to see anything up there. Clemente's hands could descend onto my shoulders any moment; I'm almost waiting for it to happen.

When I surface, gasping for air, he's standing there with folded arms.

'One minute twenty,' he says.

I can tell from his face that it's not enough. One second feels like two when you're holding your breath; I remember that from the course.

'Again,' he says.

So I try again and manage an extra twenty seconds.

'Now with my hands holding you under,' he says.

My breath sticks in my throat.

'Is like in big waves,' he says. 'You can't choose when you come up.'

I imagine myself wanting to surface and not being able to. Like Kasim must have. 'No.'

'I'm trying to help you!' Clemente gives me an exasperated look. 'I do it first, okay?' He peels off his T-shirt, balls it up and tosses it up the beach.

'What? I hold you under?'

'Yeah.' His chest and shoulders rise as he sucks in a breath.

'How do I know when you want to come up?'

'I will push up and you don't let me. We can always go longer.'

He sucks in another breath and ducks under. I grope for his shoulders and find them. Nausea rises inside me immediately. Was this what it felt like for Kasim during his final moments – the weight of the ocean holding him down? I whip my hands off and step back. Clemente remains underwater. I count seconds in my head, reach one minute and realise I'm holding my own breath in sympathy.

The water shimmers. I want to drag him forcibly up. I'm too distressed to count any more.

At last, Clemente surfaces and sucks in air. He seems perfectly calm. 'Why didn't you hold me under?'

'I couldn't.'

'You need to toughen up fast if you're going to survive here. Your turn now.'

I don't think I can do it.

Clemente glances at the trees. '*Mierda!*'

There's someone there, watching us.

Ryan steps out of the shadows and walks down the sand. 'What are you doing?'

'What does it look like?' Clemente says. 'Checking the surf.'

How long was Ryan standing there? I wait for him to say something but Clemente nudges my arm for me to go with him. Leaving Ryan on the sand, we head back to the clearing.

'Remind me again why you were helping me?' I ask.

Clemente gives me a strained look. 'I don't want any more blood on my hands.'

CHAPTER 27

KENNA

There's a symphony of bird calls from the overhead branches as we eat breakfast. It's still early and the sky is yellowy grey between the trees. Mikki sits beside me. I'm still waiting for her to tell me about the test.

Clemente hasn't spoken to me since we returned from the beach. I watch him from the corner of my eye. Blood on his hands. What did he mean?

'Time for Kenna's initiation test,' Sky announces once we finish.

I feign surprise. Mikki shoots me a guilty look. They're not supposed to warn people, clearly. And yet Clemente did.

'Can you grab the masks, Victor?' Sky asks.

'Snorkels too?' Victor asks.

'Yeah, bring them for after. We haven't been snorkelling for ages.'

'What do I need?' I ask.

'Just sunscreen and your towel.' Sky stuffs things into a backpack. 'Hey, come here, darl.'

Jack has a blob of sunscreen on his cheek. Victor scowls as Sky leans in to fix it.

'Everyone ready?' Sky asks. 'Follow me.'

'Where are we going?' I ask.

'The river.'

Sky's clearly a lot fitter than me and I'm hard-pressed to keep up with her, despite my regular visits to the gym. The others walk silently behind us. The trail branches several times. I don't think I've been this way before. I try to memorise the route but the dense undergrowth interferes with my sense of direction.

'They need more signs round here,' I say.

'There used to be more,' Sky says. 'But we moved them around or took them down. Don't want to make it too easy for people.'

'And nobody replaced them? Don't national parks have wardens who do that?'

Sky throws an amused look over her shoulder. 'Not this one.'

A bramble snags on my shorts. I pause to free it.

At last we break out of the trees, climb a bank of parched-looking grass and there's the river below, silent and wide, running out to sea. Under the heavy cloud cover the water looks dark and murky.

'At least there won't be sharks,' I say.

'Are you kidding?' Ryan says. 'The rivers are the sharkiest places in Australia.'

'Really?'

'They're full of bull sharks.'

The others are nodding.

Jack nudges me. 'Don't worry. There's plenty of fish for them to feed on. We've never had an issue with them.'

'Not in the river anyway,' Ryan says.

Before I can ask what he means, I spot a kangaroo on the grass behind him.

The others show little excitement.

'There's heaps of them round here,' Jack says. 'I think they like this grass.'

It has a baby in its pouch! Enchanted, I drop into a crouch.

'Cute, hey?' Mikki says.

The kangaroo stops eating to stare at me. In the pouch, the baby stares too.

I reach out a hand towards it. 'Will it come to me?'

'I've fed them a few times,' Mikki says.

Further away, several more kangaroos hop about.

'You just have to watch the large males,' Jack says.

'What?' I look at him, certain he's winding me up. *Let's tell the Brits we have killer kangaroos!*

'They're territorial,' Jack says.

Ryan nods. 'You should see their claws. Razor sharp.'

'But they wouldn't actually hurt you, would they?' I say.

'They have been known to,' Jack says. 'Not round here, but you hear of them kicking people in the stomach with their hind legs and basically ripping them open.'

I straighten, no longer so keen to get close. There's a little sheltered inlet this side of the river with a tiny area of sand. We scramble over the rocks and jump down onto it. I kick off my flip-flops and dip my toes in the water. 'It's colder than the sea.'

'Tide must be going out,' Ryan says. 'It comes down from the hills.'

'Bloody freezing after heavy rain,' Jack says.

I step in deeper. My next step takes me up to my thighs, then my neck. The bottom just drops away. Shit, I'm only a few metres from shore but the current is already pulling at me and I'm swimming on the spot to stay in place. Further out, the water races along, forming little peaks and troughs as it rushes out to sea. I'm not nearly such a strong swimmer as Mikki and I feel lost without my surfboard. I laugh shakily as I wade back to the bank.

'Grab your masks,' Sky tells them. 'Not you, Kenna.'

They gather round the bucket, removing masks from snorkels. Names are written on them in permanent marker.

'Can you chuck us mine?' Jack calls.

Only two snorkel sets remain in the bucket. I lift out the purple set and my heart goes still. *Elke*. The letters swim before my eyes. It has to be her, doesn't it? The missing backpacker.

Shock rushes through me, slowing my thoughts. Should I pretend I haven't noticed? Too late. Sky has seen what I'm holding. Our eyes meet.

'It says "Elke" on it,' I say.

Sky purses her lips. My insides are jittering about, my breaths shallow and rapid. Victor and Jack are laughing about something. They fall silent as they see the snorkel.

'Was there an Elke here?' I ask.

'A while ago, yeah,' Sky says.

'Was she from Germany?'

'Yeah. Why?' Sky's tone is impatient.

'There were posters saying she was missing.'

'Elke?' Clemente says.

'Are you sure?' Sky asks.

The others exchange puzzled looks.

'Nah, must be a different Elke,' Jack says.

I try to remember her surname but can't think of it. 'Blonde, blue eyes?'

'There's probably hundreds of Elkes in Germany who are blonde with blue eyes,' Ryan says.

I turn to Mikki. 'You saw that poster in the petrol station. Was it her?'

She hesitates. 'It wasn't a good photo. I wasn't sure.'

From the way Mikki reacted, I'm almost certain she recognised her, so why is she denying it? But I won't put her on the spot in front of the others.

'Does anyone know anything about this?' Sky asks.

Silence from the others. Clemente looks at me, his expression troubled.

I turn back to Sky. 'How long was she here for?'

'About six months.'

'And what happened to her?'

'She left.'

'Didn't even say goodbye,' Jack says. 'She just disappeared.'

'And now she's on a missing poster,' I say.

'Not our problem,' Ryan says.

'If the bitch went missing after she left here, that's her problem.' Sky has this way of taking on the accent of the people around her, and just now she sounds American.

'Nothing to do with us,' Victor agrees.

A shudder passes through me. I'm certain they know more than they're letting on. Clemente mentioned a girl who panicked. Was that Elke?

Sky pulls rope from her backpack. 'Initiation time. This is going to be a trust exercise, Kenna. Do you trust us?'

CHAPTER 28

KENNA

I try to calm my racing heart. 'I hardly know you, so how can I trust you?'

Sky seems satisfied with my answer. 'Well, this will help you. You must let us take your life in our hands.'

A shot of fear hits my stomach.

The Tribe will wait downriver at ten-metre intervals to carry me, Sky explains, not swimming but running underwater along the riverbed, dragging me with them. Blindfolded, with my hands tied behind my back. I try to hide my shock at this last bit.

'You don't have to do it,' Clemente says. 'We can run you to the nearest town.'

Sky shoots him an annoyed look. The nearest town is suddenly a tempting prospect, but what about Mikki? If I back out now, it'll be obvious I don't trust them and they'll never trust me either.

Mikki offers me an apologetic shrug. She won't let anything bad happen to me. 'I'll do it,' I say.

Clemente paces back and forth shaking his head, as Sky ties my hands behind my back.

She fastens the blindfold above my forehead. 'The less you struggle, the easier this will be.'

It's as though she's trying to scare me. 'Easier? To do what?' I ask. 'Drown me?'

Sky hides her smile.

'Will I be able to breathe?'

Her smile widens. 'Hopefully.'

The sight of Elke's snorkel poking from the bucket doesn't help my nerves.

'She needs a safety rope,' Clemente says.

He doesn't talk much, I notice, but when he does, everyone listens. Sky tosses him another rope and he silently secures it around my waist.

Victor immediately volunteers to man the other end of the rope, standing on the bank, gesturing to the water with a shudder. 'Too cold.'

The others have clearly done this before. They lower their masks and take their positions in the river, swimming on the spot against the current. Mikki is the first in line, with an aqua mask up on her forehead.

'Should I try to swim?' I ask.

'You won't know what direction to swim in,' Mikki says. 'And anyway, your hands are tied. So, no. Just relax and let us do all the work.'

I'm taller than Mikki and larger framed. 'You won't be able to lift me. I'm too heavy.'

'In the water you'll be lighter.'

'Fear is fuel!' Sky shouts.

'Panic is lethal!' the others reply.

154

Mikki lowers the blindfold over my eyes and guides me into the river. I must be out of my mind to go along with this but it's too late to back out; the current is already tugging at me. I take deep breaths, fighting for calm. Mikki grips my waist and I'm lifted off my feet. The water is around my neck now. I suck in small breaths as I'm jerkily dragged forward.

It's scary not being able to see the water. I can feel it lapping around my chin. Another pair of hands grip me: the first handover. Jack was next in line and I tense up, thinking of his poor back and how he'll handle my weight, but he maintains a fast pace.

There's something almost militant about how they pull together to function so smoothly and effortlessly. One thing's for sure: I wouldn't like to cross these guys.

A few breaths later, I'm passed to the next set of hands – Ryan or Sky, I can't remember the order – except they don't get a good hold of me and I slip through their grip. Caught by surprise, I swallow a mouthful of briny water and sink like a stone. Panic flares in my stomach. I strain to free my hands but they're securely tied.

Fingers rake at me, scratching my shoulder as they haul me to the surface. Mikki shouts something as I cough and gasp for air. My throat burns with the taste of salt as I'm dragged onwards. Another handover. I keep my mouth firmly closed, breathing cautiously through my nose but this time it's smoother. Another few breaths and I reach the final handover. Clemente was last in line so I know he has me now. The feel of his large fingers splayed around my ribs is strangely calming. He comes to a stop and lifts me higher, his torso warm and solid against my side, then whips off the blindfold. I blink as sunlight floods my eyes.

He unties my hands. 'Take a breath.'

'What?'

He signals to Victor and I'm dragged rapidly back upriver. Half the river has gone up my nose by the time I reach him. Victor unties the safety rope and I wade up the bank, still spluttering. Someone wraps a towel around me. I look from Sky to Ryan, wondering which of them dropped me, and if it was intentional. Even if it wasn't, it proves the point I'm trying to get across to Mikki – that in a place like this accidents can happen at any moment.

I sit on the grass while the others do running jumps into the river: backflips, frontflips and all kinds of crazy stuff. I should join in but I'm feeling pretty shaky.

Sky lowers herself to the bank beside me, black mask up on her forehead. 'You remind me of me, sometimes.'

I'm flattered but I try not to show it. 'Do I?'

'How I used to be anyway.' One blonde dreadlock sits on my shoulder, dripping cold water down my back.

'How do you mean?'

'You're a people pleaser.'

I no longer feel flattered, because that isn't how I see myself at all. It just shows how fazed these guys make me feel. Well, that's got to stop.

Sky's icy fingers clasp my arm. 'Sometimes I think about the life I left behind, doing and saying what everyone wanted me to. It took me years to break the habit. To really find myself. The people I dated before I came here? I freaked them out.'

'Yeah,' I say. 'I can imagine that.'

Her lips twitch into a smile. 'Do I freak you out, darl?'

I don't answer.

She goes on. 'I freaked out the people I worked with as well. Nobody told me outright, but I could tell. Basically, I was miserable, so I ran. Then I met Jack in the surf at Bondi. He dropped in on me, actually.'

That drags a smile out of me.

'But he seemed like a nice guy so we got chatting and I was complaining about how busy it was in the surf.' Her tone is low and intimate. '*I know a secret spot,* he said, and he took me to Sorrow Bay for the weekend. I met the others and I didn't freak them out one little bit. If anything, they freaked *me* out. The waves certainly freaked me out.' She laughs to lighten it.

I laugh too, sensing this kind of admission doesn't come naturally to her.

She goes on. 'The first time I saw it was during a winter storm. I'd never seen waves that big, not in real life. My surfing wasn't that good back then so I washed up on the beach half-drowned and felt like I'd been born again. And right now, you look exactly how I felt.'

A whoop from Victor. They're doing belly flops now – huge ones that must hurt. Mikki's belly is bright red from the impact as she scrambles up the bank. I note again how well Mikki fits in with them. She looks so happy.

When I turn back to Sky, her face is serious.

'Sorrow Bay is a special place, Kenna. It changes people in a way I can't explain. It's partly being so far away from the rest of civilisation and its distractions – shops, TV and social media. But it's partly the Bay itself. There's

157

something in the trees, an energy that belongs to this place that affects you in ways you don't expect.'

Unsettled by her words, I glance at the trees beyond her shoulder.

Sky stares at me with her strange pale eyes. 'How will you change, Kenna? For the better, or the worse? Because there's a darkness inside all of us and the Bay has a way of bringing it out.'

Chapter 29

Kenna

Ryan scrambles up the bank towards us, water sluicing off his chest. 'Good job I brought the spear gun.'

'Are there fish?' Sky asks.

'Loads of them.' Ryan lifts the gun from the bank and slots his snorkel onto the strap of his mask. His shoulders are pink and peeling and covered with sunspots.

'Grab a snorkel, Kenna,' Sky calls, helping herself to one.

The others collect snorkels and wade back in, leaving me alone on the bank. Elke's snorkel set is the only one in the bucket. Reluctantly, I pull it on. The mask blocks my peripheral vision and I feel vulnerable as I enter the water. Before I go under, I glance around to orientate myself, making a mental note of where the current gets stronger. A few steps in the wrong direction and I'll be in danger of being swept out to sea.

I inhale deeply and duck under. My hair lifts upwards, floating above my head. Sand particles churned up by the others obscure the visibility and the fish darting along the seabed are almost the same colour as the sand. I turn left into clearer water. Sky swims past, the red string of her bikini streaming behind her like blood.

Brighter fish come into view: a plump one in bold zebra stripes, a trio of spotty ones. Remembering what they said about sharks, I make regular checks around me.

Clemente dives down to lift a rock from the riverbed. I swim up for air, then dive back under, and heave a rock of my own to my chest. Rock running is a great way to build strength and stamina on flat days. Mikki and I did it all the time in Cornwall after seeing it in *Blue Crush*. You find a suitably sized rock and run along the ocean floor with it, holding your breath. In the movie, they make it look easy, but it's not.

I dig my toes into the sand for purchase and propel myself along. Something touches my shoulder and I squeak into my mouthpiece but it's only Mikki. She raises one hand and makes a circle with her thumb and forefinger: the diver's 'OK' signal. I nod and she grips my shoulders, adding resistance to make the exercise harder. I used to love doing this but it makes me claustrophobic today. Heart banging, I run forward, towing her along.

Sunlight filters through the water, turning it a beautiful shade of aqua. Fish flit past, tiny iridescent purple ones and slower moving ones with crazy yellow and black spotted tails, but I barely notice them because I'm too preoccupied. Elke swam with them like this, possibly right here, and now she's on a missing poster. They all complained how much they hate localism, yet this place is potentially an extreme example of it.

A shape to my left catches my attention. Shit, that's Ryan with the spear gun – and he's aiming it right at me. I release my rock and stop dead, causing Mikki to bump against me. I point to Ryan, but the gun is angled in a different direction now and I'm not sure if I imagined it.

Mikki mimes bewilderment and swims up to the surface to see what I want.

I surface at the same time as Ryan.

'Did you catch any?' Sky calls.

'No.' Ryan's mask obscures his eyes so I can't tell if he's looking at me or not. 'Not this time.'

Sky beckons us in. 'Training time!'

I glance at Ryan again as we pack up our stuff but he doesn't look at me once. I think I was just being paranoid.

Sky leads us along the riverbank to the beach and gets us running along the sand, barefoot, holding our breath for ten seconds, then breathing for ten seconds. We race along, feeding off each other's energy, like a pack of dogs. No, I think, when I look more closely, there's something altogether wilder about their expressions. A pack of wolves. And I'm running with them.

Chapter 30

Ryan

My heart is beating too fast, my breaths coming one on top of the other. Hoping none of the others notice, I cut into the trees. The spear gun bashes against my hip; twigs snap and crack under my soles.

What's Jack playing at, bringing another outsider here? The Bay is my haven – my hiding place. I stumble over a tree root and crash to the ground. There's a ticking sensation in my brain as I pick myself up, as though my head is about to explode. I clutch at my chest, suck in a gasp of air and run on.

The trees thin at last and I reach the tiny grassy clearing that we call the Meadow. None of the others ever come here, so it's my place, the only place I know I won't be disturbed. Lungs heaving, I dump the spear gun and stretch out on the earth.

Closing my eyes, I begin the tapping. Tap-tap-tap! Ten to my stomach, ten to either side, ten to my sternum . . . Ten different areas of my body and face. One round isn't enough so I start again, but my thoughts are twisting and repeating through my brain instead of latching onto the numbers and calming themselves.

All Kenna's questions at the river – I wanted to press my hand over her mouth and make her shut up. When it was my turn to carry her, I 'accidentally' dropped her but bloody Sky fished her out far too fast.

Stop thinking about her! I stick my fingers in my ears and hold my breath, battling to slow my racing heart.

I found great pleasure in counting things as a child. Numbers made me feel safe. Until the numbers became huge amounts of money, and then they weren't safe any more. I probably made the worst possible career choice. The best way to describe investment banking? Intense. You can never switch off from it because the market never stops. My wife had expensive tastes so I found myself taking greater and greater risks to fund the lifestyle she wanted. I would lie in bed gritting my teeth trying not to imagine what might be happening to the market while I wasn't looking. I didn't find calm again for many years.

Early one morning, when I hadn't slept for three nights running, I slipped out of bed and drove into the sunrise to a rocky outcrop to watch the waves crashing up against the land. Numbers continued whirring around my brain. I stood up on the rocks and jumped off – just to make them stop. And they did. They washed from my mind immediately.

The waves pounded me and I felt calmer than I had for ages. *Next time I'll do it with a surfboard,* I told myself as I staggered back to my car, bruised and bleeding. I waxed up a board I hadn't used since I was a teenager and surfed that vicious little reef break all winter. Suddenly I could cope with the pressure of work again. I moved on to try other sports – rock climbing and sky diving, snowboarding and motocross. The more dangerous the sport, the calmer I felt. I came off my medication because I didn't need it any more.

Then Ava was born. The financial pressure doubled because I was the sole breadwinner, the lack of sleep tripled, and there was no time to do any sports. In desperation, I snapped and did something stupid that I'll regret for the rest of my life. *Don't think about that.*

A stabbing pain shoots through me. Tap-tap-tap. Focus on the numbers.

Last year, things got so bad that I thought I was having a heart attack. I had to leave the Bay and see a doctor. Jack let me use his details on the form I had to fill in. Since then, I've tried hard not to get past a certain point. Jack's pills work, if I'm desperate. I've pinched one on occasion, but if Jack notices, he'll go off his nut.

These days, when I'm surfing is pretty much the only time I feel calm. Flat days are always the worst, with no waves to distract me from all that goes on in my head. I hate myself more than ever on such days. I think about Ava, seven thousand miles away, and imagine what she might be doing, which gets me thinking about going home. But I can't go back – I can't go to jail.

My chest tightens up again. *I'm safe,* I tell myself. Nobody's going to find me here. The Tribe don't even know my surname. I've been careful never to tell them and I hid my passport and bank cards soon after I arrived. I tried so hard to keep out of trouble but I didn't completely manage it. Elke's name chimes in my head over and over, in time with my tapping. Now that Kenna's seen Elke's snorkel, how long until she discovers the rest? I might face jail here too, if they discover what I did. I picture a windowless cell, so narrow I can't even stretch my arms out, and a cold, concrete floor. My chest tightens even more. *Stop!*

I tap and I tap but it's not working. My breaths are fast and shallow and my heart is beating so fast it's about to combust. This is Kenna's doing. I need her gone. That's the only thing that will make this feeling go away.

CHAPTER 31

KENNA

I change out of my wet bikini, slap on more sunscreen and help myself to a banana. I can't see Mikki anywhere.

Jack is at the barbecue, cutting watermelon. I approach him cautiously. 'Have you seen Mikki?'

'She's probably at the beach.' Jack holds out a piece of watermelon. Once again he looks a little spaced. 'Want a piece?'

'Thanks.' I suck juice from my fingers as I head down the track. And there's Mikki, near the rocks. Seagulls scatter as I jog over the sand. They're smaller than their British counterparts and cleaner too, with snow-white bellies and neatly spruced grey backs.

I reach Mikki, breathless. 'Are you okay?'

Mikki looks round in surprise. 'Of course. I just like watching the waves. I could watch them forever.'

I sit down beside her. The water rears up, peels over and crashes down, leaving lacy white patterns on the sand which fade and disappear before the next wave washes in. The rhythm is hypnotic.

Mikki nods to the ocean. 'That *colour*.'

'I know.'

Turquoise has always been our favourite colour. The first apartment we rented together, we filled with turquoise things: bowls and mugs, candleholders and cushion covers; canvas prints of waves breaking that we could look at when we couldn't see the real thing.

'Don't you just love this place?' Mikki says.

'It *is* pretty special.' I sift the sand through my fingers. If I squint at it hard enough, I can see every colour of the rainbow. 'You didn't tell me about Elke. That *was* her on the poster, right?'

She shoots me an irritated look. 'Probably.'

'Did you know her well?'

'Yeah, we came to the Bay together.' Mikki combs her fingers through her hair. 'I met her in the backpackers' hostel in Bondi. We met Jack and Clemente in a bar there and they brought us here.'

'So what happened to her?'

'She left. I thought she just decided to move on.'

'Yet now she's on a missing poster.'

Mikki purses her lips.

'Back in Sydney, you said there's some weirdness in the Tribe. What did you mean?'

'There's been a few arguments, that's all. Nothing major.'

A tribe member ending up on a missing poster: that's pretty major if you ask me. The fact that Mikki knows about Elke's disappearance and hasn't left tells me just how deep in she is. I need to get her out of here before she ends up on a missing poster herself, but with her wedding only eleven days away, I'm running out of time.

I take a deep breath. 'Look, I hate to say it but I'm scared Jack only likes you for your money.'

Hurt flashes across Mikki's face. 'Thanks a bunch.'

'I mean, he seems like an okay guy, and he may actually like you, but this is so sudden. You have money and he doesn't, and I'm scared that's why he's marrying you.'

She folds her arms. 'You know what? You're right.'

'What?'

'He needs money. I need a visa.' She looks at me, daring me to argue.

'Shit.' I didn't expect that. I'm totally thrown.

'We get on, so why not?'

I stare at her, realising I've never seen them kiss each other, or be physically affectionate in anything other than a platonic way. 'Are you like . . . together?'

'What does that even mean anyway?'

I force myself to ask it. 'Do you sleep with him?'

'Of course I do.' Mikki's flushing. She and I never talk about stuff like that. It's funny – I talk about sex all the time with my work colleagues.

'Do you love him?' I ask.

She hesitates. 'No. But I love this place.'

It's as though she's been brainwashed. 'I can see the appeal of surfing empty waves but you're breaking the law. Do you realise the implications? What if you get reported?'

Mikki lifts her chin. 'It's worth the risk.'

She's right here, so close I can touch her, but I might as well still be ten thousand miles away.

The ocean rises and falls like a sleeper's chest.

'Are they all overstayers?' I ask. 'Ryan, Clemente and Victor?'

Mikki looks startled. 'What?'

'I know Ryan is. He told me.'

'He's the only one. Clemente and Victor are legal.'

I look at her sceptically.

'Clemente married an Aussie. Victor came here on a sports visa, but after his accident, he switched to an investment visa. His family's loaded.'

'Can't *you* get an investment visa?'

She laughs. 'You have to have a *lot* more money than I do.'

'You haven't even known Jack for a year. It's too soon. Wait a bit at least.'

'I can't. My working holiday visa runs out in two weeks. If I don't marry him, I'll have to leave the country.' Mikki gestures around. 'This is my favourite place on earth. I'll do anything to stay here.'

Anything. The word echoes around my mind. So it's not Jack who has a hold on her, as I originally thought. It's the Bay itself.

'Shall we head back?' Mikki says.

I watch the everchanging shades of blue as we walk along the beach. In the bright sunshine, with the sparkling water lapping the golden sand, Sorrow Bay seems like a tropical paradise where nothing bad could possibly happen. But a few steps into the trees, the air has a chill to it. I sense strongly that what happens in these trees stays in these trees. And the undergrowth seems thick enough to hide all manner of secrets.

CHAPTER 32

KENNA

Late afternoon, Sky emerges from the trees in a white bikini with a spear gun over her shoulder. She looks like a Bond girl.

'Did you catch any?' Clemente calls.

'Come and see!' Sky shouts.

Three large fish flop against the sides of her bucket. Clemente gives her a high five and takes the bucket from her. He's on dinner duty tonight.

I join him at the barbecue. 'Thanks for helping me earlier.'

'No problem.' He stoops down to fiddle with the gas canister.

'What can I do?'

'Nothing.' He lays a fish onto a chopping board and slices it open with a look of intense concentration, skilful and precise with the knife.

Across the clearing, Mikki laughs as she sprays insect repellent on Victor. Once again, I notice how well Mikki fits in, but she always was good at fitting in. She's had some practice, after all – Australia's the fourth country she's lived in.

She comes over with the repellent. 'Put some of this on.'

'Thanks.' As I take it, I notice a gouge on her wrist, right where her tattoo is. 'Shit, what happened?'

Mikki gives it a casual glance. 'Must have done it on the rocks.'

I spray on repellent. My skin is smarting from the sun earlier and I'm still smarting inside that it was Clemente who warned me about the initiation, not her. Mikki's in deep with these guys. Her loyalties lie with them, not me. Hopefully that will change now I'm one of them.

'Want me to do you?' Mikki asks Clemente.

'Yeah, thanks,' he says, reaching for another fish.

Funny how he accepts her but not me. I watch her spray his broad shoulders.

'My legs,' he says. 'They always go for my legs.'

Mikki giggles and bends down. 'They're so juicy.'

I'd think she was flirting with him if I hadn't seen her do the same thing to Victor.

Clemente jerks away – did she tickle him? The movement brings his knife arm close to me and I jump backwards. Knife tight in his fist, Clemente's eyes meet mine. The darkness I see in them scares me – or am I imagining it?

Mikki turns to me, apparently oblivious to the tension. 'I'm going to wash my hair. Want to do yours? I'll show you how. We try to conserve water.'

Mikki and I take turns dipping our heads in a plastic tub.

She lowers her voice. 'What were you talking about with Clemente?'

'Nothing.'

'You can't trust him.'

I pull my head from the tub to look at her. 'What?'

She darts an anxious look across the clearing. 'There are things you don't know.'

Water trickles down my back, snaking inside my bra. 'Like what?'

Mikki shakes her head a little. 'I can't tell you.' I start to protest but she cuts me off. 'Just don't get too close to him. Hey, we need to get changed.'

I stare at her in frustration. 'What for?'

'Your initiation ceremony.'

I head to my tent, still puzzling over what she said about Clemente. Mikki and I used to tell each other everything but I guess that's the price I pay for moving to London. I pull clothing from my backpack but nothing seems right. A patterned shirt? Too hot. A black dress? Too clubby.

'What should I wear?' I shout.

'Come in here,' Mikki calls.

I crawl into her tent, where she's pulling a sequinned silver dress over her head.

Mikki hands me something. 'Wear this.'

I unfold it to find a lacy white dress I've borrowed before. 'It's so short.'

'Who cares? Soon it'll be too dark to see.'

'True.' I pull it on. 'God, I've got fatter. That's London for you. Too much food and not enough exercise.'

'You'll lose it here in no time.'

'Mikki! Kenna!' Sky calls.

As we crawl out, Mikki plucks a flower from a nearby bush and puts it in my hair. I notice her heels – silver to match her dress, so inappropriate yet somehow perfect – and snort back my laughter as they sink into the earth and she grabs my hand not to fall.

The others are gathered around the fire. My laughter dies when I see their solemn expressions.

'We are here tonight to welcome Kenna to the Tribe,' Sky says.

'Welcome,' they chorus, faces eerie in the firelight.

Sky wears a long white dress with shoestring straps, tanned bare toes poking out beneath. The men wear smart shirts: white for Victor, a stark contrast to his skin; black for Clemente; Ryan's has a Hawaiian print.

Jack's is pale blue and unbuttoned all the way. He leans to whisper in Mikki's ear. 'You look hot, babe.'

A gleam on Sky's wrist catches my eye. My stomach clenches at the sight of the engraved silver bracelet. It's Mikki's – an heirloom passed down from her beloved Japanese granny, passed down in turn from *her* granny. The one time I asked to borrow it, Mikki said no. *I'll lend you anything else, but this is irreplaceable.*

'We have only two rules,' Sky says. 'Number one: tell nobody. Most surfers would die to surf in an uncrowded spot like this. This wave is ours and we do whatever it takes to protect it.'

'Whatever it takes,' the others chorus.

'Rule number two,' Sky says. 'We share everything. And that means *everything*. Got it?'

Does *everything* mean what I think it means? The others are nodding. All eyes are on me, so I nod too.

The hem of Sky's dress scrapes the earth as she moves. She reaches her hand into the middle of the circle, over the fire. One by one, the others put their hands below hers, forming a stack. Heads turn my way and I realise they're waiting for me to do the same, so I put my hand at the bottom, beneath Victor's. It's directly above the flames and the heat licks my palm.

'The Tribe,' Sky says.

'The Tribe,' they echo.

My palm is burning. 'The Tribe,' I repeat, desperate to move my hand.

'Your strengths are our strengths,' Sky says. 'And you will use them to help the Tribe. Your weaknesses are our weaknesses and you will work to eliminate them. Do you agree?'

'Yes,' I say.

The palms lift off mine and I snatch my hand back. Am I burnt? I press my palm to my water bottle, enjoying the smooth coolness of the plastic.

Sky smiles at me. 'Let's eat.'

Clemente has made a paella to go with the fish. I watch them as I chew, thinking how the set-up here reminds me of *Survivor*. Just like on the show, a complicated web of allegiances between the tribe members have formed following past events that I know nothing about. Clemente has spoken out against Sky a couple of times; he's clearly a power player. Ryan sided with Clemente yesterday against her. Clemente and Victor are friendly, but if Clemente stands up to Sky, Victor takes her side. Clemente is protective over Jack, who seems lower in the pecking order – or prefers to avoid conflict at any rate. Mikki also seems reluctant to take sides.

I lean in towards Mikki. 'You lent Sky your bracelet.'

Mikki looks at me, guilty-faced. 'Actually, I gave it to her.'

I blink. 'Oh.'

My hurt must be obvious because Mikki's eyes fill with concern. 'Sorry.' She shifts in her seat, clearly uncomfortable. 'She really liked it.'

Ryan lifts a bowl from the ground. 'I got some sorrow fruit.'

The others nod in approval and he passes the bowl around. I've never heard of sorrow fruit before. When he reaches me, I take one. They're small and purplish red.

'Are they apples?' I ask.

'Yeah,' Ryan says. His long hair sits over his shoulders and it looks like he's brushed it, for once.

Jack raises his apple. 'To Sky.'

The others raise theirs. 'To Sky.'

Funny, they're looking at Clemente, not Sky.

They're a clean-living bunch, toasting with fruit instead of alcohol. I haven't even seen any alcohol since I arrived here. Still, I drank far too much these last two years and it'll do me good to have a break from it.

The apple is crunchy and sour, its sharp tang filling my mouth. I want to spit it out but sense it would offend so I wash it down with water.

Jack rubs Mikki's arm. 'Are you cold? You've got goose bumps. Want me to get you a sweater?'

'No, I'm fine.' Mikki shifts her arm away.

I'm pretty touchy-feely when I'm in relationships. If I was seeing a guy like Jack, I wouldn't be able to keep my hands off him. *Banish that thought, Kenna.*

Ryan produces a guitar later and strums a song: Lou Reed's 'Sweet Jane'. Victor sings along in his deep voice; Mikki joins in. The Tribe seem relaxed and happy. Unlike me. My head is still full of questions.

'You're really good,' I tell Ryan when he finishes.

'Hardly,' he says. 'I can only play the one song.'

I think I was wrong about him at the river. I was so spooked by Elke's snorkel that I imagined things. He seems unfriendly, but most of that is down to shyness.

'I still can't believe you have this place to yourselves,' I say. 'Other people must know about it. What about the people who've been here and left? Don't they ever come back?'

'Nobody else ever comes,' Sky says. 'Not any more. So nobody leaves either.'

'Except Elke,' I say.

I'm not sure if I'm being paranoid, but I sense a stiffening of bodies and a collective holding of breath. *Shut up, Kenna,* a little voice in my head tells me, but I can't resist. 'What was she like?'

Jack glances at Clemente, Victor too.

'We have an expression in Portuguese,' Victor says.

Ryan groans. 'Oh, here we go.'

Victor ignores him. '*Comprar gato por lebre.* It means you thought you bought a rabbit but you got a cat.'

'I don't get it,' I say.

Victor raises his hand, finger flexed. 'She seemed like a really sweet girl to start with. But she had claws.'

'She was competitive as all hell,' Ryan says. 'Used to play hockey for the German national team.'

There's an odd silence and I catch Jack looking at Clemente again. I'm good at reading body language after a decade of sports therapy work. From the minute someone steps into my studio, I'm scrutinising them for signs of tension: clenched fingers or jaws, shoulders higher than they should be, stiffness of the back or limbs. Bodies should be symmetrical but they rarely are. Hips and shoulders are frequently higher on one side from trauma or stress. If part of your body is hurting, you naturally lock up the neighbouring area in an attempt to protect it, and it's my job to notice it.

And right now, the tension in the group is blindingly obvious. Ryan looks everywhere but at me; Jack does the opposite and locks his eyes on mine as if attempting to hold back my thoughts. Mikki sits stiffly upright, playing with her hair. Clemente and Sky conceal it better but their shallow breathing gives them away.

Let it drop, Kenna. I'll press Mikki about it later in private.

'Hey, Ryan!' Victor says. 'Play it again!'

So Ryan begins to strum and the tension eases a little, but they're clearly hiding something and Mikki's body language suggests she's in on it.

Clemente catches me by the arm as I head off to refill my water.

'That poster about Elke,' he says quietly. 'What did it say?'

I strain to remember. 'That she was last seen on Bondi Beach in September. That's about it.'

Worry flashes across his face. Is he worried about Elke's safety or about keeping Sorrow Bay secret? He opens his mouth but remains silent as Mikki approaches.

'Fancy a swim before bed?' Mikki asks.

'Not right now,' Clemente says.

'Me neither,' I say. 'But have fun.'

Mikki gives me a funny look and I remember her warning about him. I smile reassuringly and she heads off.

'In September?' Clemente asks.

'Yeah,' I say. 'Why?'

'Just curious.'

'Was she the girl who panicked during the test?'

He hesitates. 'Yep.'

I squint into the shadows, trying to read his expression, but he's wearing his mask once again and as usual I have no idea what he's thinking.

When I crawl into my tent, something crackles on my pillow. I turn on the torch on my phone (one per cent of battery left) to see an empty surf wax packet with a note scrawled on it.

You're asking too many questions.

CHAPTER 33

KENNA

We're on the beach as the first light glances over the horizon. The waves loom like ghosts from the blackness. I wade through the shallows and splash water over my face trying to get my thoughts together as the others paddle past.

I didn't sleep well because I couldn't stop thinking about Elke. She could have left here of her own accord – perhaps after falling out with one of them – and something happened to her after that. I'm sceptical, though.

The note on my pillow proved they're trying to keep something hidden. I puzzle over it again as I paddle out. I have no idea which of them wrote it. It seems unlikely that it was Mikki – she would warn me in person, surely – and if I follow that line of reasoning, Clemente could also have warned me in person when we spoke last night. But maybe the author of the note prefers to remain anonymous because they know something they shouldn't.

Light creeps up the horizon. As the sky changes from navy to violet to pink, I watch the group on the waves, noting once again how much this reveals about them. Jack, particularly, is beautiful to watch, so smooth and light on his feet that when he snaps the board around in a sharp top turn or cutback the movement catches you by surprise. You wouldn't think he had it in him.

Clemente paddles for waves, even the ones that are obvious closeouts, with total commitment, undaunted by the monster chomping at his heels. He seems able to tune out what's behind him and focus on the wave in front. Mirroring how he lives his life, perhaps.

Ryan clearly hasn't forgiven Jack for dropping in on him the other day and snakes his waves every chance he has. Funny. Ryan's this soft-spoken guy who can barely look you in the eye most of the time, but in the surf he's a different person – and he obviously holds a grudge like nothing else.

Victor is as confident and powerful in the water as he is on land, his amazing bottom turns testament to the strength in his quads. Mikki gets a wave next. Shit – Clemente is paddling back out and Mikki's heading straight for him. At the last minute he ducks under and she rides over him.

'Oh my God, I'm so sorry!' Mikki shouts.

The others chuckle as Mikki and Clemente paddle back out.

Victor leans across to slap Clemente on the shoulder. 'She nearly took you out, brother!'

Clemente grins ruefully. 'I thought she was going to run me down!'

Mikki's right behind him, red-faced, but the rest of us are laughing.

'She's lethal,' I say. 'She nearly took my boyfriend out a couple of years ago.'

My voice peters out as I say it and they look at me curiously. It's still hard to talk about him without feeling the loss. A wave rolls my way. *Okay, Kasim. This one's for you.*

I jump to my feet as the water surges beneath me. Muscle memory kicks in and before I know it, my board is most of the way out of the water, a white arc spraying into the air and landing with a hiss.

There are moments in surfing, and perhaps in every sport, when everything aligns and you get a movement just right. 'Flow' they call it, in sports psychology books, but the four-letter word doesn't seem nearly big enough to express the feeling zinging up my legs and radiating through my body. The only problem is you immediately crave more. *You can't get sucked in again,* I remind myself, but a little voice in my head tells me it's too late.

Shells prick my feet as I walk up the sand.

'Wait up!' Mikki calls.

'This place is amazing!' I say. 'I got twelve waves. I can't remember the last time I got twelve waves.'

Mikki beams, 'I knew you'd love it.'

'You've made a good life for yourself here.'

She studies my face, unsure if I genuinely mean it or if I'm just changing tactics.

Worryingly, I'm not sure either. How had I forgotten how good it feels to simply slide through the water? Elke's disappearance is seriously disturbing, and it terrifies me that Mikki's about to enter into a huge commitment – marriage – without seeming to have given it much thought, yet I can see the appeal of Sorrow Bay. There aren't many spots left in the world where you can get such perfect, uncrowded waves.

Mikki transfers her board to her other hand and slides her arm round my waist. 'It's your life too now, remember?'

'For a while.' I don't want to mislead her.

Her eyes shine. 'This place isn't about who you are, it's about what you do, and I love that. We're living simply, close to the land, almost like we would have done thousands of years ago, when we were hunter gatherers.'

The gathering I don't have a problem with. It's the hunting part that bothers me. No matter how amazing the waves are, Mikki's not safe here.

'Let's grab something to eat and surf again,' she says.

'Great idea.' There's no point in me being here and not surfing, but in a month's time I fly home and I'll do everything I can to make sure Mikki's on the plane with me.

I glance over my shoulder as we leave, reminding myself that while the ocean can bring so much joy, it can also take it away.

CHAPTER 34

KENNA

TWO YEARS AGO

Kasim tasted of orange marmalade that morning.

'Yum,' I said and kissed him some more. I'd have kissed him for longer if I'd known it was the last time I'd do it.

My kitchen smelt of toast. The central heating was on and I was sweating inside my wetsuit. It was mid March and the promised six-to-eight-foot swell had arrived: the biggest swell we'd had all winter. Mikki and I watched the surf-cam on my phone while we ate breakfast.

'Whaaa!' Mikki said as a wave peeled and a tiny rubber-clad figure surfed down it, the water pitching up well over his head.

Kasim swore in Arabic. 'It's too big.'

I drained my coffee and stood up. 'You don't have to come.'

Kasim tried to block the door. 'You're not going out there.'

He went all alpha male on me at times and mostly it was cute – hot even – but not when he was coming between me and the surf. Over his shoulder, a set wave peeled with hypnotic power. I itched to get out there.

'I'm sorry,' I said. 'But I'm surfing.'

'All right!' Kasim flung his hands up. 'I'm coming with you.'

I looked at him in dismay. How could I tell him I thought the conditions were beyond him without offending his precious pride?

I'd gained a whole new respect for surf photographers since I'd met Kasim. Some call surf photography an extreme sport and it certainly seemed that way to me. While surfers have their boards to keep them afloat, Kasim had to keep himself afloat for hours on end, holding a heavy camera in its waterproof plastic housing. Getting the shot meant putting himself in crazy positions on the wave in order to get the best angle. He frequently got sucked over the falls, he'd had stitches on his temple from an out-of-control surf canoe and broken his ankle from being pile-driven into a reef. Anyway, he was one of the fittest guys I knew, but he didn't have much experience in waves the size they were today.

He was wriggling into his wetsuit already. I looked to Mikki for help, but she shook her head, pale with nerves. I could have changed my mind and decided not to surf. Instead, I put my selfish need over his safety.

Ten minutes later, I was sitting on my board, rising and sinking with the movements of the ocean. Being out in swell this size always made me mildly seasick. I looked round for Kasim and caught a glimpse of him in the distance, camera gripped in front of him.

We clearly weren't the only ones who'd seen the surf

report – it was surprisingly busy for March. There were four guys sitting on the peak that I was on. A wave rolled through and one guy surfed off. Three people left, then it would be my turn. Mikki was on a neighbouring peak nearby. I shot her a reassuring smile. She always got scared in waves this size. Finally, she caught one, then I caught one myself. And then another, followed by another.

It was at this point I realised I hadn't seen Kasim for a while. *I hope he's okay,* I thought. But if I paddled in to check on him, I would lose my spot in the pack.

I expected to find him waiting on the beach as usual, but he wasn't there. Mikki and I waited around, asking other surfers if they'd seen him. Maybe he'd got too cold and caught a lift home. Yet he wasn't there either. That's when fear began to wrap around my heart, making it hard to breathe. I reported him missing and a search began.

I was in my car when another surfer phoned me. *They've found him.* I breathed out in relief until I caught my friend's tone. 'Where?' I asked in a strangled voice. I parked in the same spot at the beach and raced down the sand. A huddle of people clustered around an unmoving body and everything went dark.

CHAPTER 35

KENNA

My tent smells of sunscreen. Once I've wriggled into my cut-offs, I slide the note from under my pillow to see it in daylight. It's written on an empty packet of Sex Wax, the surf wax we all pass around. I can't tell if it's written in black or blue ink until I unzip the tent door and let more light through. Blue – quite a dark blue. I hide it in my backpack.

The others are milling about preparing second breakfasts. I don't imagine these guys have many pens between them.

'Anyone got a pen?' I ask, because it seems worth a try.

'Yeah.' Jack gets one from his tent.

'Hey, that's mine!' Victor snatches it off him, then presents it to me like a rose. 'Here, Kenna.'

'Thank you.' It's a black one. Damn!

Across the clearing, Clemente is taking a Stanley knife to Ryan's foot.

I go over there. 'What are you doing?'

'Sea urchins,' Ryan says, grimacing.

Clemente is digging around with the point of the blade. I'm squirming but Clemente wears the same look of total concentration he had when he was preparing the fish.

Ryan yelps.

'Sorry,' Clemente says. 'I can't quite . . .'

'Shit, dude!' Ryan mutters.

'Stay still,' Clemente says. 'Yeah. Got it!'

'Can I see it?' I ask.

Clemente shows me the small, black, stick-like fragment on the blade.

'I've seen them on the rocks. I didn't know what they were.'

'Don't tread on them,' Clemente says. 'I've still got some in my heel from weeks ago.'

'Thanks, doc,' Ryan says.

I look at Clemente questioningly. 'Are you actually a doctor?'

'No. I didn't finish medical school.'

I can tell from his scowl this topic is off limits.

Ryan's foot is bleeding.

'We should put something on it,' Clemente says. 'You don't want an infection.'

Victor leans in to see. 'In Brazil, we put lime.'

I wince, imagining how much that would sting.

'Is there limes in the Meadow?' Victor asks. 'I can get.'

'No thanks,' Ryan says. 'I'll use Betadine.'

'Wait,' Clemente says. 'Let me see if there's more.'

I like Clemente – more than I want to – but I wish he looked a bit less comfortable with that knife.

Jack is washing up the breakfast stuff. I head over to

help. I'm not rostered on to do anything yet and I feel like a freeloader.

'How's your back?' I ask as he slips a foil packet from his pocket and pops a tablet into his mouth.

'A bit stiff.'

Now I know the truth about him and Mikki, I feel a bit differently about him – sorry for him, almost, because there's real affection in how he acts towards Mikki at times, yet he gets little back in return. Who is using who? Or should I see it as Mikki seems to: a straightforward deal between two consenting adults?

'Mikki told me about the wedding,' I say.

Jack looks defensive. 'And what do you think?'

'That you're crazy.'

'It's a private arrangement between the two of us.' His expression softens. 'I'm not a bad person, Kenna.'

His blond hair flops over his forehead as he scrubs the plates. Any straight woman would be hard-pressed not to fancy him, surely. It's fine to find him attractive, I tell myself, as long as I maintain boundaries.

With a jolt I notice Clemente watching me watching Jack, from over by his tent, with an expression I can't read. I lower my voice. 'Clemente's wife. What was she like?'

'A bit of a hippy,' Jack says. 'Kind of . . . what's that word? Earthy. She was good for him. She was estranged from her family, he's the other side of the world from his, so I guess they grounded each other. And she looked a bit like you.'

Maybe that's why Clemente stares at me so much.

'It must have been such a shock.'

Jack glances over at Clemente. 'I don't reckon he ever got over it.'

'Was it out of the blue? Like, was she depressed?'

'Not that I noticed. The week she died, the waves were amazing. We had some of the best surfs of our lives that week.'

I think of Clemente's guilty expression when I asked about her. 'Did they ever argue?'

'Sometimes. You know what it's like. When there's no surf, we get cabin fever and pick fights over stupid shit. You know our place in Bondi? It was hers. She wanted to sell up, buy land and start a sustainable farm. Clemente reckoned it would be too much work. It wouldn't leave enough time for surfing.'

Remembering the note's warning, I keep my tone carefully casual. 'When she died, her house went to him?'

'Yeah.'

The tents flap in the breeze. My thoughts race. Sydney has some of the highest property prices in the world. It sounds like Clemente benefitted nicely from his wife's death. Though this thought doesn't square with the kindness I've seen in him, I flash back to the darkness in his eyes. Was there anything fishy about her suicide? Jack isn't the right person to ask since he and Clemente are clearly very close.

Victor is nearby, changing the fins on a bright yellow surfboard. I'll try him instead. I head over, searching for an innocent way to bring up Clemente's wife. 'I like your board.'

Victor clicks in the last fin. 'You can have it. I have others.'

I blink, taken aback. The board is way too big for me and besides, it's his. 'Thanks, but I just meant I like the design.'

Victor smiles. 'Is from Brazil. Hey, look!' He snaps a stem of waxy white flowers from a nearby bush and sticks it under my nose. 'Smell. Beautiful, yes?'

'Yeah.'

He breaks off a couple more stems and arranges them carefully into a bouquet. 'I will give to Sky.'

I check none of the others are in hearing distance. 'I wanted to ask you something. You know when Clemente's wife killed herself? Was there anything strange about it?'

Victor's expression changes. 'How do you mean?'

'Like, suspicious?'

'Suspicious? Who said that?' His tone is sharp.

I backtrack, kicking myself for not being more subtle. 'Nobody. I just wondered.'

'No, it was definitely a suicide. No question.' He stabs the air with the bouquet to emphasise the point. 'She was very sad before. Like, crying all the time. Couldn't stop crying, yeah?'

He's going way overboard on the crying thing. I file it away: Victor is a terrible liar. Clearly he *does* think the death was suspicious – or even *knows* it was suspicious. It's not at all what I wanted to hear. He's friends with Clemente, so is that who he's trying to protect? The problem is they're *all* friends with Clemente. How am I ever going to find the truth about anything in such a closed group?

I change the subject. 'Mikki said you're a big wave pro.'

I thought this would be a safer topic but Victor tenses up even further. 'I used to be.'

There's a cracking sound and something hits my toe. Petals. The flowers – he's crushed them.

CHAPTER 36

VICTOR

Kenna is saying something but I can't hear her because my mind is full of churning, foaming whitewash.

Mavericks. The Californian surf spot is famous for its icy water and enormous waves. True 'big wave' surfing means waves of at least twenty feet and Mavericks could reach sixty feet at times. Eighteen metres. The size of a small apartment block.

Aren't you scared? people used to ask.

Try growing up on the edge of the biggest slum in Rio. Scared is having a gun put to your head as you speed along the BR101 on your motorbike. *Give me your bike or I'll shoot.* Scared is getting caught in a shootout between police and slum leaders, or armed robbers breaking into your home and holding a gun to your mom's head.

Survive that and you feel invincible. Waves are just water after all.

Vitão, they used to call me. *Big Victor.* Not any more. Three years ago, I drowned.

People always have a million questions when they hear that. I used to try to describe what it's like to have hundreds of tons of water pinning you below the surface. To feel your consciousness fading like a dying torch as the pressure builds inside your lungs and brain.

You're not just a beetle, stuck on your back, I would say. *You're a beetle stuck on your back under a skyscraper.* When I came round in hospital, every one of my ribs was broken.

Over time, I've realised there *are* no words to describe that amount of water, or that amount of terror, so these days I keep the story short. I wiped out on a fifty-foot wave and I was held down so long I got unconscious. My rescue team pulled me out. There was a good medic. I was lucky.

It took me three months to make a complete physical recovery. As for recovering mentally . . . I was back in the water surfing my home break in Rio, when a set wave surged towards me and in front of all my mates and several camera crews, I had my first ever panic attack.

When you know a wave like Mavericks exists, you can never forget it. I see it every night in my dreams. And every night, I drown again and wake choking. *You've got smokers' cough,* the others say when they hear me, but I've never smoked.

One day I will surf Mavericks again. I would die for that feeling. Sky alone seems to understand. My woman – she's so good for me. The others question how far she pushes me, but I want it. I want to be Victor Romano again. I hope Kenna doesn't do anything that jeopardises the set-up we have here, because I won't let anything get in the way of my recovery. The waves at Sorrow are only a few feet most of the year, up to ten feet occasionally in a storm, but if I can surf the Bay in all conditions, I can progress to something bigger.

Several times a week, Sky takes me by the hand and leads me to the ocean or the river. My body begins to shake, my palms start to sweat. I battle to get in *the zone*, knowing whatever calm I find, Sky will try to trigger my panic, which usually comes all too easily. She gets a peculiar look on her face at these times – a gleam in her eyes. Sometimes I think she needs these sessions as much as I do. We wade into the water, then, without warning, she grips me in a headlock and shoves me under. I fight for calm, not knowing when – or if – she'll let me up for air.

Big wave surfing is a mental sport as much as a physical one. When a wave holds you down, all you can do is relax and wait. As the seconds pass, you try to slow your heart rate by taking your mind to a happier place. You only fight right at the end, when you have no choice.

Big wave surfers can typically hold their breath for four minutes plus. I used to make four minutes twenty on a good day, but it's dropped way back since my accident. My sessions with Sky allow me to increase the time I can stay under, but it's my past trauma that we're really working on.

When she holds me there, her bicep slick and strong around my neck, my eyes are level with her rose tattoo, my favourite of her tattoos because it sums her up so perfectly. My woman looks and smells like a rose but she has thorns, in the same way that Elke had claws.

Sky's eagerness to nearly drown me bothers me, but

maybe it shouldn't, because a different sort of partner would be unable to give me this. My attraction to her gives me something to cling to in these sessions. In our tent afterwards, she's always particularly passionate, as if making up for what she did.

Or as if taking me to the edge turns her on. And I do come increasingly close to the edge in these sessions. This bothers me too.

Sometimes I worry that all my efforts will be in vain. That I will never make it back to Mavericks. That I will die on this lonely Australian beach, far from my homeland. Just like Elke.

CHAPTER 37

KENNA

Victor is in some sort of trance.

Sky is nearby, hanging clothes on the line. I head over to her. 'Is Victor okay?'

She looks over, uninterested. 'He's fine. His accident traumatised him, but we're working on it. It's what we do here. We work on our fears until they disappear.' She drapes an arm around me and steers me to a bench. 'Tell me, Kenna. What are you scared of?'

Nerves bubble inside me. Clemente warned me this would happen. There are many things I'm scared of – most of the insects around here for a start – but I'm reluctant to tell her that. 'Not that much, really. What about you?'

She smiles. 'I was scared of lots of things but I ironed them out.'

She pronounces ironed in a weird way, with a strong R.

Her fingers rub up and down my bicep. I'm not used to friends being so hands-on, but it's not unpleasant so I try to relax into it. A cool breeze is blowing and her hand is warmer than my arm – and surprisingly soft, considering the activities she gets up to.

'That's impressive,' I say.

'Facing our fears is an incredibly freeing experience.'

Having her this close, giving me her full attention, is addictive. Wanting to hold it a little longer, I find myself telling her about Toby and the quarry.

'Deep down, I'm terrified I'll hurt someone else,' I finish.

'You can't take responsibility for someone else's choices,' Sky says.

I look back at her, wanting to believe her. 'It wasn't just that.'

Her eyes sparkle with interest, so I tell her about the day Kasim drowned. 'Kasim didn't want me to surf that day. He was only out there because I insisted on going out. He died because of me.'

Sky looks at me with sympathy. 'You can't carry that sort of thing with you. It will weigh you down. I can help you with this. We're about to do a visualisation session. Visualising is such a powerful technique. You can use it to work on your fear and help you heal. This is what I want you to imagine. You need to picture you're in the water with Kasim and you reach out and hold him under.'

I recoil. 'I don't see how that would help.'

'It's your worst fear, right? So you need to experience it, over and over.'

I'm getting cold rushes at the thought of it. 'Okay.' I'm not sure that I will, though.

Sky calls the group together. Everyone gathers round.

'Most people run from fear,' she tells us. 'What if,

instead, you embrace it? What does that do to you? How does it change you? Whatever you're scared of, I challenge you to seek it out. It won't be as bad as you think.'

With that, she stretches out on a mat. The others follow suit. Jack and Clemente lie down, but Mikki sits cross-legged, as do Victor and Ryan. I'll sit, I decide; that way I can look out for ants.

The breeze tugs at my hair, parrots squawk overhead. Briefly I try to do as Sky advised and imagine Kasim in the water with me. I reach out my arms to his shoulders and . . . *No*. I screw up my face, trying to erase the image from my mind.

How long will this go on for? I struggle to sit still at the best of times and with the mozzies buzzing around, it's almost impossible, so I watch the others, wondering what they're visualising. There's the occasional jerk from Victor, and Jack sneezes, but apart from that they remain still and silent.

I turn my thoughts to Clemente's wife, wondering what Victor was trying to hide earlier. In the distance I hear waves. The sound soothes me. Soon I'm matching my breaths to their rhythm.

'Well done, everybody,' Sky says.

I've lost track of time but when I clamber up, I have pins and needles in one foot and my bum has gone numb. The others are looking around as though they're coming out of a trance. Jack rotates his neck. His eyes are glazed – did he fall asleep? Mikki has a serene smile on her face. I wonder what she was visualising. Moths or big waves, I guess.

'How did you go?' Sky asks me.

'I'm getting there,' I say.

'Keep at it. We'll do a healing ritual for you later.'

'Great.' I change the subject. 'You said everyone here has issues. What kind of issues are we talking?'

'It wouldn't be right for me to tell you that. They told me in confidence. You can ask them and they might tell you, but some people prefer to keep that sort of thing private.'

'Sure.' I like that she won't tell me but I'm really curious now. She knows everyone's secrets – almost like a priest.

Behind her, Clemente kneels over a tub of water, shirtless, rinsing clothes.

Sky turns to see what I'm looking at. 'You like him.'

The blood rushes to my face. I don't answer, but I don't need to.

'Be careful with him, darl.'

'What do you mean?' I ask.

She smiles mysteriously and doesn't answer.

'Jack told me about Clemente's wife,' I say.

Her smile vanishes. 'What did he say?'

'That she hung herself from that branch.'

'Right.'

I study her face. 'That's what happened, isn't it?'

For a split second, she hesitates. 'Yeah.'

I stare at her. What isn't she telling me?

She folds her arms across her chest. 'How are you liking the Tribe so far?'

'I love it.'

It's the right answer. Sky nods, apparently satisfied. 'A word of warning, Kenna. This place isn't perfect, nor are the people here. Everyone here has their secrets but we don't go looking for them, because sometimes it's better not to know.'

Chapter 38

Kenna

That afternoon, we surf again. I catch Clemente looking at me a few times, but it's as though he's making a conscious effort to avoid me.

I watch him surreptitiously as we eat dinner. There's clearly something odd about his wife's suicide, but it doesn't mean he's involved in Elke's disappearance. Truly, any of them could be behind it. Victor said he'd kill for this wave; Sky might have seen her as a threat; Ryan is the Guardian – could he have taken his role too seriously? What made him leave his country anyway? For all I know he could be a wanted criminal.

Mikki grabs my hand as we wash up. 'I've hardly seen you all day. Want to come for a swim?'

'Yeah, great!' I say, pleased she's sought me out.

'Can I come?' Clemente asks.

Mikki cuts in before I can answer. 'Sorry. We need some girl time.'

'No problem.' Clemente heads off to talk to Jack.

Five minutes later, Mikki and I are splashing into the ocean. It's nearly flat. Amazing that the swell can drop so much in so short a time. I scull the water with my hands, enjoying the push-pull as waves pass.

Mikki is wearing a string bikini I remember from Cornwall, the floral fabric faded now. 'I love that bikini,' I say, noticing also what incredible shape she's in.

She giggles. 'I can't wear it for surfing. Remember that time we surfed in string bikinis?'

I laugh too. 'Don't remind me!'

We'd bought our first ever string bikinis one summer when we were about fifteen and decided to surf in them. Bad idea. The waves weren't big – only a couple of feet – but plenty strong enough to blast our bikinis off. We had to hitch up our pants and readjust our tops after every wave to avoid flashing everyone.

An older girl paddled over. *Bit of advice. If you're going to surf in a bikini, get a fixed triangle one.*

Red-faced, we retreated to the sand.

I lie back in the shallows, with the tiny waves washing over my toes, admiring the sunset. Everything – sand, sky and ocean – are shades of pink. A bird flies just above the surface – an eagle or a hawk maybe – looking for a fish for dinner.

Life at Sorrow Bay revolves around the sun and waves under the open sky. It's so different from my urban life in London, where I wake to the ring of my alarm in my cold, dark bedroom, shiver as I get ready for work and barely see daylight.

'This place is seriously growing on me,' I say.

'I told you!' Mikki crows. 'Oh my God! Look at the state of your toenails!'

I look from my toes with the polish chipped to pieces to her immaculate ones and splash her. She giggles and splashes me back.

I sit up, aware I'm about to break the mood. 'I wanted to ask about Jack. How much are you paying him?'

Her face changes. 'That's my business.'

'God, Mikki. I can't believe you're serious about this. What if you meet someone you really like?'

'We only have to stay together for two years, then I get permanent residence.'

A dark shape in the water below me makes me yelp. Mikki ducks under and surfaces clutching a dripping mass of seaweed.

I clutch my chest. 'Shit, that scared me. Have you ever seen a shark here?'

Mikki lies back, hair floating around her head like a halo. 'The others all have. Once or twice I thought I saw one, but it could have been a dolphin.'

'Right.' As my heart rate returns to normal, I remember what else I wanted ask. 'So how does it work, your fake wedding?'

She gives me a sharp look.

'Am I invited?'

Her expression softens. 'Of course you are.'

'Can I bring a fake gift?'

She smiles. 'No. A real one.'

'Let me think . . . I could get you fake flowers. Or fake

jewellery. Plastic stuff, from the pound shop. Is there a pound shop here?'

'A dollar shop.'

'But seriously, how does it work?'

'We get a piece of paper from the registry office and go on as normal. It's no big deal, that's why I didn't invite you before.'

'Sky said something about sharing.' I feel awkward asking. 'Do the Tribe share partners?'

'Sometimes.'

'Seriously?' What surprises me most is that Mikki seems accepting of it.

'Sky had a really unhappy childhood. She left home when she was sixteen and hasn't spoken to her parents for years.'

Rather like Ryan. It's not healthy how they exist in their little bubble here, far from home and the people who care about them. I make a mental note to ask the others about their families. Some of them must get homesick, surely.

'Sky says the Tribe is her family now,' Mikki says. 'So she came up with this idea that we share everything, even partners.'

Briefly I wonder about Mikki's relationship with Sky. I'm not sure I'd call it a friendship, because there's none of the physical affection there is between me and Mikki – the warmth and laughter; then again, Sky's not much of a laugher. It's more like Mikki does whatever Sky wants and Sky rewards her by favouring her, or at least not punishing her.

Anyway, if Sky said jump, Mikki would ask how high.

Maybe Mikki senses my disapproval because she ducks underwater and swims back up. 'The water's so warm.'

'Yeah, wouldn't Kasim love it? He wouldn't even have to wear a wetsuit.' I sigh. 'God, I miss him.'

'Oh, come on. You had these massive rows when you wanted to surf somewhere dangerous, remember?'

'Not massive.'

'He held you back.' Mikki looks at me apologetically. 'You told me that yourself.'

She's right; it used to really piss me off when he did that.

I don't want to lose you, he'd say. Or: *I care about you.*

Mostly I ignored him and surfed anyway, but he gave voice to the doubts at the back of my mind and amplified them, sometimes to the point that I gave in to them. But I don't need Mikki reminding me of this.

'Sorry,' Mikki says. 'But you idolise him. And I don't think it's helpful.'

I glare at her. My precious memories are all I have left of him and they're curling up at the edges now, turning brown and mouldy. Good only for the bin. She's rubbishing them. Rubbishing *him.*

'You should try **talking** to Sky about it,' Mikki says.

'You idolise Sky,' I retort. 'And I don't know if that's helpful. That bloody **tattoo!**'

I catch the hurt in Mikki's eyes. She turns and swims off into the distance in a fast freestyle. I wade through the shallows and walk up the sand without looking back.

A scene plays out in my mind as I push through the undergrowth. Me, Mikki and Kasim standing on the rocks at Destruction Point one afternoon, watching the waves crash down. There were only two surfers in the water. Mikki and I had surfed the notorious Devon surf spot several times before, but she wasn't keen today – it was too big.

'You don't mind waiting for me, do you?' I asked.

She didn't, so I tossed my surfboard off the rocks and jumped in after it. The waves *were* a bit big, but each time I caught one, a delicious blend of fear and excitement rushed through me. I thought Kasim would take photos but he just watched me with folded arms. He was too far away for me to see his expression.

I didn't know what I expected. That he would be impressed? Proud of me? He wasn't. He was furious.

'You think I want to watch that?' he shouted when I scrambled out. 'No – I don't! I thought you were going to die!'

I felt bad, yet I'd do it again in a heartbeat. 'I'm sorry I scared you.'

'Look! You're cut!'

Blood streamed down my shins. My foot was sore too. 'I always get cut when I surf here. Everyone does. The barnacles are sharp.'

'Why did you jump off the rocks?'

'It's the only way to get in. Otherwise you have to paddle round from the beach and that's miles.'

There were many more times when he tried to stop me from surfing because he thought it was too dangerous, but I always surfed anyway, despite his protests. After he died, I beat myself up about how selfish I was to scare him like that. If you're in a relationship with someone, maybe they have the right to stop you doing dangerous things. Do they? I still haven't figured that one out.

CHAPTER 39

KENNA

Back in the clearing, Ryan is cleaning the barbecue. I grab a sponge from the bucket. My arms ache from my surfs but there's nothing like some good hard scrubbing to work off my anger. I'm not even sure who I'm more angry with: Mikki, Kasim or myself.

Ryan looks up with a rare smile. 'How good were the waves today?'

My anger melts a little. 'Yeah, I know. I still can't believe no one else ever comes here.'

'Yeah, well, that's not totally true.'

'What do you mean?'

He looks like he regrets telling me. 'Jack brought some girls here.'

Warning bells ring in my head. 'Did he?'

Ryan sees my face and tries to backtrack. 'Before he met Mikki. Just for the weekend. But we kicked up a big fuss after the first one, so after that he made sure they didn't know exactly where it was.'

I try to keep my tone casual. 'They'd know roughly, though, right? Like they'd know how many hours north of Sydney and where it was near?'

Ryan's getting flustered now. 'Well, no, because he gave them something.'

'What do you mean?'

He shifts his feet. 'He stuck something in their drink before they left Sydney.'

The sponge slips from my fingers. The temperature feels like it has dropped ten degrees. 'You mean he drugged them?'

Ryan's eyes flit from my face to the trees. 'He just gave them a sleeping pill.'

I stare at him. He clearly doesn't see how wrong that is. Ryan shifts his shoulders. 'They were foreign back-packers, first time in Australia. He made them think he was driving south, not north, and they never knew any different. When they'd had enough, he dropped them back in Sydney.'

'Did he drug them on the way back as well?'

'Yup.' Ryan folds his arms across his chest. 'We have to preserve this place.'

'He could have given them anything! The date-rape drug. And who knows what he did to them while they were drugged?'

'Aw, come on. I know Jack. Date rape isn't his style. The guy's a chick magnet. Those girls were all over him.'

Doesn't he read the news? I guess not, if he never leaves this place. He's so out of touch. So many people have been caught out by the exact same misconception.

'How many of them were there?' I ask.

'Two or three?'

Fury explodes inside me. Jack is washing his feet under the tap. I march over to him. 'Ryan just told me you drugged the women you brought here.'

Jack opens his mouth, looking from me to Ryan, who stands awkwardly behind me. *I'm not a bad person,* he told me. The bastard. I'm pleased to see him looking suitably embarrassed.

Does Mikki know her fiancé drugs people? Here she is now, walking up the trail. I'll go and try to smooth things over, once I've dealt with Jack. 'What did you give them?'

Jack seems bemused by my anger. 'Calm down. It was only a sleeping tablet.'

'Gather round!' Sky calls.

I haven't finished with Jack but he goes over to join Sky around the fire. Reluctantly I follow, still turning over his casual confession in my mind.

'Tonight, we will do a healing ritual,' Sky says.

It's almost dark by now and she hands each of us a tiny white tealight candle, then puts the fire out, so the only light comes from our candles.

'We've all done things we are not proud of,' she says. 'Things that fester inside us and weaken our spirits.'

It's still festering inside me that Jack drugged the women and I glare at him but he doesn't notice. *Let it drop, Kenna.*

'We will relive our mistakes as we watch our candles,' Sky says. 'Then, when we blow them out, they will disappear from our minds.'

Seven flames flicker. I stare into mine and see Kasim's face. It morphs into Toby Wines. Is Sky right? Should I feel responsible for what happened to Toby and Kasim? It's certainly tempting to let myself off the hook but I just don't know.

I glance up at the solemn faces of the others, crouched before their candles. Mikki is beside me. What is she reliving? Something glistens on her cheek. Shit – she's crying. I look quickly back at my candle, sensing she wouldn't want me to see.

In all the years I've known her, I've never seen Mikki cry. Even when her dog died, back when we were teenagers, her eyes remained dry. She was quieter than usual that day, but that was the only way I could tell she was sad.

'Now blow away your mistakes,' Sky says. 'Feel your guilt leaving your body and floating into the trees.'

One by one, we blow our candles out. I picture our guilt as a physical entity: little black clouds that ooze out of our chests and hang in the air like smog. I imagine all the times the Tribe must have done this over the years. And the night seems particularly dark just now.

CHAPTER 40

KENNA

Raised voices from behind me. I jump up – we all do – as two men enter the clearing, torches in hand. One is broad with a bushy blond beard, the other dark-haired and leaner. They're wearing matching navy polo shirts and beige cargo shorts, with large carryalls slung over their shoulders.

I know they're bad news from the way the Tribe huddle together doing the same sports-team-confronting-an-enemy act they did when I arrived, except this time I'm part of the team. Victor puts a possessive arm round Sky's shoulders; Jack holds Mikki's hand – the first time I've seen him do that.

'You're a week early,' Sky calls.

'A cyclone might be coming down this way,' Bushy Beard calls back. 'Thought we'd get here while we can.'

'Cyclones never come down this far,' Jack calls.

'They reckon this one might.' Bushy Beard spots me. 'Well, well, well. You got yourselves a newbie. That'll cost you.'

Clemente shifts closer, his shoulder brushing mine.

'Did the other girl come back?' Bushy Beard's companion asks.

'No,' Sky says.

Is he talking about Elke?

Sky starts out towards them. Victor makes as if to go with her but she stops him. 'Let me deal with them.'

Victor stands beside me, visibly bristling as the men negotiate with Sky. Ryan busies himself relighting the fire.

'Who are they?' I ask Jack, glaring at him to let him know I haven't forgotten about him drugging the women.

'Northy and Deano,' Jack says. 'The park wardens.'

I can see the logos on their shirts: *New South Wales National Parks*.

'Word was getting out about this place,' Jack says. 'Don't know how, because it's not in any of the surf guides, but in busy periods there could be a small crowd, so Sky had this brainwave and lined up a deal with Northy. Blond one with the beard.'

'The barricade across the road,' I say.

'Yeah.'

'How long's it been there?' I ask.

Jack glances at Mikki. 'Since before you arrived, right? About a year?'

Mikki nods. I want to ask her if she knows about Jack drugging the women but now is clearly not the time.

'There was a bad storm that caused some rockslides,' Jack says. 'It was good timing. We cleared the minimum for us to get past and asked them to leave the road like that.'

'Wow,' I say. 'And they did?'

'For a price.'

'And nobody complained?'

'Who's going to complain?' Jack says. 'It's the middle of nowhere. Plenty of other surf beaches with easier access.'

'How often do they come?'

'First Monday of the month normally.'

Suddenly I wonder what form of payment they've been taking.

A cold wind sweeps through the clearing. Branches lurch, bushes shudder. I hug my arms around my chest. 'How do you pay them?'

Jack gives me a funny look. 'Money, what else? And the occasional surfboard if we don't have enough cash.'

I study him, wanting to believe him.

Sky heads back towards us. She doesn't look happy. 'Okay, listen up. It's three hundred each.'

Furious discussion amongst the others.

'Calm down,' Sky tells Victor.

'How's it that much?' Ryan says.

'Extra maintenance, apparently,' Sky says. 'I don't like it either but we don't have much choice.' Her gaze shifts to me. 'Three hundred okay for you, Kenna?'

I jolt. 'Yeah, sure.'

She flashes an apologetic smile. Presumably they want cash, so I head to my tent and take three hundred dollars from my wallet. I'm not complaining about the cost – a hotel would cost way more and I still haven't contributed anything for food – but I wish I'd taken out more cash when I had the chance.

'So you have to pay them every month?' I ask.

'Yeah,' Sky says.

'It seems a lot.'

'For these waves?' Victor says. 'I'd pay a lot. Almost anything. Wouldn't you?'

Again, that sense of buried secrets lurking just out of reach.

After Northy has pocketed the cash, he and Deano wander around looking at everything as though they own the place.

Northy saunters over. 'It's looking nice around here.' His eyes meet mine as he says it. 'We might have to camp up for the night. What do you reckon, Deano?'

'Sounds good to me,' Deano says.

They head off down the trail, returning with a crate of beer and a tent.

Northy cracks open a blue can. 'Cheers. What's for dinner?'

'We already ate,' Sky says.

'We'll help ourselves,' Northy says.

He and Deano head to the barbecue area. I watch in dismay as they ransack our food. They're making a complete mess.

I turn to the others to see what they make of it. 'Are you just going to let them do that?'

'If we complain, they just hike up the price,' Jack says. 'Victor called Northy a shithead one time and the nightly fee doubled from that point on. Sky's banned us from talking to them. She's the only one that deals with them now.'

Northy has found some leftover pasta. 'Not bad!' he shouts. 'But it could do with more salt.'

Deano drains his beer and cracks open another.

'Hey, that's my guitar,' Ryan shouts as Northy roughly grabs the instrument.

'I'm just having a go,' Northy says.

Ryan mutters and curses.

'Don't,' Sky hisses.

I can feel all the others willing Ryan to let it drop. Oblivious to the tension, a lorikeet swings from branch to branch in the nearby tree, like a gymnast on a set of parallel bars, feeding from the blossom.

Men seem to fall into two main categories when drunk: happy drunk or angry drunk, and Northy is clearly an angry drunk. He gets angry with the food bags, ripping them all open, and with the barbecue, aiming a vicious kick at it and telling it to *Hurry the fuck up!*

We watch from a safe distance.

'They said something about a cyclone,' I say.

'Nah,' Jack says. 'Too late in the season. In all the time I've been coming here, we've only had one.'

'What happens in a cyclone?' I ask.

'Heavy rain and high winds,' Jack says.

'And *big* waves,' Victor says.

Once Northy and Deano have finished eating, I help Sky pack the food away – all that's left of it. There's grated cheese scattered everywhere. The block of cheese itself lies in the dirt. I sigh and put it in the rubbish bag.

'Shit,' Sky says. 'They're pitching their tent right next to yours.'

I glance over.

'You can't sleep there,' Sky says.

'So where do I sleep?'

'I don't know, but not there.'

214

CHAPTER 41

KENNA

I look at Sky helplessly. Mikki and Jack are in their tent already. It's a two-man tent like all the others and there's no way I'll fit in there with them.

'You could sleep with me,' Sky says. 'But I need to keep an eye on Victor.'

She's right. Victor's been brewing for a fight all evening. I look around for the others. Clemente is outside the toilet block, washing his feet under the tap. Ryan's nowhere in sight – he's either in his tent already or in the trees, doing whatever it is he does there.

'You'd better sleep with Clemente.' Sky sees my face. 'Oh, come on. I said sleep with him, not fuck him. Although you probably could if you want to.'

I'm burning up.

Sky smiles, clearly enjoying my discomfort. 'He could do with a good fucking. He hasn't had a girlfriend for a while.' Her smile fades. 'They're looking at us. Sort it with Clemente quick because I don't want to hang out here much longer.'

'Like, what do I say?'

'Make it subtle. Northy and Deano need to think you're a couple.'

I walk over to Clemente with no idea how to approach this. He's brushing his teeth now, chest muscles flexing with the movements of his arm.

'Can I sleep with you?' I say.

Clemente nearly chokes. He slides his toothbrush from his mouth.

I'm burning up. I hope it's too dark for him to see. 'They're camping here, next to my tent.' I gesture in Northy's direction.

Oh, shit – Northy is walking towards us.

A large hand wraps around mine. 'Coming to bed?' Clemente's tone is casual, as though he's asked it a million times before. His palm is warm and rough. I'm momentarily rendered speechless.

'Goodnight.' Clemente nods in Northy's direction and leads me to his tent, gripping my hand all the way.

He unzips the flyscreen door. 'After you.'

His tent smells musky but not unpleasant. He clicks on a small torch. 'I only have one sleeping bag.'

I stretch out on my back as he unzips it, looking everywhere except at him. He spreads it over us and lies back, arms folded behind his head. Outside, Northy and Deano crash about. I flinch at the sound of footsteps passing our tent.

'Ignore it,' Clemente whispers and clicks the torch off, leaving us in complete darkness.

Northy and Deano crash about a bit more.

'What are they doing?' I whisper.

'Being drunk.'

The sounds fade. Now all I hear are the usual Australian night creatures. After Sky and Mikki's warnings, I should fear Clemente as much as Northy and Deano, so why don't I? Is it my gut instinct telling me I can trust him, or is it just that I fancy the hell out of him?

Either way, I'm never going to be able to sleep. 'Are you tired?' I whisper.

'Not really. You?'

'No.' It's not that warm. I shift closer until his shoulder touches mine while I search for something to say. 'So is your family all in Spain?' I curse myself as I say it because of course his wife was family too, and he doesn't want to be reminded of her – nor do I.

'My parents are. And my brother lives in England.'

'No way! Whereabouts?'

'Bristol. He married an English girl.'

'That's only a few hours from where I live. Do they come and visit you?'

'Is expensive for them to fly here. They came only for my wedding.'

I take a deep breath and shift my head towards him in the darkness. 'How long were you married?'

In the silence that follows, I hear an owl.

'Three years.'

I tread gently, aware he might not want to talk about it. 'My boyfriend died two years ago. I'm still feeling it.'

'Yeah?'

I sense he wants me to keep talking, and *I* want to keep

talking. Out of all the Tribe only he might understand. So I tell him how my parents did their best to help, even though they hadn't been too sure about Kasim, warning me from the start that the culture difference would cause problems.

Be gentle with yourself, Dad told me.

Go and do some climbing, Mum said. She turned sixty this year and she can still raise her foot above her head on a climbing wall. Climbing is her answer to all life's problems.

I knew she meant well, but I didn't want to climb or surf or do any of the other activities I used to do. When they finally convinced me to see my GP, she made me do a quiz.

Loss of interest in activities you used to enjoy. Check. 'Apparently that's a sign of depression, so she referred me to a counsellor.'

'Did it help?' Clemente sounds genuinely curious.

'I don't know. As much as it could, I guess.' The darkness and close confines of the tent seem intimate. 'It feels like a bad break-up. Except I can't phone him in the middle of the night, drunk and crying, because he's not there. We can't grow apart, or have a domestic over who does more chores. Sometimes I feel like I lost my soul.'

I haven't talked with anyone else about this kind of stuff before. Nobody except my counsellor anyway.

'I blanked it out,' Clemente says.

'Really? How?'

'I was into boxing when I was a teenager. You get smashed in the face, in the ribs, everywhere. I trained myself to blank out the pain. You have to, or you can't fight back.' His English really is good. He has traces of an Australian accent, but that makes sense because he was married to an Aussie.

'I wish I could do that,' I say.

'No, you don't.'

'Just sometimes.'

'It doesn't work like that.' His voice is raw. 'You can't switch it on and off.'

He lies still and silent, so close I feel the warmth radiating from his body. A lump forms in my throat. 'When Kasim died, I went to pieces. I couldn't function. I feel everything so deeply – I've always been like that.'

When Clemente finally replies, he sounds his usual cool, calm self. 'We are the opposite. I don't feel anything any more.'

I don't believe that for a minute. Just because he doesn't show emotion, it doesn't mean he doesn't feel it, but I'm not going to challenge him. I want to comfort him, pull him to me and tell him it's okay, because maybe nobody did that. But it would be like hugging a sea urchin. There's a good chance he'd spike me.

'Why have you been such a dickhead to me?' I ask instead.

He must hear the hurt in my voice. 'I don't want to like you. It's not personal.'

'How can it not be personal?'

'My wife died.'

'I get that. My boyfriend died, so trust me, I get it.'

'The next girl I liked disappeared. And now she's on a missing poster.'

My breath catches in my throat. 'You were with Elke?'

'Yeah.'

'For how long?'

'Six months.' The sleeping bag rustles; he's rolled away. I lie there rigid. 'What do you think happened to her?'

'I wish I knew.'

Outside, insects chirp and hum. An ex-girlfriend on a missing poster, a wife who killed herself. While I could accept either event individually as a shocking tragedy, the combination of both, one after the other, seems sinister.

'Come on,' I say. 'Am I seriously supposed to sleep after that?'

'What do you want me to say?'

'Were there any other deaths or disappearances?'

'No.'

Just his partners then. The evidence is pretty damning.

Chapter 42

Six Months Ago

It was easier than I expected to drown someone. Elke stopped thrashing after only a minute or so, compared with the two-minutes plus that she could hold her breath in our training exercises. Panic really is lethal.

Wait an extra minute, *I told myself,* just in case. *The waves buffeted me, as though trying to fight me off, but I kept a firm grip of her shoulders. Her wavy blonde hair floated around her head like seaweed, tickling my legs. While I counted down the seconds, I searched the panorama for something more pleasant to look at. A movement on the clifftop made me stiffen.* Was someone up there? *No, it was just the trees jiving in the wind.*

Tentatively, I released Elke's shoulders. She didn't move.

I liked you, Elke, but you didn't like me back. Not enough.

Wanting to see her face one more time, I flipped her over. And dropped her with a yelp. Her mouth was wide

221

*open like a fish, her eyes bulging and bloodshot. I drew
in a slow breath, trying to erase the image from my mind,
then lifted her out, her limp body surprisingly heavy.
Red fingermarks were visible either side of the straps on
her bikini. Damn! Her body would presumably wash in
at some point – hopefully miles away from here – but this
had to look like an accident.*

*Spotting a piece of shale on the beach, I dragged Elke
up the sand and pressed it to the taut skin of her shoulder. Blood oozed up and dripped to the ground. I swore
and hauled her back into the shallows, making a note of
where the blood was. Once I'd finished, I would scuff the
sand to get rid of it.*

*With Elke's body balanced over my knee, I sawed the
shale back and forth until the finger marks were obliterated. If she was found, it would look as though a shark
had mauled her. Once I was done, I tossed the shale and
heaved Elke north to where the rip rushed out to sea. It
was running fast today. Blood streamed from Elke's
shoulders, turning orange as it diluted into the water. I
wanted a shark to find her but not yet, and I checked
around nervously. As my toes lost contact with the seabed, the rip pulled Elke from my grasp and she disappeared
into the deep.*

*I felt rather like I did when my new sunglasses slipped
off my face into the water: sad I'd lost them but I hadn't
had them long enough to get really attached. Irritated
too, because now I'd have to look for a new pair.*

*Back in the clearing, to my relief, the others were still
sleeping. I cooked bacon and eggs for breakfast.*

Before long they were wondering where Elke was.

'I haven't seen her,' I said. 'Perhaps she went for an early run.'

The others decided they would go running too – on the beach. I cursed inwardly, picturing Elke's body floating back and forth, with her vacant eyes and gaping mouth. Imagine if she washed in while they were there!

'I'll catch you up,' I told them.

As soon as they were gone, I dashed to Elke's tent, where her clothes were spread out across the ground-sheet like a patchwork rug. It smelt of dry-roasted peanuts in here. I stuffed her clothes into her backpack.

The groundsheet was bare now and it crinkled under my knees. Hang on – where was her daypack? It was blue – Rip Curl or Billabong, one of the surf brands. Knowing one of the others could return at any moment to see why I was taking so long, I hurried from the tent and checked the other tents and all around the clearing, but it wasn't there. Could it be in one of the cars? No. I'd seen her return with it the last time we went shopping. Damn!

I'd planned to hide her bags in the bushes but there was no point hiding only her large backpack. It would raise too many questions if the daypack turned up – they'd know she wouldn't have left without it.

The others would be wondering where I was. I'd better join them and think about it as I ran. I headed to my tent for sunscreen – only to find a note written on an empty packet of Sex Wax.

I know what you did. Meet me at the cliff at midnight.

CHAPTER 43

KENNA

When I wake, Clemente isn't beside me. Much as I'm getting drawn in by the waves and the lifestyle, I can't ignore the warning signs: Clemente's wife's suicide, Elke's disappearance, Jack drugging the women. And I sense there's plenty more.

From now on, I'm going to focus on one thing only: getting me and Mikki out of here. There are obvious rifts within the Tribe. Perhaps I can use this to my advantage and try to drive them apart. If the Tribe disbands and they go their separate ways, Mikki will have no reason to stay.

It's only nine days until the wedding. If I can't persuade her to leave before then, at least we'll be back in Sydney for that. I'll get her parents on the phone. Although Sorrow Bay and the Tribe have such a hold on her, I'm not sure she'll listen to them any more than she listens to me.

Mikki raises her eyebrow as I emerge from Clemente's tent. The others are chatting in angry tones around the barbecue.

'Have Northy and Deano gone?' I ask.

'Yes,' Sky says. 'So have most of our food supplies.'

'And my fucking board,' Victor says.

'We can't let them get away with it,' Ryan says.

'What do you propose we do?' Sky asks wearily.

Ryan picks up a pole spear. 'For a start, we need to keep watch on the road in so we don't get taken by surprise again. Hide our supplies better. Spread them out, stow them in the bushes. Bury them, even.'

Victor and Jack roll their eyes.

'And in the meantime we need to eat,' Sky says. 'Who's shopping?'

'I'd go,' Jack says. 'But my front tyre's fucked.'

'I would lend you mine,' Clemente says, 'but last time you got a speeding ticket and you still haven't paid me back.'

'What?' Mikki says. 'How did I not know this?'

Victor laughs in delight and slaps Jack on the back. 'Take my ute, brother. But no speeding tickets, okay?'

'Sweet,' Jack says.

I have no idea what a ute is but I guess it's either the pick-up truck or the silver four-wheel drive that Jack parked beside.

Ryan paces back and forth, clutching the spear. The others ignore him.

Jack ruffles Mikki's hair. 'You coming, babe?'

'Yeah, why not?' she says. 'I need some cash out.'

I seize my chance to get her away from this place, even briefly, so I can try to talk some sense into her without the others overhearing. 'I'll come too.'

'Sorry, Kenna,' Jack says. 'It only has two seats.'

225

I look at him in dismay. 'But I need cash.'

'Give me your bank card,' Mikki says. 'And I'll take cash out for you.'

This is all going wrong. I'm panicky now, but what can I do? I've been eating their food all week and haven't paid anything yet except for the hush money for the park wardens. Reluctantly, I get my wallet from my tent and hand Mikki my card.

'Still the same PIN?' she says.

'Yep.' We've used the same PIN number since we were teenagers. When she first got a bank card, she kept forgetting hers, so I told her mine and said to use it, that way I could remind her.

'How much do you want?' Mikki asks.

'Maybe five hundred dollars?'

'Don't look so worried. We'll only be gone a few hours.'

'Anyone would think you don't like it here, Kenna,' Sky says.

Careful, I tell myself. 'I just wanted some chocolate.'

Sky's frown deepens.

Jack winks. 'I'll get you some. Same as last time?'

'Yeah, thanks.'

Mikki gets her backpack from her tent.

I tug her aside, desperate to catch her alone before she takes off with Jack. 'Did you know Jack drugged some of the girls he brought here?'

'Talk to Sky,' Mikki says hurriedly as Jack comes over.

Damn. I wanted to talk to her about Elke as well.

Sky hands Mikki a shopping list, pausing to write *mushrooms* on it. I note with interest that her pen is blue

226

until Jack produces a blue pen of his own and scrawls *chocolate* on the list.

Mikki hugs me, Jack collects Victor's keys and they head off down the track.

'Don't forget!' Victor calls. 'Check the surf forecast. I want to know about this cyclone.'

Jack holds his thumb up above his head without looking back. I watch until they're out of sight.

The leaves shiver in the wind. It's going to be so weird being here without Mikki.

'I take it there's no surf today?' I ask.

'No,' Sky snaps.

Clemente is a shadowy figure in the corner of my eye. My thoughts return to Elke. After meeting her mum, I feel a duty to her, somehow, to learn the truth. And if my hunch is right and something bad happened to her here, maybe I can use that to convince Mikki to leave. I need to find out more about Clemente's relationship with her. Did he do something to make her run? Victor is nearby, fixing a surfboard, but I sense he's the wrong person to ask.

Ryan sets off, spear in hand.

'What are you doing?' Sky shouts after him.

'Going to patrol the perimeter,' Ryan shouts back. 'Someone's got to do it.'

Victor says something in Portuguese.

Ryan turns on him. 'What did you say?'

Victor grins. '*Cão que ladra não morde*. The dog that barks does not bite. The people who bark most have no guts to take action.'

'You Brazilians have too many expressions,' Ryan says. 'Have you got any about chickens?'

Victor is no longer smiling. 'We have lots of expressions about chickens, Ryan. Why?'

Sky mutters under her breath and grabs a towel from the line. She might be a better person to ask about Elke. I need to be subtle, though.

She sees me watching. 'I'm going to the beach. Want to come?'

'Okay.' Too late, I register the note of challenge in her eye.

What have I let myself in for?

CHAPTER 44

KENNA

The sun is high already, blazing down through the vegetation. The palm fronds stripe the trail with shade.

'Clemente said he was in a relationship with Elke,' I say, casually.

Sky flashes me a suspicious look. 'Yeah.'

'I got the impression you didn't like her?'

She frowns. 'No, I liked her a lot. Why do you say that?'

'You called her a bitch.'

She shrugs her strong shoulders. 'We got on. She seemed happy here. Then she disappeared without saying goodbye. I was pissed off.'

I study her face for signs of a lie. 'Clemente's wife died and now Elke's on a missing poster.'

Sky's blue eyes give nothing away. 'We try not to dwell on the past.'

'But it's pretty bad luck, wouldn't you say? For one guy?' *Careful, Kenna.*

'This is a dangerous place. We do dangerous things.'

The ocean lies shimmering like crumpled satin. There isn't a wave in sight. I remember the upcoming cyclone. Perhaps this is the calm before the storm.

Sky leads me towards the rocks. I'm getting nowhere with Elke, so I ask her about Jack instead. 'Ryan told me Jack drugged the women he brought here. He said everyone blew up about Jack bringing them here.'

'*Ryan* blew up,' Sky says.

Which makes sense – he's worried about being caught as an illegal.

'So Jack gave the next woman he brought here a sleeping pill so they wouldn't remember how they got here.' Sky sees my outrage. 'Yeah, I know. The rest of us went nuts and Jack promised he'd never do it again. Don't worry, darl. There's no way I'd go along with something like that. We left Ryan thinking Jack was drugging them just so he didn't get too worked up.'

I search her face and decide I believe her. Once is bad enough, though. And it's disturbing how far Ryan is prepared to go to keep the Bay secret.

Sky is different away from the men. Softer, somehow. Maybe she feels insecure about her leadership and thinks she needs to act tough to maintain control.

We reach the rocks and Sky strips down to her white Bond-girl bikini so I peel off my top and shorts too.

'What are we doing?' I ask.

She nods to the cliff. 'Climbing up there and jumping off.'

'I didn't bring shoes.'

'Me neither.' Sky gestures to the water pooling around the cliff face. 'Go on, pace it out so you know how deep it is.'

I scramble over the rocks and wade in, careful where I step. Sharp spikes rise up in places, the water frothing around them. When I turn, Sky is several metres up already, bare feet wedged against the cliff face. She reaches a narrow ledge and swivels around to face me. 'Tell me to jump,' she calls.

Suddenly I'm back at the quarry again, looking up at Toby Wines far above. I stagger backwards.

'Say it!' Sky calls.

It's as though she's *trying* to trigger me, and she knows exactly how to do it. My palms are sweating; my heart is pumping like mad.

'Do it!' Sky shouts.

I force myself to say it. 'Jump!' It comes out more weakly than I intended but Sky leaps off, tombstoning into the water between the spikes of rock. My stomach plummets with her. I clench my fingers into fists, waiting for the scream that doesn't come.

Sky's eyes shine as she scrambles out. I can't decide if she did that to help me or for her own personal amusement.

'Let's try again.' She starts climbing again before I can protest. This time she climbs higher. I dig my fingernails into my palms, replaying what she said to me. *We make our own choices.*

'Ready?' Sky calls, far above.

I muster all my strength. 'Jump!'

It's just as terrifying as before. Sky surfaces with a self-satisfied smile.

'What are you doing?' I ask.

'Trying to override your memory. Replace a traumatic memory with one that isn't. Want to try again?'

231

'No.'

Her smile widens. 'Okay. Your turn to climb.'

I wipe my palms on my shorts. Still shaky, I plant my feet cautiously, wincing at the grate of sandstone against my toes. I've never climbed barefoot before; Scotland was too cold. I'm relieved to see Sky waiting at the foot of the cliff rather than climbing up behind me.

When I turn, I'm surprised how high I am.

'Jump!' Sky calls.

And once again I'm back in the quarry, with the opaque grey water far below. I clutch the rock in panic and clamp my eyes shut. Dizziness rushes over me. *Breathe, Kenna.* When I open my eyes, the image clears and the water below is back to its usual turquoise.

Sky is watching. Not wanting to look like a chicken by climbing down, I brace myself and leap, hoping for the best. The shock of the water hitting me takes my breath away. In its place, adrenalin rushes in. That dangerous, addictive feeling.

Sky is climbing again – higher than last time. To my relief, she jumps without me prompting her. I start climbing the moment she surfaces. My feet are bleeding in several places by now but I can't feel them because every cell in my body is singing. Higher and higher we climb. Mikki balances me out with her words of caution but Sky has the opposite effect on me and eggs me on. She doesn't say anything else but her presence alone is enough.

'Last one,' Sky says. She lets out a wild scream that echoes up the cliff as she splashes in.

I climb as high as I dare. God, I love this. I *needed* this. Far below, the water glistens. I suck in a breath, knowing it could be my last. How can this feel so good? Terror and pleasure merge as I jump.

I feel Sky's gaze on me as I scramble out.

'What?' I say.

'Nearly everyone is scared of heights to some extent, but you're not, are you?'

'Not usually.' I scrape my hair back into a ponytail and squeeze water from it, unsure whether to be grateful to her for bringing me here or not. Maybe it's what I need, to help me process my guilt and grief about Toby and Kasim, but I'm pretty sure I'll have nightmares about it tonight.

Sky pulls her T-shirt on. 'Do you still feel responsible for your boyfriend's death?'

'Yeah. I think I always will.' A wave washes over my toes. It's hard to believe these pretty ripples can rear up into monsters that bite and kill.

Sky touches my arm, as though she guesses what I'm thinking. 'Keep at it with the visualisations. It'll get easier.'

As we walk back, I realise I'm getting sucked in by her when I should instead be seeking out weaknesses in the Tribe. If Sky feels insecure in her role as leader, maybe I can use that against her.

I picture Clemente next to me in his tent last night, warmth radiating from his broad shoulder, hating that I have to do this. 'You do realise Clemente wants to lead the Tribe, don't you?'

'What makes you think that?' Sky's tone is light but I'm not fooled.

'It's pretty obvious. He doesn't like how you run things. He reckons he'd be a better leader.'

'And what do you think? Would he?'

He probably *would* be a better leader – a safer one at least – but he shows no sign of wanting the role. He's still in that same headspace I was in after Kasim died, of not wanting any extra responsibility because he's dealing with issues of his own. 'No. He'd be a terrible leader. But if I were you, I'd watch your back.'

We're nearing the clearing now. Sky catches my arm. 'I didn't tell you the full story about his wife's death. There was something weird about it. The esky was next to her, like she'd climbed on it to hang herself, except it wasn't quite under her feet. It was too far away.' Sky glances down the trail and drops her voice to a hiss. 'As though someone had moved it.'

'Shit,' I breathe. 'Who found her?'

'I did.'

I shudder, imagining what it must have been like to come across something like that.

'Victor was right behind me,' Sky says. 'He helped me get her down. Jack was still surfing. Clemente and his wife had left the water about half an hour before. But Clemente was nowhere to be seen. He didn't return until a few hours later and he was just . . . odd. He said he'd been for a run but . . .'

I've noticed Sky treats Clemente with a wariness she doesn't have with the others. I took it for respect. But it's not.

She thinks he killed his wife. Or at least believes he's capable of it.

CHAPTER 45

KENNA

I lie on a mat in the clearing, imagining I'm in the icy Cornish ocean with Kasim bobbing beside me. I reach out to his shoulders and push him under. He disappears but strains upwards. Briefly I fight him, but he's too strong for me. And when he bobs up, it's not Kasim but Clemente.

I sit up in shock, trying to blink the image away. The others are silent on their mats. A movement catches my eye: a spider crawling along the ground towards my toe. I squeak and pull my foot away. Sky remains motionless on her mat. I'm glad she didn't witness that.

Ryan is nearby, wondering what I was squeaking at.

'Look,' I whisper, pointing. 'A spider.'

Ryan gets up to see.

'I don't know what bites or stings and it makes me nervous,' I say.

He peers at it. 'If in doubt, assume it does.'

As usual I have no idea if he's serious or not. Suddenly

he stomps forward with his bare foot and grinds the spider into the dust with his heel. I feel physically ill but try not to show it. Ryan wipes his heel on the earth and walks off to the barbecue area.

I join him as he helps himself to food. 'Thanks for that.'

'No problem.'

His sandy hair looks even more unkempt than usual – he badly needs a haircut. I need to get them talking about their families more. Anything to burst this little bubble they're living in and remind them of life outside the Bay. 'Can I ask something? Do you miss your family?'

Ryan's eyes flash my way.

'Am I annoying you? Just tell me to shut up if you want. My boyfriend used to tell me I talk too much.'

That drags a smile out of him. 'My wife used to tell me I don't talk enough.'

'Your wife?' I try to hide my surprise.

Ryan flushes and turns away.

Two lorikeets toddle one behind the other across the clearing and hop up into a nearby tree.

Ryan sees me watching them. 'Apparently they pair for life,' he says. 'If one of the pair dies, the other mourns for days.'

'I didn't know that.' The two birds nestle close on an overhead branch, beaks and feathery chests touching. I've often seen pairs flying side by side or dangling upside down together.

Ryan tugs his beard. 'If they can do it – choose a partner and stick by them, whatever happens – why can't we? We make our lives so damn complicated.'

His eyes reflect his misery.

'I imagine you wouldn't have left unless you needed to,' I say.

'There were other options. Leaving was the best of a bad bunch.'

He doesn't say what they were, but he doesn't need to. It's something that crossed my mind too, briefly, at my lowest point.

'Don't you ever think about going back?' I ask.

'It was too much. Work, a mortgage, bills. I couldn't breathe.' He tugs his beard again. I wish he wouldn't do that. It must hurt. 'When I flew here, I wasn't thinking ahead, I just had to get as far away as possible. I guess I imagined I'd go back but I couldn't face it, and the longer I stayed, the worse I felt. How can I go back there now?'

'I lost someone I loved and I'd do anything to have him back, but it's never going to happen. Your wife probably thinks you've died but hopes desperately you haven't. If you explained why you left, I reckon she'd understand.'

I wonder how Ryan manages financially. How much money did he bring with him? Presumably he no longer accesses his American bank account in case they could trace him.

The visualisation session has finished and Clemente is doing chin-ups – slow ones. Inch by inch, he raises his body until his chin sits above the bar. It's hard enough to do them at normal speed. Slow ones are undoubtedly harder. His jaw tightens, the only visible sign of the pain he's putting himself through.

I turn back to Ryan. 'Sky says everyone works on their fears. What's she scared of?'

'Nothing. She reckons she's worked through her fears and eliminated them.'

'Yeah, she said that to me, but there must be something. Even if she's not scared of anything else, she must be scared for the safety of people she cares about. Victor maybe?'

'Does she love him, though?' Ryan asks.

'Good point.' He doesn't mix much with the others, but he's clearly very astute. 'And why the crazy challenges?'

'When the waves are flat, I go stir crazy – we all do. You start to ask yourself difficult questions like: *Why am I here?* Better to keep busy. And it keeps us fit, if nothing else.'

Ryan may be smart, but I sense more than ever that he's not happy. I clear my throat. 'What are you scared of?'

Ryan's eyes flick to mine, as if recognising the intimacy of the question. He shows me his left wrist. There's a tiny tattoo that I hadn't noticed.

I peer at it. 'Is it a spider?'

'Yep. Victor did it for me.'

I feel touched by how he stomped on the spider for me. 'And . . .' Ryan flashes his other wrist.

There's a letter *A* written there, faint and badly formed, like the spider.

'Ava,' Ryan says. 'My daughter. I'm scared something's happened to her.'

I stare at him. 'How old is she?'

'She was one when I left. She'll be three now.'

How could he leave them? Do the others know he has a wife and child? 'Look, I meant what I said. If you went back, I know they'd be so happy to see you.' Yes, I want

238

him to leave as part of my plan to weaken the Tribe, but I'm also saying it for him – and his little daughter, growing up without him.

Ryan glances away.

'So you all have tattoos?'

'Not all of us. Only if we want to.'

'Right.' I've seen Victor's, Jack's and Mikki's, but I haven't seen any on Clemente or Sky. 'Can I ask something else?'

'What?'

This is probably a bad idea because Ryan's doing his usual impression of a cornered animal. 'What were you doing back there in the trees that day I met you?'

'What do you mean?' There are little pink spots in his cheeks. He *knows* what I mean.

'When you were lying down.'

For a while I don't think he's going to answer. His shoulder twitches. 'Tapping.' He presses his lips together. 'For my anxiety. It's—'

I smile in relief. 'I know what it is.'

Ryan seems surprised.

'After my boyfriend died, I saw a psychologist,' I say. 'Life seemed so fragile. I was convinced other people I loved would die. My nan, my parents, my friends. My clients, even. God, the stuff they did to themselves. I've got this rugby player, dad of two little kids, who fractured his neck, then recovered, and resumed playing. It made me sick to think of him in the scrum. I used to lie awake at night, worrying about them. As soon as I forced one worry from my brain, another would form.'

'I know that feeling,' Ryan says.

'It got so bad I couldn't sleep. Eventually, I booked myself in to see someone. She taught me to tap and I still do it sometimes, when I'm having a bad day.'

'Does it help?'

'A bit. You?'

'Yeah, usually.' Ryan's looking at me differently now.

I'm looking differently at him as well, glad there's an innocent explanation for why he was there.

He reaches for his guitar and cradles it like a baby. He doesn't play it, though; he just fiddles with the strap. 'I don't want the others to see. That's why I go there. They'd think it was weird. I mean, they already think I'm weird, but—'

'I get it. I used to tap between clients sometimes and I was always careful to lock the door first. I'm sorry I interrupted you back then.'

'No problem.'

I really feel for him right now. But I'm not here for him, I'm here for Mikki, and I need to drive the Tribe apart. 'I wonder if Jack will bring anyone back with them.'

Ryan stiffens. 'What?'

'You said he brings women back sometimes.'

'I fucking hope not.' Ditching the guitar, he picks up his spear and strides off into the trees.

I pushed the right buttons and it was so easy. I feel terrible, but I need to keep at it and figure out how to do the same with the rest of them.

240

Chapter 46

Kenna

Clemente is still on the pull-up bars. Sweat trickles down his cheek as he hoists his body up. When I arrived in London, I joined a gym, because I knew I'd fall apart completely without exercise, and it was one of these weights gyms full of grunting bodybuilders. So I've seen people train hard. But Clemente is something else. His face scrunches in pain as he raises himself, yet he doesn't make a sound. His discipline is incredible. How can he do it after surfing for hours yesterday?

Maybe he can do it because it isn't a workout.

It's his way of punishing himself.

It's a relief to see Jack and Mikki tramping down the trail, laden with bags. The way the others crowd in, you'd think Santa had arrived.

'Cool, you found rocket,' Sky says.

'And strawberries,' Clemente says, taking out a punnet.

'Did you check the forecast?' Victor asks.

241

'Yeah,' Jack says. 'The cyclone could be heading our way.'

'Shit,' I say.

But the others are all smiles.

'It's on track to hit us later this week,' Jack says. 'Really big swell if it does.'

'I don't know what you're grinning about,' Sky says to Victor. 'You'll freak out if it's big.'

Victor doesn't seem to hear.

'I took some screenshots.' Jack shows Victor his phone. 'Ten feet, they reckon.'

Victor pinches the screen between finger and thumb and a strange look forms on his face, wistful and terrified at the same time.

Jack nudges Mikki. 'If we get as much rain as they're predicting, the roads might flood. We're due in Sydney next week for our wedding.'

'Might have to reschedule,' Mikki says. 'If there's decent waves here, I don't want to miss it.'

Sky laughs and gives Mikki a high five. 'That's my girl!'

'I thought I was bad for missing my cousin's wedding for waves,' I say. 'You're missing your *own* wedding?'

Delaying the wedding is a good thing, I guess, but it doesn't solve the problem, and the fact that Mikki would miss it for the surf just shows the extent of her addiction. Having once been just as addicted myself, I know how hard it is to break free of it.

Mikki casts a furtive look over her shoulder and pulls a chocolate bar from her pocket. 'I got you this.'

'Yay!' I rip into it. Just a few days ago I'd have scoffed

the lot. Instead, I find myself counting how many pieces to break it into. Mikki and I eat a piece, and I tuck the rest back in the wrapper for the others.

Mikki seems mildly stressed.

I touch her arm. 'You're not having second thoughts about the wedding, are you?'

'No, I'm just tired. I had a bad dream last night.'

'Moths or big waves?' Mikki used to get nightmares in Cornwall sometimes – bad ones that made her cry out in her sleep – and it was always one of the two. I used to go in her room and wake her.

'Moths. How was it here without me?'

'Not bad. I had an interesting chat with Ryan.'

'Yeah?' Mikki seems surprised. 'He creeps me out sometimes.'

Ryan calls her over. Mikki crosses the clearing, glances all around and hands Ryan something. Cash. A wad of cash. He stuffs it into his pocket. I head over to them.

Mikki looks up guiltily when she realises I saw. 'I owed him.'

Perhaps he gave her his bank card and she withdrew cash for him, except as a missing person, surely he can't have a functional bank card. So why would Mikki owe him money?

Ryan slaps at a mosquito and reaches for the mosquito repellent. He shakes the can. 'We've nearly run out. Did you get more?'

'Sorry,' Mikki says.

'Why the hell not?' Ryan says. 'It's not like I can run off and get some myself. I put it on the list.'

Mikki flinches from his anger.

Jack comes over. 'No drama, mate. We'll get it next time.'

'Yeah, and in the meantime I get bitten to shit.' Ryan hurls the spray can at a tree.

The impact is shockingly loud. A bat flaps upwards into the sky.

Jack turns to the others. 'What's eating him?'

'Mosquitoes!' Victor says.

The two men crack up. Jack collapses to the ground, his laughter high-pitched and girlish. I clamp my lips together until I see Mikki's shoulders shaking silently and that sets me off too.

Ryan's pale face turns scarlet and for a moment I think he's going to punch someone.

'Fuck the lot of you!' he shouts and storms off into the trees.

I turn my thoughts back to the money. 'You pay Jack, and you're paying Ryan too?'

Mikki's smile fades. 'I borrowed money off him last month.'

I study her face. What isn't she telling me? 'How much have you got left?'

'That's my business.' She heads to the barbecue area.

I watch her laughing and joking with Sky as they put food away. Mikki may look like one of the Tribe, but what if she isn't; what if they're using her? If she's funding their surfing, her inheritance won't last forever. And once they've sucked her dry, what then? I need to get her out of here before we find out.

CHAPTER 47

KENNA

Spotting Jack standing alone, I pull the chocolate bar from my pocket. It's half-melted already. 'Want some?'

Jack grins. 'Ooh, yeah!'

It's ridiculous but I feel like a drug dealer. Which reminds me . . .'Sky told me about the sleeping pills. She said you only did it once.'

'Yeah.' Jack flashes his perfect teeth. 'It didn't seem like a big deal.'

From the look on his face, he *still* doesn't think it was a big deal.

'So.' Jack waggles his eyebrows. 'You slept with Clemente last night.'

He has an uncanny ability to embarrass me. 'Yeah. But not like that.'

Jack turns sombre. 'He's had some bad luck with women.'

I jump at the chance to get some information out of him. 'He told me about Elke.'

Jack glances over at Clemente. 'Yeah, he was fully into her, poor guy.'

'What was she like?'

'No filter. I loved her.'

Loved her. I remember what Sky said about sharing, and now I'm wondering something else. Did Jack share her? If so, how might Clemente have felt about that? 'Did they ever fight?'

'Funny you should ask that,' Jack says. 'The day before she disappeared, they had a massive row.'

'What about?'

'No idea, but she was threatening to go back to Germany. But they made up.'

My throat goes dry. *Nobody ever leaves*. That's what they told me. Did one of the others overhear her threats and take matters into their own hands?

'Did Elke and Sky get on?'

'Most of the time,' Jack says.

From what I've seen, Sky wouldn't take kindly to anyone who threw their weight about – especially another female.

Sky and Mikki are deep in conversation at the barbecue as they chop vegetables.

I head over to them. 'What are you making?'

'Japanese casserole,' Mikki says and turns back to Sky. 'How's it going with Victor?'

Sky glances at me as though unsure if I should be privy to this conversation, then gestures over at where Victor and Clemente are working out with battle ropes. 'Look at him. He looks so strong. But he's just . . . not.'

Mikki smiles in sympathy.

'Sometimes I get sick of him leaning on me,' Sky says. 'And wish I had someone *I* could lean on. Stupid, because even if I did, I'm pretty sure I wouldn't lean on them.'

'It's the same with Jack,' Mikki says. 'Sometimes I wish I'd met him before his accident.'

I'm amazed to hear Mikki open up like this. She never talked about this kind of thing with me.

Mikki frowns in concentration as she cuts carrots into little batons. 'But he probably only dated models and wouldn't have looked twice at me.'

It kills me that she has such a low opinion of herself. I slide my arm round her. 'What do you mean? You're gorgeous.'

'Yeah, totally,' Sky says.

Mikki pulls a face.

Sky nudges me. 'And Kenna has the hots for Clemente.'

I laugh to hide my embarrassment. Mikki looks up from her carrots with a troubled expression and I remember her warning.

'You'd better watch him though, darl,' Sky says. 'I worked in construction for a while—'

'Oh, did you?' Mikki says. 'Cool.'

'Yeah, I was seeing this girl who was project managing a build. And she told me about these tall buildings, how there might be a crack in the foundations but you can't see it, and you have no idea it's even there until one day it all comes crashing down.' Sky looks over at Clemente meaningfully.

'And he has a crack?' I say.

'Lots of them. I'm surprised he didn't collapse a long time ago.'

I study her face, wondering if she really thinks that or if it was motivated by what I said earlier about him wanting to be leader. 'So what you're saying is they're all broken. All the men in the Tribe.' I'm joking, sort of.

But Sky nods. 'We all are. All of us here.'

It's a rare admission of weakness from a woman who has until now never conceded it.

Sky seems to catch herself. 'But we're healing. That's what matters.'

Sky sits beside me at the fire that evening, leaning forward to swipe her hand through the flames. She wears a loose-fitting purple tank top, faded from the sun, and no bra, so you get a flash of her boob every time she moves her arm, but nobody bats an eyelid.

'Look at you lot,' Sky says. 'Sitting around, bored out of your brains. Time for another rock race.'

'No way,' Clemente says.

'I'm too tired, honey,' Victor says. 'Let's go to bed.'

'Not yet,' Sky snaps.

Sky seems particularly restless tonight. Clemente is sitting on the ground in front of her. She reaches forward and slides her fingers through his hair. 'Your hair feels nice.'

I catch Victor's expression. Victor whose head is shaven.

Sky combs her fingers through Clemente's hair, making the dark tufts stand upright. 'It's so thick. Kenna, you feel it.'

I shoot her a look, but I can't think of a decent excuse not to touch his hair so I lean forward and run my fingers through it. This is *definitely* about Clemente wanting

248

leadership. She's wielding power over him in a subtle and clever way.

Victor yawns.

'Why are you tired, mate?' Jack asks. 'Is she keeping you awake?'

'No.' Victor clamps up.

'I'm knackered too,' Jack says. 'I get bad dreams sometimes.'

Victor eyes Jack warily. 'What about?'

'The wave that broke my back.'

Victor listens, transfixed as Jack describes his dream.

'I never go back to sleep in case I dream it again,' Jack says. 'Next time I might not wake up. I might die in my dream and stay dead.'

Sky leans across to whisper in Mikki's ear. Mikki nods.

'Poor baby,' Sky says to Jack. 'How about I protect you from the scary waves tonight?'

Jack looks from Sky to Mikki in disbelief.

'Go for it,' Mikki tells him.

What? My mouth falls open. This is so screwed up. Jack sits there looking like all his birthdays have come at once, until he remembers Victor, who fails to mask his shock.

'Can I sleep in your tent tonight, Kenna?' Mikki asks.

It takes me a moment to find my voice. 'Okay.'

Sky tugs Jack to his feet. I watch them head to Jack and Mikki's tent, wondering how anyone can be so cruel.

CHAPTER 48

KENNA

My heart breaks for Mikki as she lies beside me in my tent. We can hear *everything*.

'I've got earplugs,' I say, because that's about the only thing I can offer.

'I told you,' she snaps. 'I'm fine with it.'

I should use this time to work on her about leaving, but the muffled sounds of Jack and Sky are too distracting.

When Mikki and I get up, Sky is sitting beside Victor, eating scrambled eggs as though it's a regular morning, but Victor's hand isn't on her leg and the mood feels tense. Unbelievably, Jack slings an arm around Mikki as she sits down and my stomach squirms.

The others seem to sense the mood and we eat in silence.

When Sky heads to the tap to wash her bowl, I confront her. 'How could you?'

Sky seems bewildered by my anger. 'We share. It's what we do.'

'Mikki doesn't fit in here. She's softer than the rest of you.'

'I don't see her that way. She wanted to see if she could do it. She's working hard to improve herself and I admire her for that.'

'She doesn't need to improve herself,' I say. 'She's fine just the way she is.'

Sky's eyes narrow. 'She said you want her to leave. Maybe you can't handle her having lots of friends now.'

This completely throws me. Is she right? Is it me who has the problem?

Clemente jogs down the trail from the beach. 'It's barrelling!'

Everyone jumps into action. I grab my shorts from the line, still reeling from what Sky said. Mikki and I never had any other close friends, so it's weird seeing her so close to Sky and the other tribe members. It makes me feel left out at times, but that's not why I want her to leave. I'm acting in her best interest.

Muffled male shouts alert me that something's not right as I put on sunscreen. Victor and Jack are on the ground wrestling. Victor punches out at Jack's head; Jack raises his arms protectively. Victor punches him in the stomach. Jack groans and curls in a ball. Clemente rushes over, shouting in Spanish. He shoves Victor up against a tree trunk, sending bits of grey bark showering to the ground. You'd think Sky would try to help, because it's obvious why they're fighting, but she stands there with a look of fascination.

Jack falls into step beside me as we hurry along the sand.

'Is your back okay?' I ask.

'Yeah,' Jack says. 'But Victor wants to kill me.'

'I hope it was worth it.'

He glances sideways at me. 'Are you asking how it was?'

'Maybe.'

'It was hot.' The wind ruffles his blond hair, flattening it against his forehead. 'But it was full on. My back couldn't take it on a regular basis.'

Too much information. I'm furious with him for doing that to Mikki, but part of me has to concede that she agreed to it.

'I didn't know Victor would be *that* upset,' Jack says.

'Has Sky slept with any of the others?' I ask.

'Only Clemente.'

Somehow I force my legs to keep moving.

'Chill,' Jack says. 'It was only once.'

'Was Victor okay with it?' I ask weakly.

Jack smirks. 'Not really, but he got over it. She's had a crack at Ryan a few times but Ryan wasn't up for it. Poor guy probably shat himself.'

The sky is china blue, the sun bright and strong. Sky and Clemente are up ahead, chatting as they stretch. I feel shaken by the idea of them sleeping together. Betrayed, somehow, which is ridiculous.

I dip my face in the ocean as I paddle out, trying to wash my mind of all the drama. The water is as clear as I've ever seen it, the sand of the seabed visible several metres below. Underneath me, a flash of silver as a shoal of fish dart past.

I look over my shoulder and see the whole ocean coming at me.

'Paddle!' Sky shouts.

The water gleams as I paddle over it. My board tips downhill and it's like I'm running down the up escalator. The ocean rushes upwards to meet me, sliding in a smooth, green sheet under my board. I jump to my feet. I have so much speed by now that I don't know how I'll be able to turn but instinct takes over. With the bottom of the wave in sight, I bend my knees and carve the biggest bottom turn I've ever done. My board shoots up the face so fast I almost go airborne. At the last minute I cut back down. The top of the wave curls over my head and time seems to slow.

It appears to defy the laws of physics that you can balance inside a loop of water on a piece of wood so puny it wouldn't hold you afloat unless it was moving. The barrel, the tube, the green room . . . Surfers have so many names for the place so dear to their hearts. I never got a proper barrel. Until now.

As a teenager, I used to devour Australian surf magazines with their glossy shots of the ocean on the other side of the earth. The words of *Australian Surfing Life* remain lodged in my brain to this day: *The safest place in any hollow wave is the barrel. Commit yourself to it. Put yourself there and stay there as long as the damn thing will let you.*

With the wave peeling over my shoulder, I commit. I have no choice. The loop closes around me, forming a shimmering blue cavern. It's as though I'm in another dimension and I want to stay in here forever.

All too soon, the roof caves in, blasting me below the surface. I paddle out to try for another – and wipeout badly, smashing myself in the shin. Clemente paddles over and I wait for him to tell me to quit before I break something, because that's what Kasim would have said.

He tilts his hand. 'You nearly made it. Take more angle.'

Two hours later, I've scored one more barrel and a dozen more bruises. I'm buzzing as I walk up the sand. I'm not thinking about Mikki or Jack right now – or Elke – or anything but my barrels.

I pause to remove my leg rope, but Clemente's right behind me and our bodies collide. We're the last ones out of the water and we're alone on the beach.

'Sorry,' I say.

He grips my arm to steady me. His chest – bare and wet – is flush with mine, but I don't pull away and neither does he. Little drops of water cling to his tanned skin. The sun shines into his eyes, turning them the same aqua green as the ocean. He's a good-looking guy, as are all the men in the Tribe, but they don't have this *pull*. It's like being caught in a rip, the way it sucks the sand out from under your toes and drags you out to sea. Fight it all you like, you are powerless against it.

Mikki doesn't trust him, nor does Sky. And nor should I.

Clemente steps backwards and I can breathe again.

I seize my chance to get him alone. 'Can we talk?'

His expression turns guarded but he gestures to the sand. 'Want to sit?'

We lay our boards down and sit facing the water.

'Look,' I say. 'I know you said you don't want to get

close to anyone, but can we at least try to get on as friends?'

His eyes search my face. I don't know what he's looking for or if he finds it, but he nods grudgingly and turns back to the water.

I study his profile as he watches the waves – his strong jaw and straight nose. He reminds me of Kasim right now: the strong silent type who struggles when it comes to emotional matters. A funny thought comes from nowhere: *Kasim would like this guy*. It's strangely freeing. Only now do I realise how guilty I've been feeling about liking him.

Elke is the elephant in the room.

'Can I ask you something?' I say. 'How can you stay here after your wife . . . and Elke . . .?'

His fingers delve into the sand. The sand makes squeaking noises as he squeezes it in his fist. 'Where would I go? My friends are here. Of course I wanted to leave because of the memories, but these guys hold me together.'

I'm taken aback by his honesty. 'The sessions with Sky. Are they helping?'

'Sky said I can either visualise the events over and over until I can accept them, or I can blank them out. I choose to blank them out.'

I don't know how this friends thing is going to work when his gaze stirs up all kinds of stuff in my stomach. 'And can you?'

Clemente stares at the water with haunted eyes. 'If people don't keep asking me about them.'

Chapter 49

Clemente

I have blood on my hands, the sort you can never wash off. Sometimes I look down and actually see it, a crimson stream running over my fingers and trickling down my wrists like it did when I pulled Elke out of the water.

One thing I've always liked about the Tribe is they don't ask difficult questions. We all have our problems, but we deal with them in our own ways. Jack and I talk sometimes, and I've talked with Sky on occasion too, but there's never any pressure. Then Kenna comes along, dragging up the memories.

Elke. The night I met her, I was with Jack in a dodgy backpacker bar in Bondi. I was tired after an early surf at the Bay followed by the long drive to the city, but when you're out with Jack there's no such thing as a quiet night, and he was up on stage alongside a bunch of mostly women in a wet T-shirt contest. (Only in Australia.) I didn't mind. Jack's a good guy. Behind his crazy antics, he's in a lot of pain and much of what he does is an attempt to distract himself from it.

'Do you speak German?' the woman next to me asked. Elke.

Music boomed from a speaker behind us and the table next door were doing vodka shots so I had to lean in close to hear her. 'No. Can you speak Spanish?'

'No,' she said. 'So we speak English, okay?'

I hadn't dated since my wife had died a year earlier – hadn't even looked at a woman since then – but she smelt amazing, an enticing mix of sunscreen and shampoo, and she had an interesting tan line around her neck from her bikini.

'Your accent is so sexy,' she said.

Was she flirting with me?

'I've never kissed a Spanish man before. I wonder what it's like.' She smiled. 'What? I like you. Am I too direct?'

I pulled myself together. 'No. But Spanish women are more subtle. If they like someone, they show it with their eyes. Like this.'

And just like that, I was flirting back.

'Can I kiss you yet?' she asked.

I laughed, no longer aware of the terrible music or the annoying crowd. 'Yes.'

Elke made everything so simple. I never had to guess what she was thinking like I used to with my wife, because she came straight out and said it. If she wasn't happy, I was sure to hear about it, and the same went for anyone else she wasn't happy with. It didn't always make for an easy life – she clashed heads with Sky and Victor in particular – but I appreciated her honesty.

At the end of every day, we crawled into my tent and I sank into her and forgot the outside world. If only I could forget what happened next.

I look down at my hand. I can't see the blood but I can feel it. I squeeze my eyes shut, only to see my wife's body swinging back and forth. I clench my fingers. And that triggers another memory. My hand, punching out. Hitting over and over.

Alejandro was my best friend ever since we'd met at a boxing class when we were about five. He always had a reckless streak, but after his parents split up when he was about nineteen, he went off the rails and started drinking heavily and looking for trouble. We'd be out in a bar and he'd seek out the biggest guy in there and try to pick a fight with him. I saved his skin over and over, sometimes taking blows in the process and even paying one guy off to help Alejandro avoid criminal charges.

We'd kept up the boxing, reaching the final in the regional championships that year. I didn't like that I'd have to fight him, but it was nothing new – we sparred all the time.

'I have something to tell you,' he said, right before the big fight.

There was something in his face that should have warned me what was to come.

'I slept with Marta last night.'

Marta was my then-girlfriend, the first girl I'd ever loved. I searched his eyes to see if he was serious, half-hoping he'd laugh and say he was just kidding. But of course he wasn't. They called us into the ring before I could respond.

In the far corner, I saw Marta watching. She raised a hand to wave. I didn't wave back. Who was she here to cheer for – me or Alejandro?

Over the buzzing in my ears, I heard the ding of the bell. My anger flooded through my fists. To lose control like that spells disaster for a fighter normally. I don't know why it didn't – maybe Alejandro let me get the first punches in because he thought he deserved them, or maybe I simply caught him by surprise. Anyway, he went down. A fraction after the ref started counting, I aimed an extra punch that I was lucky not to get disqualified for, leaving Alejandro with a bloodied nose. It was an easy win. I still remember the metallic smell of him as we shook hands afterwards.

Back in the changing room, I gathered up my stuff and left. I felt vindicated, until I heard the news in the morning. He'd got a blood clot in his brain and died in his sleep.

There's no defence for what I did. My anger exploded and I couldn't control it. And Alejandro died. That's why I quit boxing. Because it fed that dangerous urge inside me – the urge to hit and keep hitting.

We're led to believe that sports make you stronger, yet they can also destroy you, not just your body but your life as well. All of us here at the Bay have had our lives destroyed by sports in some way. Anyway, I left medical school, because I couldn't reconcile killing Alejandro with my dream of being a doctor, and the following year I left Spain.

I don't intend to tell Kenna about Alejandro. She's wary enough of me as it is, and I don't blame her. When you factor in my wife's death and Elke's disappearance, I can see how it looks. Like I'm cursed.

CHAPTER 50

KENNA

I grip the pull-up bar. The others do pull-ups daily but it's an exercise I've always struggled with. Sunlight shines through the leaves; the metal is warm under my fingers.

Sky watches as I heave myself upwards. 'Clemente! Can we borrow you a minute?'

He comes over, wet board shorts moulded to his lower body.

Sky clasps his shoulder. 'Could you please teach this girl to do a decent pull-up?'

I feel completely stupid and maybe Clemente picks up on it because he says: 'It's one of the hardest exercises to do correctly.'

He watches closely as I try another. Those eyes. They're incredibly distracting.

He walks around me. 'Where can you feel it?' He sets a fingertip to my shoulder. 'Here? Or here?'

I haul myself back up. 'There!'

'Breathe in,' he says. 'Breathe out. No. Let me show you.'

I watch his chest muscles ripple as he lifts his body. There's no sense that he's showing off or competing with me – he genuinely wants me to get it right.

Sky loses interest and wanders off.

'Now you try,' Clemente says.

Normally it's me standing there, watching my clients to see what hurts. Now that it's the other way round, I realise how exposing it is. You're laying yourself bare, physically and mentally. *This is the limit of what I can do.*

My arms are shaking. 'I can't do it.'

Clemente's voice is soft. 'You can.'

And when someone helps you surpass that limit, it takes the bond to another level.

The Tribe do this kind of thing on a daily basis. Perhaps that's how they got so close. Training with someone like this, you have to listen to their voice over your own. Do it enough and you come to trust them.

Even when you shouldn't.

The mood around the fire that evening is euphoric. I got more waves today than in an entire season in Cornwall. I've pushed Elke from my mind for now. I'm going to sit back and enjoy the moment.

Mikki catches my eye. 'Now do you see why I like this place so much?'

'I do.' I gesture in Jack's direction. He and Victor sit side by side, talking about *sick barrels*, apparently best buddies again. 'Are you really okay about . . .?'

Mikki's nostrils flare. 'Yeah, I *told* you!'

I study her, unsure if she genuinely means it. Mikki's a

hard person to read, even for me. 'We never used to talk about our relationships, did we?'

'I wanted to.'

'Did you? So did I.' I reach across to grip her hand. 'Well, in future, we will, okay?'

She squeezes my fingers. 'Okay!'

I lean back against a tree trunk. Being back on a beach has made me realise I'm not cut out for city life. Whatever happens here, I can't go back to London.

Victor is playing bongo by slapping his thighs and singing a loud Portuguese song.

'Dude, give it a break!' Ryan snaps.

'Cheer the fuck up, brother!' Victor says. 'Nobody died, so stop being so miserable.'

'Fuck you!' Ryan slinks off to the barbecue area.

He looks really upset so I go over to check on him. 'Are you okay?'

He's on his hands and knees, poking at something in the earth. 'It's too much of a crowd sometimes.'

I hide my smile. Seven is hardly a crowd, but I get it, because he's an introvert, and we introverts need our alone time to recharge. 'What are you doing?'

'Squashing ants. It's like they can smell death coming. Watch.' He flattens them with a fingertip, one by one.

Sure enough, the remaining ants go haywire and run madly in all directions. From Ryan's soft-spoken tones and nervous manner, he seems a gentle type at first. With his goatee beard and long hair and loose-fitting clothes that have seen better days, you'd take him for a hippy. In the surf, though, his whole demeanour changes from quiet to cut-throat, just like Jack. And watching Ryan now, methodically snuffing out lives with a fixated look in his eyes, challenges that view further. *The Guardian*.

Mikki's right. He *is* kind of creepy.

'I'll leave you in peace.' I ate a mountain of casserole for dinner but that was an hour ago and I'm starving again. I head to the fridge to see what I can find.

Someone taps my shoulder and I turn to see Victor offering a bowl of something purple. 'You want?'

'What is it?' I ask.

'Açaí,' Victor says. 'Try. It gives you good energy.'

'Oh yeah, I've had it before. Thank you.' I take it back to the fire with me. A fruity cinnamon taste fills my mouth as I spoon up the frozen pulp.

By the time I finish, I'm shivering. 'I'm freezing.'

'Have this.' Clemente hands me a fleece blanket.

I pull it around me. 'Thanks.'

Clemente lowers himself to the ground beside me, so our shoulders are nearly but not quite touching. Jack and Mikki snuggle nearby under a blanket of their own.

Mikki squeaks and jumps up.

'What?' I ask.

'A moth!'

'Where?' Then I realise what she's flapping at. 'It's just your tattoo.'

'Oh.' Mikki laughs awkwardly and sits back down.

My arms ache from paddling. I stretch them out in front of me, noting how they've changed shape.

'Admiring your muscles?' Clemente asks.

I laugh. 'I was, actually.'

Clemente's relaxed demeanour is a total contrast to how he was on the beach earlier.

'Surfing out there today,' I say. 'And all the other stuff you do. Do you ever feel guilty?'

'What do you mean?' he asks.

'If something happened to you, how would your family feel?'

Sky glances over, oozing disapproval, as though 'family' is a dirty word here. The more isolated they are from their families and the outside world, the more power she has over them, I suppose.

'They know I need to do it,' Clemente says. 'My mum, she took me to hospital so many times. Broken arm, broken fingers, mostly from boxing, but she never once told me to stop.'

'My boyfriend used to try to stop me doing dangerous stuff,' I say.

He looks at me curiously. 'Did he?' He hesitates. 'My wife and most of my girlfriends knew I needed it. I was lucky.'

I can tell he hates talking about them. It's as though he realises that to get me to trust him, he has to let me in – at least a little.

Victor chuckles and gestures to Sky. 'Imagine if I tried to stop her!' He flips his fingers back and forth.

'But I would never try to stop you either, right?' Sky says.

Victor blinks as though this has never occurred to him.

Clemente nods. 'If your partner wants to do this stuff, you cannot try to stop them. It's part of who they are. My mum always understood this side of me.'

Sky frowns again, which only makes me more determined to keep talking about family. I remember Clemente's brother who lives in England. 'Does your brother surf?'

Sky cuts in before he can answer, leaning across to touch my cheek. 'You caught the sun, Kenna.'

'I know.' My skin feels hot and tight.

Jack gets up to pluck a leaf from a nearby plant. 'Here you go. Aloe vera.'

It's thick and chunky with spikes down the side. A clear gel oozes out from where he snapped it off. 'Wow,' I say. 'I've had it in a tube but never fresh.'

'I'll do it,' Jack says. 'Stay still.'

Clemente watches expressionlessly as Jack rubs the leaf over my face.

'Hey, Ryan!' Victor shouts. 'Play a song. I wanna dance!'

Ryan comes reluctantly over with his guitar and launches into 'Sweet Jane'.

'No,' Victor says. 'This song is . . . not cheerful. Is . . .' He looks to us for help.

'Mournful?' I say. I don't think it's supposed to be a mournful song, it's the way Ryan's playing it.

'Yes!' Victor says. 'Play a cheerful song.'

'I told you,' Ryan snaps. 'I don't know any other songs.'

'Is okay,' Victor says quickly. 'I dance anyway.'

Victor tries to get Sky to dance with him but she shakes her head, so he dances on his own, a kind of samba, jiving his hands and looking down at his feet as he does a complicated sequence of steps. He's a great dancer and his goofy grin is contagious.

Jack jumps up. 'I'll dance with you, mate!'

'Oh God,' Victor says. 'Two men dancing together is not good. Sky, *please*!'

Sky rolls her eyes and gets up. The rest of us get up too. So we're dancing like idiots around the fire to Ryan's mournful song, and everything is good in my world. I still have my concerns about Mikki's safety and Elke's disappearance, but I'll worry about that tomorrow.

I'm so caught up in the dancing that it takes me a moment to realise the music has stopped. I turn to Ryan to see why.

And see two women standing there. Once I've recovered from my shock, I realise who they are. It's the Canadian couple we met at the service station five days ago. The pretty redhead is wearing the same denim playsuit she wore that day.

They nod at me in recognition but they're not smiling.

CHAPTER 51

KENNA

The Tribe do their usual thing of bunching together like a sports team. They stand there looking hostile, arms folded across their chests.

'Who are you?' Sky asks sharply.

'I'm Tanith,' says the pretty redhead.

'And I'm Shannon.' Her wife has dark hair cut in a pixie crop.

'We're here for my wallet,' Tanith says, looking at Jack.

Sky turns on Jack, furious. 'Do you know them?'

Ryan, Victor and Clemente stare at Jack with incredulous expressions. I can guess what they're thinking: *Jack's done it again.*

'We met them at the service station on our way here,' I say.

Sky turns back to the women. 'How did you hear about this place?'

Shannon nods in my direction. '*She* told us about it.'

All eyes turn my way.

I can feel their rage. 'Back then I didn't know this place was secret.'

'My wallet?' Tanith repeats.

The others all start talking at once.

Sky pounces on Jack. 'See? This is what happens when you bring people here!'

'You absolute *dickhead*!' Ryan tells him. 'If they bring the police here . . .'

Tanith steps towards Jack. 'Did you take it?' she asks loudly.

The others fall silent. I think of Jack's hands all over Tanith as he swatted 'mosquitoes'. Jack's in pain. Is it possible he was desperate enough to pickpocket for cash so he could buy codeine?

Jack raises his hands to proclaim his innocence, but I'm not sure. After all, he drugged some poor woman and seems to have no concept of how wrong that was.

Tanith backs down a little. 'If it wasn't you, I just don't know what else could have happened to it.'

Jack looks her in the eye. 'I would never.'

Tanith looks uncertain suddenly, as though she was expecting Jack to admit he had it. 'We called in at the service station on our way back but nobody had handed it in. And that was the last time I had it. I just thought . . .'

Jack nods stiffly. 'I get it, but like I say, I would never.'

Tanith and Shannon glance at each other. I sense they're not quite convinced, but what can they do? An awkward silence follows.

Tanith gestures around. 'Nice camping spot.'

Shannon smiles brightly. 'How're the waves?'

Nobody answers and I feel terrible. They seem like good people. 'It was pretty fun earlier,' I say.

Sky gives me an icy look.

I ignore her. 'Where did you guys end up?'

'We drove all the way up to the Sunshine Coast,' Shannon says. 'Then we realised her wallet was missing so we had to order new bank cards and wait around while they mailed them out to us. It took forever.' She turns to Tanith. 'We should get the tent from the Jeep before it gets too late.'

'You can't camp here,' Ryan says.

'Why not?' Shannon asks.

'You have to book with the park warden.'

Shannon pulls a phone out. 'There's no signal, so how can we?'

'You have to do it in advance,' Sky says.

I feel so uncomfortable. This wave doesn't belong to Sky – or Ryan – or anyone else.

'If the park warden turns up, we'll pay,' Shannon says. 'Otherwise we'll pay online as soon as we leave.'

'The warden's a real dickhead,' Sky says.

Shannon folds her arms across her chest and says quietly but firmly: 'We came all this way, there's no way we're not going to surf here.'

With that, the women head off to the vehicles, returning with bags and a tent.

'They're not surfing here,' Victor says.

'Come on,' Jack says. 'Two chicks. What's the harm?'

'Are you kidding?' Sky says. 'If it's barrelling tomorrow like it was today, the minute they leave, they'll get on the phone and tell all their friends how good it was.'

'And next week, we'll have half of Canada here,' Ryan says.

Clemente nods but says nothing.

'So what are we going to do?' Victor asks.

The women are struggling to pitch their tent – it's too dark, so I go over to help.

'Kenna, right?' Tanith says. 'How long have you been surfing?'

'Nearly twenty years,' I say. 'You?'

They tell me about Canada's surf scene; I tell them about Cornwall and my sports therapy work. A dangerous undercurrent hangs in the air as we chat. When I can't bear the tension any longer, I head back to the others.

'We need to get rid of them,' Ryan is saying.

'Don't worry, we will,' Sky says.

Suddenly I'm wondering how safe it is for the women to stay here. Jack is at the barbecue. A prickly sensation creeps through me as he picks up two mugs and carries them over to the Canadian women. He wouldn't, would he? But I can't risk it.

I hurry towards him, pretend to trip and crash into him. The impact is harder than I intended. The mugs go flying; Jack falls to the ground.

'What the fuck?' he shouts.

'I'm so sorry,' I say.

His face is a snarl as he picks himself up.

I feign dismay at the overturned mugs. In the bottom of one is what smells like hot chocolate. 'I'll make new ones.'

'I'll do it,' Jack says.

'I insist.' I wash out the mugs and heat more milk, then carry the drinks over to the women, who are eating a makeshift dinner of sandwiches and crisps. I'm probably just being paranoid. Even so, I feel like I should warn them. But Sky and Jack are hovering right there, too close for me to say anything.

CHAPTER 52

KENNA

A buzzing vibration wakes me. An insect? I peer into the darkness, ready to bolt from my sleeping bag, and realise what it is. The unzipping of a tent. Now, though, all I can hear is the crash of waves. Did I imagine it?

A crack of a twig snapping underfoot. Someone's out there. Further away, the unzipping of another tent, then, after a moment, low voices. Is it the Canadian women? More faint sounds, like something – or someone – is being moved. My breath catches. I grope for the zip of my tent. Quietly as I can, I slide it upwards, but all I hear now is bats.

Someone probably just nipped to the bathroom. But as I'm drifting back to sleep, I hear footsteps of someone returning from wherever they went. I switch round so I'm lying on my belly and peek out the gap at the bottom of the zip. Total darkness, just as I expected, but I hear someone climbing back into their tent and zipping it up.

I know whose tent that is.

Clemente's.

When I next wake, it's light outside. I creep out of my tent and my stomach drops. The spot where the Canadians pitched their tent is empty.

Clemente is frying bacon and eggs on the barbecue. None of the others are in sight.

I march over to him, feeling terrible that I didn't go out there last night. 'Where are they?'

Clemente swings to face me. 'They've gone.'

'What did you do to them?'

He blinks. 'What do you think I did?'

'I don't know. That's why I'm asking. I heard you in the night.'

'Are you accusing me of something?'

The bacon is burning, I can smell it. 'Are you deliberately being evasive or do you have something to hide?'

His expression is unreadable. Why's he being so maddening?

A zip opens and Sky pokes her head out of her tent. 'What's going on?'

'Nothing.' Clemente calmly tips the bacon onto plates.

'Have they gone?' Sky asks, nodding to where the Canadians were pitched.

It seems a genuine question – either that or she's a very good liar.

'Yeah.' Clemente gives me a pointed look. 'They didn't like it here.'

Mikki emerges from her tent. I can tell from her face that she's overheard some of the conversation.

'Want bacon and eggs, Mikki?' Clemente asks.

'Yeah, thanks.' Mikki looks at me inquiringly.

Later, I mouth.

We eat in awkward silence.

'What was that about?' Mikki asks quietly, as she and I wash our plates.

'I heard Clemente in the night with the Canadians,' I say. 'I'm worried he . . . did something to them.' It sounds outrageous saying it out loud.

'Like what?'

'I don't know. Threatened them.' Or worse.

'Let's take a walk,' Mikki says. 'And see if their Jeep's gone.'

Clemente has gone to check the surf, Sky is doing yoga and none of the others are up, so Mikki and I slip off down the trail. Insects swoop and buzz in the early morning sunlight. I flap my arms when they come close.

'I'm sure they're okay,' Mikki says. 'I can't believe he'd hurt them.'

'I don't know what to think any more. Sky seems to think Clemente's wife's suicide was suspicious.'

Mikki darts a look my way. 'She mentioned that to me as well.'

'And then Elke. It's a lot of bad luck for one guy.'

'I know what you mean,' Mikki says. 'That was my reaction when I saw the poster. I like him, but he has issues.'

'Do you think . . .' I glance over my shoulder, not wanting to finish the sentence.

Mikki glances over her shoulder too. 'This might sound ridiculous. But he has guilty eyes.'

Scuffling sounds from the bushes ahead. I yelp as a

large bird rushes across the path. It's an ugly thing, plump and black with a red head, yellow ruff and sharp claws.

'Bush turkey,' Mikki says.

'Do they bite?'

'No.'

I punch the air. 'Finally, something that doesn't bite.'

'Come on, it's not that bad.'

'I'm getting used to it. There was a mosquito in my tent last night, buzzing about, but I was so tired I just put my towel over my head and went to sleep.'

There are little bags under Mikki's eyes.

'You look tired,' I say. 'Another nightmare?'

'Yeah.'

This fear therapy, I don't think it's helping her. My thoughts return to the Canadians as we reach the parking area. The yellow Jeep isn't there, which is somewhat reassuring, but last night the women seemed determined to surf here today, so how did Clemente make them change their minds?

Mikki goes stiff beside me. 'Oh my God.'

At the side of the track, there's a figure standing so still I didn't notice it at first. It's Ryan, holding a pole spear, arms and face smeared with mud. We keep a careful distance back from him.

'What are you doing?' I ask.

'Keeping watch,' Ryan says. 'Don't want anyone else sneaking up on us.'

'Have you seen the Canadian women?'

'They've gone.'

Am I imagining it or is there a spark of madness in Ryan's eyes?

And then I see it: a splash of red on a rock beside Jack's car. From the way Mikki has frozen to the spot, I can tell she's seen it too. I stare at it. Is it what I think it is? We can't let on that we've seen it. I tug Mikki's arm and we walk rapidly back down the trail.

As soon as we're out of earshot, I turn to her. 'Was that blood?'

Her brow furrows. 'I don't know. I don't think Clemente would . . .'

'But would Ryan?'

'No! I know these guys. There must be a reasonable explanation for it.'

'Like what?

'Maybe they spilt something. Wine or something.'

'It didn't look like wine.' While the wildlife may not bother me as much as it used to, the human inhabitants of the camp become scarier the longer I stay here. 'We have to get out of this place, Mikki.'

'Calm down.'

I lower my voice as we near the clearing. 'What are we going to do?'

Mikki shoots me an exasperated look. 'I'll talk to Jack. Just act normal, okay?'

The others sit around, sullen-faced.

'How are the waves?' Mikki asks.

'Flat,' Clemente says.

'Damn,' she says. 'I *so* need a surf. Is there really nothing?'

I'm impressed by Mikki's acting skills. I'm too busy wondering about the blood – if that's what it was – to think about the surf.

'Trust me,' Clemente tells her. 'It's like a lake.'

'Ryan's guarding the perimeter,' I say.

'With a pole spear,' Mikki adds.

'Fuck me,' Jack says. 'He's lost it.'

'He seems pretty stressed, but he's harmless, isn't he?' I say.

Victor laughs. 'Not with a pole spear.'

The others murmur in agreement.

Sky and Victor go off fishing, leaving the rest of us to work out in pairs or alone. I want to go back to the vehicles to look more closely at the blood but I don't fancy facing Ryan. Mikki promised to talk to Jack but she's busy staring at her moth, so I make a half-hearted attempt at yoga, my mind still in overdrive.

Clemente doesn't speak to me all morning. His workout continues for two hours. It bothers me to watch him. Mikki's right. There's a darkness in his eyes and a heaviness in his posture that could be one of two things: grief or guilt. Anyone who can block out pain as successfully as he can can surely block out everything else as well.

Even their own conscience.

CHAPTER 53

KENNA

Across the clearing, Clemente and Victor are sparring. They wear padded helmets and boxing gloves but it's terrifying to watch. Nimble on their feet, they dodge about. The force in some of Clemente's punches makes me wince, but Victor hits back just as hard.

Clemente catches me watching him and turns back to Victor, pounding him – *bang, bang, bang!* – until he's up against a tree trunk.

Guilty eyes, Mikki said. But guilty of what?

'Steady, brother!' Victor calls.

Clemente peels his helmet off and comes over, breathless. 'Want to know what happened with the Canadians?' His voice is low and furious. 'I heard them packing up in the night. They'd changed their mind about surfing here so I helped them carry their stuff to the car.'

'Why?' I ask.

His hair is damp with sweat. 'Because they seemed like

278

nice girls and I didn't want anything bad to happen to them.'

The words send prickles through me.

'Happy now?' Clemente asks.

I blurt it out before I can think better of it. 'I saw blood.'

Clemente flinches as though I've punched him. 'The boot of their van fell on Shannon's head. It bled a lot. Head wounds always do.'

With that, Clemente stalks off to resume boxing. I stare after him, unsure whether to believe him.

The leaves in the trees rustle and shake as we eat lunch. Sky has made a tuna salad but I'm not hungry. I'm kicking myself for not warning Tanith and Shannon last night, but I thought I was just being paranoid. I still don't know for sure if they're okay. I only have Clemente's word for it.

Clemente presses an ice pack to his ribs, Victor presses one to his cheek. I can't tell who came off worse in the fight but at least Clemente seems to have worked off some of his anger. He chats quietly to Victor as they eat.

A high-pitched scream from the bushes makes me drop my fork. I look round in shock.

Victor laughs. 'It's just a bird.'

'Really?' I freeze, listening hard.

The sound comes again, screeching and horrible, like a woman in agony. The others are obviously used to it because they don't react.

As we wash up, Ryan comes down the path, spear in hand.

Jack marches up to him, face tight with rage, and grabs him by the scruff of his T-shirt. 'Have you been in my tent?'

Ryan splutters. 'What? No.'

Jack shakes him. 'Tell me the truth.'

'Hey,' Clemente calls. 'Calm down.'

'He's been stealing my codeine,' Jack says. 'Admit it.'

Ryan pulls free of Jack. 'Yeah, okay! I took two. That's all.'

'Fuck, man!' Jack shouts. 'I need them!'

Ryan shrugs. 'Sorry.'

Jack aims a punch at Ryan's solar plexus. The viciousness of it takes my breath away. Sky's right. He has the killer instinct. Ryan doubles over, but he recovers quickly and advances on Jack, fingers white around the spear, and I can see he has the killer instinct too. Come to think of it, maybe Sky, Victor and Clemente do as well.

Clemente rushes in between Jack and Ryan. The lorikeets are making a racket so I don't catch all of it but there's a shouting match between the men. Clemente eventually forces them to shake hands, then Jack retreats to his tent and Clemente lets out an audible sigh.

Muttering under his breath, Ryan looks in the fridge. I show him the salad. The wild look I saw in his eyes earlier is gone and I wonder if I just imagined it. All I see now is exhaustion.

'Are you all right?' I ask.

Ryan sighs and rubs his ribs. 'Yeah.'

'Have you broken anything? I can check you if you want.'

'No. Thanks.' Ryan eats the salad robotically.

I remember his miserable expression as he told me about his wife and daughter and feel a pang of pity for him. But I need to keep the pressure up, and to see if I can uncover anything more about him. 'Do you think more people will be turning up when they see the surf forecast?'

Ryan's expression darkens. 'Better not.' He looks around as though he expects people to come bursting from the trees and jumps up to pick up his spear.

A leaf crunches behind me and I turn to see Sky.

'Why did you ask him that?' she asks as Ryan strides away.

I raise my hands. 'I didn't know he would react like that.'

Sky looks at me curiously and I can't tell if she believes me.

'He's a loose cannon,' I say. 'If someone came here right now, I worry about what he'd do to them.'

Brow crinkling, she looks after Ryan thoughtfully.

CHAPTER 54

KENNA

The mood is restless; tempers are fraying. Seven frustrated people, bubbling with energy. It flows harmlessly out of us into the water normally, but I can feel it crackling in the air above our heads after a day without waves.

'Time for a trust exercise!' Sky announces.

Is she serious? I glance around, waiting for someone to protest, but nobody does. 'Is that a good idea?'

'Why?' Sky asks. 'Don't you trust us, Kenna?'

'I just meant . . .' My words fizzle out under her gaze.

'It's exactly what we need right now.'

Her smile seems like a bad omen. What does she have in store for us?

'Should I look for Ryan?' Clemente asks.

'No,' Sky says. 'Leave him be.'

I glance at Mikki, who shrugs and reaches for her towel. We slap on sunscreen and follow Sky to the beach. The wind is howling off the sea, blowing sand everywhere. I shield my eyes, wishing I'd put my sunglasses on.

The seagulls don't seem to like the wind either. They toddle ahead of us like small children wearing their mothers' shoes. When a gust hits them, it blows them backwards a few awkward steps and they open their wings to stabilise themselves. The strongest gusts blow them off the ground completely, and at this, they hover on the spot with what looks like a scowl on their small, pinched faces until the gust subsides.

Jack's warm fingers wrap round my arm, making me jump. 'Careful. Bluebottle!' He points to a bright blue ink-splat on the sand ahead.

I lean in to look. 'What is it?'

'Jellyfish,' Jack says. 'Gives a nasty sting. There's another. Look at the stinger on that one. We often get them on a north wind.'

A thin blue thread stretches across the sand for half a metre. 'Would it sting me?'

'If you trod on the tentacle, it would.'

There are more on the high-water line. The gulls dash about, pecking them up. They scatter as we approach and resume the feast the moment we pass. I hope they don't miss any.

By the time I reach the rocks, sand encrusts my scalp and eyebrows. Sky and Victor are wearing backpacks. They heave them off.

'See the bluebottles?' Jack calls.

'No,' Mikki says. 'Are there any in the water?'

We peer into the shallows.

Victor points. 'I see one.'

'Another one here,' Mikki calls.

'It'll add to the challenge,' Sky says.

Victor and Jack shake their heads, half-laughing, but I'm worried.

Jack nudges me. 'They won't kill you. They just sting a bit.'

One of the backpacks contains ten white rocks. Sky has us distribute them in the water just beyond head depth. I check for jellyfish as we wade back and forth, ferrying the rocks.

I give Mikki a pointed look. 'Are we really going to do this?' I ask quietly.

She nods, face taut with nerves.

Jack grabs Sky's arm. 'Bluebottle!'

For a moment I think I see fury in Victor's eyes. Just as fast, it's gone.

The sun blazes down on my arms, its blistering strength taking me by surprise once again. My poor skin is already red from yesterday. The sun seems to burn straight through the sunscreen I just applied.

The bright blue sky is marbled with white feathers.

Jack sees me looking at them. 'Horsetail clouds.'

'What do they mean?' I ask.

'Rain, and a lot of it.'

Sky interrupts. 'Ready to hear the teams? We're in pairs today.'

Jack glances uneasily at Victor. She wouldn't, would she? Victor's shaven head gleams in the sunshine as the two men eye each other.

'Me and Victor, Mikki and Jack, Kenna and Clemente,' Sky says.

Clemente gives me a resigned look. It's no real surprise that we're paired together. Like any good trainer, she sniffs out our weak points and attacks them. Clemente's my weak point and maybe I'm his.

There's a worse shock to come. Sky pulls out sports tape and tapes her and Victor's inside legs together. It's a three-legged race with a horrible twist: it's going to take place underwater. Can I trust Clemente? I look to Mikki for help but she's busy with the tape.

Sky notices my hesitation. 'When you wipe out in big waves, you can't always come up to the surface when you feel like it. Sometimes you get held down. We're mimicking that.'

I feel queasy, just like I did when Clemente took me to the beach early that morning and proposed holding me under. This is what he was preparing me for. I've only ever had a few bad hold-downs. In the worst one, I breathed in water and came up choking. If you get seawater in your lungs, you can get an infection, so I took myself to hospital to get checked over but fortunately I got away with it.

Clemente beckons me over. Fear skitters across my stomach. I don't want to do this, but can I afford to make a stand? Reluctantly I position my right leg next to his left one. Sand blasts me, pricking my calves. It's a hot day so I'm wearing just my bikini with a T-shirt over it to ward off the sun. Now I wish I was more covered up.

A feeling of unreality sets in as Clemente winds the tape expertly round our ankles. It looks really strong. I tug my leg apart from his, testing the bonds.

Clemente winds it several times more. 'Don't want it to come undone.'

He watches my face as he smooths the tape down, but

I have no idea what he's thinking – or planning. I think about how powerless I'll be down there, able to move only if Clemente does. Attached to him by the ankle, how easy will it be to stay afloat? And that's if he so chooses. What if he doesn't? He's bigger and stronger than me, as well as far more at home underwater. If he wants to stay under, we'll stay under. It's a trust exercise like no other.

'The winning team is the one to get the most rocks,' Sky says. 'If two teams have the same number, they'll wrestle for them at the end.'

It's like another one of the crazy challenges on *Survivor*, except they probably wouldn't allow this one – it's too dangerous.

'Let's practise,' Clemente says. 'When you feel me lift my leg, you lift yours.'

I'm panicking big time but Clemente shows no emotion. We walk jerkily forward.

'We signal left or right to change direction.' Clemente points his forefinger left and we walk left. He points right and the tape cuts into my skin as he changes direction.

'One more thing,' Sky says. 'The males will wear blindfolds.'

Clemente's head jerks up. 'No.'

I remember his fear of losing his vision. Maybe this is more of Sky's payback, thinking he wants to be leader.

'We can always do the crunch challenge instead,' Sky says.

'Fine!' Clemente snaps. 'I'll do it.'

Why? I've seen how many pull-ups this guy can do. Crunches aren't going to be a problem for him. Then I realise why. He isn't worried for himself, he's worried for

Jack. Crunches are a definite no-no for Jack, but knowing him, he'd be too proud to admit it and do them anyway.

Clemente mutters in Spanish as we pass the black ties around. I help him secure it above his forehead.

Clemente nods at Victor. 'Look. He's freaking out. We can't do this.'

Victor does look pretty shaky.

'You want to do this?' Sky asks.

'Of course,' Victor says.

'Watch out!' Mikki swishes at something in the water – jellyfish.

I move my leg just in time, nearly pulling Clemente off his feet, and it sails past.

'Let's vote on it,' Clemente tells Sky.

She lets out an exasperated hiss. 'I vote yes.'

Victor and Mikki vote yes, Clemente and Jack vote no. They turn my way. I don't have a choice. If I want to learn the truth about Elke, I need to remain in Sky's inner circle, so I can't let her see me doubting her any more.

A little muscle in Clemente's jaw tightens. Sky hands out masks. I pull mine over my head and tug the strap tight.

'Forget what I said about the hand signals,' Clemente tells me. 'You lead us to the rocks. When you find one, pass it to me and I carry it.'

As we wade through the shallows, I try to calm my thoughts.

Mikki nudges me urgently. 'Are you okay?'

I flash her a thumbs up, then dip my face in to test the mask. Visibility is good today and the white rocks stand out against the darker ones. We swim the last few metres until we're directly above them.

The men lower their blindfolds. I imagine how it will feel to them down there: not completely helpless but close to it. Trusting their partner. It's so bloody dangerous.

Sky pumps her arm. 'Fear is fuel!'

'Panic is lethal!' we chorus.

Is it just me or do the others sound as low in enthusiasm as I feel?

'Ready?' Clemente's hand gropes for my shoulder.

'Yep.' I can't shake the bad feeling I have about this.

'Go,' Sky shouts.

When we duck under, it's as though I've joined a beautifully choreographed ballet and I'm the only one who doesn't know the moves. Sky and Victor move in smooth tandem motion. She picks up a rock and passes it to him. Jack has one already.

Clemente's leg is warm against mine. I jerk forward, tugging Clemente with me, until I can reach a rock. He shifts obligingly and I place it into his arms, but I need air now and the only way I can get to the surface is by pulling Clemente's leg with me. He tips forward, rock clutched against his chest. I snatch a breath and duck under, expecting him to need a breath too, but he yanks us back down. Sky is coming towards us, dragging Victor alongside her. She dives for the rock in Clemente's arms. He seems to realise what's happening and twists his torso to protect it.

It's funny to start with but all the air bubbles out of me when I laugh and I immediately need to surface to get another breath, except I can't because now we're full-on wrestling with Victor and Sky in a tangle of arms and legs. Mikki and Jack are miles away, and Mikki hasn't noticed what's going on.

There's a strange sound like water spluttering in a blocked plughole and I realise it's coming from Victor's mouth. He's taken his blindfold off and he's freaking out big time. Sky is still trying to get Clemente's rock.

I rip Clemente's blindfold off, then grab Victor by the arm and try to haul him to the surface but we're all tangled up. Victor scrabbles at his ankle, trying to get the tape undone, but he's panicking so much he can't do it.

Sky watches him with the detached curiosity of a scientist. What's wrong with her? If we don't get Victor up fast, he's going to drown. I try to get his tape off but he's lashing out everywhere and I'm desperate for air. Clemente releases his rock, points to me, then grabs Victor's left side. Catching on, I grab Victor's other arm and between us we haul him and Sky to the surface. As I gasp for air, Clemente ducks down again and manages to loosen Victor's tape enough that Victor can pull free of Sky.

Coughing and choking, Victor runs through the shallows and sinks to the sand, where he rocks back and forth, arms wrapped around his head.

I've only ever seen PTSD attacks on telly. This is the first one I've seen in real life. I turn on Sky. 'That was so fucking dangerous.'

She raises her eyebrow. 'And your point is . . .?'

'It's not normal, doing stuff like this.'

'We aren't normal people. Do you want to be normal, Kenna? Because I don't.'

The irony doesn't escape me. Not so long ago I might have said the same thing. 'You go too far. Way too far. You're playing with death.'

A slow smile spreads across Sky's face. 'And it feels so good.'

CHAPTER 55

KENNA

Back in the clearing, as soon as I've changed out of my wet clothes, I confront Mikki. 'Someone could have drowned this afternoon.'

Mikki is putting on her running shoes. 'They didn't, though, did they?'

'More from luck than anything else. Sky knows Victor has a problem. Clemente warned her that exercise was a bad idea.'

The others are going about their normal business as though nothing happened. Sky is stretched out on a yoga mat, Jack too.

'What are you doing here, Mikki?' I say. 'These guys are so fucked up.'

'They're my friends.' She glares at me, but there's doubt in her tone.

'How well do you really know them? You were just as freaked out as I was when we saw the blood on that rock. Anyway, they only like you because you're funding

291

their surfing.' I catch her hurt look and I instantly feel terrible.

'They only let you join because you're a sports therapist,' she retorts.

This hadn't occurred to me, but she's probably right. Considering I only joined to buy time to convince Mikki to leave, it's ridiculous how stung I feel, but this is about Mikki, not me. 'What happens when your cash runs out?'

'I'll find another job.' Mikki straightens, bottom lip trembling.

I gesture to her shoes, hating that I've hurt her. 'Going running? Can I come?'

She hesitates. 'Is it okay if I go on my own?'

'Sure.' I'm so frustrated. How can I get through to her?

Clemente is at the barbecue frying onions. Victor's supposed to be on dinner duty tonight.

I tap Clemente on the shoulder. It's a warm evening and he's bare-chested, as usual. 'Want a hand?'

He swings to face me. He doesn't speak; he just looks. In the tension of the challenge, a level of trust built up between us, despite me siding against him in the vote beforehand. There was touching – a lot of it – but our interaction was practical and efficient and I felt surprisingly comfortable with him. Now it's as though he's flicked a switch. The heat in his eyes makes my insides tighten with a different sort of tension. It's a long time since a guy looked at me like that.

I step backwards. 'This sharing thing. I'm not into it.'

His eyes don't leave mine. 'Neither am I.'

The nearest tree is covered in cream blossom. Its

heady smell fills my nose. 'Yet you slept with Sky.' I throw it at him.

'Yeah.' Slight defensiveness. 'It was a few months after my wife had died. She . . .' He searches for a word. 'Jumped on me. I was single; it was a one-off.'

'And how was it?'

Clemente's eyes soften. 'You don't need to know that. I can tell that from the sound of your voice. The sharing thing was Sky's idea. Most of us, our parents split up or they're so unhappy we don't know why they're still together, and we didn't want to repeat their mistakes, so we all agreed to it because it made sense at the time.'

'But now?'

He sighs. 'It makes life pretty complicated, but maybe that's how relationships are.'

A crash from behind us makes us spring apart. Victor grips his surfboard with two hands and rams it at a tree. I watch in shock as he backs off and raises it again. He runs at the tree, yelling at the top of his voice, and snaps the board in half around the trunk. Gripping the front half, he rams it nose first into the ground.

From the resigned looks of the others, I guess that they've seen this before. Sky watches with little emotion. After his shouts have stopped, she walks over and says something I don't hear. Victor jerks her round to face him and I stiffen, scared he's going to attack her.

Sky doesn't flinch. 'Come with me.'

The broken surfboard drops from Victor's hand.

'Goodnight, guys,' Sky says and leads Victor away.

The others exchange looks but nobody comments. I hug my arms around my chest, shaken by Victor's anger.

Now I'm wondering if he's taken his anger out on anything besides his surfboards.

The moment between me and Clemente is broken. Suddenly I long to be in the water, to wash off the tension of the day. I help Clemente cook a basic pasta and as soon as we've cleared up I head down the track to the beach.

The sand is deserted. The peachy sky rings with the raucous squawks of the white cockatoos that flap above the treetops. The isolation hits me afresh. From this vantage point, you can't see a single sign of human habitation. It feels like a scene from *The Lost World*. Any moment now a T-rex is going to come rampaging out of the trees.

There's a flash of movement to my right and I'm realise I'm not alone after all. I'd assumed Sky and Victor had gone to their tent, but Sky is lying back in the shallows, topless. The water recedes and a head bobs up: Victor. Their clothes are further up the sand.

I hear Sky's voice, low and honeyed: *That's it, baby.*

Victor gasps for breath. Sky clasps the back of his head and pushes him back below the surface. Seconds pass and Sky's head tilts back in pleasure. It's certainly a novel way to practise breath control. I'll swim another time. Not wanting them to see me, I back away into the bushes, needle-sharp bristles spiking my ankles.

A noise from behind makes me twist around in fright.

Clemente puts his hands in the air. 'Sorry. I didn't mean to scare you.'

Embarrassed by my overreaction, I gesture to Sky and Victor. 'Look.'

'Yeah. They do it a lot.' Clemente remains a careful

distance away, as though he knows I'm wary of him. As though he expects it, even.

And that makes me sad, somehow. 'There's something sadistic about it.'

'All the best trainers are. And he wants it.'

'Our training exercise earlier, you can't say that was good for him. And the way she makes him work out. She *hurts* him. She crosses a line, don't you think?'

Clemente looks thoughtful. 'No. If my partner asks me to do something to them, I try to do it.' His jaw tightens. 'Even if it hurts them.'

I turn the words over in my head, wondering if they relate to Elke.

Chapter 56

Kenna

It's almost dark by the time we return to the tents.

Ryan approaches with a strained expression. 'Can I talk with you?'

'Sure,' I say.

'Over there?' Ryan points to the trees.

I follow him cautiously, remembering his fingers around the spear.

Ryan turns to face me. 'I've been thinking about what you said about my family and I've decided to fly back.'

Wow, that's a turnaround. 'I'm glad.' And I *am* genuinely happy, partly for little Ava, even if Ryan doesn't work things out with his wife, but more importantly because it means one less tribe member. He's clearly a guy on the edge and the Bay will be a safer place without him.

He clears his throat. 'Only I don't quite have enough for the air fare.'

'Oh. How much do you need?'

'Another hundred or two? I'll pay you back as soon as I get back home. You can write me your address.'

I hesitate. Since it was me who talked him into leaving, I feel obliged to help him but I'm reluctant to give him my address – I hardly know him. 'I can give you a hundred, but I don't have much more to spare.'

'Thanks.'

I get my wallet from my tent and he stuffs the money into the pocket of his shorts.

'How are you getting to the airport?' I ask.

Ryan looks cagey. 'Same way I got here. Walk to the highway, then hitch-hike. But I don't want them to know I'm going so I'll slip off in the night.'

He disappears into the trees, leaving me wondering if it was just a complex ploy to get money out of me. Where's he going? Glancing around to check none of the others are watching, I decide to follow him.

In the twilight his pale blue T-shirt is easy enough to spot amongst the greens and browns. He's heading for the cliff. I hang back as he reaches the railing. He crouches down. I can't see what he's doing, but he takes the cash from his pocket and reaches down with both hands over the cliff edge. Half a minute or so later, he straightens and returns my way. Just in time, I shift back into the bushes.

Once I'm sure he's gone, I head to the railing. I'm too scared to climb over it – the sign says erosion after all and the rock is visibly crumbling, so I lie on the earth and crawl forward, trying to see what he put here. Far below, the waves rumble and crash. There's a hole in the rock a few inches down. I can't see it, but I can feel it. I delve into it, hoping there aren't spiders, and feel smooth, cold metal. I pull it out to find a small rectangular tin that once held biscuits.

I move back a little and open it. Inside is a thick wad of money. Unlike the rest of the group, Ryan doesn't have a car where he can lock his valuables away, so it makes sense that he'd stash stuff here, rather than risk leaving it in his tent. Below the cash is a bank card that expired a month ago and two books, one dark blue, the other burgundy. The first is an American passport for *Ryan Higgs*. My breath dies in my throat when I see the other one. *Deutschland. Reisepass.* A German passport.

My hand shakes as I flick through it. At last I find the photo page. A young blonde woman, and the name: *Elke Hartmann*.

In my shock, I almost drop it. My mind is jumping to some dark conclusions right now. Did Ryan keep it as a trophy after he killed her? I shiver, remembering his expression as he squashed the ants. He needed money. Maybe he killed her in order to rob her? A leaf falls onto my shoulder, making me jump.

Think logically, I tell myself. I take deep breaths, searching for an innocent reason why he might have it. Maybe Elke dropped it and Ryan found it on his wanderings after she'd gone, but if that was the case, surely he'd have shown the others. It seems likely they don't know he has it or he wouldn't keep it here.

The stunted trees along the clifftop look like monsters. I don't want to hang about here in case Ryan comes back.

Elke's mother's tearful face appears before my eyes. This passport might be all that's left of her daughter. If I put it back, it might disappear like the rest of her. I slide it into my pocket and hurry back down the trail. I'll show it to Mikki and see what she thinks we should do.

Yet the clearing is empty when I return. The others must have gone to bed. I crawl into my tent and lie there with the passport digging into my hip, wondering if I've made a terrible mistake.

CHAPTER 57

RYAN

I lie still and silent in my tent, waiting for the others to fall asleep. Did Kenna ever see the note I left her? She hasn't stopped snooping around, asking questions and stirring things up. I get flustered every time I talk to her in case I let something slip.

Anyway, I have all the money I need now – as much as I'm going to get out of these guys at least – so I'm out of here. When I'm sure the others are sleeping, I creep from my tent and hurry down the trail to the cliffs to retrieve my tin.

The sky is navy blue and it's pitch dark in the shadow of the trees. I don't know why I told Kenna about Ava; I haven't told any of the others. It came out before I could stop myself. Still, maybe it wasn't such a bad thing, since it prompted her to cough up a hundred bucks. Annoying as she is, it's hard to dislike her because she actually seems to care. Not that much, though – she only gave me a hundred bucks and I saw several hundred more in her wallet.

Despite what I told Kenna, I'm not going home, no matter how much I want to see Ava. I can't risk going to jail. There are plenty more beaches in Australia. I'll find a nice quiet one where nothing bad happens.

When I flew out from the States, I had twenty thousand dollars in cash. Obviously I couldn't leave that much in my tent. The hole in the rock, hidden and dry, seemed the best option available at the time. Now I have just three thousand left. I've done well to stretch out my funds this long – thanks mostly to Mikki.

I duck behind a tree trunk and listen for anyone who might be following me. Nothing: just birds, leaves and the ocean. I get nervous up here. I check around once again to make sure I'm alone before I lean over the edge of the cliff and reach down into the hollow.

The waves splash up against the rocks, far below. My hand gropes into empty space. Where's my cash box? There's a plummeting feeling inside my stomach as though I'm tumbling over the edge. My money – it's gone! This is a disaster. Who the fuck . . .?

My fingertips touch cold metal. But I didn't push the tin in this far. Someone moved it. Is my money still in there? I scrabble at the box, nails scraping painfully against the rock, trying and failing to get a grip on the smooth metal. It's stuck, wedged in place. Fuck! The chances of it having money in there are just about nil, but I need to check so I shuffle forward and climb a few steps down the cliff.

At last I see it: the gleam of silver in the dark hole. The rock grazes my knuckles as I wiggle the box, which finally shifts enough that I can slide it out, but I need two hands to open it so I dig my toes in to make sure I have solid footholds. Blood smears the tin as I claw off the lid.

I'm barely breathing. If it's empty, I don't know what I'll do. The lid comes off and . . . relief. The cash is still there. As I lift it out to count it, a shadow falls over the box.

I look up in shock to see a figure standing there. By the time I realise what's happening, hands are pressing on my shoulders, forcing me backwards.

And then I'm falling . . .

Chapter 58

Kenna

A scream wakes me – long and loud. Mikki!

I struggle out of my sleeping bag, bolt from my tent and hurtle straight into Sky. 'Sorry!' I gasp.

Sky grips a torch in one hand; her other hand is on the door of Mikki's tent. It takes me a moment to realise she isn't opening the tent but holding it shut.

Mikki draws breath and screams again.

'What are you doing?' I ask.

'Fear therapy.' Sky grips a string looped through the puller of the zip. Around her neck is a stopwatch.

In the shadows behind her are Clemente and Victor. Jack is presumably with Mikki; Ryan must still be in his tent.

Another long scream from Mikki. Sleep still has a grip of me and I'm struggling to make sense of what's happening.

Jack's voice from inside the tent: 'Breathe! You're doing well.'

Three sharp screams, one after the other.

My brain latches on. There's only one thing that could make Mikki scream like that. Moths. Did Sky put moths in there?

'Get me out!' Mikki pummels the tent door.

'She's had enough,' I say.

Sky glances at the stopwatch. 'Not yet.'

More screams from Mikki. I tug at Sky's arm. 'Let her out!'

Sky doesn't budge. I try to wrestle the zip from her. Arms circle my waist and Victor lifts me off my feet. I flail at him in vain as he carts me across the clearing. When he puts me down, I try to get back to Mikki's tent, but he blocks me.

'You can't think that's helping her,' I shout.

'It's on me!' Mikki shrieks.

I appeal to Clemente. 'She's losing it!'

I can tell he doesn't like this but he makes no move to help her.

Mikki releases scream after scream.

I can't bear it. 'She's hysterical. Help her!'

At last, Clemente steps forward. 'Okay. Enough.'

I dodge Victor and launch myself at Sky as Clemente reaches her. Between the two of us, Clemente and I wrestle her from the door; the tent unzips and Mikki stumbles out.

She's clawing at her wrist hard enough to draw blood. As I rush to help her, her arm flails, catching me on my ear. I step backwards in shock. She scratched me. Clemente jumps in and restrains her hands. I pull her tight. 'It's okay.'

She sobs into my chest, arms still moving as if of their own accord.

Jack emerges from their tent.

I turn on him. 'What's wrong with you? Why would you go along with this?'

Jack looks sheepish. 'We do it every month. Mikki reckons it helps.'

Mikki's arm is dripping blood, her tattoo all but obliterated by her nails.

'Have you got a bandage?' I ask.

'I'll get one.' Jack produces a first-aid box from somewhere.

'Put her in my tent,' I say, once he's stuck a plaster over her wrist.

I hold the flyscreen open and Jack ushers Mikki inside. She curls in a ball in the corner.

'No moths in here,' I say. 'See? Shine the torch around.'

Clemente steps forward to shine a pen-torch into the tent but Mikki keeps sobbing.

'Stay with her,' I tell Jack. 'I'll get your sleeping bags.'

It's too dark in Mikki's tent to see if the moth's still in there. I shake out their sleeping bags and pass them in to Jack.

'Where will you sleep?' he asks.

'In your tent.' The moth is presumably in there somewhere, which isn't a pleasant thought, but moths are one of the few insects I'm not afraid of – they don't bite or sting, as far as I know – so I'll deal with it.

I'm still wearing the shorts I had on earlier, too scared to take them off in case the passport disappears. It stabs into me as I grab my sleeping bag from my tent, crawl out and zip the tent shut behind me.

I turn to Sky. 'Look what you've done to her!'

Sky folds her arms. 'The exercises we do. You think we're training to be better at surfing? No. We're training to be fearless, because that will make us better full stop, not just at surfing. And who doesn't want to be better?'

'I wouldn't call that better, would you?'

All is quiet in my tent, so presumably Jack has managed to calm Mikki down. Fake marriage or not, it's clear he does actually care for her.

'It's your choice to be here, Kenna. If you don't like it . . .' Sky angles her head towards the vehicles.

But that's the whole problem. I'm stuck here, because Mikki needs me more than ever.

'Fear is fuel,' Sky says. 'We should experience it every day. The waves are small here most of the time, so we have to seek fear elsewhere.'

'So you *aim* to scare people?'

Sky looks at me coldly. 'You interfere with something you do not understand.'

Her words replay in my head. The stiltedness of them. I realise for the first time that she isn't a native English speaker. 'You're not Aussie, are you?'

'I never said I was.' Her tone is muted now. Caught out.

Now I'm wondering why I didn't pick up on it sooner. The funny way she pronounces certain words, how her Js are more like Ys. But my mind was on other things. My heart thumps as I process what this might mean.

Clemente and Victor stand at a distance, listening in.

For once I have Sky on the back foot. I seize my chance to get some answers from her. 'Where are you from?'

She shrugs. 'Sweden.'

I've noticed how Swedish people often speak amazing English. There's a Swedish masseur who works from a studio opposite mine and you can hardly hear his accent. 'Do you have permanent residence?'

Sky holds my gaze as if to say she has nothing to hide, but I notice her eyes have widened just a bit. 'Yeah. Through my work.'

Now I realise how little I actually know about her. Funny, the others chatted about their lives and backgrounds but somehow she always avoided it. 'What do you do?'

'I'm a clinical psychologist.'

All the air leaves my lungs. No wonder she's so good at getting in our heads. I'd imagined she must do something related to sport. I know from what Mikki told me that it's not easy to get residence here; they don't grant it to just anyone. One way to get it is through marriage, another is through your profession. They're short of certain skilled workers and if your occupation is in demand, you can apply, but from what I've heard, it's a long process.

'Do you have an Australian passport?' I'm not sure why I'm asking; it's a stab in the dark as I hunt about for more to attack her with.

She blinks. 'Yes.' Her slight hesitation gives her away.

'How long have you been here?'

'Two, three years?'

Again, a split-second hesitation. Something's not right. Clemente and Victor stand still and tense. What do they know that I don't?

I turn back to Sky. Whatever it is, she's clearly not going to volunteer it.

'It's late,' she says. 'I'm tired.' With that, she heads to her tent.

Suddenly I remember the article about missing back-packers. One of them was Swedish. I might be clutching at straws here but I hazard a guess and I call after her: 'You're one of the missing backpackers.'

Slowly she turns and shoots a look at Clemente. He shrugs, expressionless. I only saw the photos briefly. Ryan stood out in his smart suit, but I don't remember what the others looked like, yet I think I'm onto something.

'Yes.' There's a note of defiance in Sky's tone.

'Let me guess,' I say. 'You came here on holiday and liked it so much you decided to stay.'

'A working holiday visa, yes.' She turns and ducks into her tent.

I stare after her. Have I got to the bottom of it? Is she simply an overstayer? Clemente's guilty expression suggests otherwise.

'I want to talk to you,' I tell him.

'Okay.' Clemente clicks his pen-torch on and leads me away from the tents.

I follow him, sleeping bag draped around my neck like a scarf. 'I want to get this straight. First it was you and your wife, Jack and Victor who were coming here. Then Sky joined you, started training you and sorted the deal with the wardens.'

'Right.' Clemente's face looks eerie lit up from below.

'What was your wife's name?' I say, realising I've never asked.

He looks at me uncertainly, and resignation passes over his face. 'Sky.'

All the breath rushes out of me once again. Clemente looks at me, braced for the questions he knows will come.

'It's not a common name,' I say.

'Yeah.'

'What happened to her?'

Clemente looks away. 'I don't want to talk about it.'

'No. You can't go silent on me again. I need to know.'

'You don't want to know. Trust me. You really don't.'

I hug my sleeping bag around me. 'Sky isn't really called Sky, is she?'

Clemente purses his lips.

I strain to make the connections. 'Let me guess. She took on your wife's identity after she died because she wanted Australian residence?'

Clemente sighs. 'Yeah.'

My skin prickles. 'What's her real name?'

'Greta.'

Greta. It suits her somehow. 'Why do you call her Sky?'

'She asked it,' Clemente says. 'To make it a habit, you know? Otherwise we might call her Greta in front of someone else and give it away.'

'How long was it after Greta joined the Tribe before your wife died?'

'A few months.'

I give him a pointed look. Victor said the best trainers get in your head. Did Greta see an opportunity and get in Clemente's wife's head, in a way that prompted her to kill herself?

'No,' Clemente says, apparently realising what I'm thinking. 'They were friends.'

He seems certain. Yet she gained residence papers from Clemente's wife's death, which gives her a motive for killing her.

'Why would you let her take on your wife's identity?' I ask.

'I asked myself what my wife would have thought, and she would have wanted it.' Clemente's voice cracks. 'It was the only positive that could come from it, her friend being able to remain in the country she loved.'

'You don't think Greta might have . . . done something to your wife, because she wanted her identity?'

Clemente's answer is instant. 'No.'

I reach to my pocket to finger the passport. 'What about Elke? Do you think Greta did something to her?'

He sighs. 'I really don't know.'

I study his face and sense he's hiding something from me.

CHAPTER 59

KENNA

I crawl out of Mikki's tent, feeling like I hardly slept. Elke's passport is still in my pocket.

A hand grabs my shoulder and I squeak in shock.

'Morning, Kenna!' It's Victor. For a big guy, he's incredibly light on his feet. I didn't hear him approach.

'Are you okay?' There's concern in his dark eyes.

'Yeah, just tired.'

The others are eating breakfast. Ryan and Mikki aren't up yet. I hurriedly help myself to muesli.

'Kenna is so nervous this morning,' Victor announces as I sit down.

'Why are you nervous, Kenna?' Sky asks in a caring tone.

'The waves,' I lie, remembering the upcoming cyclone. 'They're going to be huge.'

'We need to surf them,' she says. 'So you get a chance to work on your fear.'

I force myself to nod. No matter what Clemente thinks,

311

I suspect she's involved in the death of his wife – and possibly Elke's as well. It was dangerous challenging her last night. I need to be more careful in future.

Victor seems his usual loud and cheery self, slapping out a rhythm on his thighs as he eats. The broken pieces of his surfboard have magically disappeared; one of the others must have cleared them away. I search Victor's face for a sign that he remembers yesterday's outburst: embarrassment, awkwardness – even looking around for his board – but there's nothing. It's as though it never happened.

Mikki emerges from my tent.

I hurry over to her. 'How are you?'

'I'm fine. Look, I appreciate that you wanted to help last night, but I want to cure my phobia.'

'But you don't want to go that far, surely?'

'It's working.' She sounds snappish. 'Soon I'll be fixed.'

'What does it matter if you're scared of moths? I hate most insects but I just try not to get near them.'

'It's not just about the moths. Overcoming a fear – any fear – makes you stronger.' Mikki is parroting Sky now. 'And I *am* stronger, haven't you noticed? I used to be terrified surfing waves above head height. Now I'm not.'

I lower my voice to a whisper. 'Sky isn't who she says she is.'

Mikki frowns. 'What do you mean?'

'She's a psychologist from Sweden and she's here illegally.'

'I know,' she snaps. 'Just drop it!'

I watch helplessly as she heads off to get breakfast.

I didn't get a chance to tell her about Elke's passport. Still no sign of Ryan.

'Anyone seen Ryan?' I call.

Nobody has.

I've never known him to sleep in before. I head cautiously to his tent. 'Knock, knock!'

No answer. I peer inside to see a bulging backpack, sleeping bag strapped on, but no Ryan.

Something clamps around my leg. Stifling a scream, I turn to see Sky.

'What are you doing?' she asks.

'Looking for Ryan.'

'He'll be off in the trees, doing Ryan-stuff. And if I were you, I wouldn't go in there. He's pretty protective over his stuff.'

Elke's passport is burning a hole in my pocket. Maybe it's for the best that Ryan's not here. I feel certain that Clemente doesn't know Ryan has it – he would never have let Ryan keep it. I wonder how they'd react if I showed it to them.

I follow Sky back to the others. Hoping I'm doing the right thing, I pull out the passport. 'I found this.'

'What is it?' Clemente asks.

There's no sign on his face that he knows what it is, and the others look equally bewildered.

I flick through the pages. In my hurry I can't find the photo. *Calm down, Kenna*. Here we go.

Clemente has a plate of nuts on his lap. It slips to the floor, sending the nuts flying as he lunges for the passport. He peers at the photo, then inspects the other pages before looking up with a baffled expression. The others crowd in and pass the passport around.

What happens next is terrifying. They glance at each other, Mikki included, drawing almost imperceptibly closer until they're huddled in like they were when I arrived. Turning on a common enemy.

Me.

Are they *all* in on it? Even Mikki?

'Where did you find it?' Clemente asks.

'I followed Ryan yesterday. He has a hiding place near the cliff.' I'm careful not to say exactly where it is. 'He keeps his passport and money there. And this.'

A hushed silence falls over them. The towels flap on the line, like war drums.

Predictably, Sky appoints herself spokesperson. 'It was strange,' she says slowly. 'Elke disappeared in the night. We assumed she must have gone swimming or fallen off the cliff or into the river, something like that.'

'Right.' I keep my voice casual. Whether I believe her or not, I'm outnumbered, so I must pretend that I do.

Sky goes on. 'A storm was raging. Clemente wanted to call in a search party but the road was flooded so we couldn't call for help. Then we realised her little daypack was gone. Her big backpack and board were still here, as though she'd left in a hurry.'

Surely Elke wouldn't have left without her passport. 'So you didn't report it, once the flood had gone down?'

A look passes between Clemente and Sky.

'She washed in a day later,' Clemente says.

Sky's lips tighten as though she didn't want him to say that.

'Dead?' I ask.

'Yeah.' Clemente's voice is strained.

I study his face wondering if I'm finally hearing the truth.

'She had some shark bites,' Mikki says.

I stare at her. She *knew* and didn't tell me?

So Elke's dead. I'm embarrassed to find my eyes watering. I don't know why I feel so crushed when I never even met the girl.

'We aren't sure if the shark got her before she drowned or after,' Sky says.

I swallow hard. 'Then what?'

'Shark deaths are international news, Kenna.' Sky's tone is calm and reasonable. 'If we reported it, we'd bring the authorities here and all the news channels. Sorrow Bay would be seen and talked about by every surfer in Australia.'

Clemente looks at me as though begging me to understand. 'I wanted to report it. But what was the point? It wouldn't bring her back to life.'

'So where's her body?' I ask.

Another look passes between Sky and Clemente.

'We let the ocean take her.' With that, Clemente lowers his head and presses his knuckles into his eye sockets.

His sadness is all too convincing. I picture Elke's poor savaged body sinking to the seabed, never to be found, leaving her mother to search in vain.

'You never found her daypack?' I ask.

'No,' Clemente says.

'What did you do with the rest of her stuff?'

'We discussed it and decided it would look bad if someone found it here. People might think we'd robbed her. So we buried her large backpack in the trees. The surfboard we kept.' Clemente gestures to a board nearby, grimacing as though it gives him a bad taste in his mouth.

'So why did Ryan have her passport?' I press.

Nobody seems to know.

'I suppose she dropped it and he found it,' Sky says finally.

'But why didn't he tell anyone?' I say. 'It's odd, don't you think?'

'This is a dangerous place,' Sky says. 'Accidents happen.'

The others nod sadly. There's an awkward silence. Eventually Jack changes the subject to the upcoming cyclone. Victor makes a few lame jokes but he's the only one who laughs and even that sounds hollow.

When the group disperses, I head for Mikki. 'I can't believe you didn't tell me about Elke.'

'Sorry.' Mikki gives me a pained look. 'I wanted to, but we had a pact.'

I glance at Ryan's tent, puzzling over his packed bags. Did he realise Elke's passport had disappeared from his tin? Was that what drove him into hiding? 'Will you come with me? I want to see if his tin of money is still there.'

'Sure.' Mikki slips her toes into her flip-flops.

The trail looks dark in the shade. I wrench off a branch from a nearby tree and finger the sharp end. Better than nothing.

Mikki gives me a funny look.

'For the snakes,' I say.

I'm grateful for Mikki's company. The trees and bushes are playing tricks with my eyes, and I'm seeing things that aren't there, getting spooked out by creaks and movements of branches. Something crashes through the undergrowth away from us. I freeze but I can't hear it any more.

'Just an animal,' Mikki says.

I feel like Ryan is going to jump out any moment.

We reach the clifftops and I delve into the hollow. The tin isn't there and I have no idea what that means.

Something occurs to me. 'Sky said in the joining ceremony that nobody ever leaves. Ryan told me he was planning to leave.'

Mikki's eyes reflect her surprise. 'Really?'

'Yeah, he was sick of it here and missing his family. He'd packed his bags. What if someone saw and did something to him?'

Mikki stares at me. 'No. They'd never go that far.'

'Jack brought some girls here before he met you, right? Do you know if they joined the Tribe?'

'No, I think they were only here for a few days.'

'So as far as we know, no fully fledged members of the Tribe have ever left. Not alive anyway.' In my head, Ryan has gone from perpetrator to possible victim in the space of just a few seconds. But the more I think about it, the more likely it seems.

Mikki frowns. 'Ryan goes off all the time.'

I reach for her arm. 'Please, Mikki. We have to get out of this place or we might be next.'

She snatches it away. 'I've had it with you trying to get me to leave. This is my life now and it's yours too. It's sad that Elke died but it was an accident. These guys are my friends and I trust them.'

CHAPTER 60

KENNA

Just visible in the gaps between the leaves, an aircraft passes thousands of metres above. The pale shape is a jarring reminder of the outside world, which suddenly seems even further away. Right now, I would give anything to be on that plane.

Clemente and Sky are sparring under the trees when Mikki and I return. Despite Mikki's resistance, I haven't given up on getting her to leave with me. I just need to go harder at my plan to cause a rift – make the Tribe turn on each other and they might rip each other to pieces.

Victor is working out nearby. I head over to him. 'Aren't you jealous?'

'What?' Victor says.

I nod in Sky's direction. 'She likes him. Can't you tell?' I hate that I have to do this. Despite all that's happened, it feels like Clemente and I are beginning to trust each other, but if he finds out what I'm doing, the trust will be broken.

Victor's eyes darken and there it is again: fury. This time I know I didn't imagine it. Shit. Now I want to take back what I said. I think I've put Clemente at risk.

A gust of wind lifts one of the mats and blows it into the trees. Victor chases after it.

Sky pulls her boxing gloves off. 'That wind's really picking up. We need to secure everything.'

I join the others hammering down tent pegs. Oh God – a cockroach just ran over my toe. I snatch my foot away. Somehow I manage not to scream and it scuttles away under a pile of dead leaves.

Sky looks at me with amusement. Oh, shit. I can't have her knowing about my fear of insects. The idea of being trapped in my tent with one . . .

'I nearly trod on it,' I say, as though I'm worried about the cockroach's welfare rather than my own, but I don't think she's convinced.

She turns to the others and raises her voice. 'Let's put all the gym stuff in the men's toilet, and everyone use the women's for now.'

'The clearing won't flood, will it?' I ask.

Clemente is halfway up a tree, tightening the tarpaulin. 'No, but the road might. Hey, Victor, can you pass me that twine?'

I watch nervously as Victor hands him it.

'We need to get that firewood bagged up ahead of the rain,' Sky calls.

Mikki finds some bags.

'Have you ever been in a cyclone?' I ask as she and I work side by side.

'Back in Hawaii we had a few, but I can't remember

much. We had some good thunderstorms in Sydney this summer. Jack's windscreen got smashed by hailstones.'

Jack picks up a bag of wood. 'Shit, I didn't think of that. Better put something over the cars, hey?'

Mikki glances sideways at me.

'What?' I ask.

'You're not going to stay here, are you? I can feel it. Your heart's not in it.'

I don't want to lie to her, but I'm nervous about the others hearing. 'I only have a tourist visa,' I say carefully – although the lack of a valid visa didn't stop Sky or Ryan.

Mikki's face falls. 'It won't be the same here without you.'

I've been here for eight days now but somehow it feels like double that. 'I'm not going back to London, though.'

'Really?'

'I need to be by the beach. I'm moving back to Cornwall.'

Mikki stares at me. 'Right.'

I squeeze her hand. 'Don't worry, I'm not going anywhere yet.'

I look at her slim fingers, thinking again how soft she is compared to the rest of them. I can't leave without her. I really can't.

Sky is rolling up yoga mats outside the toilet block. I've talked to Ryan and Clemente about their families, with varying degrees of success, but I haven't yet tried it with Sky. Without her there isn't a Tribe. I'm getting desperate now. A dangerous plan forms in my mind.

Before I can think better of it, I go over to her. 'Clemente told me last night your name is Greta.'

'Yes?' Sky's expression is guarded.

'I wanted to tell you last night but I didn't want the others to hear. I met your mum in Sydney.'

She gives me a startled look.

'She was handing out missing posters. I didn't recognise you from the photo but I remembered when I heard your name.' I'm taking a huge risk by doing this, because her mum might be well aware she's here in Australia, but Mikki did say she hadn't spoken to them.

Emotion flickers over Sky's face.

'I'm sure you had your reasons for leaving, but I thought you should know. She looked really sad.'

Her eyes soften. 'How was she?'

'She cried on my shoulder. I think she'd love to see you, or even just to hear you're okay.'

'It's so long since I saw her.' Sky's voice is strained. 'Does she still have her blonde curls or has she gone white?'

'Still blonde.' I hardly dare to breathe but I think I'm getting somewhere.

'Was she walking okay? She had knee surgery before I left.'

'As far as I could tell.'

'Does she still have her weird glasses?'

I gulp and hope for the best. 'Yes.'

Sky's expression changes. 'My mum died ten years ago, Kenna.'

I stare at her in horror.

'So why would you tell me that?' Her voice is soft but the look in her eyes isn't.

'Really? Sorry, I must have got it wrong and she was

your auntie.' I'm gabbling now. 'I don't think she said. I just assumed.'

'I don't have any aunties either. So why would you say that?'

I want to sink into the ground. 'It must have been a different Greta. Is it a common name?'

'I heard you talking to Ryan and Clemente about their families. So this was my turn, right?' Sky purses her lips. 'Clemente's a pain in the ass but we need him here. *Victor* needs him here. I prop Victor up as much as I can but he responds differently to another male. And of course Jack needs him too. So I'd appreciate if you could just shut up about families.'

'Okay,' I say weakly.

She regards me in silence for a moment. 'I lied to you. My mum isn't dead, as far as I know, but I haven't heard from her since I left Sweden.' She smiles a tight smile. 'You almost had me. For a moment I actually thought Mum had flown all the way to Australia to hand out posters and cry on strangers' shoulders over me. But she didn't even bother to come to the police station at the end of our road when I got in trouble as a teenager, because she was too drunk. I doubt she gives me a passing thought.'

I cannot think of a single response.

Sky tosses her dreadlocks over her shoulder. 'Anyway, guess what? I love this place. I'm not going anywhere. And neither is Mikki or any of the others. So whatever you're trying to do here, *stop it*.'

I look from her to Mikki in despair. I've tried everything I can and I'm all out of ideas.

'By the way, you have it,' Sky says. 'I wasn't sure, but I saw it just then.'

'Have what?' I ask.

Her smile returns. 'The killer instinct.'

The trees are closing in on me. It's as though the leaves and branches are knitting together to block out the sky. I have to get out of their shadow. Glancing around to check nobody's watching, I retrieve my stick and hurry down the trail to the beach.

It's a relief to be out in the open with the familiar horizon spreading before me, but the beach is an eerie place this morning. The sky is overcast with a ceiling of grey cloud so thick and low it's as if a roof has been erected over the world overnight. There are specks of liquid in the air – drops of rain mixed with sea spray.

The wind roars in my ears, flapping my T-shirt. The gulls face into it, shoulders hunched, or shelter in the hollows of footprints. A large white bird – a stork or an ibis? – strides along and takes off with much flapping, great body inching upwards. Watching it brings home how trapped I am.

Wet sand squidges under my soles as I head to the water. Stirred up by the storm, the waves are huge misshapen wedges. The tide's coming in. Dark blobs streak the sand. Are they . . . raisins? No, I realise, as I draw closer. Dead flies. Hundreds of them, washed into neat curves by the waves. Some are still moving, crawling up the sand in a hopeless race against the tide. Others are stuck on their backs, pedalling spidery legs in the air. A wave washes a group of them afloat like a miniature fleet of ships.

The gulls are having a field day gobbling up these juicy morsels. It's too much. My stomach heaves. I stoop and hurl my breakfast onto the sand. A couple of gulls take fright and flap up into the air. One settles again and takes a cautious mouthful of my vomit. I drop to my knees and retch, over and over, eyes screwed shut. Wishing that when I open them again, I might find myself somewhere else.

Something touches my hand. Startled, I open my eyes to see a fifty-dollar bill floating away. Is it Ryan's? I scan the ocean for more but don't spot any. A shadow passes overhead as black clouds race across the sky. Before long, they cover it entirely, turning day to night, at not even nine in the morning.

Lightning flashes on the horizon. A growl of thunder. Ahead, I make out a dark shape on the sand. At first I think it's a rock. All at once the world lights up in neon violet and I realise it's a person. As I race towards them, an almighty crack makes me flinch. It reverberates back and forth, only to be drowned out by an even louder crack.

Ryan lies motionless on his back, eyes closed, in pretty much the same position he was in the first time I met him. I hurry towards him, expecting him to jump up like he did before, but he doesn't move.

CHAPTER 61

KENNA

A wave washes up around Ryan's ankles. When the water subsides, I see his legs properly. They're swollen and bruised and his feet stick out at odd angles.

'Ryan!' I say.

No response, so I pat his cheek. It's damp and icy cold. I squeeze his shoulder and gently shake him. He flops back to the sand. For a moment the body before me isn't Ryan but Kasim. Dizziness overwhelms me. I stagger forward, place one hand on the sand for balance and screw up my eyes. When I open them, it's Ryan again. *Get a grip, Kenna!*

I scan in both directions down the beach but I can't see his surfboard. Maybe his leg rope ripped off and his board's floating about out there. Surely he wasn't swimming in these conditions? Either way, judging by the state of his legs, he got smashed on the rocks. I don't want to move him in case he's damaged his spine but another wave washes up to his waist, so I grip him under his armpits and drag him further up the sand, to the high-water line, where I start CPR, pumping his chest and breathing into his cold mouth.

The storm continues to build. The thunder comes in several varieties. Sometimes it's a jumbo jet taking off close by, scraping ever so slowly off the ground and roaring directly overhead, leaving an echo after its passing. Sometimes it's an awful accident on a building site: something – or someone – plummeting from a great height. Sometimes it's a sudden and deafening crack accompanied by a giant fork stretching across the sky as though the whole world is splitting apart.

I hear the rain before I feel it, spitting on the sand in a furious hiss, and then it's upon me, showering onto my head. By now, the thunder is almost constant and lightning flashes several times a second like a strobe light.

Minutes pass. *Breathe, Ryan!* But he remains unresponsive. I struggle to my feet.

Freezing water showers down as I run back. Tears roll down my face, mixing with the rain. Faster and faster I run up the track, bare feet skidding in the mud. Around the corner I crash into someone coming the other way. Clemente.

'He's dead!' I gasp. 'Ryan.'

Clemente gets over his shock quickly. 'Show me.'

We race back along the beach until we reach his body. I stand there as Clemente examines him.

'I tried,' I gasp. Then I'm crying again.

Clemente wraps his arms around me. I cry into his shoulder, my legs nearly collapsing beneath me. I'm crying for Ryan's wife and his daughter. And I'm crying for me. I'm really scared now.

*

'Dead?' Sky says.

'Are you sure?' Victor says.

Jack rubs his head. 'Shit.'

Back on the beach, the wind tears at our hair and clothing as we stand around Ryan's body.

Jack frowns. 'He was surfing?'

'It looks like it,' I say. 'Or swimming.'

Jack gestures to the ocean, where the wind is churning the surface into spiky peaks like egg white. 'Why would he surf in this? It was rubbish yesterday too.'

Ryan often surfed early before the rest of us, and given the tensions of the last few days it's hardly surprising if he preferred to surf alone. But Jack's right, it's barely surfable this morning.

Now that the shock is wearing off, the logical part of my brain is kicking in. Another death, which appears to be a tragic accident. Ryan wiped out on a large wave and his leg rope came open – possible in surf of this size, especially if the Velcro was worn – and he drowned before being washed back in. His surfboard could have washed up miles down the coast. Or maybe he went swimming and got smashed on the rocks.

But Ryan planned to leave and this brings the count to three deaths now. A suicide, a shark attack and a drowning. Unrelated tragedies? Or something else? I look down at Ryan's face, as though his pale lips might tell me the answer.

'We'll take him to the Meadow,' Sky says.

'I'll get spades,' Victor says, and jogs off.

Spades? I look at Sky in horror. 'You're not going to bury him?'

Sky's tone is sad but firm. 'What else can we do?'

'Call an ambulance,' I say.

I turn to Clemente, willing him to see reason.

'It's too late for that,' he says gently.

'Or the police . . .' Even as I say it, I see the problem. Ryan's an overstayer and once they figure that out, they'll wonder about the rest of us. Sky in particular can't risk that happening. Of course the visa issue is the least of it if one of them did, as I suspect, kill him. Even if Ryan's death is deemed an accidental drowning, Sorrow Bay will make the news, which is the last thing any of them want.

We stand there with the rain pelting our heads. I study their faces. Is one of them a killer? Sky's eyes meet mine as though she guesses what I'm thinking. Did she see Ryan packing his bags?

The rain goes up a notch. I've never seen it rain this hard. The sand is deserted; the gulls have taken cover.

When Victor returns, he, Clemente, Jack and Sky each lift one limb and carry Ryan along the beach, leaving me and Mikki to follow with the spades. As we turn into the trees, a wave washes high up the beach, erasing our footprints, leaving the wet sand pristine. As though we were never here.

Victor starts to whistle and the others join in. 'Sweet Jane'. At first I think we're heading towards the river, but they turn onto a different trail. Rain hisses down onto the leaves.

Sky's foot slips out from under her. Jack drops Ryan's ankle, leaving him in the mud to rush to her aid; Victor yanks Jack backwards and helps Sky up himself. Jack rubs his arm as they lift Ryan back up.

A familiar ridged trunk catches my eye, and soon after it

the tree with orange fruit that Ryan climbed up. We reach a tiny clearing, where they set him down. This must be roughly where I saw Ryan for the first time, lying in the dirt.

'What tree is he going to have?' Jack asks.

'Lime?' Victor says.

'Or peach?' Mikki says. 'He loved peaches.'

I listen in, puzzled. And notice the fruit in the tree behind her: purple apples like the ones we ate recently. *Sorrow fruit.* My stomach heaves as I make the connection. *To Sky,* they'd said as they raised their apples. I thought they were toasting Sky – Greta – as their leader but they were toasting the real Sky – it's her tree. They planted the tree on top of her grave, letting the rotting bodies feed the fruit. Which *I* ate. I retch and manage to disguise it as a cough.

Clemente sees me registering it and guilt flashes across his face.

The rain drums down on the leaves above. A kookaburra watches from a nearby branch, looking wet and dejected, as they dig a grave. They take turns with spades. The practised way they do it is chilling. How many times have they done this before? Beside the apple tree is what looks like a plum tree. Oh, shit. I think Elke's here too, buried beneath the earth.

Why would Ryan come here and lie on top of them? To grieve? Or to gloat?

Tearless and far too composed, Mikki sings 'Sweet Jane'. Eyes closed, she sways on the spot, her clear high voice rising above the sound of the shovel. I don't know her any more. She continues singing as she takes a turn with the shovel.

I watch her, appalled. I have to face it: she's in so deep with these guys that she's beyond saving. I need to save myself or risk being buried here in this lonely spot. I'm going to steal one of the vehicles and drive away.

Once the hole is dug, they lower Ryan into it. Lightning flashes, lighting up their faces. Six sad friends, gathered around a grave. Except they're dry-eyed, all of them.

Victor steps forward. 'You and me didn't always get on but we had some good times. Hope you find some waves up there, brother.'

Jack goes next. 'Ryan, you were a good bloke. Sorry I dropped in on you so many times.' His voice wavers.

I notice again how Jack shows the most emotion out of all of them. I feel terrible about leaving Mikki but at least she has Jack looking out for her. He's far from perfect but I think he'll protect her.

From the looks of it they're going to be tied up here for a while longer so I fake a sob. Heads turn in disapproval. It's not hard to summon tears. My grief is genuine. An intelligent man lying cold and still in an unmarked grave. I cry for Ryan's wife and most of all for his daughter, growing up without him, never knowing how much he loved her or what happened to him.

I lower my head, press my hand to my mouth and melt away into the bushes. As soon as I'm out of sight, I break into a run, bracing myself for someone to shout after me – but they're too caught up in the ceremony to notice.

This might be the only chance I have to make a break for it. My body is chilled through from the rain and my knees seize a few times as I run. I reach the clearing and check over my shoulder. Nothing, so I dive into Jack's tent. Where would he keep his car key? His black Quiksilver backpack is in a corner. It has pockets all over it. I check them one by one and in the fifth pocket I find it.

The trail is ankle deep with water in places. I splash through the puddles, key fob tight in my palm in an attempt to keep it dry. I can't wait to get away from this place. Halfway there, I remember that Jack said his tyre was fucked and curse inwardly but I don't have time to go back and look for the keys for the other vehicles, so I'll just have to hope the tyre will hold up long enough to get me to the motorway.

Damn! Why didn't I bring my phone? I could have recharged it in Jack's car and called for help as soon as I found a phone signal. Too late. If I can make it to the service station we stopped at, I can get help from there.

I reach the vehicles, gasping for breath, and stab the key fob. Jack's car opens with a click and I jump inside. My shorts squelch as I sit. It's an automatic transmission. I haven't driven one for years and it takes my panicking brain a moment to remember what to do. *D* for drive. No – *R* for reverse.

The chassis bumps up and down as I back out of the spot. The windscreen is running with water. It takes me several tries to locate the wipers. Good job the vehicle is a four-wheel drive. The track is thick with mud, the potholes full of water. As I creep round the corner, I glance over my shoulder to see if anyone's coming after me, but the back window is too fogged up to see out of. The engine roars as I drive up an incline. Tyres skid as I drive down. Around another corner my heart sinks. The weir. It was only a few metres wide on the way here, but now it extends as far as I can see. My foot hesitates on the gas. Should I try to drive through it? I'm tempted to, but I have visions of being trapped in the vehicle and swept all the way to the river.

Leaving the engine running, I jump out to see how deep it is. The water is cold and muddy. I splash through it up to my ankles, then my knees. Already the current is pulling at me. Two more steps and it's thigh deep. I can't drive through this.

I take deep breaths. I'll have to try again once the rain stops. Have they left the Meadow yet? If I hurry, I might get back to the tents before they do. I wade back to the car and climb in. The track is narrow. I'll have to do a three-point turn.

Wheels slithering, wipers flashing, it ends up taking me a dozen careful manoeuvres back and forth. As I pull into the original parking spot, the front left tyre sticks in a pothole and the vehicle refuses to budge. I find reverse and shove my foot down. The vehicle bounces backwards and the glove box falls open to reveal a wad of money.

I wonder immediately if it's Ryan's. No, Jack and Mikki probably just keep cash here because it's safer than leaving it in the tents. I lean across to see roughly how much there is and see something behind it. A wallet in lurid pink leather. I switch off the engine and reach for it. It could be a spare one of Mikki's but somehow I know it isn't – it's not her style. My hands shake as I rip open the Velcro. Half a dozen cards sit inside it, but no cash except a few dollars. I pull the cards out. There's a familiar photo on one of them. A pretty redhead. *Tanith O'Brien.*

CHAPTER 62

KENNA

A sound outside the car makes me jump. There's someone at the misted-up passenger window. I shut the glove box just in time.

The door is wrenched open. Victor leans in. 'What are you doing?'

Rain blows into my face. I have two seconds to come up with an answer. 'My period started. I didn't want to interrupt the ceremony. Mikki always has tampons in her car.'

This at least is true. Years ago, Mikki's period started suddenly when we were far from the nearest shop and she was wearing a white bikini. She had such a horror of it happening again that she kept an emergency tampon stash in her car, my car and everywhere else you could imagine.

Victor frowns. 'Why did you drive it?'

'The mud. It looked like it was sinking, so I moved it back a bit.' I can't tell if he believes me or not. 'Can you see if there's any tampons in the back?'

Wordlessly, he shuts the door and goes around to the rear. As he rummages, I open the glove box again. I don't know if he knows about the stolen wallet or not, and even if he does, I don't want him to know that *I* know.

Please let me find some tampons. My story will hold up better if I do. Sure enough, there are several shiny pink packets tucked away. I grab them, shut the glove box and jump out into the rain. 'Yay, I found some! Look!'

'Okay.'

Just as I'd hoped, Victor finds it hard to meet my eyes. He slams the rear door and doesn't say anything else as we head back. The thunderstorm has moved off but the wind has strengthened. Rain pelts us as we climb the small mound. The ground squelches underfoot. Mud and rocks have slid down from the hillside above, across the trail. I step carefully from rock to rock.

A flash of royal blue in the mud on the left. Victor is in front of me. I pause to look. Squinting through the rain, I make out a logo I recognise – the Rip Curl wave logo. I'm immediately thinking the worst. Is it a body? Victor glances back at me and I quickly walk on.

Breathe, Kenna. It's probably an item of clothing that was dumped – or buried – and washed down the hillside by the storm. It might have been there for years and be nothing to do with the Tribe.

The others are huddled under the tarpaulin, sheltering from the rain. They watch us approach.

'Here you go,' I say and hand Jack his car keys back.

He looks at them, bemused.

'My period started. I knew Mikki would have tampons in her car.' I show them the tampons.

Jack and Clemente suddenly have Urgent Things To Do. Clemente heads to the barbecue, Jack goes off to his tent. Victor looks uncomfortable but loyally remains beside Sky.

'I needed them in a hurry,' I say. 'It was pretty messy.'

That's enough for Victor; he practically runs off to join Clemente in the rain. Mikki says nothing but I'm sure she guesses I'm lying; she knows me too well. Sky doesn't seem fully convinced but doesn't say anything, so with shaky legs, I head to the toilet block.

I'm desperate to go back up the trail and see what the blue thing was but Sky keeps a close eye on me for the rest of the morning. Lunch is a sombre affair. We eat standing up, huddled together on the muddy ground beneath the tarpaulin. We're running low on food and Sky has mixed kale from Ryan's little vegetable patch into a scrambled egg mixture.

Jack picks the green bits out. 'Why would anyone eat this shit? It's the bitterest thing on earth. I'd kill for a meat pie right now.'

'A steak,' Victor says. 'A nice bloody steak.'

There's a hard edge to Jack's smile. It could be his back pain, yet there's something ugly about it. Now I know he lied about the wallet, I know for sure he can't be trusted. Panic flares inside me. Mikki's due to marry him in just six days.

It's cold enough that we're wearing jeans and sweaters. Leaves and twigs swirl around our legs; the tarpaulin rattles overhead. The wind drives the rain this way and that, streaking us on all sides. I feel damp to the bone. The only good thing is it's too wet for the mosquitoes.

'At least we won't need to wash up,' Jack says. 'Watch this.'

He sets the plates out in the rain and the scraps wash off them in no time.

'I hope that wind dies down,' Sky says. 'And we might get some waves this afternoon.' She nudges Victor. 'Big ones.'

To talk about surfing so soon after Ryan's death seems callous. I turn on her. 'You're not sad about Ryan at all, are you?'

She blinks. 'Of course I'm sad.'

'Think of his family. His little daughter.'

Her forehead wrinkles. 'His daughter? Is that what he told you?'

'Yeah. Ava. She's three.'

'He asked Victor for money because his son was sick back home. He told Jack he had terminal cancer. He was a compulsive liar, Kenna.'

I turn to Victor. 'That tattoo you did on his wrist. *A* for Ava.'

'He said it was his wife,' Victor says. 'Anna.'

'I sneaked a look at his passport before he hid it,' Sky says. 'And googled him the next time I was in Sydney. He was involved in insider trading. If he goes back to America, he'll face jail.'

'So why did you let him join?' I ask.

'He swindled some rich corporations so he could go surfing for two years? That's my kind of person.'

The others are nodding.

'Plus it suited us to have him here while we were in Sydney,' Sky says.

A surfboard lifts off the ground and blows into a tree. Victor swears and runs to get it.

Clemente paces around the toilet block. 'It's more sheltered round here,' he calls.

We stack the boards beside the wall and hurry back under the tarpaulin.

'That reminds me,' I say. 'Are any of Ryan's surfboards missing?'

'No,' Clemente says gesturing. 'He only had two and they're still here.'

'So he was swimming.'

'Apparently.'

Clemente seems as troubled by this as I am. 'I keep thinking about his family,' he says. 'Whoever they are.'

'I know.' I stare at the dirt, wishing again that I was anywhere but here.

He blows out a long breath. 'Sometimes I ask myself what I'm doing here.'

Mikki's head turns his way in surprise. 'Are you missing home?'

'I don't know where home is any more, but I think I'm ready to move on.'

I catch Mikki's stunned expression. *Careful, Clemente.* It's dangerous to admit such things around here. With a jolt, I realise Sky has also heard. She seems just as amazed.

'Where to?' Mikki asks.

He sighs. 'No idea.'

Sky gives Clemente a disgusted look. 'So you're selling out?'

He folds his arms. 'I didn't make any promises.'

'Oh, but you did.' Sky leads him off into the trees and they stand there arguing. I'm desperate to know what they're saying but I can't hear over the rain. Victor watches broodingly, then marches over.

I want to join them, but Clemente is a big boy who must know what he's doing so I turn to Mikki instead. 'Where's Jack?'

'In our tent,' she says. 'His back was hurting.'

I lower my voice. 'There's a wad of cash in his glove box.'

'Yeah. Safer to leave it in the car.'

'There's quite a lot.'

'We took some out when we went shopping.'

Watching her carefully, I tell her about the wallet. *Please don't let her be in on it.*

Mikki's face crumples. 'Oh, shit. I sensed something was going on. He said he was working for his friend, fitting solar panels? But perhaps his back was too sore. The pain is too much for him sometimes. He's a good person, I swear.'

I can't tell if she actually believes that but I'm relieved she didn't know. Behind her, Clemente, Sky and Victor are still arguing. 'In the Meadow. Clemente's wife – Sky – is buried there, isn't she? And Elke?'

Mikki sighs. 'Yeah.'

Hearing her confirm it just brings home how she really is one of them. 'And you went along with it? It didn't occur to you to go to the police?'

'What good would it do? It wouldn't bring them back to life. No one was to blame. What would the police do?'

I tell Mikki about the blue thing I saw on the path. 'I want to see what it is. Will you come with me?'

She gestures to the rain still streaking down. 'Seriously? You want to go now?'

'It might be important. Please?'

Mikki sighs. 'Fine.'

The trail is strewn with leaves. Our bare feet slip and slide as we hurry to the mudslide.

'It was somewhere here,' I say.

'Where?'

Branches creak and crack overhead as I scan the mud. 'Or a bit further.' I walk on, trying to remember.

Mikki flinches as a branch crashes down nearby. 'Are you sure it wasn't a flower or some rubbish?'

'I saw the Rip Curl logo.' But I can't see it now.

We wander back and forth.

'Damn! I know it was here.' Has someone moved it?

Mikki wraps her arms around her chest. 'We're getting soaked.'

I give up. 'Okay.'

Jack's in their tent. When Mikki confronts him about the wallet, he admits it immediately. 'It was a stupid impulsive thing. This guy I know, he's been selling me codeine but it's not cheap. I used to steal stuff when I was a teenager when Mum didn't have enough money to buy food. Never thought I'd do it again.'

I think about how he lied to me about robbing Tanith and how easily we were taken in. 'How many people have you robbed?'

'Just her, I swear.'

He grins sheepishly. There's something childlike about

the way he thinks he can do something terrible, then apologise and all will be forgiven.

Mikki hugs him. 'I have money. I'll buy you codeine if I have to, but let's talk with your doctor. She has to help you.'

'What about the wallet?' I ask, amazed Mikki is letting him off so easily.

'We'll post it back to them,' Mikki says.

'If there's an address, it's probably a Canadian one,' I say.

'We could hand it in to the police as soon as we're back in Sydney and say we found it,' Mikki says.

Jack's eyes meet mine. Now I'm wondering what else he might have done.

CHAPTER 63

KENNA

'Surf's up!' Sky shouts. 'The wind's eased.'

I crawl out of Mikki's tent to see Sky, Victor and Clemente pulling on wetsuits. The rain is still bucketing down.

'You're not seriously going to surf in this, are you?' I say.

The waves were huge this morning. Without the wind spoiling their shape, they'll be even bigger.

'Of course we are,' Sky says. 'We train all year for conditions like these.'

If she's sad about Ryan, I can't see it. Then again, surfing might be her way of coping.

Jack crawls out of the tent. He has his wetsuit on already. Mikki is stepping into hers. The Tribe are quieter than ever, but they wax boards with expressions of concentration, the shock of Clemente's announcement that he's leaving pushed aside in their rush to get to the surf.

'You coming, Kenna?' Sky asks.

I catch the challenge in her tone. *Are you with us, or against us?* That's what she's really asking.

Mikki gives me a pointed look. I can't tell if she really wants to surf these waves or not, but the others are already suspicious of me now – Victor especially – so I have to maintain the illusion that I'm one of them until I can get out of here.

'Of course,' I say.

'I have a spare wetsuit if you want,' Sky says.

I force a smile. 'I'm Scottish. I don't need no wetsuit.'

Clemente flashes me a smile as he picks up his board, although he looks tense and I can't tell if it's because of the waves or the drama earlier. One by one, the others jog off down the trail.

'We'll catch you up,' Mikki calls.

Victor comes running back. 'I forgot this!' He peels his Brazil band from his wrist and tosses it into his tent.

Once he's gone, Mikki turns to me. 'You don't have to surf.'

I feel torn. The last time I surfed big waves was when Kasim died, but if Mikki's going out, I need to go with her to keep an eye on her. 'If you're surfing, I'm surfing.'

Mikki fingers the neck of my T-shirt. 'The waves will blast this right off. Put a rash vest on at least.'

'Good point.'

She gets me one from her tent. Nerves jitter in my stomach as I pull it over my head. I gesture to the leaden sky. 'At least we won't need sunscreen.'

Raindrops glisten on the leaves. Battered by the storm, the delicate peach blossom on the nearby bush has withered and the petals, once beautiful, now look like wrinkled flesh. A stench rises up from them, musty and rotten. The waves sound like thunder. My nausea builds.

Rain showers our heads when we break clear of the trees. A sea mist has come in and we can't even see the ocean until halfway down the sand. In the shallows, a dirty scum of foam sails back and forth. Out the back, glimpses of waves peaking and crashing through the fog. I glance at Mikki. Are we seriously surfing that? They're bigger than anything I've ever surfed, but Mikki seems in a hurry to get out there so I have no choice.

Fishy-smelling seaweed litters the shore, garnishing one inflated and very dead pufferfish. *Ugh.* The eye that I can see is wide open, giving it an expression of shock. Do they inflate like that after death, or was it a last-ditch effort for survival?

As we near the rocks, I see the others: little figures bobbing in the mist.

Mikki points. 'Look!' A dark shape on the sand ahead.

For a terrible moment I think it's another body, but as we get closer, I realise it's a tiny dolphin. Shit. Has it beached itself?

Mikki breaks into a run. I jog alongside her, with visions of pushing it back into the water. Then we reach it and my stomach heaves. Half its face has been bitten off.

Mikki turns away. She nods to the shoreline where the water sucks out to sea, then caves over and crashes back down. 'That shore-dump is savage.'

The word repeats in my head. This whole place is savage, really. Waves, wildlife and human inhabitants alike.

We continue to the point in silence. Waves crash onto the rocks, sending spray high into the air.

Mikki fastens her leg rope. 'Follow me.'

Once again, I'm struck by how we've switched roles. I was always the leader, she the follower. Her time at the Bay really has changed her. She doesn't seem scared at all. I hold my breath as she scrambles over the rocks, jumps in, then bobs about, dodging oncoming waves. I'm not going out there. I'll get thrown onto the rocks and smashed.

The rip at the other end of the beach – will it be working? I race back towards the rock wall and there it is: a narrow channel clear of waves. I fasten my leg rope and wade in. The rip sucks at me with alarming power, tugging my feet out from underneath me. I shove my chest over my surfboard and hold on tight as I'm swept out to sea.

It feels like it'll drag me all the way to New Zealand, but halfway out, a set approaches. It's coming right at me. I duck-dive, driving my board hard under the surface. Even underwater I feel the impact of the wave breaking, but I cling to my board and pop back up. Rain lashing my face, I paddle hard towards the point, keeping a constant watch for oncoming waves. Here and there, black neoprene-clad mounds poke up from the ocean like tombstones, but I can't tell who's who; they all look the same with wetsuits on.

The mist thickens until I can only see a few metres ahead. An enormous wave looms from nowhere. Like a rabbit in the headlights, I freeze. At the last minute, I duck-dive and a mass of white water crashes down onto my back, forcing me far below the surface. My ears pop.

When I come up, another huge wave rises from the mist. I ditch my board and dive under. Bad move. The wave tumbles me like a sock in a washing machine. I fight my way to the surface, knowing there are only seconds until the next wave arrives. One snatched breath and it hits me. All I can do is tuck into a ball, arms wrapped around my head for protection. Saltwater floods up my nose and I no longer know which way is up. Taking a guess, I swim in that direction, really wanting some oxygen by now. Too late. The next wave hits, tossing me over again.

At last I surface and haul myself back onto my board. I barely have my breath back before another wave looms. I can surf it or get smashed by it, and surfing it seems the best option so I paddle hard. My board surges forward and I jump upright. I daren't look behind but I can feel the wave's power. *Don't fall, don't fall.* Falling off would mean I'm stuck in the impact zone getting the waves behind on my head.

I glimpse a dark wetsuit-clad figure. Distracted, I wobble and overbalance. I snatch a breath and wrap my arms around my head as the wave crashes down on me, then swim upwards to snatch a breath before the next wave but as my head breaks the surface, hands grab me and force me back under. At first I think they're trying to help me, whoever they are, but when the hands remain there, resisting all my attempts to come up, I realise the truth.

They're trying to drown me.

I flail and tear at the hands, trying to break free. A tiny part of me remembers I'm supposed to keep calm to preserve oxygen but it's impossible. I'm going to die like this in this lonely spot, just like the other missing backpackers, and nobody will ever know the truth.

Desperate for air, I renew my efforts, but they're above me, so they have the advantage. The urge to open my mouth becomes almost irresistible. Subconsciously I know that if I do, I'll breathe in water and die, but I've gone beyond fear to pure panic.

Fear is fuel, panic is lethal. Sky's mantra plays in my mind like a stuck record. I'm not even in a state to take the words in but it gives my brain something to latch onto. A wave hits, blasting us forward in a tangle of leg ropes and boards. Fibreglass strikes my hip – my board or theirs, I don't know. A dozen more seconds and the next wave will hit. An idea forms. Fighting is getting me nowhere. If I play dead, they might release their grip enough that when the wave hits, it'll tow me with it. My board will drag behind, slowing me down, so I grope for my leg rope and rip open the Velcro to release my board, then go limp.

The pressure in my lungs grows. I'll burst if I don't get a breath soon. The hands shake, like they're testing, then the wave arrives, ripping me free. I bring my arms out in front of me, keep my body rigid and bodysurf the wave. Five seconds, ten seconds . . .

I raise my head and gasp in sweet, beautiful air. Over my shoulder, the mist obscures the ocean. Ahead, the beach comes into view. Exhausted, I dog paddle towards it and a wave rears up and hurls me at dry land.

Light-headed and heaving for breath, I stagger up the wet sand. My board is nowhere in sight. With the rain streaking my face, I bolt for the trees. Branches creak in the wind, drowning out the sound of a possible pursuer. When I reach the tents, I keep running without stopping to get my things. The flooded weir was too deep to drive over but maybe I can wade across it – or even swim it. It'll be a long walk to the motorway, but I have no other option. More mud and rocks have slid down across the trail. I scramble over them. As I near the spot where I saw the blue thing with the Rip Curl logo, I look down the bank to the left. And see something else.

Clemente stands there, ankle-deep in mud, holding the shovel. Beside him is what can only be a half-dug grave.

CHAPTER 64

KENNA

I turn and run back down the trail. I'm not going anywhere in particular, I'm just running. Branches crash behind me. I can't tell if it's the storm or him chasing me.

'Kenna!' Clemente shouts.

I keep running, bare feet sliding all over the place. A trail branches off to the left. I don't want to bump into any of the others so I run that way. And stop dead. A large kangaroo blocks the path ahead. It stands there on its hind legs, dark ears shifting back and forth in indecision. I double back and run down a different trail.

'Let me explain!' Clemente shouts.

I run faster, mud splashing up my legs, but it's no good, I can't lose him. Branches tear at my face. The trees are lurching about, leaves and twigs ripping off and crashing down all around me. I cover my head as a branch narrowly misses me.

I can't keep up this pace much longer. Spotting an opening in the undergrowth, I dart through it and press myself behind a tree trunk to hide. My chest is heaving but I clamp my hands over my mouth so as not to make a noise. Water showers down through the leaves onto my shoulders.

'Kenna!' Clemente shouts.

I wait, still and silent. My shoulders throb from where the hands held me down. I can't hear anything except the sound of running water. I think Clemente has gone. Now what? I daren't return to the vehicles, but where else? The river! If I had a surfboard I could paddle across it. There are plenty of boards in the clearing. Could I sneak back to get one? Then I remember the current. It was strong enough last week, when it hadn't rained for days. After the torrential rain, it'll be raging and full of debris washed off the land by the storm. I'm better off heading to the trail along the clifftops. It'll be miles before I reach a road but surely there's a footpath. Cautiously, I step out from the tree.

'Kenna.'

I nearly jump on the spot. There's Clemente, just a few metres away. I raise my arms protectively, but he remains where he is.

He's gasping for breath. 'I came up there earlier to see how high the flood water had got. I was worried about my car. And on the way, I saw a bag in the mud.'

Was that really what it was? He seems genuine, but I'm still wary. Then my curiosity gets the better of me. 'Whose was it?'

'Elke's. Her little daypack.'

'Wow! Did it have anything in it?'

'All her things. It's evidence that something happened

to her. I want to take it to the police. Maybe they can get fingerprints. I wanted to bury it before anyone else gets hold of it or it might disappear again so I sneaked off while they were surfing.'

I study him, still sceptical. 'Why didn't you report her death to the police six months ago?'

'Sky didn't want the police here. If they questioned her, what name would she give? The police have my wife in their computer. Climate change protests. Sky said if I call the police, she will tell them I sold her my wife's identity. I thought it was a shark death. What could the police do?' Clemente tips his head back against a tree trunk. 'I regret it now. Elke's parents, I think about them every day.'

I'm still not sure I believe him. 'Someone tried to drown me,' I say, because this, at least, couldn't have been him.

'What?' Clemente steps forward, shock in his eyes.

I step back. I can't trust him – I can't trust any of them. 'I had to play dead to survive. When they let go of me, I washed into the beach and ran.'

'*Mierda!* Who did that?'

I touch my sore shoulders, straining to remember the feel of the hands. Were they big or small, strong or weak? But there was too much going on. 'I don't know. What does it mean, that you found Elke's bag?'

'Her wallet isn't there, so maybe they robbed her. Or maybe there was some kind of accident and someone covered it up and made it look like she left.'

A gust blasts the trees sideways, showering us with water.

'How come Ryan had her passport?' I ask.

'I have no idea. Everyone liked her.' Clemente sounds choked up.

'Do you think Sky felt threatened by her?'

'No. They got on.'

'What about Victor?'

Clemente hugs his arms around his chest, rubbing his hands up and down his biceps. 'The night before Elke disappeared, Sky slept with her, so I always wondered.'

'Whoa.' This has my head reeling. I saw how Victor felt about Sky sleeping with Jack. 'You think Victor got jealous?'

Clemente flashes me a miserable look. 'I don't know. Maybe.'

'But you two seem so close.'

'We are.' Clemente rakes his fingers through his wet hair.

Shit. If Clemente is right and Victor is killing people out of jealousy, then Jack is in danger of being his next victim.

'And Jack has a codeine addiction,' I say.

Clemente shoots me a guilty look. He *knew*. 'Jack would never . . .'

'Wouldn't he? If he was in pain and needed money? Ryan needed money too.' I turn reluctantly to the possibility of Mikki. 'Maybe Elke made a pass at Jack and Mikki didn't like it.' I'm only saying it to cover all possibilities. I don't seriously think that. As far as I can tell Mikki isn't even that into Jack.

'And me?' Clemente says.

'Do you really want me to speculate on that?'

'Why not?'

I think of what Sky told me about his wife and force

myself to say it. 'You could be a monster. You could make women love you and then – I don't know, maybe when they love you too much, you get scared. Or you kill them for kicks. Or you love them so much you can't bear it. Or you love them and they want to leave you . . .'

Clemente stands there still and silent.

I suck in a shaky breath. 'Or you could *all* be in on it. You sacrificed Elke and your wife for the good of the Tribe. To steal their money or their identity, or because they intended to leave.'

Clemente reaches for me, but the darkness in his eyes makes me stay back.

A strange look passes over his face. 'You're right to fear me.'

I back away further.

Clemente looks me in the eye. 'I didn't kill Elke. But I killed my wife.'

Chapter 65

Kenna

An icy wave crashes over me. I open my mouth, but nothing comes out. After all this, it was him? I should run but my legs won't move, and anyway it's too late.

'She had cancer in three places.' Clemente's voice is so quiet I can barely hear him over the storm. 'They said it was untreatable, it had already spread too far. She had one year to live, max.' His dark hair is plastered to his scalp. 'A friend of hers had died from cancer a year before. My wife helped her through it and after she died, she told me: *If that ever happens to me, I want to end it before it gets too bad. Go out on a high.*' His voice falters. 'She didn't want the others to know. Didn't want their pity.'

I can imagine it might be that way. The Tribe are all about strength and vitality and being invincible, but this was something nobody could fight.

'So life continued,' Clemente says. 'But she started feeling the effects. She'd never been into drugs before but she started smoking weed. She thought it might help with the pain.'

'And did it?'

'No, I don't think. It just made her depressed. I was happy when Greta took charge of our diets and made us cut out drugs, alcohol and all junk food. I thought it might help Sky's cancer.' Clemente bites his lip. 'But she lost weight and got . . . how do you say? Nauseous. She kept surfing but she became tired more quickly than she used to. One morning we were all surfing and she left the water before the rest of us. After a few minutes, I got out to check if she was okay and I found her hanging from that tree.'

I cringe inside, imagining the horror of the discovery.

'She had made a noose from the leg rope of her surfboard, but it was too stretchy. The esky was on its side under her. It must have fallen when she suspended herself. Her feet were resting on it. She was still alive.'

I hold my breath, scared of what might come next.

'*Help me,* she said.'

My fingers curl into my palms. I'm dreading how this story might end.

'I rushed over to get her down. *No,* she said. Her feet were . . .' He mimes a pedalling motion with his hands, then screws his eyes shut as though he can't bear the image in his mind. 'She was trying to kick the esky away but it was too heavy. She wanted me to move it.'

He pauses a moment to collect himself. I can feel how painful it is for him to put this into words.

'There was no question. I had to respect her wishes. She asked it, so I did it. I moved it. And put my hands over my ears and ran.'

354

The wind howls through the leaves.

'By the time I got back, the others had taken her down from the tree and she was dead.'

I take a few deep breaths, trying to get my head around this. 'And you buried her where you buried Ryan?'

'Yes.' Clemente watches me, waiting for me to react.

'And the others? Elke and Ryan?' If he confesses to killing them as well, I don't know what I'll do.

'No.'

I let out my breath.

Clemente's voice cracks. 'Just her. Isn't that enough?'

Water pelts down on our heads and shoulders. My teeth are chattering. I wrap my arms around my chest. 'If I was in that situation and someone asked me to do that? I don't know if I could.'

'You could. Trust me, if you loved them, you could.'

The trees are jumping black shapes behind him. Night has arrived early, the dense cloud cover obscuring the moon.

Clemente rakes his hand through his hair. 'I always wondered if I did the right thing. Maybe I should have tried to get her some kind of treatment? To keep her alive longer? A miracle cure might be discovered. Perhaps the doctors were wrong.'

He leans against a trunk, looking broken. I reach for his fingers and squeeze them. They're icy, like mine.

'The last days of her life, the waves were so good.' His voice is raw. 'I'm grateful for that. Her earliest memories were of the ocean and her last memories too.'

I squeeze his fingers tighter. He slumps back against the tree.

'What now?' I ask.

He draws a deep breath. 'We go back to the tents.'

'One of them tried to drown me.'

Clemente reverses his hand, wrapping his fingers round mine. 'I stay with you every minute. And where else can we go?'

He's right. We need shelter, so we have no choice except return to the campsite. I feel safer with him at my side.

He gestures to the darkening sky. 'We must go now, or we'll never find our way back.'

We race through the trees, stumbling over roots and sticks.

'Wait,' I gasp. 'What about Elke's bag?'

'I do it in the morning,' Clemente says.

We reach the campsite, gasping for breath. Heads poke out of the tents: Mikki, Jack, Victor and Sky, shielding their faces from the rain.

'Where were you?' Mikki demands.

'Someone tried to drown Kenna,' Clemente says.

I flinch, because I hadn't intended to confront them so directly. Clemente shifts closer, the warmth of his body radiating against my hip.

'Oh my God!' Mikki says.

'Are you sure?' Jack says.

I pull aside the neck of my rash vest to show him my shoulder, red hand marks visible in the dim glow of his torch.

I watch their expressions carefully as I explain what happened. One of them *knows* what happened. Poor Mikki is beside herself. She looks from face to face, wondering, just like I am, which of them it was. Jack puts a protective arm around her and glances from Sky to Victor.

Sky's cheek is swollen and she has a gash below her eye.

'What happened to your cheek?' I ask.

'I went over the falls and my board hit it,' Sky says.

I search her face. Did it happen as she wrestled me?

'The waves had some power today,' she says. 'Victor snapped his leg rope.'

'Jack lost a toenail and I smashed my shin.' Mikki lifts her leg to show me a bruise. 'Look!'

An appalling notion crosses my mind, but of course it couldn't have been her. She's my best friend. No. Out of all of them, Sky seems the likeliest option. I've seen how protective she is over the Tribe.

'Go back to your tent,' I tell Mikki. 'You're getting soaked.'

'I'm already soaked,' she says. 'What about you? Someone tried to drown you!'

Clemente cuts in. 'I'll stay with her.'

Mikki's eyes widen. She clasps my arm. 'Can I have a word?'

She leads me round to the back of her tent. 'What if it was him?' she hisses.

'It's okay,' I whisper. 'He was already in the trees when I ran from the beach, so it couldn't have been.'

Her long black hair is plastered down the sides of her face. 'So who was it?'

I open my mouth to share my suspicions about Sky. And stop myself. I no longer know where Mikki's loyalties lie. 'No idea.'

'You can squeeze in with me and Jack, or Jack can sleep in Clemente's tent, he won't mind.'

'I trust him.' As I say it, doubts creep in. It wasn't Clemente who tried to drown me – but as for the other deaths . . . I need time and space to process what he told me.

'All right,' Mikki says, clearly still dubious. 'I put your sleeping bag back in your tent.'

She and I return to the others.

'There's leftovers on the barbecue,' Sky says.

'Thanks,' I say, and they retreat into their tents.

It's too dark to see what they've left for us – beans and rice and egg, I think. I eat hurriedly, so cold my entire body is shaking. I collect my sleeping bag, Clemente unzips his tent and I throw myself inside. He scrambles in after me and zips it up.

The canvas flaps as though the tent is about to take off. It's pitch black in here. Coldness overrules my shyness. I peel off my rash vest and shorts, fingers stiff with cold. My bikini top is soaked so I peel it off too.

Rustling sounds. Clemente is removing his clothes too and our elbows bash in the cramped confines.

'Want a dry T-shirt?' he asks. 'Here.'

I grope in the darkness until I feel soft cotton. 'Thanks.' I pull it over my head.

'Give me your wet clothes.'

I slither into my sleeping bag. My fingers are icy. I curl them into fists and blow on them.

'Still cold? Come here.' A second later, he adds: 'If you want.'

He's asking if what he told me changes how I feel about

him. I haven't processed it all yet but I grope for him in the darkness and he wraps his arms around me.

The rain beats down on the canvas, a soothing sound now I'm warm and dry. Clemente strokes my hair, the gentleness of the movement hitting me in the gut. Shock is really setting in now. I came as close as I've ever been to dying this afternoon.

'I think it was Sky,' I whisper. 'Who tried to drown me.'

'We will talk to her in the morning,' Clemente whispers. 'Demand the truth.'

The softness of his T-shirt against my face and his familiar musky smell makes me crack. Then I'm crying again, big heaving sobs that shake my body. Clemente holds me tight.

'Sorry,' I mutter from the depths of his shoulder. 'Am I crushing you?' I pull away.

Clemente pulls me back to his chest. 'Have you *seen* the size of my shoulder?'

My laughter mingles with my sobs. Not being able to see focusses all my senses on touch. He strokes my back, flattening his palm around the angles of my shoulder blades. I breathe in his smell, thinking how precarious our existence here is. Life is short; time is precious. My mouth finds his in the darkness.

The rain comes down harder and the frogs croak out a raucous chorus, off-key and out of time, like drunks in a pub.

CHAPTER 66

KENNA

I wake with a start, remembering. Hands on my shoulders, drowning me. Ryan dead. Then I feel the warm body curled around my back.

'Hi,' Clemente whispers.

He wraps his arm around my side and pulls me close. The wind is still howling. The canvas flaps overhead, raining drops of moisture onto us.

I roll over to face him. 'Hey, your hair's wet.'

He presses his palm to the canvas above his head. 'Is leaking.'

I'm not surprised. The storm lashed the tent all night. 'Did you sleep?'

'Yeah.' Clemente's intense grey eyes hold mine. And shift to my lips.

Rustling sounds from outside make me tense up. Clemente sits up to pull clothes on. I *so* don't want to go out there. I want to stay here, warm and safe. My head isn't working properly.

Clemente unzips the flyscreen. 'Don't go anywhere without me.'

I crawl out behind him, wearing his T-shirt and my knickers. Mikki and Jack are up. No sign of Sky or Victor. Mikki sends me an anxious smile. Judging from the bags under her and Jack's eyes, they didn't get much sleep either. Clemente waits at the entrance to my tent while I get a pair of shorts, then we huddle under the tarpaulin eating overripe bananas, rain streaming down on all sides.

The birds are silent, as if in protest over the storm, or perhaps I just can't hear them over the wind. The air is so damp my clothes seem wet through already. I'd feel cold, except Clemente grips my hand, radiating heat.

The zip on Sky and Victor's tent opens and Clemente grips my hand tighter.

Sky crawls from her tent, rubbing her eyes. 'Have you seen Victor?'

'No,' Clemente says. 'Is he surfing?'

Because on a day like today, that's pretty much the only reason you'd get up early.

'I'll see if any of his boards are missing.' Jack springs off round the side of the toilet block. 'Yeah, his yellow one's not here.'

'I'm going to the beach,' Sky says.

'Wait,' Clemente says. 'We should all go. Stick together.' He releases my hand to reach for the zip of his lightweight rain jacket. 'Take this, Kenna.'

'Thanks, but I'm fine.' I'm seeing a different side of him now.

He takes my hand again. Lowering our heads to the

rain, we hurry after Sky. The trail is thick with mud, the smell of decaying vegetation filling my lungs.

The wind blasts us as we leave the trees. The mist has cleared and I suck in my breath at the size of the waves.

'Surely Victor wouldn't surf that?' Jack says. 'How would he even paddle out?'

The others look equally worried. Shielding our eyes from the rain, we search the ocean for a tiny figure, but there's no sight of him. Sky jogs to the water's edge. The wet sand is gritty underfoot. Someone walked along here before us and their footprints are filling with seawater, topped with dirty froth like the foam on a cappuccino.

Sky breaks into a run. Then I see it: a dark shape on the sand. *No!*

Victor lies on his back not far from where we found Ryan yesterday. His broken leg rope curls across the sand, his board nowhere in sight.

Sky reaches him and falls to her knees.

Clemente pushes her aside. 'Let me.'

A sense of unreality grips me as Clemente goes through the motions. Minutes pass. Clemente straightens, shaking his head. Sky stares down at Victor's lifeless form while the rest of us stand around in stunned silence.

Sky looks up at us, shock on her face. Guilt, too. All those times she teased him about being scared . . . She must blame herself for him going out there. I know what it's like to be in that position. She's not crying yet; it hasn't sunk in. The tears will come later.

I check either way along the beach for Victor's board. Snapped leg ropes are common in big surf, but my suspicions are creeping in and from the looks passing between

Clemente and Jack, they're thinking the same thing. Yet another 'accident'. This is a dangerous place – especially now, with double-overhead waves – but were these latest tragedies caused by nature or by one of us? Someone tried to drown me; that's the only thing I know for sure.

With a small exclamation, Sky reaches for Victor's wrist – his Brazil band. She presses her hands over her face and lowers her head. Her shoulders shake. 'He never wore it in the water,' she says in a funny tight voice. 'He was scared he'd lose it.' She presses her hand across her mouth.

As Mikki and Jack try to console her, I stare at the Brazil band. As Sky said, Victor never wore it in the water, so why today? Did he put it on for luck, as Sky seems to assume, or did someone rouse him from sleep, murder him and drag him here? Clemente is looking at it too. I catch his eye. Is he thinking what I'm thinking?

He gestures to the ocean. 'Nobody could paddle out in this. Why would he even try?'

Jack nods. 'Yeah, you'd need a jet-ski to get out into the bay today. Hey – there's his board.' He runs along the sand to where it bobs in the shallow, and returns holding it awkwardly out in front of him like an unwanted gift.

My teeth are chattering. We're shivering, all of us.

'We need to get back,' Clemente says.

Sky walks alongside us a short distance, then runs back and reaches down to Victor. As she comes back towards us, I see the Brazil band around her wrist. She walks in silence, face tilted to the rain – which is lessening now.

Back in the clearing, Clemente halves the last remaining apples and hands them out. 'We need some sugar, for the shock.'

As I crunch it, I picture the sorrow fruit trees, blowing in the wind. I feel like I'm holding my breath for something else to happen. I suspect all of them right now – even Sky. Clemente hands a piece of apple to her, but she just stares at it as though she doesn't know what to do with it.

Five sorry friends sheltering from the rain. I look from face to face. Jack eats his apple with a little too much relish, Clemente seems rather too composed, while Sky's shock seems extreme to the point of overreaction. I even wonder about Mikki, whose eyes look weirdly vacant.

Jack takes Sky's apple gently from her hand and lifts it to her mouth. 'Eat.'

The intimacy of it is disturbing. He's wasting no time in muscling in on her right after Victor's departure, but Mikki doesn't seem to notice – or perhaps she doesn't care.

'We have to call the police,' Clemente says. 'Once the rain stops.'

Panic sparks inside me as I remember that we're trapped. Until the water goes down, we can't call anyone.

'He drowned,' Jack says. 'What can the cops do? Do you really want them snooping round? Think about it, mate. We've got three bodies buried there and we're all implicated, because we helped bury them.'

Jack seemed childlike in Mikki's tent yesterday; now he seems anything but. He's taking control in a way I haven't seen him do before.

Sky doesn't take part in the discussion; she's too locked away in her shock. If this is an act, it's an impressive one. She places her apple on the barbecue and walks off into the trees.

'Where are you going?' I call, but she doesn't answer.

There's a crash from behind the toilet block.

'What was that?' Jack asks.

'The surfboards,' Clemente says.

We hurry around to see. The topmost board in the stack has blown to the ground. It's Clemente's board. The leg rope tangles round my ankle as he picks it up.

'Shit!' I say, wondering how I didn't notice it before. 'Victor's goofy. The rest of us are all left-footers.'

They stare at me as though I've lost my mind.

'But when we found him lying on the beach,' I say, 'his leg rope was fastened around his right leg.'

Jack frowns. 'Was it?'

'Are you sure?' Mikki asks.

'Kenna's right,' Clemente says. 'I remember it now.'

They fall silent as they realise what it means. Someone put Victor's leg rope on after he was dead.

And there's only one reason why they'd do that.

CHAPTER 67

KENNA

For a moment the only sound is the water splattering down on all sides.

'Sky!' I shout, because she needs to hear this, but there's no answer – she's out of earshot already.

I turn back to the others. 'Can anyone suggest an innocent reason why Victor would have his leg rope on the wrong leg?'

They can't. Because there isn't one.

I've heard of good surfers occasionally swapping their stance to ride with the opposite foot in front – Mikki and I even tried it once – but it's the sort of thing you try when the waves are small. No way on earth would you do it on a day like today.

There's panic in the air now. Clemente remains at my side but Mikki has shifted away from Jack. I try to catch her eye. Does she suspect him?

Jack is looking at Clemente – a logical first choice, I suppose, since Victor is – *was* – a big guy with a martial arts background, so whoever killed him would have needed considerable strength.

'Clemente was with me all night,' I tell Jack. 'I would have heard him leave the tent.'

As I say it, though, I wonder about it. Could Clemente have sneaked out, lured Victor to the beach and drowned him before slinking back into the tent? He'd have got soaked, but he might have changed his clothes. I was so tired I might have slept through it.

My breath sticks in my throat. *His hair was wet this morning.*

No. I trust him. I turn my thoughts to Jack, remembering his punch-up with Victor three days ago. Jack has seemed wary of Victor since then, but he might have been waiting to get Victor alone so he could get revenge. I picture the way Jack is in the water: snaps of aggression one minute, graceful curves the next. He clearly has issues, and I've seen how good a liar he is.

Jack sees me looking at him and hurries off to fetch something from his tent. 'I took a sleeping pill last night. See?' He holds up a foil packet, as though that proves anything.

There's no way Mikki could have overpowered someone the size of Victor.

What about Sky? I've seen how devious she is. She's strong, too. It would have been easy enough for her to creep back into her empty tent and change into dry clothes afterwards.

A branch crashes down behind me, making me jump. The undergrowth is in constant movement, trees and bushes snapping back and forth. I keep thinking someone is going to come bursting out, but there's nobody here. Nobody except us. We have to face it: there's no faceless stranger to blame this on. One of us killed Victor.

'Ryan's death may have been an accident, so might Elke's,' I say. 'But this one, there's no doubt. We have to go to the police.'

Jack's face changes. 'Concealing a body is a crime. We had a pact.'

He really is keen to avoid the police. Yes, they had their pact but it's gone too far. Clemente clearly thinks so too, yet Mikki seems swayed.

'I'll go after Sky,' Jack says. 'You lot stay here.'

'Be careful,' I call.

'Don't you go anywhere, right?' Jack jogs off.

The tension eases a little now there's only the three of us. Clemente makes coffee and I tip cereal into bowls – we'll have to eat it dry because we're out of milk.

I offer one to Mikki.

She pushes it away. 'I can't.'

Her bottom lip trembles. I put my arm around her, remembering how well she got on with Victor. She's upset after all, but trying to be brave.

Jack pelts down the track towards us. 'She jumped!' he shouts. 'Sky jumped off the fucking cliff!'

CHAPTER 68

KENNA

Jack reaches us, heaving for breath. 'Oh my God.' He clasps his hands around his head. 'Oh my fucking God.'

I look at him in shock.

'Did she hit the rocks?' Clemente asks.

'I couldn't see,' Jack gasps. 'We have to get down there, check if she's alive.'

Clemente is shaking his head. 'There's no way . . .'

But Jack rushes for the trail to the beach. Clemente and I are about to follow when a stifled scream from Mikki stops us in our tracks. I turn to see her coming at me, wielding a knife. I don't have time to run; all I can do is raise my hands protectively. Clemente dashes over, but he's too slow; she's upon me already.

It's a terrible sight. My best friend, knife in hand, the gleaming point of it aimed at me.

'Help me!' Mikki gasps.

And I realise she's not turning the knife on me but on herself, aiming the tip at her wrist where her tattoo is.

I find my voice. 'Stop! What are you doing?'

'Get it off me!' Mikki cries.

I grab the knife hand but she won't let go. Jack stands frozen in the distance as Clemente dives in to help.

'It's him!' Mikki whispers, darting a terrified look in Jack's direction. 'He killed Victor.'

Clemente is first to react. 'I've got this,' he shouts to Jack. 'You go to the beach.'

Jack bolts off.

Mikki is shaking. She darts another wide-eyed look at Jack's retreating figure. 'He said he'd kill me if I told anyone.'

'What?' I'm still reeling from the way she came at me with that knife. I never knew my best friend was such a convincing actress.

'Slow down,' Clemente says. 'Jack killed Victor?'

'Yes,' Mikki says. 'I saw it.'

Clemente and I exchange horrified looks.

Mikki hugs her arms around her chest. 'And now I think he might have killed Sky too.'

'What?' It's too much to take in.

'Let's go back to Victor,' Clemente says. 'What did you actually see?'

'I heard a noise outside the tent last night.' Mikki gabbles her words in her hurry to get them out. 'I looked out and saw Jack and Victor fighting in the dirt. Victor's hands were wrapped round Jack's throat.'

I remember the look of fury on Victor's face yesterday morning.

'I rushed out to help Jack and I guess it startled Victor and he lost his grip. Jack flipped him over and wrenched

Victor's neck sideways. There was a crack and Victor went still. Then Jack said, *We have to make it look like an accident.*' Mikki's eyes flit from us to the trail Jack disappeared down.

I check the trail too, to make sure Jack has really gone.

Mikki goes on: 'He got Victor's yellow board, cut the leg rope off and put it round Victor's ankle, then dragged him to the beach and made me follow with the board.'

Clemente blows out a long breath. 'Whoa. But why were they fighting?'

'Over Sky,' I say, 'I'm guessing.'

'Yeah, probably.' Mikki shudders. 'The way he could kill his friend so easily! But he does it in the water too. Every time he surfs, it's like he changes into someone else.'

'Yeah,' I say. 'I noticed.'

'And I don't think Sky jumped. I think he pushed her.'

I stare at her. 'But why would he do that?'

'I think she was onto him. Guessed he killed Victor. Maybe she accused him of it, so he took her out.' Mikki grabs my wrist. 'Come on! We have to go.'

I'm still trying to get my head around it. 'The cliff. Do you think there's any chance Sky . . .' Even as I ask it, I remember the drop.

Mikki shakes her head. Clemente too.

I can't bear to think of it. That Jack would do that just days after he slept with her. Now I'm wondering something else. 'What about Ryan? Do you reckon Jack pushed him off the cliff too? Because his injuries . . .'

From Clemente's expression, I can tell that he thinks it's all too possible. I found that wad of cash in Jack's car, after all, and wondered if it was Ryan's. And if Jack killed Ryan to rob him, did he do the same to Elke? To fund his codeine addiction? It's all falling into place in the most horrible way.

'And me?' I say. 'Did Jack try to drown me?' But why? Again, the answer is obvious. I was asking *a lot* of questions. I'd discovered the money in his car and knew he was a thief. He must have feared it was only a matter of time before I realised the rest.

'Fuck!' Clemente shouts.

Mikki's face twists. 'I'm so, so sorry.'

I try to pull myself together. 'It's not your fault.'

She tugs my arm again. 'We have to get out of here.'

She's right – Jack could return any moment. 'But the road's flooded,' I say. 'We can't go anywhere.'

Clemente raises his face to the sky. 'The rain is less now. We might be able to get across at low tide. It's risky, but . . .'

'When's low tide?' I ask.

He frowns in thought. 'It was going out earlier when we found Victor. So the low will be . . .'

'Around now,' Mikki says.

'Grab what you can!' Clemente says and we dash to our tents.

I stuff what I can into my backpack, still trying to process it all. I remember how well Jack played the part of a shocked and grieving friend this morning. I was totally taken in by him.

Clemente is waiting outside my tent. 'I've taken his car key so he can't follow us. What do you think?'

I clock his guilty expression. 'Yeah, we can't risk it.'

Jack can walk to the road once the flood goes down and call a tow truck or hire car. It'll give us time to escape.

'We should take Victor's keys as well,' Mikki says.

'I looked for them but I couldn't find them,' Clemente says.

Mikki swears. 'Quick. Let's go before he comes back.'

We hurry through the mud. Mikki and Clemente have surfboards under either arm; I have bags in both hands. The trees along the trail are bowing so far over in the wind that I'm sure they'll be ripped out of the ground but they spring back upright as each gust subsides, lashing us.

We stuff everything into the boot of Clemente's car and I jump into the back beside Mikki. The tyres slip as Clemente reverses out.

Mikki puts her hands over her face. 'I didn't know if I should tell you. He's my fiancé. *Was* my fiancé.' She starts sobbing quietly.

I take my seatbelt off and move to the middle seat so I can pull her close. 'Hang in there. We're getting out of here.' I held her like this once before, when she pulled out of a surf competition because the waves were too big.

Branches scrape the back of the car as Clemente turns down the trail. The windscreen runs with water even though he has the wipers on high speed.

I check out the back window and see a moving figure. 'Shit! Jack's coming!'

Clemente slams his foot down on the accelerator, making the tyres spin.

On foot, Jack is faster than we are and draws level with the right-hand side of the car. He bangs on the driver's window. 'Stop!'

Mikki squeaks in fear. Branches are strewn across the track. Clemente swerves around the biggest ones and bumps over the rest.

Jack yanks the passenger door open. Shit! Mud sprays over me as I lean out to try to shut it. Jack grabs hold of my wrist and pulls me forward. I'm dangerously close to falling out.

Mikki screams and grabs my other arm. They tug me back and forth between them.

Jack is hardly recognisable, his handsome face twisted into a snarl. 'What the fuck are you doing?' he shouts.

'Faster!' I tell Clemente.

The car surges forward, sliding over the mud. I yank my arm free, grab the door handle and slam it shut. Clemente hits a button and I hear the click of central locking.

Jack is still running alongside us. 'Fucking stop!'

Mikki whimpers. I pull her tighter against me and cover her ears with my hands. I can't imagine how it must feel to know you've been dating – and sleeping with – a murderer for all this time.

Ahead, the weir comes into view. Clemente swears. 'I don't know whether to go fast or slow.'

'No idea,' I say. 'Watch out! We're aquaplaning!'

Clemente is already slowing.

Jack bangs on the side of the car. 'Stop, you fuckers!'

'Let me know if it's getting too deep,' Clemente says.

'Okay.' I watch anxiously as the water rises around the car.

Jack falls back a little, the water over his knees.

'It's above the wheels,' I say.

'*Mierda!* Keep going?'

I glance at Mikki. 'Yeah.'

Then the water is going down and we're through.

'Whoa,' Clemente says. 'We made it.'

I turn to see Jack standing in the water behind the car, arms folded. Relief washes over me. Soon we'll be back in civilisation.

'Shit,' I say. 'We forgot Elke's bag.'

Clemente swears. 'Too late now.'

My heart is pounding. 'We need to call the police as soon as we get phone reception.'

Silence from Clemente and Mikki.

'If that's what you want to do,' Clemente says.

I stare at him. 'You don't think we should?'

He steers around a pothole. 'I hate to say it, but from what Mikki said, Jack and Victor were fighting, right? So even if they prove it was Jack who killed Victor, Jack could argue it was self-defence.'

Mikki is nodding.

'As for the other deaths, I don't see how we can prove anything. There were no witnesses.'

Dismay fills me as I realise he's right. The chance of getting fingerprints from Elke's bag was always a longshot.

Something occurs to me then. I turn to Mikki. 'Your visa runs out. So if the wedding's off . . .?'

'Yeah,' she says. 'I need to leave the country.'

'Come home with me,' I tell her.

'Okay,' she says in a tiny voice.

It's what I wanted all along, but she looks so defeated my heart breaks for her. My flight back isn't for another two weeks but it's a flexible ticket. Better if we leave as soon as possible, before Jack finds us.

I lean forward to pass Clemente my phone. 'Can you plug this into the charger so I can check flights? I'll see if there are any seats left for this evening.'

Clemente glances over his shoulder. 'Three seats.'

My breath catches. 'What? You mean . . .'

'If you're okay with that,' he adds.

A giddiness rushes through me, briefly overriding all my other emotions. 'I'm okay with it.'

He reaches back to squeeze my fingers. I don't know what this is going to be, but I'll take each day as it comes.

The trees are thinning, the river visible between them on our right now, muddy brown and high with floodwater.

I remember something. 'The house in Bondi. It's yours, isn't it?'

Clemente hesitates. 'Officially my wife is still alive, and it's still in her name.'

'And you can't . . .?'

'Think about it,' he says.

He has a point. To claim it, he'll have to report her missing and all sorts of questions will be asked. At worst, he could face murder charges.

Clemente turns onto the highway and we pass a sign: *Sydney 300km.*

I crane my neck to watch the national park disappearing out the rear window. It's ridiculous how much the sight tugs at my heart, when I've been trying to leave this place for days, but I know I'll never surf waves like that again.

Chapter 69

Sky

My name is Greta Nilsson and I'm afraid of heights.

I stand on top of the cliff. The waves look a lot smaller from up here. On either side, the national park continues as far as I can see, the patchwork of greens shifting and lurching as if alive, tents hidden somewhere beneath the leafy canopy.

Why do I feel like this? As though I'm a balloon and someone has punctured me, all the air inside me hissing out; soon there'll be none left. I never realised I liked Victor this much.

His Brazil band: that's what sent me over the edge. I finger it now. This grotty rubber band had sentimental value as a memento of his homeland and Victor never once surfed with it on, for fear of losing it. Yet he kept it on today, like a good luck charm. Some luck it brought him. The rain runs down my face like the tears I cannot summon.

A crack of a twig attracts my attention – but it's only

the wind. Clemente and Jack questioned why Victor would surf in such unfriendly conditions. I could feel them blaming me – and they were right. This is all my fault. All those times I goaded Victor about being scared . . .

Our therapy sessions were for me as much as for him. Growing up with an abusive father, I'd played the victim for so long. My control over Victor – and the rest of the Tribe – gave me a power I'd never experienced and allowed me to recast myself in a different role.

The others don't know about the ultimatum I gave Victor last night. The tightness in my chest grows as I replay what happened.

Someone tried to drown me, Kenna told us as the rain beat down. And I knew immediately that it was Victor, because he'd grabbed me like that once too, but I managed to knee him in the balls and swim half-choking back to shore. I'd worked intensively with him ever since, to ensure it never happened again. Clearly I'd failed.

'It was you, wasn't it?' I whispered to Victor as soon as we were in our tent.

He admitted it straight away. 'I feel so ashamed.' His muffled sobs were loud in the darkness.

'If Kenna had died, I would never have forgiven myself,' I told him. 'What about Elke? Was that you?'

He swore it wasn't. I'd asked him many times before, but it had to be him, didn't it?

'I thought you were getting better,' I told him.

'I am!' he insisted.

'Prove it!'

My words ring through my head. I know what I must

do. Victor faced his greatest fear, and now so must I. I look down at the waves far, far below, steeling myself for what is to come.

None of the others know about my fear of heights. For the past few years, I've been climbing higher and higher up these cliffs and jumping off. I've been so scared at times that I've actually vomited, but I embrace that feeling. Fear is fuel, it really is.

This cliff is so high I don't know if it's jumpable. The impact would certainly kill you if you didn't know what you were doing, or if you got it wrong. But I watch the cliff diving championships whenever I'm back in Sydney with an internet connection and read up on techniques, then try them out.

I put both hands on the wooden railing now, which creaks under my weight, and climb over it. Nausea spirals up my throat. I clamp my lips tight. *Fear is fuel.*

The only person I told about my fear of heights was Elke. She was scared of heights too. Sometimes it stems from a traumatic past experience but genetics and environment may also play a role. Elke and I used to sit up here and talk about it. Exposure therapy at its best.

When Elke disappeared, I thought at first that she must have jumped, at least until we realised her daypack had also gone.

I shift forward until my toes are over the edge. Pebbles spill over and drop through the air. I force myself to watch them land. Some bounce off the rockface, others shatter into pieces. A single lucky pebble lands in the ocean. Dizziness rushes over me and I clench the railing so as not to fall.

Another noise from down the track: the snapping of a twig. Someone's coming! I need to do this fast, before they try to stop me. But my fingers don't want to let go of the rail.

Come on – focus! By the time I land, I'll be travelling at eighty kilometres an hour. The impact will be immense – like hitting concrete. But I know what to do: keep my toes slightly flexed and brace as I hit.

I unclamp my fingers from the rail. I can control my breaths, but I can't control my heart and it's banging away no matter how hard I try to calm it. I gaze at the ocean one last time.

And step off.

Chapter 70

Kenna

Two Days Later

Clemente and I are in a quaint little guesthouse in Cornwall, complete with squeaky floorboards, draughty windows and lacy white bedlinen, with a view of the sea from the window. It's just down the road from where my parents live. Tomorrow, Clemente will meet them but right now it's just the two of us, behind a locked door for the first time ever.

Clemente eyes me from across the room, barefoot in jeans and a hooded Billabong top. Judging from his expression, he's as nervous as I am. Ever since we met there's been something between us, an inexplicable pull that only intensifies the more time I spend with him. This moment feels long overdue but now it's finally here, it's as if we're afraid to act on it.

He breaks into a smile. 'Come here.'

I step forward into his arms. He takes my face in his hands and kisses me.

For the first time in ages, I feel excited about what lies

ahead, though I doubt I will ever be quite the same as I was before my visit to the Bay. On the long flight back to the UK, we made plans. Clemente wants to train as a paramedic in England; I'm going to pack up my stuff in London and return to sports therapy work here in Cornwall. Mikki will resume her job as a surf instructor at her parents' store.

After an awkward moment at the airport when Mikki seemed to think Clemente would go his own separate way – travel to Bristol to see his brother or something – Clemente hired a car (since mine was in South London and Mikki's was on her parents' driveway) and drove us here. The minute he'd dropped Mikki off, he turned to me. Did I want to stay with him? Of course I did. My parents could wait.

His palms cup the sides of my head, covering my ears, pinning me in the moment, so I'm aware of nothing except the pressure of his mouth against mine.

Needing more of his skin, I peel off his hoody and T-shirt. When he presses back against me, I feel the warm hardness of him through his jeans. I tug at the waistband. 'Get them off.'

Clemente catches my hand. 'Slow down,' he says, and kisses me some more, gentle and soft, along my jaw and down my throat.

Sky said he has cracks in his foundations, but don't we all? Look at what he's been through and he's still standing. He has a super-thick shell, and it will take a lot to soften it – so far I've only had glimpses of what's underneath – but that's part of the pull and I can't wait to get to know him better.

He pulls away. 'We should go on a date. Let me take you to dinner.'

'I've waited two weeks to get you behind a closed door.'

He hides a smile. 'We hardly know each other.'

I think of all the things we've been through: the mistrust and accusations, followed by crisis after crisis. What doesn't kill you makes you stronger, the saying goes, and in our case it seems particularly true. 'No. I reckon I know you pretty well.'

'Yeah? What's my favourite food?'

'No idea. But that's just detail. It doesn't matter.'

He leans back against the wall. 'Ice cream. And you?'

Distracted by the view of his chest, it takes me a moment to respond. 'Chocolate.'

'See? I didn't know that. What's your least favourite food?'

'Kale.' I say it without thinking but my voice peters out as I remember Ryan, who grew it.

'Me, I hate prawns. It's weird for a Spanish person to hate prawns. But I do.' Clemente is squirming.

Amused, I step closer. 'Why?'

'I don't know. They are too soft.'

'You don't like soft things?' I prod the smooth olive skin of his bicep. 'Because you aren't soft?'

'Maybe.'

I explore his chest and shoulders with my fingertips. Across his pecs, down to his abs and around his side to his lower back.

'What are you doing?' he asks.

'Checking if anywhere is soft.'

His eyes spark with laughter. 'Right now, nothing is soft, I promise.'

We look at each other.

'You're lucky I have so much control,' he whispers.

'I *love* that you have so much control. It's hot.'

And it will be even hotter if I can shatter it.

CHAPTER 71

MIKKI

You've probably heard of one-person cats and one-person dogs – the antisocial pet who hates everyone but his owner. Well, people can be just the same. Some people have lots of friends; others have only one special friend. And I'm that second type. I like to have one special friend and I prefer it if they feel the same way. I'm not good at sharing.

On Kenna's first day in primary school, we were climbing the monkey bars in the playground. Fearless and daring, Kenna was unlike anyone I'd ever met. I longed to be as brave as she was. Some of the other girls came up to ask if they could join in but I wanted her all to myself.

'Kenna doesn't like you,' I told them. 'She only likes me.'

Word got around and soon the others left us alone.

The week before Kenna's eleventh birthday, she brought party invitations to school. It was hurtful that she wanted

385

to celebrate with twenty others, as if I wasn't enough. I spread word that she'd only invited them because her parents had forced her to, and none of them showed up to the party. Kenna was upset but admitted it was her mum's idea to invite them.

'Don't worry,' I told her. 'You've got me.'

She had a crush on a really annoying boy called Toby Wines for months. I told him she wasn't interested but he kept sniffing around. When we went to the quarry, he followed Kenna all the way up to the ledge at the top. I climbed up after him, the shale sharp as razorblades under my bare soles. Toby was teetering on the ledge. If I was scared, he was terrified. He was never going to jump, I could tell from his face, so I helped him by giving the shale a little nudge. It cascaded around his ankles and off he went.

Through our teen years, Kenna had a succession of boyfriends. 'He's so boring,' I told her. Or: 'He's a total flirt.' And she didn't get serious with any of them. I had a couple of boyfriends myself but they didn't compare to Kenna. Her fearlessness washed off on me and I was a different person whenever I was with her – braver and stronger.

When we were twenty, Kenna and I moved in together. She was dating this idiot called Connor who she'd met in the surf, and before long he moved in with us. When I got sick of him, I told her he'd made a pass at me and she kicked him out.

All was great until she met Kasim. 'He's my soul mate,' she told me.

The Bay

She did her best to include me, inviting me along wherever they went, but it was awkward being the third wheel. The things she used to share with me, she shared with him instead, and I couldn't bear it. I just wanted him to disappear. And then, one day, he did.

Chapter 72

Kenna

A hideous ringing jars me from sleep. After two weeks without hearing it, it takes me a moment to recognise my ringtone. I grope about for my phone. 'Hello?'

'Surf's up.' Mikki's voice. 'I checked the cams and it's pumping. See you in ten?'

It feels like the middle of the night, but the light creeping in at the bottom of the blackout curtains tells me otherwise. Bloody jetlag. Beside me, Clemente's eyes are open, his face lined from the pillow. Last night's activities have left me feeling dazed and all I really want right now is to snuggle back into him.

Yet I don't want to say no to Mikki. While I was with Kasim, there were too many times when I turned her down in favour of spending more time with him. I'll never forget her breaking down on me at the Bay and crying about how I'd moved to London. I never realised until then quite how much our friendship meant to her. It means the world to me too, and I intend to be a better friend in future.

'Great.' I strain to focus. 'I'm at the Little Abberton Guesthouse with Clemente. We'll need a coffee and something to eat.'

'I'll sort it,' Mikki says.

'We'll need wetsuits, right?'

'Yeah. You can use my spare one, and I'll bring you a board as well.'

'Thanks.' All my boards are still in my parents' garage. I hope Clemente's wetsuit will cut it here at this time of year. My excitement is building now. 'Where are we surfing?'

Mikki hesitates. 'It's too big for Sandy Point. The nearest place that looks good is Archer's Cove.'

A tremor of shock ripples through me. It's the beach where Kasim died. I glance at Clemente and he smiles at me. I can do this.

'Great,' I say.

I check my Instagram as Clemente wriggles into his wetsuit. I'm still wading through all the messages and notifications of the past two weeks. Spotting a message request from someone I don't follow, I click on it to accept it.

Hope I got the right Kenna! Don't know when you'll get this but we just wanted to say sorry to disappear on you like that. No offence, but we didn't like the vibe. We left in a hurry, while you were sleeping. Tell that Spanish guy thanks for helping us with our tents. Tanith.

Clemente sees my face. 'What?'

'Nothing,' I say, feeling terrible about how I suspected him.

Clemente looks pensive as we go down the stairs. 'I

keep thinking about Elke's parents. I could try to contact them and tell them I surfed with her and say I think she drowned. To give them . . .' He searches for the word.

'Closure?' I suggest.

'Yeah. Is better for them to think it was an accident from doing the sport she loved than imagine something worse.'

I remember the way Elke's mother grabbed me like a drowning woman clutching at a log in a fast-flowing river. 'That's a great idea.'

Mikki is outside, leaning against her car, with a spare wetsuit and a bag of takeaway. She flashes us her wrist. Her moth is now a brilliant shade of turquoise.

'Wow!' I say. 'A butterfly!'

'Yeah. I found a place open late last night.'

We laugh at the ridiculousness of it: a moth changing into a butterfly!

'Wait,' I say. 'Aren't you supposed to keep your tattoo out of the water?'

Mikki rolls her eyes. 'Like that's going to happen.'

It's just like old times as I jump in her car, except better than old times, because Clemente's here too. We eat while she drives.

The waves come into view, bigger than I expected. 'Shit,' I breathe.

Clemente squeezes my fingers, and I squeeze back, drawing calm from him. By the time Mikki pulls into the car park I'm back in control.

We wax our boards, then jog down the sand.

'Brace yourself,' Mikki says, as a wave rushes up the beach.

I gasp as icy water wraps around my ankles.

'*Mierda!*' Clemente exclaims.

Mikki pokes him in the ribs. 'Wuss.'

Finally, I have a boyfriend that she likes. She's comfortable with him in a way she never was with Kasim.

CHAPTER 73

MIKKI

As a surf photographer, Kasim had surfboards flying at him on a regular basis. What was one more? The first time I tried to run him over, he ducked under me. The second time I only nicked his ear. Third time lucky – I cracked him on the head with my board and he sank like a stone.

I hadn't foreseen how upset Kenna would be. I thought things would return to how they were before she met him, but she shut herself away, turned her back on surfing and moved to London.

Cornwall wasn't the same without her. I decided to make a fresh start and got a working holiday visa for Australia. Elke was staying in my backpackers' hostel and we clicked from the start. I was overjoyed to have found a new best friend. A keen surfer with a fearless streak, she reminded me so much of Kenna.

We met Jack and Clemente in the bar below the hostel. Elke made a move on Clemente, so when Jack made *a move on me, I went along with it. They took us to the Bay and we couldn't believe our luck.*

But Elke started spending more and more time with Clemente, inviting him along wherever we went, so we never had any one-on-one time. I invited her for a swim early one morning: just the two of us. She didn't want to come – she wanted to lie in with Clemente.

'I hardly see you any more,' I protested.

Elke sulkily agreed to come along.

'You have a problem,' she told me, as light crept over the horizon. 'I can't cope with this. You're too . . .' She searched for the right word. 'Clinging. Back off.'

I didn't plan to kill her. I was just so hurt.

After I dragged her body into the rip, I learnt Ryan had seen me from the clifftop and hidden her daypack and passport before I could get to them. He proposed a deal. His savings had nearly run out. Unless I paid him every month, he'd tell the others what he'd seen. He wasn't asking for much, not at first, so I went along with it.

After Elke disappeared, Clemente wanted to call in a search team. Luckily, the storm meant he had no way of contacting anyone. I didn't expect her body to wash back in, but the sharks had really had a go at her and none of the others suspected anything.

Elke's words weighed on my mind. Sky was already helping with my fears so I told her I wanted to be less possessive and a bit less of an introvert.

Meanwhile, Ryan was becoming a problem. He kept asking for more money. I sensed a time might come when I wasn't prepared to keep paying.

It was weird when Kenna turned up. I'd just about

managed to wean myself off her – to forget about her almost, apart from our occasional calls – yet there she was, expecting everything to be just like it used to be. And I wanted that so badly, but I didn't think she would stick around. Then I saw how Clemente was looking at her and realised there was a greater danger. If they got together, I would lose her all over again. I had a soft spot for Clemente – he held his emotions back like I did and never asked awkward questions – but I couldn't have him coming between me and Kenna. I hinted to her that he was dangerous, but it didn't seem to put her off.

One day, Ryan asked for three thousand dollars. It was too much.

'I have Elke's passport,' he reminded me. 'It proves she never left the country. If you don't pay, I'll post it to the police along with your name.'

Ryan wouldn't have wanted to bring the police to the Bay any more than I did, but he knew my address in Sydney and I couldn't risk it. I gave him three hundred dollars, which was all I had until I went to a cash machine, and followed him to the cliff. One sharp push was all it took.

CHAPTER 74

KENNA

I never thought I'd surf Archer's Cove again – especially not in swell of this size – but I feel ready for it. Perhaps there was something in Sky's methods after all. I bite my lip. Of all the deaths, hers is the hardest to accept. She was so full of life; it just doesn't seem possible that she's gone.

There's a small crowd out there: a dozen shortboarders with serious expressions, a couple of older guys on longboards and a heavily pregnant woman on a bodyboard. We paddle out to join them.

Soon we're sitting on our boards with the cold Cornish sea lapping around our waists.

'Hey, you know that apartment on Muscat Street?' Mikki says. 'I phoned them last night and we can view it this afternoon.'

'Brilliant,' I say. We'd spent half the flight checking out local rentals and there was very little available.

I glimpse Mikki's tattoo again, poking out below the

sleeve of her wetsuit. How apt it is. She's so much more confident, in and out of the water. Sorrow Bay really did change her. It changed me too, in just ten days, not only by helping me come to terms with Kasim's death but by restoring my passion for surfing, allowing me to embrace danger again and strengthening my friendship with Mikki. I will never forget my time at Sorrow, nor the people I met there. Ryan, Victor and Sky surf on in my mind, golden and strong, racing along the waves.

As for Jack . . . I *hate* it that he's still out there.

Clemente reaches for my board, tugging me up alongside him. 'Are you okay?'

'Sky and Ryan,' I say. 'Do you honestly believe Jack pushed them? Sky was so upset about Victor. You don't think she might have jumped? And Ryan might have fallen trying to get his tin.'

Clemente's jaw tightens. 'We only know for sure that he killed Victor.'

'What about me? Do you really reckon it was Jack who tried to drown me?'

Clemente's eyes darken and I remember how close they were. 'I try not to think about it.'

Mikki is nearby, watching us intently. 'I try not to think about it too. Now stop yapping or you won't get any waves.'

A wave looms just then and I catch it, managing a couple of turns before it shuts down, plunging me head-first into the icy water. I didn't intend to get hooked on surfing again, but whatever. There are worse things to be addicted to.

I paddle back to Mikki and Clemente. 'I got smashed.'

Clemente laughs. 'I saw.'

I laugh too. I don't want a partner who wraps me up in cotton wool. I want one who picks me up when I fall and tells me to try again. Clemente doesn't hold me back, like Kasim used to. He does the opposite, inspiring me to go harder.

Mikki looks from me to Clemente with a troubled expression. And I get it. She had her doubts about him – about his wife's suicide in particular (and rightly so, as it turned out, though it's not my place to tell her that) – and she doesn't want me to get hurt.

It's okay, I want to tell her. *We can trust him. Everything's going to be great.*

But her gaze shifts to the horizon. For long moments, she stares at the dark lines forming there as if struggling to make a decision.

Finally, she turns to Clemente and addresses him in a strange high voice. 'Just so you know, I'm warning you . . .'

Goose bumps come up on my arms. I don't like that voice one bit. It reminds me of the way she sang at Ryan's funeral, shovel in hand, clear high notes rising above the storm. *Stop, Mikki. You're scaring me.*

But she hasn't finished. She fixes Clemente with her eyes. 'You better treat her well.' A weird little laugh comes out as she says it. 'Or I will kill you.'

CHAPTER 75

MIKKI

I liked Victor a lot. Right up until a few hours before he died.

Someone had tried to drown Kenna in the surf, and from the sounds of it, they'd almost succeeded. I lay in my tent, with my sleeping bag sticking to my legs, in complete shock.

Then Jack dropped the bombshell. 'I reckon it was Victor,' he whispered. 'He did it to me last year. Snapped his leggie and lost his board. When I paddled over to him, he freaked out and grabbed me. I had to fight the fucker off.'

The more I thought about it, the more likely it seemed. Victor had snapped his leg rope earlier, after all. Anyone would freak out to be boardless and at the mercy of the swell that day. Anger boiled inside me. Rain drummed down on the canvas as loud and fast as my heartbeat.

I must have eventually drifted off, because I woke to a noise outside the tent that didn't seem to be coming from the storm.

'Jack?' I patted the space beside me, but he wasn't there.

I crawled out. Freezing rain drenched me, waking me up in an instant. In the half-light I saw Jack and Victor wrestling in the mud. Victor had his hands round Jack's throat. The wet ground squelched under my bare feet as I dove in. I got Victor in a choke hold, the mud cold and slimy under my knees.

Victor's hands left Jack's throat and he tried to pull my arm away. He twisted and writhed and we toppled sideways into the mud but I didn't let go. Victor had been teaching me jujitsu for months and he'd taught me well. Jack, still red in the face and gasping for breath, restrained him. We were a good team, me and Jack.

I squeezed tighter.

'What are you doing?' Jack whispered. 'Mikki, stop! You'll kill him!'

But he'd nearly drowned my Kenna. I squeezed as hard as I could.

A horrified look formed in Victor's eyes. He was always ridiculously gentle with me whenever we sparred together, clearly seeing me as small and delicate, terrified of hurting me. I could imagine what he was thinking now: I thought little Mikki was a rabbit. But she's a cat.

I didn't let go until Victor stopped moving.

'Oh my fucking . . .' Jack wrapped his head in his hands. 'You killed him!'

'You started it,' I reminded him.

'I only went out for a piss,' Jack said. 'He came out of nowhere and started attacking me!'

I was cool and calm like I was in the surf, thinking

ahead to my next move. This had to look like an accident. We needed to drag him to the beach and make it look as if he was surfing. I headed to the barbecue area for a knife. Jack flinched when he saw it, as though he feared I might turn it on him. I pretended not to notice.

'Get his biggest board,' I said. 'Now hold out the leg rope for me.'

The leg rope on Victor's board was brand new. I caught how Jack looked at me as I cut through the cord. He was wondering if I'd killed Ryan and Elke. I was grateful he didn't ask – just like I never asked where his sudden cash windfalls sometimes appeared from.

Jack dragged Victor's body along the trail; I followed with Victor's board. The waves were thundering navy mountains. We dunked Victor in the shallows to wash off the worst of the mud – the rain would wash away the rest – then arranged him and his board on the beach. Hurriedly I fastened the broken leg rope around his ankle – the wrong one. I'm still kicking myself for that.

Jack looked pensive as we returned to the clearing.

'I can't marry you,' he whispered, back in our tent. 'I'm sorry.'

It blew my chance of securing Australian residence, but by then Kenna and Clemente had announced their plans to leave the Bay.

In the morning, when Kenna realised Victor's leg rope was on the wrong leg, I knew that before long she'd wonder about the other deaths as well. I needed someone to pin it on, fast.

Sky seemed a likely candidate at first. Kenna had positively hated her ever since she'd slept with Jack, not realising it had been my idea for them to sleep together as part of my self-improvement programme, to test if I was able to share him. But I didn't trust Jack to back me up and keep his mouth shut about what we'd done. When he announced Sky had jumped off the cliff, I saw an opportunity to make a clean break from him and changed my plan. And it worked out for the best, because it brought me back to Cornwall with Kenna.

I hadn't foreseen that Clemente would come with us. I feel torn about him being here. Kenna looks as happy as I've ever seen her. And I want her to be happy, I really do. Can I share her? I don't know yet.

Chapter 76

Sky

Bondi Beach is more crowded than ever. I wonder where Kenna, Mikki and Clemente are right now. On the other side of the world, I'm guessing.

The low sun shines into my eyes. In the distance, a surfer carves up a wave, throwing a plume of spray into the air. With his broad shoulders silhouetted against the golden backdrop, for a moment I think it's Victor. But of course it isn't. I'm still surprised by how much I miss him. How did it creep up on me like that?

Wave after wave rumbles past, several surfers on each. The cyclone swell has made its way down here and it's six-to-eight foot, conditions I'd normally be nervous about, but I've felt invincible since I jumped off the cliff. I twisted my ankle and bruised my ribs as I hit the water, which kept me from surfing for a few days, but it was worth it – the memory will fuel me for months to come. The hardest part was the swim in afterwards, in huge surf with a sore chest and ankle. Jack was waiting for me on the beach, looking frantic. I was stunned to learn the others had driven off. I knew Clemente planned to leave, but to do a runner like that, taking Mikki and Kenna with him, without even saying goodbye? The heartlessness of it tore me up. If Jack hadn't been there for me, I don't know what I would have done. I watch him paddle for a wave now, strong forearms cutting through the water, and wince as he drops in on someone.

Jack has been a good friend to me this week. He helped me drag Victor's body to the Meadow and bury him. My ribs were seizing up by then, and shock was kicking in, so back in the clearing, when he presented me with his last remaining codeine tablet, the gesture seemed incredibly romantic. When he led me to his tent, I let him. I've been losing myself in his warm body every night since.

Just a pretty face. That's the expression that sprang to mind the first time I met Jack. I saw how he looked at me, but half the reason he wanted me was because I didn't want him back. He wasn't used to women being immune to him, and while I enjoyed being desired by such a conventionally good-looking guy, I didn't think he was my type.

I'm beginning to change my mind.

'I don't believe in relationships,' I warned him yesterday, just as I warned Victor long before. I saw the pain – physical and mental – that my dad inflicted on my mum, which drove her to become an alcoholic, and anyway I pride myself on being strong enough that I don't need anyone else.

'Fine with me,' Jack said.

As much as the Tribe pretended to endorse our policy

of sharing, I knew they struggled with it. Humans are hardwired to be selfish. If they like something, they want it to be theirs alone, and this tends to include partners. Jack was the only one who seemed genuinely okay with it.

Victor knew my dad used to hurt me. I told him in a weak moment and regretted it ever after, because he'd try to make me talk about it when all I wanted was to forget. Jack is a very different person, happier to stay on the surface, and I don't intend to tell him anything about my past.

I took a knife to bed with us last night.

Jack jerked away from me when he saw it. 'What the hell?'

'Relax,' I told him. 'It's an experiment. Your back hurts, right? Let's see what happens if I give you a different sort of pain. See if it takes your mind off your back.'

For the next half hour, whether it was from the knife or what I was doing with my mouth, I'd say I was successful.

I saw him chatting up a couple of backpackers earlier – rich ones, hopefully. We need to find some new tribe members fast because Northy and Deano will be wanting their fee next month.

This weekend, I'm working at the nightclub where Mikki used to work. It's a far cry from my job in Sweden, where I had my own immaculate office and a good salary, but thanks to my weak-willed clients and the male colleagues in my practice who conspired against me, I was discharged. I still hear their voices in my head: *She has no empathy, she's not fit to work in this profession, she's a danger to all around her . . .*

Anger flares in my belly every time I think of them, but it was for the best. If I'd stayed in Sweden, I would never have discovered the Bay.

A wave rolls my way. I adjust my ankle brace and lie flat on my board to paddle, wincing at the pain from my ribs – perhaps they're actually broken rather than bruised – but a dozen other surfers are already paddling for it. Damn! I picture the waves at Sorrow Bay breaking unridden. I can't wait to get back there.

Some people say the Bay is cursed and I can see why they think that – it certainly has a weird energy. The trees have a way of crowding in on you and casting you in their cold, dark shadow; the cliffs and waves seem weirdly malevolent at times. But wild places attract wild people. Victor, Ryan and Elke knew the risks. I choose to believe that their deaths were simply tragic accidents.

Besides, even if there *is* a curse, it's worth it. Where else am I going to find such empty waves?

ACKNOWLEDGEMENTS

To my incredible agent Kate Burke, for her fantastic editorial advice and story-doctoring once again as well as endless support and encouragement these last two years. I'm incredibly fortunate to have her as my agent. To my TV/film rights agent Julian Friedmann for his expertise and enthusiasm in selling my work. To James Pusey and Hana Murrell in foreign rights for selling my debut *Shiver* to so many different territories, and the rest of the team at Blake Friedmann.

To my amazing editors, Jennifer Doyle at Headline UK, Danielle Dieterich at Penguin Putnam in the USA, and Rebecca Saunders at Hachette Australia, for their amazing editorial assistance, meticulous attention to detail, endless patience and being an absolute pleasure to work with. I'm so grateful to you all for investing so much time and effort in this book. Huge thanks also to Alara Delfosse, Joe Yule, Rebecca Bader, Chris Keith-Wright and the rest of the team at Headline, and the teams at Putnam and Hachette Australia.

Massive thanks to all the authors who read and provided quotes for this novel and *Shiver*. To all the book bloggers and reviewers who review my work. I was blown away by all the enthusiasm for *Shiver* and I'm incredibly grateful for your support.

To Sue Cunningham, first reader of this and all my other projects for your advice, moral support and always being there for me. To the many writer friends who helped, supported and encouraged me including Anna Downes, Lucy Clarke, Sarah Pearse, Roz Nay, May Cobb, Samantha M Bailey, Kyle Perry, Emma Haughton, Sharyn Swanepoel, Amy McCulloch, Gabriel Dylan, Kirsty Eagar, Ann Gosslin, JA Andrews, Rebecca Papin, Jessica Payne, Tobie Carter, Kelly Malacko, Terry Holman, David Thomas and so many more.

To the Brissie writers for welcoming me to their gang including Poppy Gee, Grant Ison, Rahnia Collins and Ray See.

To my boys, Lucas and Daniel. And to their dad for being an amazing dad and supportive co-parent. To Jon: thanks for everything. To all my friends for their endless moral support through a tough two years, including Jodie, Anita, Celine, Mandy, Anne and Mick.

To Gold Coast city council and library staff for their fabulous library system. The friendly staff at the Coolangatta branch give me a warm welcome every time I visit.

To all the surfers out there, wherever in the world you are.

And to my readers. Thank you so much for choosing this book. I hope you enjoy it.

Discover another exhilarating thriller by Allie Reynolds . . .

When Milla is invited to a reunion in the French Alps resort that saw the peak of her snowboarding career, she drops everything to go. The five friends haven't seen each other for ten years, since the disappearance of the beautiful and enigmatic Saskia.

When an icebreaker game turns menacing, the group realise they don't know who has really gathered them there . . . and how far they will go to find the truth.

Available now from

Allie Reynolds was once a freestyle snowboarder in the UK top ten at halfpipe. She spent five winters in the mountains of France, Switzerland, Austria and Canada.

She's had many jobs including nanny, barmaid, London primary school teacher, bookshop assistant and French teacher/translator. In 2003, she swapped her snowboard for a surfboard and moved to Gold Coast Australia, where she taught English as a foreign language for fifteen years.

Allie became a full-time writer in 2018 and her debut novel, *Shiver*, was published in 2020. She has two young children and a cat who thinks he's a dog.

Keep in touch with Allie at

www.allie-reynolds.com

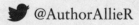 @AuthorAllieR

 @AuthorAllieR